Mistress and Mage

BLYTHE BRANDENBURG

5 PRINCE PUBLISHING
5PRINCEBOOKS.COM

Published by:

5 Prince Publishing and Books, LLC

DBA 5 Prince Publishing

PO Box 865

Arvada, Colorado 80001

This is a work of fiction. Names, characters, places, and incidents are the product of the author's imagination or are used fictitiously. Any resemblance to actual persons, living or dead, events, or locales is entirely coincidental.

Digital ISBN: 978-1-63112-432-7

Print ISBN: 978-1-63112-433-4

Cover design by Marianne Nowicki

Interior design by 5 Prince Publishing

First Edition

F01072026

For more information about this title, visit: www.5princebooks.com

To Rochelle.

You were the first piece of serendipity in my writing life. If we hadn't met at the pool so many years ago, I would never have started writing again or kept with it so long.
This book wouldn't exist without your friendship and support.

Acknowledgments

Many Thanks to Cassia Hall, who first urged me to write short stories for her indie anthology project. It was a key part of my growth as a writer.

Thank you to both Erica Damon and Paska D., who edited those anthologies. Erica, your patience with magic, pointy ears, and green people was above and beyond. Paska, I will never have an editor tougher than you; I trust none of them will suggest I add an entire book to a series.

Although they were not part of my professional journey, many thanks to Margaret, Rashel, and MaryAnn. Look how far we've come, ladies!

Finally, thank you to Bernadette, Cate, and the rest of the team at 5 Prince Publishing.

Mistress and Mage

CHAPTER 1

Debts and Obligations

DELPHINE

"Mr. Stokes, I am not quite sure I understand." Delphine pressed her cold palms against the rough table. "My husband died over four months ago. I've paid off every debt on record." And there had been many; David had owed every merchant and banker in Rockhaven. "How can these have been overlooked?"

Mr. Stokes stroked his thin mustache. He was thin all over, small, with a pug nose and nervous eyes. Although his coat was of good quality, he made it look shabby.

"I am not your usual creditor, Mrs. Leighton. Your husband came to me frequently to borrow money, as you can see." He slid the pile of papers across the table, each one a record of the gold thalens David had borrowed over the last year of his life.

She rifled through the thick pages. "But why now? Oh."

She had already paid off loans from bankers. Mr. Stokes was the other sort of lender. Bookies were less polite than bankers, although the difference was slimmer than she'd expected.

"Threatening you with debtor's prison would do me little good. It doesn't put money in my pocket. Mr. Leighton had rich relatives. I suggest you prevail on them for help." He retrieved the pile of notes but left her a single sheet with all the amounts neatly listed with the total at the bottom. "If I receive one hundred gold thalens by the end of the month, I will consider that a proper start, and things won't get more serious."

He didn't need to be specific; the vague threat was enough.

"You can see yourself out."

Her tiny, rented rooms closed in on her. The narrow bedroom barely held one small, hard bed and a chest of drawers. The front room where she sat now was the kitchen, dining room, and sitting room all in one. People lived like this all their lives, with no servants, cramped into dirty spaces.

But even a space like this required rent, and she had to eat. The last bit of her money from selling the house, furniture, jewels, and artwork would not stretch long. By her estimate, she had two more months before she started to starve, instead of being merely hungry each night. She laughed bitterly. Her stays already didn't fit quite right, the baleen boning poking in odd places, and she'd no idea how to adjust them beyond tightening the fraying laces.

After the door closed, she tapped the final number at the bottom of the page the bookie had left. David had borrowed seven thousand gold thalens. Even her generous dowry had only been six thousand. How could he have taken on so much? How could he have hidden it from her?

She had three weeks to find one hundred thalens. Impossible. People lived for a whole year on less than that. No position offered that type of salary.

She groaned. Father had died four years ago. Two years after that, Mama and Alastair, her brother, had sailed for her mother's home country of Elethen—an ocean and a war away. She had no family here to fall back on.

Her only recourse was David's sister, Edwina, and her husband, Michael; Lord and Lady Havemshire. Edwina was vaguely kind but fluttery, uninterested in anything but breeding

2

and showing her tiny lap gryphons. Over the eight years of Delphine's marriage, Michael had gone from affable, to distant, to disapproving. Once the war between the country of Torlund and the commonwealth of Elethen broke out, he'd forbidden Edwina to invite Delphine to social events. As an important member of the House of Law, entertaining a half-Eletheni relative would cast doubts on his loyalties.

"I can't be what I'm not." Delphine buried her face in her hands.

She couldn't be Torlish, and she couldn't be rich. Maybe she could convince Michael that a poor relative perishing in squalor would be a stain on the family reputation, even more so than David dying penniless in a bar fight.

The column of numbers stared back at her. Nothing would be solved sitting here and brooding over the bill. She couldn't afford pride anymore. Pride was for the rich.

Time to beg.

Varrick

The rowboat scraped softly against the sandy shore. In the thick darkness of a cloudy night, Varrick stepped out, hopping to avoid wetting his boots in the surf. The irregular crescent of sand curved against a steep, rocky slope that led to higher ground.

He flared his wide nostrils. It smelled different here, cold and salty in the wrong way, with none of the lavish greenery of the duchies of Istalia far to the south. He didn't belong here. The conviction washed over him like storm-driven waves. Torlund was no place for jaglin. He'd be too big. His green skin, slitted eyes, and feline ears would be remarkably strange to a population that was solely human.

Rejecting the urge to climb back into the boat, he scanned the top of the ridge. He could see better than humans in the dark, even better than the elven sailors in the rowboat. It was no trouble to find the two humans standing at the top of the slope. One raised a hand. He copied the gesture, touching one of his horns, unsure if it was a greeting or signal.

The figure lowered their hand. Varrick laid his ears back. They'd called him here, demanded he leave his work and sail halfway around the world, but insisted on all this cloak and dagger secrecy.

"Catch." A sailor tossed Varrick's heavy canvas bag of possessions at him.

Varrick caught it out of the air and whistled softly for his drakes. Talon and Sable leapt from the center of the rowboat, sprinted about the sandy slip of shore and returned to him, forked tongues lolling over their scaly lips. Varrick rubbed their crests. They'd gotten restless, then listless, during the two months at sea. He wouldn't begrudge them a quick dash now.

"We'll be off then," one of the elves said, pushing the boat off the sand with an oar. "You'll make a decent sailor, jaglin, if magery doesn't work out."

Varrick bobbed his head, ears out to the sides. He didn't have much choice. He owed his benefactor for his education—as her summons had pointed out. But the sailors meant well, and he'd enjoyed their easy camaraderie. That sort of fellowship was a rare thing in his life.

"Thank your captain for me," he called, "and may you have favorable winds and cowardly enemies."

They waved and applied the oars to return to the three-masted ship waiting dark and silent on the open water. An urge to splash after them and beg to go back welled inside him. Back on the water, back to Istalia and the Scholarium with its familiar halls and ambitious, taciturn professors.

Instead, Varrick patted the side of his thigh to call the drakes close, shouldered his bag, and picked his way up the slippery path.

The human who'd signaled was an older woman, hair gone white and skin soft and wrinkled, but she stood straight as a blade, dark skirts full under her cloak. The man was younger, perhaps forty, broad and stocky with dark hair slicked back. He wore a sort of uniform with knee-length breeches and a long open coat over an equally long buttoned vest. Beside the woman, he was barely noticeable. Varrick tried to pick emotion or intent out of their auras, but both were shielded. He could discern nothing.

The woman spun her innate magical energy, her anima, into a golden sphere in her hand, surveying him by its light. "Varrick Allard?"

He tapped a horn in acknowledgement. "Yes, Ma'am."

She smiled, some of the tension leaving her stance. "It is good to finally meet you. Do you know who I am?"

"My patron." He didn't know her name. It had taken the first four years of study to even learn that his patron was a woman, then another two to discover that she was Torlish.

"Lady M." She held out her hand. "Did they teach you protocol on the voyage?"

In answer, he took her hand, bowed over it as he'd been taught, and brushed his lips on her knuckles. In Istalia, people greeted one another with exuberant kisses on the cheeks. This was more intimate and more distant all at once. He didn't want to kiss her cheeks though.

Her smile grew to a grin. "Very good. Shall we get on our way? Rain is expected."

"It's Rockhaven in the autumn," the man said. "Rain is always expected." He nodded to Varrick. "Basil Morrow. I'll be your butler for this charade."

"Butler?" Varrick readjusted his bag. Why did he need a butler and all the prancing manners the elven captain had taught him? Morrow looked like the sort of man who fixed things by making people disappear.

Lady M was walking toward an enclosed carriage drawn by four horses. It waited by a copse of trees, where a pale dirt road snaked inland over the hills. Morrow and Varrick caught up in two strides.

"Butler?" he asked again. He was used to questions with answers, not being stonewalled at every turn.

"We'll explain in the carriage." Morrow pointed to the sky. "Rain."

As if on cue, it began to sprinkle. Varrick gritted his teeth and followed.

The carriage was made for humans, and humans were short. Lady M barely came to Varrick's shoulder. He shifted, trying to get comfortable and make space for the drakes. They would have preferred running alongside, but he wanted to see their reaction to Lady M and Morrow. Drakes were much more sensitive to emotions than dogs, making their assessment of people more accurate.

"What exactly will I be doing here? My mentor was vague, and I was in the middle of studying refracting glow through different gem lenses. It's important for creating safer glow-mining practices."

"I understand." Lady M adjusted her skirts. "A magus has summoned an elemental creature. We've had eleven attacks over the course of four months now, feeding on auras. Five of the victims are from families of rank."

Varrick winced. Attacks on auras—the visible manifestation of people's emotions—narrowed down what type of elemental being it might be, and all were dangerous. It would grow stronger with each attack.

"Why can't someone from the University of Magi deal with it?" The rite to dematerialize elementals required power and finesse, but Rockhaven's university ought to have someone who could do it. Then Varrick could go home.

Lady M and Morrow exchanged looks.

"The university is involved or at least responsible," she said. "They've already tried to cover up the evidence of a rogue magus."

"All of the high-ranking victims were rich young men who frequented gambling dens and exclusive clubs," Morrow added. "To lure him in, you will play the part of a rich foreign gentleman here to enjoy the less respectable parts of Rockhaven. You should draw the summoner's attention."

Which explained why Varrick had to learn Torlish card games as well as deportment on the journey here. He sighed and flicked his ears. The sooner he finished this business, the sooner he could go back to his lab and research. If Lady M was satisfied with his work.

She held out her hand for Sable to sniff. The drake showed no alarm, instead licking the old woman's fingers. "How do you feel about taking a mistress?"

CHAPTER 2

Of Grief and Gryphons

DELPHINE

Delphine took her bonnet from its peg and tied it on. With her hair and ears covered, she blended in better as she walked along the street, only her height making her remarkable. She'd been protected by rank, money, and favorable politics her whole life. With those stripped away following her husband's death, walking alone on the street was less safe than she'd ever imagined.

If she found a position as a governess, she might be able to escape Stokes's vague threats. Her father had been Torlund's ambassador to Elethen, and she knew both languages, as well as Low Elven and Istalian, even a little Doonish. Her geography and history were solid, and she played both the pianoforte and harp. Sweet rivers, she was overqualified. But she was part Eletheni, and Torlund was currently at war with Elethen. Worse, David's indiscretions had damaged her reputation as well as his own. No one of rank would hire her.

Some of the businessmen would not be so picky, especially if Michael wrote her a good reference. The influx of new money from the colonies in Alladoon meant every banker wanted to live like a duke, and have their daughters as accomplished as duchesses. The rich daughters of the middle class could be ladies of rank someday and save a few old family lands with new money. Lord Havemshire's word would carry weight with them.

An autumn rain shower had left the city damp and chilly. Delphine dodged puddles and mud as she made her way to the affluent neighborhood where lords and ladies enjoyed the autumn season of balls, parties, and politics. Her new neighborhood was too poor for smoothly cobbled streets or boardwalks, and the streetlamps, when lit at all, were oil or candle stubs. The wagons and riders made no room for pedestrians, forcing her and others against the buildings as they haphazardly passed. It was a relief to cross the invisible boundary into her old neighborhood, with its raised stone walkways and lamps lit with elemental magic glow every night. What should have taken ten minutes in a carriage had taken her nearly an hour on foot, and every toe felt it.

Havemshire House sat across the street from the Grand Promenade, the exclusive riding and walking park reserved only for those of proper rank. Delphine would no longer be allowed past its ornate iron gates. She'd taken the private gardens for granted although there were other parks and gardens.

It was past luncheon and not time for formal tea yet. At this time of day, Michael would be attending to political duties. The chance of catching Edwina alone was high.

By the time Delphine arrived at the front door of the Havemshire winter residence, her hands and feet were chilled through from the wind. She abhorred the cold and the thought of trying to keep her room heated through the coastal sleet and gales of Torlund's winter made her want to weep. Her only wool coat offered no protection from the bitter weather that would come as autumn turned to winter.

Delphine clanked the knocker and listened for the cries of Edwina's gryphons. Every lady of the court owned miniature gryphons and competed to have the rarest coloring and smallest breed. Edwina's favorites were of the falcon variety; when alarmed, they made enough noise to wake a dragon.

Delphine found the creatures charming from a distance. Up close, they were caprice armed with talons and beaks. Their cries came from the front of the house, which meant Edwina was in her sitting room. When Edwina wasn't home, they confined the featherballs to one of the upper rooms so they didn't terrorize the maids.

Cooper, the Havemshire's tall, thin butler opened the door. He'd probably been born with an expression of reproach. The image of a sour, disapproving baby flashed in her mind. She swallowed a giggle and covered it with coughing. Even his aura was a sort of judgmental green, swirled with dark gray-blues—utterly drab and unpleasant. He'd kept his dislike of her hidden until David's death. Now he didn't have the civility to pretend.

"May I help you?" He raised a skeptical eyebrow.

"I must speak with Lady Havemshire about something important." Delphine made sure to look him in the eye. He was no taller than she was and disliked being reminded of it.

His lip curled, but he allowed her in. "I will see if her ladyship is available."

"Thank you."

She was left to wait in the hall. A cup of tea wouldn't have gone amiss.

Eventually, he returned. "Her ladyship will see you." *Sniff*. "May I take your coat?"

He made a sound of disapproval at her dark red, curly hair with its odd, purple undertones—a legacy from her mother and the secret family scandal. There were things she'd never confided to David, much less Edwina.

He ushered her into Edwina's sitting room, where two miniature gryphons lounged on the back of the sofa, one shredding the golden upholstery while the other dozed. Edwina sat at one end, cuddling another that had white feathers and pale gray tabby fur.

It chirped as it attacked her hand. Her unshielded aura spun in lazy gold and pale pink swirls of contentment.

"Oh, Dellie! I am so glad you stopped by." Edwina set the white gryphon on a cushion and rose in a puff of fur and feathers. "My newest clutch has hatched. You must come see them, they're at the cutest age."

Edwina had little ability to control her aura. Her emotional resonance spilled enthusiasm through Delphine, no matter how well she shielded her own aura.

Delphine let Edwina take her arm and pull her out of the room to what had once been a study. As delighted as a child on their birthday, Edwina grinned and opened the door without a sound.

"She laid six eggs, can you believe it?" she whispered, tugging on Delphine. "Three females and three males, a perfect set."

The mother gryphon, white and gray like the one in the sitting room, sat on a perch above the opulent nesting box, where six fluffy, fuzzy kits tumbled and played. Their soft yellow baby down was giving way to sleek white feathers. They pounced on one another's tails, mock-fought with flapping wings and tiny beaks, and let out a variety of squeaks and peeps.

"They're adorable." Delphine crouched beside the box, wriggling her fingers. The nearest one batted at them. Any one of them was worth more than her whole debt.

Edwina sat in the one shredded chair, opening her arms for the mother to glide over and sit in her lap. "Oh Dellie, you look dreadful."

Delphine flinched. The phrase and tone of Edwina's voice were exactly like David's. Edwina had the same fair hair and round blue eyes of her brother, and sitting there now, the family resemblance was almost too much for Delphine. David had always used that tone to criticize, but Edwina's aura only showed concern.

"We don't appreciate our lady's maids enough," Delphine said. "I fear my lack is showing."

"I cannot imagine living without one. How do you care for

your hair?" Edwina leaned forward slightly, as if to better study the loose mess of Delphine's braid. "I suppose it's a terribly tedious business to attend to it yourself."

When Delphine had been a young woman with a dowry and small inheritance coming, her vibrant curls had been the subject of much discussion. Men praised it and the young women at the balls sighed at how it set Delphine apart.

"I am finding many things tedious lately," Delphine said. Edwina didn't mean ill, but some observations could be cruel.

Edwina frowned as she stroked the gryphon. "I didn't expect a visit. We are still in mourning."

"It's about David." Delphine hated this. She'd never been comfortable asking for favors, and ever since David's death, she'd done nothing else.

"I can't believe he's gone." Edwina slumped. "I don't think a year of grieving is really enough."

Delphine bit her tongue. It was easy to speak of grieving when one had a full stomach each night, warm quarters through the winter, and no worries for the future. "David left me with a great deal of debt. I have done my best to sort it out, but I was visited this morning by a man who loaned David considerable sums of money. He wants some by the end of the month."

Edwina hunched over her pet, biting her lip. "Michael said we weren't to—to waste any more money on David. I gave Davie my allowance once, and he yelled at me." Edwina winced. "You and David were endlessly running up bills. Michael said 'no more'."

Delphine hadn't known that David had ever borrowed money from Michael, and certainly not that he'd taken his sister's money as well. By rights, Michael could join the list of creditors. There was no law except decency that required him to help.

"I am asking for a loan. I need enough for the first payment. And if you or Michael will write me a reference, I can find a position as a governess and pay back the rest of the debt, every copper cuer, and you as well. I promise."

"I will try, Dellie, I really will." She set the gryphon aside and clasped Delphine's hand in hers. "They are saying the most indiscreet things about Eletheni women, especially the baronesses. I can't even repeat it, it's so filthy."

"I've heard it." The barons and baronesses who ruled Elethen took lovers as freely and openly as they wished. The lords of Rockhaven had spread lurid tales just before they declared war. It had turned the tide of popular sentiment within a month.

"Can't your mother's family help? They're quite wealthy. You could go abroad."

Delphine winced. Her grandfather was one of those barons. Her debt was probably a pittance to him, but Torlund had a blockade in place. Not even a letter could get through.

"I can't reach Elethen." That would be such a simple solution to everything.

"No, of course not." Edwina paused, thinking. "What about Alladoon? The governors there would be thrilled to have a proper lady teaching their girls. They won't know a thing about David. You might even remarry."

She hadn't considered Alladoon. It was a remote continent, even further south than Elethen and Istalia. Stories said it was full of steamy lowlands, dark jungles, and soaring mountains. "I'm not sure I have the constitution for it."

"You know I would help if I could," Edwina said. "I'd lend you the money or even give you a piece of jewelry to pawn, but Michael would be so angry. I must speak with him first."

"I understand." She had three weeks. Edwina could convince Michael, or Delphine could visit his office and plead her case. Or would that be scandalous?

"Leave your direction with Cooper, and I'll send you a note when I know." Edwina looked satisfied with herself, as if her promise alone would fix Delphine's problem. "I'll even ask around about a position."

If only it were so easy.

CHAPTER 3

Desperate Times

DELPHINE

Back in her rooms, Delphine stretched her shoulders, concentrating on the point between her shoulder blades to bloom her anima. The tingling warmth started on her spine, and with effort, she produced two strands of magic no thicker than fingering yarn. They were so weak and pale that they would have been invisible in a brighter room.

She wrapped them around the kindling in the fireplace and concentrated on the image of heat. In her mind's eye, she pictured the tea kettle from her childhood, sitting on the stove as the maids made tea. She drew on every detail, the brilliance of the copper in the firelight, the whistle of it as the water boiled, to send the command through her anima. *Heat.* The kindling smoked and caught. Delphine relaxed, pulling the magic back in. Such a small act of Craft had nearly exhausted her abilities.

Her rooms looked no better by firelight. Compared to the colors of Edwina's sitting room, the narrow space felt more dismal than ever. Her whole world was a muddle of gray and brown. Not for the first time, the contrast sparked jealousy toward Edwina.

Her sister-in-law not only had fortune enough to be frivolous, but Michael was indulgent and responsible.

What would life be like if she had married a steady, boring man? David had been exciting; handsome, engaging, and well-liked. He hadn't been intimidated by Delphine's height. She could look him straight in the eye, and he'd loved that.

She hadn't noticed his vices at first. For the first three or four years, they had been a nuisance, not serious enough to sap her happiness. His appetites grew steadily. More games. More drinking. More women. In the grief over her father's passing, she hadn't noticed how much he was spending on cards and dancers until it was too late.

Delphine held her fingers closer to the growing fire. She'd needed him, and he'd abandoned her. This was the natural end to being dazzled by excitement and a fine figure with no substance behind it. When things went badly, David's only concern had been himself. Her own worries and needs had been brushed aside.

Desperation made Delphine restless. She spent the following days walking until her feet were sore, checking the postings in shop windows. She could not sew or embroider well enough to work for a dressmaker. She'd had a lady's maid her entire adult life but no training. She had no experience cooking or baking, and no one wanted a scullery maid of thirty. No one wanted to hire an Eletheni for anything; Torlish applicants only.

Among the upper classes, her parents' story—a Torlish father and Eletheni mother—had been considered romantic. The libertine morals of the Eletheni were waved away when it benefited trade. Mama had kept the secret of her family's particular scandal, avoiding the disastrous social repercussions of it. They'd fit in by shedding everything of her mother's culture and heritage. What a stupid, empty sacrifice.

She returned home after dark on the third day, aware of the women gathered on the street corners. That was the other way for a woman to earn money, on the corner or as a mistress, but she wasn't that desperate. Yet. If no note arrived from Edwina, she would see Michael face-to-face before selling her most obvious assets.

Delphine shut the door behind her; if only she could shut the idea out as well. After eight years of marriage, Delphine knew the pleasures of bed play. The last few years, when David had come home drunk and angry more often than not, she'd also learned how humiliating it could be.

Governess. Governess would be a far better position than mistress, which might require any number of positions.

She cringed.

Respectable ladies didn't joke about such things. She could hear Edwina's gasp of shock at her indiscreet thoughts.

Exactly a week later, almost to the hour, Edwina's footman delivered a letter in her own elegant hand.

"From Lady Havemshire," the footman said as he handed it to Delphine.

When he had gone, she leaned against the grimy window and tore open the envelope with shaking hands. The smell of Edwina's favorite rose perfume and the slight musk of gryphons filled the room.

Dear Delphine, Although it caused me great embarrassment, I made several inquiries concerning a governess position. Unfortunately, there are very few at the moment and none available for you. It is too well known that you and David entertained rather questionable company at times, and he was not frequenting respectable clubs that last year.

"That was David's choice, not mine." But it had stained her, just the same.

Even many of our newly wealthy upstarts pay careful attention to such things. I don't wish to alarm you, but I am afraid I found nothing.

Nothing. Seeing it in writing made it more real.

If you wish to go to Alladoon, we might be able to pay your passage, but Michael refuses to do more.

Alladoon. Home of the Doonish jaglin, strange green people with feline ears and slitted eyes. Delphine had heard the stories from the returning officers. The Torlish had dealt brutally with the jaglin, and she could not stomach living there.

But if she went to Alladoon, Mr. Stokes and his list of debts couldn't follow her.

Perhaps if she spoke with Michael directly. He would be busy at the House of Law most days. She would have to make an appointment with his office to see him, and that would have to wait until morning. More waiting. More time ticking away. She needed one hundred thalens and only had a few weeks left.

Frustrated, she counted out her remaining money. She'd already sold all her jewelry, hanging onto Mama's prized pearl necklace as long as she could, but even that was gone. After the month's rent, she had a few silver dahls left, and a good handful of copper cuers.

Unsure of her goal, Delphine pocketed some of her coins and went out. Maybe something would occur to her, some shop or profession she'd overlooked. She had a fine head for figures, if someone would hire a woman as a clerk. Ha, there was no chance of that here. Managing money, either at a bank or business, was for men. Respectable women only handled family or household accounts.

She was beginning to loathe that word.

Delphine passed out of the rough neighborhood and into a better one, occupied by the wives of sailors, men and women who worked in service but didn't live in the family houses, and lower level merchants and shopkeepers.

She relaxed. If she could earn enough to live here, it wouldn't be so bad.

But debt meant she must earn quite a lot more than any of these people to even consider that.

The gray sky grew darker, and the mist turned into raindrops. Delphine ducked into the nearest shop, a haberdashery full of thread, ribbons, and buttons. Several other women crowded in as the sprinkle turned into a downpour. Delphine stepped into the front corner by the window.

"Fourth time this week," an older woman said as she entered. "I am tired to death of walking back and forth in the wet."

Her younger companion stopped to admire a card of pins. "I told you to find someplace where you can live for the winter. You complain every year."

"Someone let that big house in the hills south of the city. Maybe we could both go. It would be a nice place until things warm up."

"No one stays there long, Mum, and it's too far to walk anywhere. You don't want to be stuck in the country, not with your hip."

"No, I suppose not." The older woman picked up a set of ribbons. "That's a pretty blue. Matches your good shawl."

"Besides, they've got staff, I heard." The daughter shook her head at the ribbons. "Only person they need is someone *accomplished*."

Delphine stepped closer to the women, pretending to decide on buttons.

"Miss Shaw was upset because they wanted someone who spoke Istalian," the daughter said. "Although who knows why."

"Folks like the exotic," the mother said.

Accomplished. Speaks Istalian. Delphine's fingers froze on a card of cloth buttons. That meant a governess. If it was just the language requirement, she would assume a clerk or secretary but accomplished was a word only applied to women.

The downpour began to ease.

Rockhaven itself sprawled down the coast and had built up along the river that cut through the city. South of the city, the country was hilly and rough, full of gorse and scrub with few trees. Delphine couldn't remember the name, but there was a large manor house with extensive grounds there. And, if the townswomen were to be believed, someone rich enough to lease it who needed a governess.

Although it was still raining, she slipped out of the shop. She had no time to waste. As much as she resented it, she would need to spend some of her precious coins on a cab.

It had grown dim enough that the streetlamps were being lit. Light reflected off the puddles and wet stonework. The damp drove the cold deep into her skin.

Delphine didn't know which she missed more: her lady's maid, her fireplace, or solid meals. Hopefully, this family would be as desperate for a governess as she was for a position.

She found a cabbie a few streets away, waiting by a glow-lit streetlamp for a fare. He was a lump of a man with a bulbous red nose and the reek of heavy drink, but he seemed cheerful and did not ask questions. The alcohol dimmed his aura, but it was soft and clear with honesty.

He tapped his beaten hat with his whip as she climbed into the cab. "Oh, nasty evening to be out. Likely to get worse. This will be real rain before long. Where d'you want to go, now?"

It was dirty inside and smelled of vomit and drake scat. She gathered her skirts tightly around her so they touched as little of the interior as possible. "Do you know the big house south of town? In the hills?"

"Oh that one, yes. Sayledon Manor. Being let to some foreign gent this time. Well, I don't know if he's a gent. Rich as anything, I hear." He tapped the horse into motion. "It's a bit of a way out of the city, and I normally wouldn't go, but there's no business tonight, is there?"

"What type of foreign?" Delphine asked.

"What's that?"

"You said he was foreign. What type of foreign?" *Eletheni, maybe? Although that's unlikely.*

"I ain't rightly sure on that one. People ain't seen him that I heard. Private sort of fella. Most closed-lipped servants ever."

That was a good sign. Happy servants were discreet. Unhappy ones would spread the most vicious gossip, and even fearful ones would find ways of spreading rumors, usually for money so they could leave.

His chatter died down as they left the city. In the thick, misty night, he bloomed his anima, sending the glowing thread of his personal vitality questing ahead to light the way. They went along at a steady pace with few bumps and jostles until he pulled to a stop.

"Here we are. I don't go up the drive. 'Fraid you'll have to walk it. Can you see where it curves there?"

Delphine stuck her head out and squinted. The manor stood on a hill with its three-story face frowning down at them. Only the first floor's windows were lit, but they shed enough light to see the long, curving drive that led from the road to the front portico. "Yes, I think so." She had her own weak anima for light, if necessary. "Thank you." She counted out coins—more than she had planned on, but she couldn't quibble now that she was here.

The cabbie waited until she was several yards up the barely

discernible drive before he jingled his reins and drove away. Perhaps he thought she would change her mind, or maybe he was just being kind.

If she kept her eyes on the windows, she stumbled. She twitched her shoulders so her anima arcs would bloom from the spot between her shoulder blades and focused them into a spherical lantern hanging ahead of her. It was pale and faint, and the rain had gotten heavier again, but it shed enough light to avoid the bigger puddles.

Her anima had been stronger once, brighter and hotter, but both it and her aura were faded now, stolen by grief or something else.

CHAPTER 4

A Mistaken Interview

DELPHINE

By the time Delphine reached the manor house, her feet were wet, her hems muddy, her shoulders and back soaked, and her bonnet dripping. This was not a good way to convince someone to entrust their children to her.

She banged the knocker and hoped for an understanding butler.

Delphine counted to one hundred, started over, and reached sixty before he opened the door.

"I apologize. We were not expecting company." His voice carried a slight dockside accent.

Somehow he packed all the authority and dignity of a butler into a short, stocky frame. His aura was locked down tight, with not a wisp to tell Delphine more about him.

"My name is Delphine Leighton. I came about the open position for an accomplished lady." She'd acted on an overheard bit of gossip. She braced to have the door shut in her face.

"Of course." He stepped aside and swept his arm for her to enter. "May I take your hat and coat?"

It was a grander hall than she'd expected, with pale marble floors and wood paneling so dark it was nearly black. A wide staircase at the far end led to a second floor gallery. This late in the evening, none of the sconces were lit, casting the space in deep shadow and turning the mood ominous.

"Thank you." Her hands shook as she removed her gloves and bonnet.

He raised his brows, but otherwise didn't change expression at that or when he saw her hair.

"Mr. Allard is presently occupied, but if you don't mind waiting, I can send a maid with tea to the library. It's warmer than the sitting room this time of day."

Tea and a warm room. Luxury. "Thank you."

While warm, the library was not well-lit. He guided her to a high-backed chair by the fire and rang for a maid. Within a few minutes, Delphine had a lamp lit by glow, a cup of excellent tea and, to her eternal gratitude, two thick slices of bread spread with butter and jam.

She couldn't analyze Craft as well as she used to, but she was sure some talented cook had woven an anima spell for comfort and warmth into the tea. Delphine sighed with contentment. She was warm, full, and comfortable for the first time since losing Leighton House.

Hopefully, the mysterious Mr. Allard wouldn't want her to teach Skilling or Crafting to his children. Although she could Craft spells with her anima, as she had used it to light her fire, it was so weak that they dissipated almost immediately. She was unable to affect others' feelings with her aura. Skilling was useful with distraught children and necessary for spells that involved emotions, like the comfort in her tea. At least she could teach them how to read others' auras. She'd never lost her talent for that.

A warm nose pushed against Delphine's hand, and she startled, nearly upsetting the teacup. Unperturbed, the drake jogged her hand again with its nose. It was a tall, lean coursing drake, a female, since it had a lower crest. Her dark bronze scales shimmered in the firelight against black brindling. Seated, Delphine's eyes were even with hers.

"You're a pretty one." She stroked the ridge between the drake's eyes. The creature made a groaning hiss of pleasure, exposing heavy teeth. "Ah, you like that, don't you?"

A silvery-gray male with a high crest and dark dapples across his flanks slunk out of the stacks behind her and laid his heavy, narrow head on Delphine's lap. He rippled the spikes on his spine until she stroked his head as well.

Father had always kept several smaller drakes, claiming they read people well. More trainable than gryphons, the friendly affection of these two raised her hopes. Good drakes meant a good master.

She scratched the male behind the jawline, and he licked her arm. These two were exceptionally fine and probably expensive. Not as expensive as one of Edwina's tiny gryphons, but costly enough. Was Mr. Allard rich with a passion for drakes and hunting, or was he a spendthrift? It didn't matter. If she failed to procure this position, her only option was the ship to Alladoon.

She couldn't stomach the prospect.

As a child, she'd spent five years at Grandpapa's frontier barony in Elethen. Snugged up against the mountains, as far from the sea as possible, it bordered jaglin lands. Grandpapa worked closely with the large, green people. She'd played with their children and learned their songs. She could not go to Alladoon, where the children of the Doonish jaglin were treated as disposable property.

She'd rather be a mistress.

The library door opened and the butler frowned at the drakes. "I apologize. I didn't realize the other door was open."

"No apology necessary." As she stood, they moved away, no longer interested if she wasn't there to scratch their heads.

He raised an eyebrow. "Mr. Allard is ready for you."

The dark-paneled hall was long and lit only by the candelabra of glowlights the butler carried. It made the way feel menacing, as if she were walking toward some unknown doom. *Allard.* It was an Eletheni surname. Maybe he was a countryman.

"Miss Delphine Leighton," the butler said, introducing her with a gesture.

Delphine opened her mouth to correct the title and stopped, staring at the man behind the massive oak desk.

She had expected a man much like the bankers she'd dealt with, someone past his prime, going soft in the belly and bald on top. Having the drakes had adjusted her picture a little, but she had expected a human.

Mr. Allard was a jaglin.

In Rockhaven, she'd only seen a few from a distance on the docks, and one who had poured poor, drunk David onto their front step late one night. She hadn't seen one up close since she was a child.

He was the color of ivy in summer. Undertones of blue shone in the dark green of his hair, which was slicked back into a queue instead of worn in the short, fluffed style of the day. Two horns curled back from above his temples and around his cheekbones, gleaming like highly polished jet and neatly capped with brass on the tips. Silver hoops hung from his long, feline ears. He stood to greet her, rising taller than the average human man, taller than Delphine.

She was not used to looking up at a man.

She stepped back, staring. No one would do business with him here. No one would invite him to a ball or to speak to the House of Law. The magi at the university would disdain him. It made no sense.

"I startled you, Miss Leighton." He had a deep, smooth voice, but the glint of nerves in his aura confused her.

"*Mrs.* Leighton. I'm a widow." She took a step forward. "I was expecting a fat human with a receding hairline."

He broke into a grin and chuckled, motioning her toward a chair. "Sorry to disappoint you." His accent was Istalian.

Delphine marched to the chair and sat. Torlund insisted that jaglin were primitive. The governors of Alladoon claimed that jaglin sacrificed captives to strange gods. They were bigger, stronger and faster than humans. *They're just naturally violent,* a faceless, nameless voice from some past salon sneered in her memory.

The rumors that ran rampant in Rockhaven's sitting rooms clashed with her memories from her early life in Elethen. Jaglin engineers had designed the locks and support for steadying barges as they were loaded. Grandpapa's accountant was a jaglin woman who had snuck Delphine and Alastair honey candies. The jaglin lord of the bordering lands had come to dinner regularly; he'd had a big, sky-blue beard and a deep, infectious laugh.

This man in the elegant coat and jewelry felt far less threatening to her than Stokes had.

Delphine struggled to read his aura. It shimmered in a blue-green halo, a corona, around his head, misty except for the silvery ripples of interest shimmering across it. His slitted pupils widened and his ears flicked forward before settling back to their previous position.

"I hope the shock was temporary," he said. "It would be hard if you're afraid of me." Pause. "But being a widow should make it easier. You look the part." His ears flicked forward again.

Look the part? "Jaglin are rare here, and I was surprised." Delphine tumbled over her words to explain her shock. "I am sure I'll grow used to you quickly." Why would being a widow make anything easier? Perhaps he assumed she had experience with children.

He leaned his elbows on the desk. "Your aura is very well controlled."

"I am very private. As are you, I see."

He looked down, hesitating. "I have never hired anyone for

this position before. I understand some things are customary, however, the expectations will be different than usual, and I want discretion guaranteed, both during and after your employment."

"Of course." How different from usual could children be? She supposed they might require special teaching or periods of intense calm and quiet. "I can speak, read and write Eletheni, Istalian, Low Elven and a smattering of Doonish. It is never too early to start that, or geography and reading."

His brow furrowed. "It is usual to rent you an apartment in the city, however, we are some distance from Rockhaven, and I need you to live here. Will that be a problem?"

When has an apartment been customary for a governess? "I'm sure it would be far more convenient if I'm here."

"I can pay a stipend instead, and the manor is big enough to ensure privacy."

A stipend! She could use that to pay off Stokes. "A stipend would be preferable."

"I would, of course, purchase an adequate wardrobe, which would be yours to keep at the end of your employment."

Delphine was acutely aware of how shabby she looked. His own coat was expertly tailored from excellent cloth. "That is very generous of you. You mentioned the end of my tenure. Is this a temporary position?"

"I will only be in Rockhaven for a few months, until my business is finished. Now, for your duties—"

He kept talking around something, but she wasn't sure what. Was something wrong with one of the children? "It would help to know the ages of the children and how many?"

He blinked at her as if she had suddenly sprouted horns like his, and a flush of purple spread across his cheeks. "What position do you think you are interviewing for, Mrs. Leighton?"

The room began to shift, like stones sliding under her feet. The sense of being seconds away from falling twisted her throat shut so she gulped like a fish. He waited silently, drumming his fingers lightly on the desktop and looking confused.

"Governess." With one word out, a cascade followed. "I overheard two women talking in a shop. The manor asked for an accomplished woman who spoke Istalian. I've been looking for work, but no one wants to hire me." *Never mind why.* She forced herself not to explain further. "I need a position."

He bit his lower lip and flicked his ears forward, then back. "I—I am not married, nor do I have children. I wanted a... um... female companion."

Companion. *Mistress.*

"Oh." The comment about a widow made more sense now.

The slipping sensation overtook her. Even gripping the arms of the chair until her knuckles ached didn't keep the room from spinning.

Tears crowded up so thick that Delphine could hardly see. She rose, grasping the chair for support. She'd wasted her money and would have to walk back to town in the dark.

A hard lump in her throat strangled her voice. "I'm very sorry to have wasted your time."

VARRICK

I told Morrow I wasn't ready for this. I made a mistake, upset her, and now the beautiful woman is crying.

"No. No need to apologize. Please, sit down, Mrs. Leighton." His plea earnest, he rang for Morrow. "Please."

With a half-swallowed sob, she sank back into the chair.

Morrow arrived, and Varrick slipped into the hall with him. "She thought she was interviewing to be a governess. She's crying. What should I do?" He felt as if he'd kicked a pup.

This ruse had been Lady M's idea, and her reasons had been sound. He'd agreed to it, but all had gone awry. He needed help.

"Governess?" Morrow peered through the slit in the door. "Give her a drink and let her calm down."

"Right." She just needed a little time. He needed a little time. Bad enough he was supposed to interview a woman as a companion. He thought she'd understood and she hadn't. Mortification for both of them burned to the tips of his ears.

"You have a drink, too," Morrow said. "You're a rich, decadent gentleman, remember?"

Taking a deep breath, Varrick returned, giving the distressed woman a wide berth. He wanted to pat her shoulder and reach out with his aura, as he would with a frightened animal.

"Would you like something? There's brandy or wine, and we have tea. Something warm?" He cast around for anything else comforting. Was it proper to offer her a blanket?

She wiped her cheeks. "Brandy is fine."

He sloshed out two glasses and handed her the smaller one. "I am terribly sorry about the confusion. I ought to have been clear from the start." She'd walked into the room with such confidence, despite looking cold and unkempt. He'd assumed the wrong thing, obviously.

Her hand trembled as she took the glass. "It was silly of me to not ask first."

Her aura's shield hadn't cracked. *Incredible control*. Most people, even shielded, had a slight halo of aura around their heads, glimmering faintly with emotions. He was used to reading that for clues, but she gave him none.

After the first few sips, her breathing slowed, and her tears stopped.

He returned to his seat and sipped his own brandy. "Don't worry about it. Please."

Lady M had explained that having a mistress on his arm would add credence to the part he was playing. A local woman who knew the city would also help them narrow down suspects. Varrick had resisted the idea, but so long as it was all an act, he would go along with it. Certainly no one was supposed to be crying.

"Please." He relaxed control of his own aura, so it became a misty swirl of concern around his chest and head. Hesitantly, he reached a strand of it toward her to offer comfort. "Don't be embarrassed. I'm so sorry—"

Mrs. Leighton flinched from the strand and bolted to her feet, sloshing brandy. "I must leave."

He laid his ears back. "You don't have a horse or cab outside. Join me for dinner. Afterwards, the carriage can take you back." Mrs. Edward, the cook, fed him like he was still an orphaned refugee; there would be plenty of food.

"You don't need to do any of that." She wiped at the corner of her eye.

He tapped his glass. "It's pouring like a monsoon outside. You'll be knee-deep in mud. Dinner, then a ride. Please."

He couldn't send her out in the rain, and he liked her. Expecting a fat human with a receding hairline! He'd almost lost his composure right then. What he'd give to bring that determination back to her eyes.

She stood there, holding the brandy, eyes wide like a rabbit watching a drake. Somehow, he'd scared her or made her feel trapped.

He should give her time alone to think. "Would you rather wait in the library?"

Some of the stiffness flowed out of her shoulders. "I—yes."

He escorted her there, and she sat by the fire, sipping the brandy and shivering as if she would never be warm again.

He knelt and added wood to the fire, encouraging it with his anima until it roared.

CHAPTER 5

Dinner Between Strangers

VARRICK

Varrick closed the library door with a soft click. He would explain the situation to Morrow and the woman who ran the house, Mrs. Halsey. They would agree that Mrs. Leighton couldn't walk back to town. Her dress was already muddy and damp. Rain thundered down, punctuated by howling winds. She'd be soaked before she reached the end of the drive and might not make it back to Rockhaven at all.

He stopped in the large entry hall. She'd assumed she'd be left to make her own way back, despite the weather. What sort of company was she used to?

There was also the matter of how she'd heard about the position. Morrow had discreetly inquired about a mistress a few weeks ago, as soon as Varrick was settled. A contact in town had suggested a few names, but Morrow had rejected the list; he knew the lay of Rockhaven's social landscape better than the rest of them.

Mrs. Leighton had come out of nowhere, expecting to be a governess.

Varrick continued to the dining room, slipped past the table and took the servant's stairs down to the kitchen, where the maid, Bethie, and Mrs. Edward were preparing dinner. Lady M insisted on making him live like a Torlish lord; he must practice before his public debut.

He would tell Mrs. Edward they had a guest for dinner. Then he would speak with the main three staff helping to arrange the hunt for the elemental: Morrow, Mrs. Halsey, and Gertrude Tanner, their supposed lady's maid and main way of communicating with Lady M.

"Mrs. Edward?" Entering the kitchen intimidated him. Mrs. Edward was very comfortable with knives.

"Don't hover in the doorway." Mrs. Edward didn't slow her stirring.

He stepped in, ducking his head. The ceilings all felt too low downstairs. "The lady is staying for dinner."

"She'll take the job then?" She removed the pot from the heat.

"I have to speak with Mrs. Tanner first." No, the lady would not be taking the job because she was looking for a position as a governess. "Do you know where she is?"

"Upstairs." Mrs. Edwards grabbed several jars of dried spices from the shelf and seasoned the pot.

Varrick backed out of the kitchen. It would be nice to eat down there, where it was warm and everyone could be at the same table. At the Scholarium, he'd eaten with his mentor or other students. The empty dining room here was lonely. The whole house, despite being far smaller than the vast halls and buildings of his school, felt enormous and empty.

He took the back stairs to the second floor. Mrs. Tanner spent part of each week at clothiers and the market, gossiping with other maids for news. She wouldn't be happy to keep looking.

Pity. Mrs. Leighton was—she was tall. And had lovely eyes, blue and expressive. And had an abundant figure that made him feel warm all over. He was compelled to comfort and impress her but couldn't explain why. It was best that he didn't. She wouldn't be staying beyond dinner.

He found Mrs. Tanner in his rooms, putting away his shirts. He could do that himself. He didn't want her in there.

"I need to talk to you." He stopped to shuffle his thoughts into order.

"Morrow told me. We'll keep looking." Mrs. Tanner straightened. "We are running out of candidates."

Mrs. Leighton had said she could get used to him. "If we explained it to her, maybe she could do it?"

Mrs. Tanner shook her head. "No! Hiring a woman who has been a mistress is very different from asking a respectable lady to play the part." She pinched the bridge of her nose. "I cannot understand how anyone could confuse the two."

Varrick scratched one ear. Did she mean Mrs. Leighton or himself? "I invited her to stay for dinner, and I'll drive her home afterwards."

"You will stay here. We don't know a thing about this woman, and we don't need trouble before we start." She shook out a shirt with more energy than necessary.

"She's on foot." He rubbed the brass cap on his horn. "Dinner would give me time to find out more about her."

She was educated and elegant, but her dress and coat were worn. There'd been a despairing note in her voice and a slump in her shoulders. He laid his ears back as lightning lit the window, followed by a peal of thunder. Why was a woman like her so desperate and alone?

"Very well. I suppose dinner won't hurt." She put her hands on her hips. "It will be good for you to practice dining etiquette. But Henry will drive her home."

"You'd make me practice while sleeping if you could."

"Don't tempt me," she sighed heavily. "Off you go."

Delphine

Dinner was awkward. How could it not be? Delphine was not properly dressed for it, and although the jaglin's staff was impeccably trained, and their auras well contained, their perfect manners made her feel even more like an intruder. She didn't belong in the world of respectable ladies and gentlemen anymore. *Where do I fit?*

"What do you think about the news that Elethen has retaken part of Maythem Island?" Mr. Allard asked once the footman, Henry, had withdrawn.

"I didn't know they had." *Good. Torlund has no right to the island.* "I suppose it means the blockade will continue." *Blocking any passage to Elethen.*

"It looks that way." Mr. Allard took a bite, but his yellow eyes stayed on her. "Torlund's navy has taken a beating, though."

She had heard that. Even tradesmen and washerwomen spoke of ships not returning. More and more women wore black armbands to signify mourning.

It was too dark a night to discuss the war, so Delphine changed the topic. "Where do you hail from, Mr. Allard? Your accent says Istalia." Istalia had a large jaglin population, but she wondered why one would be here.

He looked down at his plate, ears out. "From Istalia, yes."

He didn't elaborate. She studied him. Well-fitted coat. Silk cravat. He oozed affluence. Wine and brandy from Istalia commanded high prices here. "Are you in trade?"

He hesitated, his aura rippling around one edge. "Of a sort. Fortunately, one that isn't affected by the war."

Coal or glow, then. Something within Torlund that utilized river or overland shipping. He'd made it clear he would only be here for a season, though. Perhaps he had some interest in this session of House arguments. If so, he might be familiar with Michael.

"Lucky for you." The staff here was small for such a large

house. One footman, and she'd only seen a butler, when there ought to be maids in the background. If he didn't require a governess, and she wasn't going to be a mistress, maybe there was some other opening. "I don't suppose you could use a secretary or clerk? I've a fine hand and a good head for numbers."

He looked to the side and ran his finger along the edge of the table. "I have all the staff I need." But he didn't sound certain of it.

He turned back to her. "You're Eletheni, aren't you?"

Delphine looked down. She had the darker golden complexion and loose curls common to Elethen, but maybe he'd seen more. Had he noticed the tip of her ears, too pointed to be fully human? Or had the glowlights caught the purple in her hair?

"My mother is the daughter of an Eletheni baron. My father was the Torlish ambassador when they met and married." She took a sip of wine. It had been so long since she'd met someone who didn't know the story. "I haven't been to Elethen for twenty years."

"Since you were a toddler, then." He angled his ears down.

She couldn't read his body language, and his aura gave nothing away.

"I am thirty, Mr. Allard. I remember Elethen reasonably well."

For some reason, admitting her age brought his ears forward again. Was he pleased? How old was he? She couldn't tell. All the signs she would look for in a human man were absent or so changed, they were meaningless.

Discussing her own history left her tense. It was more comfortable to talk about him. "Are you familiar with Elethen?"

If he'd grown up in the frontier area where the boundary between jaglin Istalia and human Elethen met, he could know of her grandfather and the family history.

"I spent time in its capital. I didn't travel too far inland."

"Ah." He wouldn't know anything about Mama's side, then. Delphine let her stiff shoulders relax.

She turned her attention to the meal, casting covert glances at him through her lashes. The fish and sauce were quite good—

better than her cook's had been. He should keep her a secret, or she'd be poached by another estate.

Mr. Allard was doing the same thing, sneaking glances, a glimmer of nervousness at the edge of his aura. The corona around his head was a slight shimmer in the air, only noticeable because the light was low.

He tapped his fingers, sipped his wine, set it down, and looked away, obviously working up to something. "Which baron?"

Delphine froze, mouth full. She swallowed, washed it down with too large a gulp of wine, and ended up coughing. "What?"

Mr. Allard grimaced. "Sorry. I didn't mean to catch you off guard. You said your mother was the daughter of a baron. I wondered which one."

"My grandfather," she wheezed, "is Baron Bollenbaucher." If he'd spent time in Elethen's capital, he would know the stories.

"Oh!" He brightened. "The timber baron. He's done fascinating things with water glow."

Delphine stared, catching her breath. It made sense that he'd connect them to timber. The Bollenbauchers provide most of the building timber used by the lowland cities. She'd never even heard of water glow.

"Has he?" She was at a loss to say anything else.

"Of course! They used to have to haul barges upstream with mules or anima. Very taxing and expensive. But by creating resonance wells on each of the barges, a trained pilot and half the crew can propel it back upstream to his docks. The Scholarium in Istalia would love to know the details."

"If there wasn't a blockade, I could introduce you." And she could get away from Mr. Stokes, and miserable, soggy winters, and everyone who knew about her marriage to David. "I think Grandpapa would be happy to meet you."

She missed Grandpapa's house. Father had always been distant; Grandpapa had given her more memories in five years than her father had in the other twenty, but Grandpapa and her parents had cut ties at the end of her childhood trip.

Mama and Father had found the libertine morals of Elethen and the Bollenbaucher family history embarrassing. Father had accused Grandpapa of undermining his authority. Delphine and her brother, Alastair, were sent back to Rockhaven with Mama while Father stayed in Elethen's capital alone.

The subject of Elethen had drawn Mr. Allard out. He spoke about the river docks, since the capital sat far up a deep, wide river that even sailing ships could traverse. He described the massive falls half a day's travel up from the sprawling city. His feline ears would come forward or lay back as he recounted studying the ruins of the old skydock there. He'd even visited Maythem Island before the Torlish invasion.

"You sound like you enjoyed your time there," she said as his enthusiasm wound down and the footman cleared away the last course.

"It holds many pleasant memories." He signaled for the footman and asked for coffee, a Doonish drink that was new to the city. "Would you like to try some?"

She would never have another chance. "Please."

In no time at all, the footman returned with the rich, novel drink. Delphine sipped hers slowly, savoring the new taste and wanting the comfort and warmth to last before returning to her cold rooms. Mr. Allard watched her over the rim of his cup, yellow eyes bright, corona glittering with interest.

"You have something to say, Mr. Allard?"

"Yes." He set his cup down with a delicacy his size belied. "You came here under a false notion, but if you wanted to fill the actual position, you would be very welcome." A purple flush spread across his cheeks.

He was asking her to be his mistress. She would live here and allow him to undress her. She would share his bed, and he would

37

enjoy her body. The heat rose in her cheeks. "I hadn't considered it. Although the offer is...flattering."

"I would be honored if you would." His ears came forward again, and the odd purple-green flush tinged them as well. His aura glimmered with admiration before he locked it.

She smiled into the cup of coffee. "If I change my mind, I will allow you the right of first refusal." She couldn't. The humiliation of being a mistress would be excruciating.

He grinned, teeth bright in the green face. Would she become desperate enough to make good on that promise? It wasn't something she wanted to think about right now, not with him watching.

CHAPTER 6

The Lonely Night

DELPHINE

When Mr. Allard handed Delphine up into the coach, his eyes lingered on her face, and he held her hand a little longer than necessary. The night was biting enough that she almost begged him for any position. She'd scrub pots or wash windows for a warm, snug room in the manor. But a rug and heated stones for her feet were already inside the carriage, and he would be in a hurry.

The enclosed carriage and warm rug made the long drive pass quickly. They finally clattered down her dark street, and her heart sank at the thought of her chilly rooms. The rain had ended, but bitter draughts still moaned between the buildings. The carriage couldn't go down Delphine's alley, but the driver dismounted, handed her out, and escorted her to her door, carrying a heavy bundle under his arm. Delphine eyed it suspiciously, wondering what might have been sent along.

"I was instructed to stay until you had a proper fire, ma'am," the driver explained, and kindled it with his anima and the wood he'd brought.

"Thank you. Thank Mr. Allard for me." She said it too many

times, until they were both embarrassed, but she couldn't express her gratitude enough. Mr. Allard had done more for her than any of her old friends and acquaintances.

Sitting in front of the little fire, she had to blink back tears. It was such an unexpected kindness—he didn't have to make sure she was warm.

She still needed the money to pay Mr. Stokes. The column of numbers weighed on her shoulders like lead. Edwina offered nothing. Delphine could go directly to Michael, at his office, and beg and then, if Michael refused to help then she would have no more options. It would be a ship to Alladoon or remain under Stokes's thumb.

Or, she could return to Sayledon Manor and accept Mr. Allard's offer. She was reluctant to warm any man's bed. It required too much trust. A curl of frank curiosity wound through her. She'd seen the glamorous women lords hired for company. What would it be like to be a woman like that, luxuriating in admiration, so far outside of society that scandal and disdain could not taint her? What would it be like to let a man touch her again, to feel his hands on her skin?

Mr. Allard's smile bloomed in her mind. Admitting her interest left her uncomfortable. It was a risk. Even the most courteous man in public could be vicious in private. David had been charming and genteel enough to fool everyone, even herself.

But the thought of Mr. Allard touching her wouldn't go away. She slept badly.

Varrick

"I don't object to your kindness, Mr. Allard," Mrs. Tanner said. "But telling her to consider the position ... we haven't even had time to find out who she is or if she's trustworthy."

Varrick crossed his arms. "You said that time was of the essence. We can't hunt the elemental without putting me out into society, and a mock mistress was part of that plan." He laid his ears back.

He understood subterfuge. It was bread and butter in the Istalian streets where he'd grown up. But misdirection and lies while negotiating an agreement or causing a distraction so a comrade could sneak past authorities was different than this. He had to pretend to adore a woman he barely knew. He had to give the impression they were lovers, which might be easier if he'd ever had a lover.

Had he explained to Mrs. Leighton that it was just a pretense? He couldn't remember. Her realization that it wasn't a governess position had cut off his first explanation and later he'd been too intent on calming her. Surely he had, but he couldn't remember.

He had to comport himself well here, not just in the hunt but in this ruse Lady M had suggested. Impressing her would open more doors at the Scholarium and disappointing her could close them forever. He couldn't afford foolish mistakes.

Mrs. Halsey laughed softly. "Mr. Allard is right. We don't have more time, and the available escorts and courtesans of Rockhaven are all unsuitable." She glanced at Morrow, who nodded in confirmation.

"It's made quite a stir. A new, mysterious, very rich man. Gossip runs rampant." Morrow grinned. "That's probably how it reached Mrs. Leighton."

"You said there'd been another attack," Varrick said.

Morrow's face went grave. "A young man who'd just been accepted into the University of Magi. He was found in the street outside the Iron Dragon."

A sober chill swept the room. The last attack had been less than two weeks ago. The intervals between them were getting shorter.

"We need someone," Morrow said. "Even if they aren't a perfect choice."

"But an unknown?" Tanner shook her head.

Varrick cleared his throat. "We know a little. She's the daughter of the Torlish ambassador to Elethen, and she's Baron Bollenbaucher's granddaughter." Although the latter might mean nothing to them.

Mrs. Halsey shrugged.

Mrs. Tanner raised her eyebrows. "An Eletheni baron?"

"The baron is brilliant, and his land borders Istalia." Varrick thought it a point in her favor, especially since she was in poor circumstances. Family was important to the barons. "If we help his granddaughter, the baron would owe Lady M a favor."

"She refused you," Mrs. Tanner said. "Don't expect her to come back. She's a lady, after all."

Mrs. Halsey nodded. "It will ruin her. She'll be a pariah."

"But the lady was desperate enough to come here based on overheard gossip. I think she already is."

She had refused him, although she'd said she was flattered by the offer. Had he explained that it was purely a ruse?—he laid his ears back, trying to remember. Might she consider it if they offered the right price? She was a widow, but she had family overseas. Lady M had brought him from Istalia; she might arrange passage for Mrs. Leighton to Elethen.

Mrs. Leighton had looked embarrassed when he asked about her family and had relaxed again when he'd gone off about the new developments for barges. He must have bored her to tears.

In Elethen, the affair between Baroness Bollenbaucher and one of the elven sea captains, decades ago, was well known. Was it known in Rockhaven? Neither Mrs. Halsey nor Morrow had recognized the family name.

Mrs. Halsey and Mrs. Tanner were discussing the locations of the attacks. The pattern wasn't as strong as he'd been told. Six were from the richest section of town, near the university, but others looked random, like targets of opportunity. There was nothing new, but they kept going over it, again and again, hoping they'd missed something.

"Time to turn in," Mrs. Halsey finally said. "I'll be at market tomorrow and I'll put out more feelers for a possible candidate. Perhaps there's an actress or singer who would do."

Varrick hoped not but couldn't put his finger on why. He wouldn't be forming an attachment to whoever they hired. He would attend operas and strut around in public in velvet and lace until he found the elemental. He'd be happy to go home to Istalia and the Scholarium and leave ruffles behind for good.

Mrs. Tanner waited until the doors to the library shut before pinning him with a skeptical eye.

Varrick eyed her back. "Yes?"

"Is it just that she has family connections to Elethen?" She put her hands on her hips. "Or is there some other reason you offered her the position?"

"Like what?" He was trying not to follow her line of thought, but Mrs. Leighton had such bright eyes, and she'd finally smiled while he spoke about Elethen. He'd like to see her smile again.

"She's a beautiful woman." Mrs. Tanner softened. "And some men can't resist trying to rescue anything that's trapped."

"I'm not trying to rescue her."

Henry hadn't returned yet from taking her home. That would be the end of it. She'd find someplace where she could sit and teach children Elven conjugations. He couldn't argue on one point, though. She was beautiful.

CHAPTER 7

Nowhere to Turn

Delphine

Delphine had never visited Michael's office. It sat facing a small courtyard and crossroads not far from the domed House of Law, where lords, magi, and the king made decisions for everyone else. The austere building loomed, both foreboding and rich, with imported stone facades and warding spells woven into the windows. It took several minutes for her to find the right number, and several more for her knock to be answered.

The doorman frowned at Delphine when she asked to see Michael. "Lord Havemshire is not in his office, Mrs. Leighton."

Her heart sank. "Do you know when he will return? I have an important matter of business to discuss with him."

"I am afraid he is engaged on House business and may not be available for some time. Perhaps not until the session is over for the season." He started to close the door.

"He can't be busy every minute of every day. I need to speak with him for a moment only." Her voice sharpened with frustration. He might not lend her money, but she'd expected him to see her at least. "The session doesn't end for a month!"

"I am very sorry. Perhaps you could inquire with his solicitor, *if* it is a matter of business," the doorman suggested, a smirk tugging at his lips.

Anger and despair lodged in her throat, blocking her reply. Michael had been David's friend once, and family by marriage. Did it mean nothing to him? "I will."

The door shut, and she glared at it before turning away and striding across the windy courtyard. Her mind spun in circles. *Will Michael help, or will he refuse and leave me with no recourse?* His solicitor wouldn't give her a loan without Michael's say-so, but he might send a message directly to her brother-in-law.

She did not realize someone had fallen into step with her until he spoke.

"You seem a little short on resources," Mr. Stokes said. "I am getting anxious that I won't get my money."

She quickened her stride. "Why don't you go talk to David's grave about it? I have no more money than his bones."

He matched her pace. "Now, now, don't despair. Pretty lady like you, there's always someone willing to put up payment."

Delphine glared down at him. "That statement could be considered highly improper."

He took her arm. "You don't want to make a scene now, do you? You and me, we're just a pair of people walking along having a friendly conversation about my money. I've got a gentleman—a couple of them—willing to pay off your debts in exchange for a little of your time. As it seems your relations can't be bothered, I thought I would mention it."

Anger simmered in her chest. "And how much extra will you get for prostituting me?" She tried to pull her arm away, but he held it fast.

He sneered. "Oh, I could make a lot off you if that was my racket, but I don't want the bother."

"You're revolting."

"I'm giving you a choice now," he said. "End of the month, I'll just give your direction to the highest bidder. He can come pick you up."

The chill of fear stopped her in her tracks. He would not. "You would condone kidnapping?" she demanded.

"I condone whatever gets me my money."

"I have over a week before your deadline, so take your hand off me." This time when she pulled away, he allowed it.

"So proud for an Eletheni whore, ain't you? No one's going to want you on the honest side of the sheets." He leered at her and licked his lips. "Everyone knows what those foreign women is like."

Her skin crawled. "Good day, Mr. Stokes."

He touched the brim of his hat, gave her another repulsive glance, and moved away into the traffic. *I hope he gets run over by a coach and four.*

When he was out of sight, Delphine stumbled to the nearest building and leaned heavily against it. She yearned for a friendly face, someone on her side.

She wanted Mama, with her slow, indulgent smile and rich red hair, or her brother with his mischievous eyes and roguish laugh. Even Grandpapa, his deep voice and gentle hands, teaching her how to plant a sapling or skip rocks. Father ... they hadn't been close, but even he'd rage at her circumstances now.

Eletheni whore. The insult had become popular since the war started. But it had never been aimed at her before. She squeezed her eyes shut until the sting of tears passed. She'd never truly fit into Rockhaven society. She was a wildflower at the garden show: beautiful until someone pointed out that she was a weed. She didn't belong here anymore. She never had.

Delphine ran through the list of people she'd once known, even David's old crowd. He'd been desperately alone at the end, having driven all his real friends away, leaving him with only parasites and predators.

Unbidden, the thought of Mr. Allard crossed her mind. She

wrapped her arms around herself, chilled suddenly. Was she seriously considering that choice? But she would not be safer with the sort of man who did business with Mr. Stokes—she'd been married to one, after all.

Mr. Allard had been a thorough gentleman. He hadn't trapped or coerced her or even pressured her. He'd treated her like a lady, even when she arrived looking like a drowned seagull. He'd made sure she was warm and fed.

If the choice was Mr. Stokes' clients or Mr. Allard, she would walk out to Sayledon Manor and tell Mr. Allard she'd be very happy to stay. At least she'd get the stipend and put off Stokes for another month. Surely Mr. Allard would run him off if he called on her at the manor house.

And she was curious. Why was he here in the first place? Rockhaven would be nothing but hostile to him. The drawing rooms and ballrooms of the city were the last place she would expect to see a jaglin.

Her father's crisp voice returned to her, his voice sharp, angry. *Nothing stupider than a jaglin. Frogs are good for cannon fodder and nothing else.*

She pressed a hand to her stomach, because the words brought back the whole memory. They'd been at Grandpapa's. Father was back from his business in the capital, and the jaglin lord had come for supper again. She'd been amused by his funny cat-ears, which he'd flip back and forth to make her laugh. Father had been furious. He'd dragged her out of the room to spill his ire and prejudice on her.

She didn't need those memories now.

Mr. Allard was well-spoken and rich enough to take a house to let that once belonged to a lord. It was a grand hall, not a place for the average tradesman. He disproved everything Father had said.

Father was dead. His opinions should be buried too.

Jaglin or human, green or pink, horns or not, being a mistress led to the bed chamber, naked bodies, vulnerability. How much of herself was she willing to trade for the promise of safety, security, and comfort?

Michael's solicitor refused to see her, sending her away with explicit instructions never to come again. He'd had the audacity to threaten to call the constables and have her committed for hysteria. She hadn't shown him hysteria, oh no.

That night, Delphine woke from a light sleep to muffled shouts, rattling at her door, scuffling, banging, and more shouts. A man's scream drove into her brain like a frozen nail, squeezing her breath away. Pale gold anima glimmered then blinked out. Feet trampled on the cobbles. As she peered out her dirty window into the night, she could barely make out the running shapes. The commotion in the alley had attracted the scavengers of the area; nothing would induce her to open her door.

Delphine huddled in bed, too afraid to stoke up the fire. The light might attract attention. Those long dark hours until dawn gave her ample time to think about Mr. Stokes' threats and to sort again through her very short list of friends who might help her. She could contact one of Alastair's old fellows from school, but it would take weeks for a letter to get to one. She didn't have weeks.

She hated being cornered. No doubt Mr. Stokes thought she was trapped. He might have counted on it from the very beginning. She had one clear avenue of escape, one the bookie couldn't have anticipated.

She spent the chilly hours before dawn racking her brain for any other way to pay the debt or escape Rockhaven. As a widow with a good name, she might marry again, although that held no appeal. What if she chose another David? Marriage was as irrevocable as ruin.

Light crept through the cracks around the door and filtered through the dirty window. Sunrise. She had to make a choice. She had to leave. One ocean away, on the other side of a war, she had family who would welcome her. Giving up or giving in to Stokes was not an option.

Although she had no plan, she dressed and prepared to leave. Something would come to her as she walked—a name, a direction, an old connection. One step out the door, she confronted what remained of the night's commotion. The man was alive. His chest rose and fell in a shallow rhythm. He'd been stripped of his clothing and anything valuable.

His aura had been shredded. It wafted around him like thin, tattered smoke, dead gray and white. Any Skilling he'd had would be gone, for it required touching others with one's aura. He wouldn't remember what happened. He might not remember anything about himself, and he would spend the rest of his life unable to fully connect to others and the world around him. *If* he ever regained his mind.

If Delphine let her aura open, it looked like that, too. She had no memory of how it happened, just that months ago, she'd woken to a shredded, gray aura and her feelings just as flat and colorless. If she had looked outside last night, would she have seen what had done it? Her throat and chest grew cold and tight. His ragged aura curling like candle smoke around him sent a frisson of terror through her limbs. It had happened here, right outside her door. The rattling had been a desperate bid for escape. Something had hunted him, ravaged him, and left him for the scavengers.

Delphine bolted out of the narrow alley. What if the same thing that had shredded her aura found her again? Would it finish the little she had left, taking memory and self, leaving her staring and mindless like that man?

She could not go back to the street, the alley, or her rooms. She needed crowds, people, safety so she could hide from the nameless dread washing over her. She made for the nearest public park, barely noticing the traffic around her or the voices that cursed when she stumbled into someone. The unknown thing frightened her more than Stokes and his threats.

Near Rockhaven's public gardens, Delphine found a bench where she could watch the carriages of the rich pass and feel safe within the constant flow of foot traffic. Even on such a dismal day, women strolled on footpaths that wound between the massive, ancient oak trees. Regaining her breath was harder; it wasn't the running that left her panting.

She could not wait in those dingy rooms for some last ray of hope. The attack in the alley showed exactly how vulnerable she was. Stokes would not wait until the end of the month to seize her. The surety of it was thick and bitter on her tongue.

She would end up in a man's bed, one way or another. At least Mr. Allard had offered to negotiate terms and made it clear it was temporary. It was not quite entering the relationship on her own terms, but it was far closer than waiting for someone to seize her off the street. Spinning panic filled her chest and throat.

Most of her scant copper cuers had been spent. She did not have enough in her purse for another cab. She set off for Sayledon Manor without further thought. Such a large house and grounds could not be missed, and only one main road went that way.

The manor offered security she would find nowhere else, no matter how long she looked.

CHAPTER 8

Desperate Measures

DELPHINE

Panic was short. The sore feet and legs trembling from hunger lasted for hours. By the time the sun reached its zenith, Delphine regretted not paying for a cab to bring her partway. The hills were steeper than she'd expected, the road rutted and muddy. Walking alongside it meant dodging clumps of yellow-flowered gorse, then releasing her skirt when it caught on the rough plant's stems. When the sun touched the horizon, turning the gray day hazy pink, she finally sighted the manor, still too far to reach before dark.

As the light faded, so did her remaining confidence. Was it possible that Mr. Allard had merely been polite in his offer, an attempt to soften the blow of disappointment? Delphine's feet dragged. What if she arrived, only to discover that he'd hired someone else? Or worse, that he'd not meant it at all. It was too late and too far to turn back.

Her rap at the door was answered more quickly this time, and the butler did not quite hide a ripple of both surprise and pleasure as he allowed her in. "I am sure Mr. Allard will be pleased to hear you've returned, Mrs. Leighton. If you would wait in the library again."

"Of course." Sweet rivers, was she really going to accept his offer?

She followed Morrow to the library again, but as she sat in the same seat as before, the full reality hit her. The weight of it was staggering. Once her time with Mr. Allard was up, she could not return to her old life, even if she had money. Appearing publicly with him was not just crossing a bridge but burning it behind her.

But so was waiting for Mr. Stokes.

Her grief at leaving respectable society carried the same relief as David's death. There would be no more pretense of acceptance, only new speculation about her private life. Speculation she now deserved. What a difference that made.

She would not think about what being a mistress entailed, not until everything was set. Not about how it was to stretch out face to face with a man and let the light reveal the geography of their bodies, nor how it felt to explore and be explored. Widows might reach a point where they desired a man in their beds again, but she was not there yet.

The nuzzling of a drake sent her thoughts flying. Delphine stroked the brindle female until it closed its eyes and grimaced in pleasure. If only she could feed Stokes to the drakes, or maybe just all his records. She was scratching the brindle between her hot nostrils when the butler returned to fetch her.

"She likes you," he said, the glimmer of approval shimmering again.

"What is her name?"

"That's Sable." He clucked for her to follow them. "Talon is waiting with Mr. Allard. He thought they would put you at ease."

"That's very kind of him." Put her at ease? Was he expecting to unsettle her again?

Mr. Allard had been extravagantly kind to her, even when it

did not benefit him. Why? Few people were kind for kindness's sake. Maybe his consideration was nothing more than a lure. What was he hiding behind it?

When she entered the office, Mr. Allard sat back in his chair, ears perked up, corona bright. The door clicked closed behind her.

"I didn't expect you back." He motioned to the chair. Sable trotted to the side of his desk, sticking her nose into his face.

"You made a very strong first impression," Delphine said. "I hope you meant what you said, and that I haven't made an eternal fool of myself."

"Hardly. You made sure I knew you spoke Elven and Eletheni."

"And Istalian. Will that be an advantage?" Surely he was jesting to make her relax.

"It may be." He removed a stack of papers from a drawer and laid it in the center of the desk, then took a quill from another drawer. "I, um, may have given a false impression of the position when we first spoke."

She steeled herself for disappointment. She could not afford it. She couldn't afford not to be here. "Go on."

"I said companion, but escort is more accurate." He wiped his quill. "You would accompany me in public and to certain private affairs."

"Only a—" A companion. Her knees went weak, and she dropped into the chair. "So, there would not be any ... intimate expectations?"

"No, Mrs. Leighton." His tone made it clear that he hadn't even considered it. That was a relief, if less than flattering. "In public, you will play the part. In private, our arrangement is strictly business." He stared down at the stack of papers, then back up at Delphine. "I hope I haven't insulted you."

Her cheeks and ears flushed with heat. What a fool she'd been, making assumptions. "I am sorry, I thought—" She stopped herself. She'd made it obvious what she thought. Mortification tied her tongue.

He stared at the far corner of the room and shook himself. "I feel privileged that you returned at all then."

Did he think she was attracted to him? She wasn't *not* attracted, but there was a vast gulf of feeling in between those two things. It was too strange to think about. But she had, when she thought she was coming to share his bed.

"So, I'm doing what any lady does, just as a mistress—in name only. Correct?" She'd made a fool of herself twice. She wanted to be clear this time.

One side of his mouth quirked upward, but it wasn't quite a smile. "Many places I will be frequenting might send gently raised ladies into fits and vapors. I need someone who can keep their head and poise in the face of lewdness and revelry, and who can listen and remember what she hears."

Delphine considered that as he pulled out a pen knife and trimmed the quill. This was not the sordid agreement she'd expected. "You want a spy, Mr. Allard?"

He raised his eyebrows. "I want a charming, lovely companion, mistress in name only. If she happens to hear and notice certain things, so much the better. I also enjoy the opera, and it's better with company."

No matter how finely dressed, if he arrived at the opera house or the Glass Gardens alone, he might be refused entry. With her at his side, he would be more acceptable to high society, if not polite society. Having a mistress—a *human* mistress—proclaimed a financial status few men could attain while leaving the ladies and lords feeling safely superior to him.

"I understand." Where else might he take her, that would give a lady fits and vapors? "It won't be just the opera, will it?"

"Rich gentlemen like to gamble, so I will be joining them. I may be attending performances reserved only for men of certain tastes. Will it put you off to be surrounded by card games, betting, and ribaldry?" He held the quill ready.

She took a deep breath, sorting that out. She'd hosted gambling parties back when things with David were good. It had been a lark, tiptoeing the line of acceptability. All the men invited had been friends of David or Michael. They'd been raucous and rowdy, but never out of hand. David had even taught her to deal and play.

"I've lived in the penumbra of that world." Her voice sounded more confident than she felt.

He looked up at her through his lashes. "I am glad you came back."

"I have few options, and your offer sounded generous." Embarrassment turned her voice tart. She needed money to pay off Stokes, and all Mr. Allard wanted her to do was dangle on his arm and eavesdrop. "I would like to discuss the stipend you mentioned. Is it per week or per month?"

"Per week would be better. I am unsure how long my business here will take." He dipped the quill and began writing out a contract, adding their names.

Varrick Allard. An Eletheni name, but an Istalian accent. *Very mysterious.* "Do I get to know your business?"

"Not at this time." On the contract, he began to list his obligations but left the amount for the stipend blank. "The rent for a furnished, appropriate apartment in the better part of Rockhaven would run close to one hundred thalens per month. Would twenty-five per week be appropriate?"

Delphine's heart sank. She needed a full month's worth to give Stokes his first payment. Would someone come after her? Her empty stomach churned with bile.

When she didn't answer, he opened his aura, sending thin, misty tendrils of pale orange reassurance toward her. She let them wash across her hands, but kept her aura shielded. She could read his sincerity and concern but couldn't risk letting him Skill her into agreement. With her own aura so damaged, she had no defense against someone imposing their emotions on her.

His aura retreated, wrapping around him and fading into a calm blue before being completely shielded. He knew she could see his aura, knew she would feel his touch, and he was carefully watching her reaction. His deft talent with the Skill was impressive. She'd been as good, once.

Stokes would not dare come for her here. He probably wouldn't know where she was until they made a public appearance. If she completely escaped his reach, he could wallow in David's debts until he died.

She straightened her shoulders, swallowing down the nausea. "Twenty-five is fair, but I also want safe passage to Elethen when we part ways." It was a daring request. There had to be smugglers slipping through the blockade, but a ship safe for a woman on her own would be harder to find. "And I would like the first payment in advance." Perhaps it would be enough to put Stokes off until she escaped.

He tapped the quill to his lips, thinking. "I can see that you get to Elethen." He added the stipend amount, even made a note that the first portion would be paid immediately, then added the stipulation for the journey. Ears perked, he looked up. "May I add an introduction to your grandfather as part of the arrangement?"

She almost scoffed, but he let a twinkle of amusement show in his corona. Delphine pursed her lips. "If I am satisfied, yes."

"I shall make an addendum, should you be pleased with the outcome." His quill scratched across the page. "Motivation for me to do my part well." He set the quill back in the ink. "We ought to set out boundaries for our public and private, um, affections."

"You mean how and where we can or cannot touch one another and under what circumstances?" She wasn't sure how serious he was.

"I don't want to put you in an uncomfortable situation, particularly not in public where everything must look real." He laced his fingers, ears forward, all attentive focus. "What would be appropriate?"

"Um." Where in the world did she start? A flurry of things she had done with David poured through her mind. She remembered places he had kissed her, and where she had kissed him. She knew the exact way his fingers had traced the lines of her neck, the angle of her collarbone, and the circle of her breasts. Delphine swallowed, furious that those memories could still stir feelings in her.

Allard flushed and put his ears half-back. "I think touching hands and arms would be allowable. Shoulders?"

She nodded. "Yes, shoulders would be acceptable. My back would be fine. Yours?"

"Mine as well." He noted it. "I don't mind my horns being touched but my ears are quite sensitive."

"So, I'll avoid them." Pity. They looked soft. "You may touch mine, if you wish."

He gulped and added that to the contract. "I shall assume that all clothing stays on."

Oh. She hadn't thought that needed to be said. "Yes." She tried to be emphatic, but ill-timed giggles threatened to ruin it.

His quill stopped, poised above the paper. He made a sound in his throat, like a deep, barely audible purr, and looked away from her, cheeks almost as dark as his sleek hair. "Kissing?"

Delphine studied his mouth. Wide, with well-formed lips. His teeth were white and clean. There would be no difference between kissing him and kissing a human man.

"So long as I don't get my eye poked out by a horn," she said, "I think that would be quite acceptable."

He blinked, flipping his ears back and forth. "I shall let you take the lead."

Delphine ducked her chin. "Thank you."

"I can't imagine we would need much else listed." He rubbed the curve of his horn with his thumb. "Addendums can be added if necessary." His blush slowly faded, and he slid the papers across the desk towards her. "See if everything is clear and agreeable."

She scanned each line. He would provide the stipend, housing, appropriate clothing, a lady's maid, transportation, and such. Delphine would play the part of his mistress in public, including introductions to people she knew. The image of introducing Mr. Allard to Edwina flashed across her mind. *Oh dear*.

She was also to agree not to pry into his business. He would tell her what was pertinent as they went. She didn't like that part. Was he spying for another country? Was she unintentionally declaring a side in the war?

"Is it acceptable?" Mr. Allard asked.

Delphine wound a curl around her finger. "Is this going to put us in jail?"

He tipped his head. "I have been legally hired by a person of rank to deal with a delicate situation. So, I don't think so."

Not as encouraging as she'd hoped, but again; if she refused, where was she supposed to go?

"Yes." She held out her hand for the quill and signed her name on the contract. How binding was it? A Rockhaven court wouldn't take him seriously, but they might listen to this *person of rank*. She wasn't intending to break it, in any case.

She returned the quill to him.

"I would like to move in tonight." She could retrieve her few belongings tomorrow.

His brows rose. "Are you sure?"

"You sent your man to start my fire, so you know my circumstances. Why wouldn't I want a decent meal and warm room starting tonight?" The empty stare of the man in the alley haunted her. She couldn't sleep there.

He stood. "We'll need time to become more comfortable with one another before we're seen together in public. Do you wish to dine with me again, or would you prefer to eat privately tonight?"

"Privately, please." A pleasant dinner when she knew she

would not be staying was far different than eating across from a man she would be affectionate with, even if it included no true intimacy. She was too exhausted and rattled to eat in company tonight.

He nodded. Was that a touch of relief in his corona? "Tomorrow, we will retrieve your belongings and make an appointment with the dressmaker. Mrs. Halsey, the housekeeper will help acquaint you with the staff."

CHAPTER 9

A Lady at Sayledon

DELPHINE

Delphine waited in the study until a shorter, plump woman with fading golden hair arrived. Mrs. Halsey showed her to a set of rooms on the second floor—what had once been the suite for the lady of the manor. There was a small entry room before the main bedroom, a separate dressing room off to one side, and a fireplace with a settee placed perfectly for lounging in front of it.

Delphine nearly melted at the sight of the merry fireplace. The room's heat embraced her, easing her apprehension.

"Now," Mrs. Halsey said. "I'll send Bethie up with a tray, then Tanner will help prepare you for bed. We'll see about getting your things—" she hesitated— "laundered."

Delphine looked ruefully down at her muddy, shabby skirt and boots. "They sorely need it."

Mrs. Halsey made a noise of agreement. "Dinner first."

The maid, Bethie, said little, although she surveyed Delphine from the corner of her eyes as she set the tray on the small side table and laid out a napkin. Later, after Bethie had removed the meal and brought a pitcher and basin for washing, Tanner arrived.

Tanner was a tall, stout woman with the olive-gold skin and dark hair of an Eletheni. She reminded Delphine of a horse trader, ready to seize her by the chin and check her teeth. However, after a stern study, the lady's maid assured her that she had impeccable training and could do wonderful things with Delphine's thick hair.

"Such an unusual color," she commented as she unbraided it, "almost purple in some light."

"Just a trick of the glowlights." If Mr. Allard and his staff didn't know about the family scandal, she wouldn't enlighten them. What had her great-grandmama been thinking? Taking a sea captain lover, an *elven* sea captain at that.

"We should show off your curls." She loosened one to fall in a spiral down Delphine's temple. "We will order a basic wardrobe tomorrow, but until then, we have nightgowns and chemises. They'll be a bit short on you, but no one will see."

Clean, warm nightgowns sounded wonderful.

Tanner rebraided Delphine's hair, helped her out of her skirts and stays, and presented her with a thick, wool nightgown.

"Wait a moment." Tanner laid the garment out on the turned-down bed and bloomed her anima—four strong, golden tendrils unfurling. She split them into finer threads and split them again until they were as thin as hair. Her aura followed, opening and turning deep, midnight blue. *Rest. Relaxation. Safety.* The blue threads of aura twisted around the anima, weaving the spell into the fabric of the nightgown and sheets. It was a spectacular display of Crafting. Delphine had only seen better once, by a master Craftsman who used it to strengthen his glassware.

Delphine crawled into the Craft-warmed nightgown and sheets with a sigh of contentment. The emotions in it soaked through her. None of her fears could catch hold. She still had to worry about Stokes and who he might sell her debts to, but for tonight, she was warm and safe.

. . .

In the morning, Tanner accompanied Delphine to the dressmakers for measurements and fittings. Tanner had a list detailing not just the desired gowns and dresses but also preferred colors and details. Much to her relief, Delphine was not familiar with this dressmaker. She didn't want gossip to reach Edwina or anyone close to her. Her sister-in-law would never understand.

The experience was surreal. Measurements, fabric and color choices, this for the opera, that for a private gathering. Delphine ought to have felt something about her change of situation. Trepidation, at least. The most she could muster was curiosity and a low-simmering concern that perhaps Mr. Allard was involved in something dangerous.

With the immediate danger of Mr. Stokes gone, Delphine could find dark amusement in the situation. As relations with Elethen broke down and David's carousing had drained the coffers, many fine ladies of society had made her feel unwelcome in dozens of tiny ways. Now, she had simply stepped out of that ill-fitting role into another one, firmly outside their purview. Only respectable women worried about their reputations and good names.

By afternoon, the driver brought Delphine and Tanner to Delphine's former rooms. Much to her relief, the man who'd been attacked was no longer in the alleyway, and her few possessions took no time at all to gather. There were only letters, a shawl that had belonged to Mama, and clothing she wouldn't need soon. No jewelry, not even a sentimental brooch.

Tanner stayed in the alleyway, although Delphine couldn't understand why. It smelled out there and was colder and damper than inside. No one bothered her, though. Tanner's severe countenance seemed to be a deterrent for onlookers and cutpurses.

As the driver bundled her things into the coach, Delphine watched the usual flow of foot traffic through the dingy streets. Many slowed for a peek at the carriage before hurrying on, but there was a tall, blond man a little way down the street who stood and watched. He didn't move until Delphine looked directly at him, then he pulled up his high collar and nipped around the corner. She frowned. There was something vaguely familiar about him, but nothing she could place.

One of Stokes' men? Or—rivers forbid—another bookie who'd tracked her down for money? Thank the skies that she'd accepted Mr. Allard's offer when she had.

Once Delphine returned to Sayledon Manor, her nerves rose to a full boil. After all, it would not all be gowns and cozy suppers. Men's games of chance and drinking could make them rash and violent. She had to trust that Allard would play protector as earnestly as she played mistress.

She had no proper dress for dinner, but Tanner arranged her hair, making it more elegant than necessary.

"From the neck up, I'm ready for a ball," Delphine said, admiring it.

What a stir Mr. Allard would make at one of the grand balls of the season! If he had a title and money, would all the over-eager mamas throw their daughters at him, jaglin or no? The image of him decked out in a full long vest and coat for a dance, with stockings and buckled shoes, brought a smile to her face.

Once one was used to the shocking amount of green, and the horns, he did cut a fine figure—tall, broad-shouldered, and fit. She suspected many mamas and their daughters would secretly look, even if they sneered in public.

CHAPTER 10

The Study of Speckles

DELPHINE

Mr. Allard was dressed for dinner in a dark blue coat. Delphine felt shabby sitting across from him, but he chatted so amiably about the news from Rockhaven that her discomfort passed. Afterwards, they retired to the library with the two sleek drakes for company.

"Once your gowns are in, I will take you to the opera," he said. "As a debut of sorts." He offered her one of the chairs before the fire and sat in the other one.

Delphine patted her knee to entice Sable closer. It was easier to look at the drake than him. "I look forward to it."

"Do you enjoy the opera?"

"Yes. I appreciate music a great deal." Her objection to the opera was what David had done with the opera dancers afterwards.

"There's a jaglin opera in Istalia that's incredible." He drummed his fingers on his thigh, looking distant. "How do you feel about being the center of attention?"

"I don't mind it." During her debut, she had basked in the glow of attention, urged on by Mama. She couldn't discern Allard's aura just now and did not know him well enough to read the expression on his face. "Are you expecting a great deal of attention?"

"I can't avoid it. I am of an unusual aspect here in Torlund." He grinned at his own understatement. "And I have a box that shall be highly visible."

Unusual aspect indeed. "You want attention."

He nodded, a slight smile playing on his lips. "I hope you shall help me garner it."

"And what am I to do with such attention?" Being half-Eletheni had always drawn casual notice and rumors, if only for the novelty. David had enjoyed the notoriety among the gentlemen. Delphine had endured the insinuations of certain ladies with less amusement.

Everyone knows what foreign women is like. Stokes' words haunted her. Mama had tried so hard to distance herself and Delphine from it, but disdain was persistent.

"You have a good eye for auras. Look for anything out of the ordinary."

She acknowledged the compliment with a nod, although she wasn't sure what would be out of the ordinary. "Anything else?"

"Be attentive to me. Extravagantly so." He looked down and traced the sprawling floral pattern on the upholstery of the chair.

"Oh. My." A warm flush crossed her cheeks, and she squashed a nervous laugh. She knew the sort of attention he meant. She'd seen mistresses do it. "You wish to set all sorts of tongues wagging, don't you?"

Talon laid his head in Mr. Allard's lap, and Allard scratched the drake's crest. "Will it bother you to be exposed to all your former society so publicly?"

Delphine shrugged. "I think they will be delighted to see that I have come down in the world." Her father's star had fallen, then David's. It was her turn, but only for a little while. It would be over in a month or two, and she would sail away to Elethen.

"But how do *you* feel about it, Mrs. Leighton?" He looked up, catching her eye.

She didn't want to examine her feelings, much less talk about them. "That you are too perceptive by half, Mr. Allard."

"And you're evasive." He cradled Talon's head, stroking the delicate scales along the drake's cheeks.

"I will play my role. My reputation was already teetering on the edge. If I must go down, I shall do so spectacularly, in flames."

"Reputations are of great concern to the ladies of Rockhaven." Worry crossed his face and flickered in his corona.

"I am no longer a lady." She stood on the shores of her old world, watching it ebb and flow, but its storms could no longer sink her unless she let them.

Good dress shops could turn out gowns in days. She might be playing her role within the week. She could stand the stigma of being a fallen woman in society's eyes, but not the humiliation of them seeing that it was a farce.

"If you want extravagant affection at the opera, perhaps we ought to—" her cheeks burned, and the heat of it rose to the tips of her ears, "—practice."

He rubbed Talon's neck with both hands, then ordered the drakes to lie to one side. His ears flicked forward, then back, almost lying down, and he wouldn't meet her eyes. "I suppose we should."

Well, at least she wasn't the only one who felt as awkward as a duck at a gryphon show.

She reached across the small space between the chairs and took his hand. It was quite large, not just broad, but long, and she was struck by the contrast of his ivy green fingers against her warm copper ones. Darker pine-green stripes started on his knuckles, faintly banding his fingers and hands like Sable's brindling.

He inhaled, watching as she turned his hand palm up and traced the lines of it, not very different from a human's. His skin had an odd texture, like finely flocked paper. Delphine stroked her fingers along the back of his hand, enjoying how the texture felt against her fingertips. Did his whole body feel that way?

She pushed the thought away. She would never know. There was no point in speculating.

He inhaled sharply again, and Delphine looked up. Allard's eyes had gone wide, his pupils full and round, ears fully forward.

"Was that acceptable?" she asked. Had it been unpleasant for him, like petting a gryphon backwards?

"Perfectly acceptable," he said, voice rough.

Acceptable, but he was definitely rattled by it. She studied the palm again before bending down to kiss it. The sensation of his skin against her lips, warm, not quite smooth, was interesting enough that she kissed it a second time before looking up at him. This would not work if he didn't stop looking like a kitten seeing its first glowlight. Perhaps he was shy.

Delphine withdrew her hand from his. In public, he must be more confident. "You should touch me, also. Imitate what I did."

He cleared his throat. "Give me your hand."

Delphine offered him her fingers, as if they'd been introduced at a ball.

Allard touched the underside of her wrist with one finger, coaxing her hand up until he kissed the back of it. He drew her hand toward him, kissing it again, more firmly. Delphine closed her eyes, savoring the steadiness of his hand around her wrist, the pressure of his kiss, the way her pulse beat a little harder from both.

It had been a long time since she'd felt anything worth savoring.

"That's good," she whispered, flushed.

He ran his thumb across her knuckles, then mirroring what she had done, turned her palm up. Pausing, he looked up at her, face uncertain. Delphine nodded encouragement. Delicately, he kissed the tip of each finger. A breathless frisson shot through her, and again when he moved from her fingertips to her palm.

He glanced up through blue-green lashes, pupils wide, and moved to her inner wrist. She licked her lips, caught in how such a simple touch on the wrist could stir heat elsewhere.

His dark hair gleamed in the firelight, with hints of blue at this angle, green in that. She stroked it, expecting it to be coarse like horsehair. It was dense and thick, but smoother and softer than any Torlish man's. She followed it back to where it was bound at the nape of his neck.

"How much more practice do we need, Mrs. Leighton?" His breath whispered hot across her skin.

"Delphine." Calling her Mrs. Leighton made her feel like David's wife, and stirred guilt she didn't want to feel. She was doing nothing wrong. She was not dishonoring her husband or even his memory. He'd done that well enough himself.

He guided her hand to one horn. "Delphine. And you, call me Varrick."

Her fingers slid around the curl of it, smooth as blown glass, all the way to the brass-ornamented tip, careful not to brush his ears. Subtle striping started at the edge of his hairline and continued along his jaw and down his neck.

He exhaled in one long sigh. "Enough for one night?"

Delphine drew back from his horn and tucked both her hands in her lap. She wanted to touch him again, to sort out the different textures of skin and horn.

"You have stripes." Once the words left her lips, she felt foolish. She didn't remember patterns like that on any of the jaglin she'd seen.

"All jaglin have stripes, spots, or dapples." He tipped his head. "The Doonish jaglin say it's a gift from Ashanti, the jungle mother."

Delphine shook her head. She'd never heard the story. "They are—" *fascinating*, "—striking."

"Some humans have spots." He tapped the end of her nose.

"Those are called freckles!" And the smattering of them across her nose and cheeks, bronze against gold, were only the beginning.

"They're spots." He half-closed his eyes and made a pleased rumble. "Speckles."

"Freckles. Not speckles." She crossed her arms, trying to scowl, but a chuckle rising in her throat ruined it. She leaned back and laughed, the first real laugh in months. Years maybe. "Oh dear. Eggs are speckled. *Trout* are speckled."

"So are some flowers. Tiger lilies. Foxgloves. Certain orchids." He tipped his head, considering. "Not delphiniums, though."

Delphine sat up, regaining her composure. "Far better to be a foxglove than a trout."

"You'd make a lovely trout."

"If you call me that, I will throw something at you. Do you have any idea what my brother used to call me?"

"I do not." Amusement and curiosity swirled through his aura.

"Dolphin! Delphine dolphin. Which was quite bad enough, so I refuse to be a trout." She crossed her arms. "Although I do not mind being another flower."

Grandpapa had delphiniums planted at his manor just for her, towers of blue, white, and purple flowers.

"If I ever call you a trout, know that I am in desperate straits." He rose and offered her a hand up. "Do you wish to retire for the night? We can practice again tomorrow."

She took his hand and stood, making both the drakes lumber to their feet. "I think it's best. It was a long day."

They strolled to the stairs, where he stopped and pointed to Talon and Sable. "I have to take these two out for a final run. I shall see you at breakfast?"

Delphine climbed a few steps and turned to look back at him. "Yes, of course."

"Then goodnight." He paused. Grinned. "My speckled ..."

He wouldn't dare.

"... orchid." He tipped his head, tapped one horn like a salute, and walked away, leaving Delphine to smother another round of laughter.

VARRICK

Varrick took Sable and Talon to the foyer and shrugged into his heavy capelet coat. A walk would clear his head and cool off everything else. Practice! The idea seemed so simple, he just hadn't been prepared. He'd be ready next time.

"Why in the world are you going out this late?"

Varrick turned to Mrs. Halsey, who stood in the door to the main hall, arms folded, expression quizzical.

"I'm going to run the drakes." He buttoned the coat.

"It's raining again," she said.

Perfect. "I like the rain."

"And quite chilly." She raised her eyebrows, as if that information might deter him.

"I enjoy the cold." He flipped the hood up. He would let the rain drive the confused, pent-up feelings away. Everything felt hot and flushed, like he had a fever, except he wasn't ill. Not at all.

"It sounded like you and Mrs. Leighton were getting along well," she smiled, "I heard laughter."

"We had a discussion about speckles." He'd been fine until she'd kissed his palm and run her fingers along his hand. He couldn't explain it to Mrs. Halsey. How was he supposed to play the cool, condescending foreigner if every time Delphine touched him, it lit his nerves on fire?

"Speckles?"

"Freckles. Speckles. I am not allowed to call her a trout. I am going for a walk. In the cold." He opened the door and the drakes bounded out into the rain without hesitation.

"Trout? Oh, never mind." She followed him to the open door and laid her hand on his sleeve. "It's good to relax with her. If you two can laugh together, it will fool everyone more than any amount of touches and affection."

"I know. I'm fine. I just need a walk." He gave her a quick nod.

He stepped onto the portico and shut the door, happy to block out the lights of the manor His eyes adjusted to the rainy darkness, making out Talon at the curve in the driveway and Sable, further along, waiting for her mate.

Delphine had given him a new experience. He knew what went on between men and women—he was uninitiated, not naive. And they weren't actually going to do anything. A few kisses ought to be fine.

He strode through the rain after the drakes.

Her lips on my palm.

Her fingers on my skin.

"Trout," he muttered to himself to bring back the mirth of the moment, but it refused to come. Instead, he was thinking of orchids and lilies and other beautiful, speckled things.

CHAPTER 11
Overture

DELPHINE

The days before the opera passed in a blur. Delphine's wardrobe arrived, sending a new wave of apprehension through her. Could she play her part well enough? She knew what she was risking, but what would happen if Mr. Allard failed?

Attempting to practice affection with him ended in laughter or an uncomfortable silence as she tried to manage feelings and he sat there looking embarrassed. She liked having her hand in his. She liked the texture of his skin and the warmth of his kisses on her palm, but was she allowed to like it? Did she only enjoy it because she was starved for affection and courtesy?

They would attend the opening night of a new production. All of society's elite would be there, perhaps even women she'd once considered friends. Delphine ran possible scenarios over and over in her head. If she saw this person and they said that, she would respond in this way, but what if they didn't say what she expected? Then she would need a different response, and she couldn't possibly plan for every old friend and acquaintance she might meet. The only choice was to be someone who didn't care what any of them thought.

As Tanner organized the new dresses, Delphine tried to picture the night going perfectly. Rockhaven's opera house was a jewel of the city, the walls and woodwork imbued with Craft to preserve and strengthen them, glowlights illuminating the halls, the way to the seats and boxes, and the stage itself. She had never been able to quite make out the trick of Craft used to enhance the acoustics.

Delphine hadn't been there in over two years. She should have realized how badly in debt they were when David no longer reserved seats. Tonight, she would shed all the bad memories and give the illusion of enjoyment.

More concerning, she hadn't found an opportunity to give Mr. Stokes his money. The twenty-five thalens lay securely in a drawer. She did not want to involve Allard—Varrick—but Stokes would not simply accept the paltry payment and wait quietly for the next one. Once she was seen publicly with Allard, Stokes could find her.

Allard didn't strike her as the sort to meekly allow trouble to come to his door. What if he decided Delphine was too much trouble and terminated the contract prematurely, leaving her at Stokes's mercy? She shuddered at the thought.

Varrick. She must get accustomed to calling him by his familiar name. Such little intimacies would make their ruse more convincing. In private, the familiarity felt odd, like a glove with the wrong number of fingers. It would take more practice, the same way they practiced touching hands, hair, and horns. It felt strange to be the leading actress in a private play, all lines improvised.

"You should rest this afternoon," Tanner said after she finished pressing and organizing the dresses, skirts, and underpinnings. The gowns hung in a jewel-toned rainbow, deep blue, rich red, and emerald green, in brocade, velvet, and satin. The familiar smell of pressed hot cotton permeated the room. "Mr. Allard won't be back until later, and you're to dine with him before the opera." She pulled an elegant dress in rose brocade from where it hung with the others. "This is for dinner. I shall surprise you with your opera gown."

"They're all so beautiful." She shouldn't be awed, but the details and quality of fabric were far finer than anything she'd worn in a while. "Is it really necessary to dress for dinner when it's just the two of us pretending?"

"It is good practice." Tanner adjusted a ruffle.

Delphine spent much of the day in the library, enjoying the luxury of the fire, company of the drakes, and the simple pleasure of reading —as much to distract herself as for enjoyment. She heard no hooves or doors, but Tanner prodded her to her rooms to change for dinner after sunset. For Delphine, stepping into the rose dress felt like stepping into her new part. She would never be Mrs. David Leighton again. The woman in the glamorous dress would be bolder. Happier, she hoped.

Allard met her in the dining room. His ears flicked back and then forward as she entered and took his hand. They would both wear gloves for the opera, but for now, they actually touched, skin to skin. Tiny intimacies. A thrill shivered up her spine.

"You look lovely," he said as he pulled the chair out for her.

"Thank you." She took her seat, and he took his.

Where had he been all day? Investigating the delicate matter he'd mentioned, no doubt. What would require bringing him here from Istalia? He'd referenced the Scholarium, which was one of two things she knew about Istalia: they produced the finest wines and had the oldest arcane academy in the world.

Delphine barely wet her lips with wine. "Is there anyone I should watch in particular tonight?"

"We are looking for anyone who has an odd aura, or who keeps theirs very strongly locked." He raised his eyebrows. "Present company excepted."

She returned the expression. "I prefer being a woman of mystery. Anything else?"

"If you recognize anyone associated with the Gaillston family, I would like to know." He took a bite. "Are you familiar with them?"

"I recognize the name. I think I would know Lady Gaillston on sight, but not any of the rest of the family." Delphine searched her memory. She had certainly attended balls or soirees with them, but nothing else came to mind. She was best acquainted with the women she'd debuted with and their families. The Gaillstons did not count among that number. "They're rather minor nobility. Why?"

"Some of their friends might be able to answer questions for me."

What sort of questions? She had no right to his secrets, so long as they didn't endanger her, and she was keeping secrets of her own. If she knew more, though, she might be more helpful. "I hope you don't think I can convince anyone to speak with you. I've never had that much social sway. If you'd tell me what to listen for ..."

"I won't be quizzing anyone tonight. We're just noticing people and being noticed. We'll compare notes afterwards." He stared at the far wall as if looking through it. "The Gaillston's son had been accepted at the University of Magi. He was attacked recently. It may be connected to my work here."

"Oh. How awful." She couldn't picture the young man. He would be five or ten years her junior. If he'd been accepted to the University, he must have been talented. The Gaillstons weren't rich enough to buy their way in.

A pall fell over the table.

Varrick was preoccupied for the rest of the meal, which left Delphine's nerves with no distraction. It was one thing to picture herself swanning about in public without a care, but quite another to actually face people she knew.

Afterwards, Tanner arranged her hair in a high, elaborate style, adorned with fake birds and flowers, which she insisted was the only appropriate style for an Eletheni lady at an opera.

"If you're sure," Delphine said, twisting and turning to see all the details in the mirror. "I feel a bit ridiculous." She was tall enough without adding half a foot of hair.

"You're to have all eyes on you, so let's make them envious, yes?" Tanner coaxed a curl into place. "Did you never see the baronesses at a ball?"

"I only visited as a child, and we stayed in the country." Delphine glanced up at Tanner in the mirror. "Are you from there?"

"Yes. I started as a housemaid there and moved up to lady's maid." She gave a proud little smile. "Now, when the baronesses of Elethen gather, they try to out-do one another with the most elaborate and outrageous gowns and hairstyles. Every ball is like a sculpture museum."

"Goodness." Delphine tried to picture it and failed. Rockhaven favored sedate colors and sleek styles. Tanner had saved every hair from her brushes over the past days to create rats of Delphine's own hair. She'd used them to create the height and fullness of the style. "So I am to be a baroness tonight?"

Tanner adjusted a flower. "Yes. Enter the opera house as if you own it."

Delphine touched a curl left dangling on her neck and smiled. "I shall." She liked how Tanner thought.

"Now, we rented jewelry for the occasion, but dress first." She pulled a stunning gown from the wardrobe. The stomacher was deep red embroidered with gold thread in a geometric pattern reminiscent of roses, with an underskirt to match it, but the overdress was gold spangled with garnets. Coupled with the gold birds and red flowers in her hair, only the blind would overlook her.

Delphine hardly breathed as Tanner helped her dress and added a sophisticated choker dripping with garnets, long gold gloves, and a matching cuff. "I feel too elegant to move. I'm afraid I'll fall and break the spell."

The gown revealed far more of Delphine's decolletage than she had ever exposed before, leaving her conflicted. She wanted to be daring but also felt like wrapping a shawl across her cleavage and partially bare shoulders. She started to spread her hands across her chest but then lowered them. This was part of the act.

Tanner laughed. "Aren't you used to this sort of thing?"

"Not quite like this." She'd never worn such finery, not at the opera, not at a ball, not even at her wedding. She felt extravagant, and it felt good.

As Delphine descended the stairs, the outer layers of her skirts flowed around her like billowing waves on the sea. Mr. Allard waited at the bottom of the stairs, adjusting his cuffs. He looked up as she came around the curve of the staircase, ears coming forward, full alert. His gaze was so focused that she stopped to avoid stumbling.

He wore severe black with a perfect, complex white cravat and a black pearl pin. The caps on his horns winked in the glowlight, matching the gold of his eyes, and he'd traded out his hoops for small jade studs. He looked like one of the gentleman pirates in the saucy novels younger women passed around: sinister and impeccable.

"You are like a priceless jewel," he said.

If she were a jewel, he was the velvet case, chosen to show her in the best light. A flush of heat crept up her neck. Was his compliment sincere or merely practice for the night? She took two more steps and decided she didn't care whether it was playacting. It was sweet to hear.

"Thank you." She finished her descent and looked up at him. She would not tell him he looked like he was about to ravage the coastline. "Whatever you pay your tailor, it is not enough. You look very fine."

He tipped his head in acknowledgement. She hoped he knew she was sincere, even though she wasn't as poetic as he was.

Did his grooming include polishing his horns? They gleamed so beautifully in the glowlight.

A delicious shiver of excitement crept up her arms; they were playing a trick on the cream of Rockhaven, putting on a show that, if successful, might outshine the opera itself. Delphine reveled in the sensation before trepidation set in. Excitement with David tended to turn out badly for her. Her body tensed at the thought.

She pushed the worry away. Although she suspected Mr. Allard was involved with something illegal or dangerous or both, he wasn't David.

"Ready to watch an opera?" he offered his hand.

"Ready to watch the audience," she took his hand.

He grinned.

CHAPTER 12

The Ensemble

DELPHINE

Memories flooded back as the coach pulled up to the opera house. Columns guarded the entrance, carved with twisting vines, flowers illuminated by glow, and frolicking figures in flowing robes. A light fog made it more magical.

Delphine had first attended as a debutante, escorted by her mother and brother. Her father had been at the House of Law on business. The thrill of finally being there had been intoxicating. It had been the height of both the debutante season and the opera season and had felt as if every lord and lady, from the lowest knight to the highest duke was there. She had hardly known where to look. The brilliant performances on stage dazzled her, the glittering assembly of people enthralled her, and the ebb and flow of the crowd as they watched one another swept her along.

In the earlier years of marriage, David liked to bring her and show her off. Delphine had never pinpointed when he'd become restless and discontented with their marriage. With her. The years that followed, especially after Mama had left, had soured her love for the music and opulence of the opera.

Delphine steeled herself before leaving the carriage. She was someone different tonight. Same body, same face, but she could wear a different persona the same way she wore her gown. She wished she had a different name, so she could leave Delphine behind for the night.

Allard stepped out of the far side of the coach and came around to open her door and help her out. Delphine took a deep breath of cold night air and took his hand.

Varrick. Call him Varrick. She must throw herself into the role of attentive and affectionate mistress and revel in the stares, the sneers, and the simmering envy.

The light and heat of the grand foyer of the opera house washed over her as they swept inside. Varrick held her arm and wore that same distant look he'd had at dinner, as if watching something far away.

They paused under an arch to do what everyone did: see who was there and be seen. Oh, how the heads turned. Delphine focused on hairstyles and gowns, skipping faces. After the first tense minute, she could hear the whispers. Tomorrow's teas and salons would be ripe with gossip.

They gaped at Varrick first, at his height and his horns, his greenness. When she did allow herself to look at their expressions, they ran the gamut of anger and disdain in the men to disgust and curiosity in the women. Delphine was nearly an afterthought, eyes drawn to her after the shock of a jaglin walking into the opera.

The men paused, eyeing her in appreciation. Torlish women wore dusty pinks, stormy blues, and soft greens. Delphine's gold and garnets shone like a flame in a forest. Tanner had added an extra petticoat, the fullness of the skirts emphasizing the balance of Delphine's figure. She lifted her chin, keenly aware that her hair and skin had always set her apart as much as her height, and that tonight was no time to fit in. The women stared, then shook open their fans to cover the sudden surge of gossip. Eyes were narrowed in envy or calculation; lips curled in judgement or delight. A pair of older women hurried a flock of debutantes away. Delphine sent a silent blessing to the two girls who dragged their feet, casting curious glances back at her. One even peeked around the corner after they'd gone.

The only person who didn't do this dance of double takes was the young man who directed them up the stairs to the proper box. Varrick tipped him well.

"Did the opera staff know you were coming?" Delphine asked when they stopped on a landing. "They seem quite unruffled."

He looked back the way they had come. "Money is a fabulous lubricant."

Most of the younger men and fops hesitated to follow them up, but an older gentleman approached them. Delphine blinked in shock; he was one of the bankers who had taken her house a month ago. He looked as startled as she did.

"Mr. Allard," he said. "I hadn't expected to see you here tonight. I trust that the little, ah, misunderstanding this morning hasn't put you off Rockhaven." He clasped his trembling hands and smiled hopefully. As was polite, his aura was well-locked in public, but a keen eye could see the pale green nerves vibrating in the corona around his face. He was afraid.

Varrick laid his hand over Delphine's where it rested on his arm. "Certainly not. I'm looking forward to enjoying the city, and I hear this particular cast is excellent. I won't be mixing business with pleasure, this evening."

The man nodded and stroked his goatee. "Of course not. I simply wanted to greet you and your lovely companion." He made as if to tip a hat he wasn't wearing. "Mrs. Leighton."

Her mind finally connected a name to his face. Delphine put on an indulgent smile. "Mr. Browly, how nice to see you. It's been so long since I was out in company. A friendly face is always welcome."

His smile, already stiff, went bone-brittle as he tried to parse whether she was sincere or not. He had not been particularly kind about the house, nor had he extended any mercy or sympathy, and now she was on the arm of someone he feared.

"Very nice to see you," he stammered. "Excellent that you grace us. With your beauty. Considerable. You look well. I must see to my wife."

Delphine extended her free hand, savoring his discomfort. "Of course. I would not dream of stealing one more second of your company from Mrs. Browly."

"You enjoyed that," Varrick said as Browly disappeared into the crowd.

She looked up at him. Had she misstepped before the evening started? "Should I not?"

He led her to the second flight of stairs. "Please enjoy yourself. I like to see your eyes twinkle. I wouldn't mind knowing why, though."

At the top of the stairs, where the hall led to separate boxes, it was more crowded than she expected. "I will tell you once we are seated, if you'll tell me about the misunderstanding."

She didn't want to tell him about Mr. Browly, but it would take very little for Varrick to discover what happened to young Mr. Leighton's estate. Any number of the gentlemen here tonight had played cards with David knowing he didn't have the funds to make good his bets.

They paused as the crowd in the upper hall dispersed. Delphine recognized too many faces up here, and many of the women's expressions mingled pity with their surprise. A distinguished gentleman—Lord Monteshreve?—stepped back in shock, although she wasn't sure if he was reacting to her, Varrick, or the two of them together.

Varrick placed his hand on the small of her back, under the sumptuous fur she wore, and guided her to the box.

Delphine took her seat, shed the fur, and scanned the opera house's sea of familiar faces.

"So, the banker?" he prompted.

"Mr. Browly foreclosed on me and forced me onto the streets a month ago. He was not kind about it."

Varrick scowled, rumbling deep in his chest.

"It's of no consequence now." Delphine turned to the audience below. "And the misunderstanding?"

"A line of credit was opened for me at his bank. He was skeptical about my identity," he sniffed.

Opened by that mysterious person of rank. What was the delicate matter, and what did it have to do with the Gaillston boy's attack?

This wasn't the place to ask. She scanned the crowd.

Several of the ladies were familiar, by face if not by name. She knew fewer of the gentlemen but could usually make guesses by the female company they kept. "It's an extraordinarily busy night."

"Opening night, so everyone who is anyone is here to be seen." He settled, looking grumpy. "I don't know any of the lords. Your background will be extremely helpful."

"What would you have done if someone without my connections had come to your door dripping from the rain?" It was easier to talk to him when both of them were looking somewhere else. She waited for him to ask more about Mr. Browly. He had never directly asked her about her circumstances, and the banker had handed him the perfect excuse for questions.

"I'd have politely said they were not what I was looking for. Although I'm sure some would make fine governesses." He smiled at her, but when she didn't smile back, it faded.

Varrick frowned, tapping his fingers on the edge of the box railing. "Do you believe in fate or serendipity?"

"I might have once." She ran her fingers along the polished wood of the box. "Life has beaten it out of me."

Varrick's box was well situated for someone who wanted to observe, and she could see a great portion of the other boxes as well as the seats below. As people shuffled to their places before the performance started, they were relatively anonymous. As soon as things started, so would the social game of seeing who was with whom, who sat in which box, and how sumptuously they were dressed. It was a silent choreography of reshuffled social status and would replay at every ball and opera all winter.

Delphine should be in mourning, wearing black and refusing all but the most sedate invitations—as if she'd had any. As details of David's death and debts spread, even those she considered close friends had quickly disappeared.

She wound her arm through Varrick's and leaned on him. If people were going to gasp and gossip, the least she could do was give them a good show. He laid his other hand possessively over hers. Delphine willed herself to relax, enjoying how solid he felt. If he was nervous or uncomfortable, she couldn't detect it in his body language or at the edges of his aura. His confidence made it easier for her to pretend.

Afterwards she and Varrick would go to his house together and the evening would be done. She would not lie awake wondering when or if he would return—not that it ought to matter to her.

Across the opera house, an elderly countess glanced their way, flinched, and raised her opera glasses to look again. Two young men sat with her. The countess leaned to the elder of them, waving her opera glasses in Delphine's direction. Delphine looked away.

She should be watching the crowd below, but the soft hair on the back of Varrick's hand held her attention. It felt like close-cropped silk velvet. Only the low angle of the dimmed glowlights made it visible. She stroked from his knuckles back to his wrist. His hand flexed under her touch.

She recognized Lord Severson, tall, red-haired, and lucky. He'd been a frequent companion of David's, and when their eyes met by chance, he gave her a wink and a nod. She would have cheerfully stabbed him.

A ripple of movement caught Delphine's eye. Someone below had seen her and passed the word along. Multiple ladies whispered behind their fans. No one was indiscreet enough to point, but more than one accidentally made eye contact with her as they glanced up, and they turned away, fans and eyelashes fluttering.

Lord Monteshreve's three daughters sat together. Delphine had been right about the old man's identity. They would all be married now. The eldest, who had always been bold, nodded when their eyes met, surprising her. Whom had she married and how secure was her position to publicly acknowledge such an obviously fallen woman? Delphine scrambled to remember the woman's suitors. Had there been a duke? Judging by her dress, she was not just following fashion trends but setting them. The only man in their party was their father.

Out of all the seething crowd, she saw no aura she would describe as unusual. Many lost control when they first saw her, or in response to others, but everything was the expected blend of excitement, jealousy, boredom, desire, and anxiety.

Delphine shifted restlessly in her seat. Observing who was present and how they reacted to her sounded simple, but what was the purpose? It would be easier to play Varrick's game if she knew how to score points, or where the playing field was. Or what the teams and stakes were.

Instead, she stroked the back of Varrick's hand and watched for more familiar faces. Far too many of David's old crowd peppered the audience for her comfort. Not the dregs he'd landed with in the last years of his life, but respectable fops and dandies, and a few rakes, with both fortune and name. Well, fortune for now. Fortunes had a way of abandoning that lot. They would glance up at her, some with blinks of recognition, but as soon as their eyes slid to Varrick, they looked away.

Delphine had been comfortable, even amused, at the whispers and glances of the womenfolk. On some level, she was used to them.

As the men started noticing, however, she became suddenly self-conscious. Her presence with Varrick had declared a situation that would interest them far more than gossip. She hadn't considered that until now.

Being dependent on the protection and good graces of a man was normal for a lady. First her father, then her husband, and now Varrick Allard, but this was the first time she'd had neither respectability nor money to go with that protection. The room spun; she was a squirrel, perched in a tree, safe for now, but foxes prowled below. This must be how singers and dancers felt. They padded their income with gifts from men like David, and if he was devoted enough, it was a shield against others.

In the minds of all those men in the audience, she was now as available as any of the women on stage. *Nothing more than jewels in a shop, sold to the first man with enough money.*

Delphine's aura gave nothing away, she was sure of it, but Varrick must have noticed something in her face or posture. "Are you well?"

"Adjusting to my new status, that's all." She met his gaze for the first time since they'd entered the box. "I've had admirers before, but now they think I'm available."

"Ah." He shifted in his seat and swept the boxes and gallery with a glower. "I hadn't thought of that."

Neither had she, until this moment. She took a shaky breath. "There is an acceptable level of admiration for married women. Poems and tokens are allowed. Some husbands even see it as flattering." David had. "When my father brought my mother home from Elethen, she was suddenly the most admired lady of the city. She used to pull out all the old letters men had written to her and read them to me, very dramatically of course." Delphine smiled, remembering. "There are an astounding number of things hair, eyes, and lips can be compared to." Not all of them as flattering as the writers imagined.

"Is her hair like yours?"

"Yes. Curly and dark auburn," Delphine said, "With stronger

purple undertones. Of course, everyone compared her skin to sunshine and copper."

He leaned over to speak in her ear. "The pattern of water droplets on fine golden silk? A golden speckled butterfly? An orchid of surpassing beauty?"

The tickle of his hot breath raised gooseflesh on her arms. "You'll have to work harder to beat my mother's admirers for poetry, Sir."

He was close, his whisper barely audible. "A certain fish?"

Delphine choked back a giggle. "No. No, never. Now you've got me laughing."

"I like it when you laugh." He lifted her hand and brushed his lips across her knuckles. "I like making the sadness leave your smile."

Delphine caught her breath, mirth draining away, and resolutely turned toward the stage. For a moment she'd forgotten her troubles, the past year, and that this was all pretend.

If she saw this through successfully, she would have time to let the wounds heal. She could walk in the woods with Grandpapa, listen to the loggers chant as they loaded the barges, catch up with Alastair and Mama, and not think about how Varrick's skin felt under her fingers.

He turned back to the stage. "If you are worried, I will make sure you have an escort anytime you leave the house."

"No one will do anything while I'm under your protection. If I were staying once we parted ways, it would be different."

Stokes and his list of men hovered in the back of her mind. Were any of them sitting in the opera house now? What if they confronted her, Varrick's presence notwithstanding? They might, if they'd paid Stokes already.

While a fabulous soprano sang, Delphine took better note of which men kept watching them. A big blond man glanced their way several times. She tried to catch a better look at him without staring, but he slipped away.

The soprano opened her aura, projecting the emotions of the song across the audience, most of whom opened their auras in return. Delphine closed her eyes against the waves of combined emotion. The singer's projected aura Skilled the willing crowd, but she couldn't open up and let herself drown in it. She might never come up.

It was the perfect time to look for the anomalies Varrick was interested in. She cracked her eyes open, scanning the other boxes and the crowd through the haze of visible emotion.

Nothing strange. There were pockets of people like her, auras locked. There were people with emotions unconnected to the sad story of the song—lust for the singer, fear of something, exhilaration and joy. And a flicker of ... not dark, exactly, but like a tiny tear in the world had opened, then been mended. Delphine stared at the edge of the box where she'd seen it, but it was gone. The mixed group of men and women in the box seemed unaware of it.

The songs continued, the emotion of them building throughout the vast chamber relieved a little when the singing gave way to dances, and building again with the next chorus.

CHAPTER 13

Aria

DELPHINE

Before the second act, the initial scandal of Delphine's appearance had faded. She marked who glanced their way and looked for odd bits in auras or another one of those strange tears, but there was nothing out of the ordinary. She relaxed to the music and enjoyed it as much as she could.

As Delphine and Varrick waited for their carriage in the foyer, surrounded by the milling crowds and subcurrents of servants moving among them, the blond man she'd noticed earlier came down the steps to the grand foyer. He was almost as tall as Varrick and burlier, with a flat, bland face. The tickle of recognition annoyed her again. He could have been the man she'd glimpsed in the street outside her old quarters, but she couldn't be sure. That man had been dressed like a workman, and this one was dressed like a lord. A small woman dripping with jewelry spoke with him, her dark hair tinted blue in the evening glowlights.

Delphine laid her hand on Varrick's sleeve to catch his attention but froze.

Coming down the steps behind the man were Michael and

Edwina. Delphine was speechless for a moment, but Edwina went pale and stumbled when their eyes met. Delphine recovered first, although her heart roared in her ears, her chest squeezing tight.

She gulped. "Edwina! I had not expected to see you here. Did you enjoy the performance?"

Edwina's eyes widened. Her aura crackled with orange flashes of surprise and dull green fear. "Dellie, what are you doing here? With that ... person?"

Michael met her eyes and pulled his wife closer. "Exactly what are you doing, Delphine?"

Edwina pulled away from him, and grasped Delphine's free arm. "If you gentlemen will excuse us." She dragged Delphine off to the private ladies' salon. "Dellie, are you alright?"

"I am fine." She caught Edwina's hands, trying to calm the hysteria she saw rising in her sister-in-law's aura.

"On a jaglin's arm? Michael said he went to your direction and you were gone. What is that person doing to you? Did he force you here?"

Michael had sought her out? Surprising. And doubtful. Delphine crossed her arms. "I have David's debts to pay. What other options are left?"

Edwina wrung her hands, waves of distress rolling off of her until the other women fled the salon. "But," her voice dropped to a whisper, "he's not human."

"No." Delphine huffed. "I tried life with a human. I think I'll see if a jaglin treats me better."

Embarrassment and discomfort swirled through Edwina's aura. "I don't know what you mean."

The roaring in Delphine's ears drowned out propriety. "You knew David gambled away every cuer we had and then some. You knew he made a mockery of me by bringing his women to balls and operas for show." *The things he said in private.* "I didn't tell you how he'd come home drunk and demand his rights as a husband, and take them, would I consent or not?"

Tears flooded Edwina's eyes. "I know he gambled, and he drank too much, but he would never have hurt you, Dellie. He loved you."

Delphine could have endured anything but Edwina's defense of David. There was always an excuse, always professions of David's love, never anything for her. "Do you want to know what the best part about David being dead is?" Delphine bore down on Edwina, trapping her in the corner and leaning in, nose to nose. "I know exactly where he is every night."

Edwina's chest heaved. The blood drained from her face, and she pushed past Delphine and rushed to the door.

Delphine pressed her forehead to the wall, gasping for breath and shaking. She hadn't meant to go that far. Silly, well-meaning Edwina couldn't imagine cruelty beyond Michael raising his voice. She pressed a hand to her chest, willing her heart to slow. She refused to leave the salon in tears and disarray.

Thank the skies, no one had witnessed the scene. She checked her hair as her breathing returned to normal. Not a flower out of place.

Edwina and Michael were gone by the time she returned to the foyer. So was the blond man and his tiny escort.

Varrick was deep in conversation with a fidgety gentleman. Several couples and groups milled about the grand foyer, awaiting their coaches. Delphine took her time weaving through them. Her heart was finally returning to a normal rhythm.

"Mrs. Leighton, is it?"

She turned toward the man's voice. Lord Monteshreve inclined his head. None of his daughters were with him.

"Lord Monteshreve," she curtsied, "I am flattered you remember me. It's been a long time since I debuted with your daughter."

He leaned on his ornate cane and looked her up and down. "I'd swear Stokes told me I was the highest bidder."

All the hot temper she'd vented on Edwina was snuffed out,

replaced by cold shock. Her throat closed, and she fumbled for a response.

He thumped the cane on the floor, the sound echoing off the columns and walls. "I was going to set you up in style."

"Whatever your offer, *Sir*, I assure you that Mr. Allard's was preferable." If only she had the fur with her, she could clutch it around her shoulders and cover herself. Instead, she walked slowly, head high, to Varrick.

She was the same age as his daughter. How could he imagine she would be flattered by what he said? She had to pause as an older couple passed in front of her. No, he hadn't expected her to be flattered. He'd wanted her to be intimidated. He wanted her to know how far she'd fallen. Her breath came in fast, shallow bursts as her heart galloped.

Delphine rejoined Varrick, who was still chatting with the nervous gentleman about hunting drakes. She draped herself gratefully on his arm and gave the man her most pleasant smile. His anxious aura settled a bit, and they kept on about breeding lines and new scale variations.

A lady, perhaps ten years Delphine's senior, came out of the ladies' salon and joined a gentleman who was waiting for her. Delphine didn't know either of them, but for a moment, as the man passed between Delphine and one of the glowlights, there were shards of a darkness scattered around his head. Tears across the corona of his aura. They were gone in less than a blink.

Delphine tensed, watching the man go, but it didn't happen again. Had she actually seen it? Varrick's arm shifted under hers and he ended the conversation with the other man.

"Anything interesting from Lady Havemshire?" Varrick asked as he handed her into the coach.

"Nothing important." Her mood was fragile. She wanted to throw things, scream, and cry, all at once.

Instead, Delphine settled among the rugs. She leaned back and closed her eyes. It hadn't been horrid, being the object of attention and speculation this time. In many ways, it was better than having rumors of David's newest lover swirling behind the fans as she passed. With the doors closed, the coach windows shaded, the world shut out, she let the woman she'd been tonight fade away.

They'd been Varrick and Delphine for the opera. They were Mr. Allard and Mrs. Leighton again.

"Who was the older gentleman who approached you at the end?"

Delphine grimaced and opened her eyes. Lord Monteshreve's comments made her ill. The more she thought about them, the more revolted she felt. "I was a debutante with his eldest daughter."

The coach rumbled on, leaving city cobbles for a country road. Allard plucked at his cravat. He pulled his gloves half-off then back on.

He cleared his throat. "He upset you. More than Lady Havemshire."

If she explained what Lord Monteshreve had said and why it upset her, she would have to explain Stokes and the debts. What if he thought it a danger and canceled their agreement? He was doing something secret and dangerous, and her debts could compromise it.

"He was vulgar. I didn't expect it from him." That should be enough.

How many other men she'd met, danced with, even received in her home, might have been on Stokes's list?

Allard tipped his head to one side, studying her. He must know she hadn't said everything. He might not be reading her aura, but he was too good at interpreting her expression and body language. He turned to stare at the shade on the coach window, flexing his fingers, ears laid back, unhappy.

CHAPTER 14

Duet Finale

DELPHINE

Back at Sayledon Manor, Delphine was ready to retire immediately. Despite the lap rugs and heated bricks for her feet, the night's damp chill clung to her bones. She rushed to the staircase.

"I would like to speak with you," Allard said.

She stopped on the bottom step and turned. "What do you need to say that you couldn't say in the coach? You spent half the ride sulking."

His ears lay back again as he scowled, "I was not sulking."

"I am cold. I am tired. I wish to go to bed." The shine of the evening had worn off, and Delphine felt foolish. Monteshreve had soured it.

Varrick took a step toward her, hands clasped behind his back, ears relaxed again. "There's a fine fire warming the library. The kitchen will have tea ready, or we can have wine or brandy, if you prefer."

Delphine ran her gloved fingers along the carved end of the

banister. Something warm to drink sounded good. "Tea. With plenty of milk and sugar."

"Thank you, Delphine." He held out his hand to her.

She ignored it and walked past him to the library. Talon and Sable lay in front of the fire, snoring. As soon as she plopped in a chair, Talon pawed his way across the rug on his belly to lay his head in her lap.

Resigned, Delphine scratched the ridge on top of his head. He made a rumbling, steamy sound, the drake's equivalent of a purr. Talon's head radiated heat, and her chilled fingers began to warm. "If you think the drakes will soften me up, you are unfortunately correct."

Allard relaxed in the other chair, where Sable immediately demanded similar attention from him. "I didn't plan on it, but I'll remember that it works." He scratched Sable under her bronze chin. "Jaglin have better hearing than humans." He cocked an ear at her without turning away from Sable.

"Thank you for telling me?" She blinked sleepy eyes at the fire. The heat made her want to doze right here. What did his hearing have to do with anything?

"So, I'm curious about who Mr. Stokes is, and what the father of your friend meant by being the highest bidder."

How much did he overhear? How clearly?

"We're not really friends." Delphine leaned forward so Talon could rest his head on her shoulder, a barrier between her and Allard's probing gaze. "We just debuted together."

"And Mr. Stokes?" He fiddled with his cravat, finally removing the black pearl pin and setting it on the small table between them. Pulling the cravat loose, he let it trail down his chest. "I am not just being nosy. I want to know if you are in danger."

She covered her gulp with a cough. Couldn't someone interrupt with that hot tea now?

He pulled the cravat off and folded it. "Are you?"

She wrapped her arms around Talon, grateful when he

accepted the embrace with a contented sigh. "I should not be in danger of anything more than vulgarity."

"You don't sound very certain."

Delphine peered over Talon's neck. Allard's aura was locked down so tightly, she couldn't catch anything on its edges. "My husband took out many loans before his death. The debts to Mr. Stokes are the last." *At least I hope they are.*

There might be a dozen like him out there, waiting for the right moment to squeeze money out of her. After tonight, they'd know she had money to pay. Or someone who might pay it for her. It was less Mr. Allard's responsibility than hers.

A maid entering with tea and Doonish coffee—spiked with something, from the smell of it—saved her from more questions.

The spiked coffee smelled good. Perhaps she should have asked for some.

They took their respective cups, thanked the maid, and ignored one another while they drank. Delphine finished first and half-turned to stare out the dark window. The fire had died down enough that she could just pick up the woven glow around the windowsill, creating a ward against break-ins.

It wasn't unusual in rich houses; Michael and Edwina's homes had it. Perhaps it was the dark or their distance from the city, but tonight, the presence of the ward sparked a shiver of unease instead of comfort.

Allard set his cup on its saucer. "How much is owed?"

She shifted in the chair but kept her eyes on the window. "The stipend will cover the first payment." It was a ridiculous lie. The stipend barely covered a fraction of it.

"We will settle it." He sounded grim. *Angry?* She couldn't tell.

"If you want me to be more open with you, try doing the same with me," she said. "Will I ever know what you're doing here?"

"I needed someone to play a supporting role. You weren't what I expected, but you know about the world I need to enter."

Nettled, Delphine's voice turned tart. "That doesn't answer my question."

He stretched his legs out and crossed his arms. "It's rather irritating, isn't it?"

She narrowed her eyes at him. "Seven thousand thalens."

He choked. "Was your husband trying to buy an entire ship?"

"A ship would have been useful, so no." Careless of her gorgeous gown, she pulled her knees to her chest and wrapped her arms around them. "He wasted it on horse and drake races, card games, and—" She didn't want to call his women whores. "Companions."

Allard sighed.

"I'll understand if this makes me useless to you." She set her chin on her knees. "Although, it would be easier to evaluate if I knew more."

"There's a … problem." He rubbed his chin. "Do you know about magi? Or formal magic at all?"

"Skilling with your aura to connect to, encourage, or persuade people, like the singers tonight. Crafting spells with both aura and anima to make things stronger. I've seen people weave spells that keep flowers or food fresh longer or warm or cool things. Tanner does that with my bed each evening. I've lit my fireplace with it. There's elemental magic, which can also be Crafted into things. I know it's used for glowlights and wards." She shrugged. "That's all."

Her father had been very good at subtly Skilling people with his aura to influence the mood of a room or the tone of a negotiation. Crafting was more structured and less intuitive, like sewing a gown instead of painting a watercolor. It drew on the individual energy—anima—of a person instead of the emotional projection of the aura. The best cooks used it to enhance food. The best seamstresses and tailors could reinforce their stitches and add shine to a pattern of embroidery. She'd once heard of a cloth crafted to be as strong as steel and act like armor, but she wasn't sure that was true. If so, it was a rare, well-protected process.

Everyone naturally had strong auras, but most had very little expressive anima. They lit fires, kindled glowlights, or used it to reach and touch things, but little else.

Magi were men who had more than a little and learned to use it for more than the basics of life. Those trained to take raw elemental glow and fashion it into harmless, usable lamps and other things were a separate discipline, as highly skilled and prized as any expert craftsman.

Allard nodded. "Elemental magic has many uses." He gestured at the glowlight. "It powers lights like those. Sailing ships use something similar, but with water and air for movement."

Delphine shook her head, embarrassed that she didn't even know enough to ask a question.

"But there are also elemental creatures. Some are powerful enough to be worshipped like gods. Some are less intelligent than these two." He patted Sable's ribs. "One of the semi-intelligent ones is attacking people in Rockhaven."

Her tea turned sour in her stomach. "Attacking...How? How dangerous is it?"

"We don't think it's loose. There's a magus controlling it. There's been a dozen victims, a sort of pattern to them, but all we know are a few places to start looking."

She forced herself to relax and set her feet back on the floor. "Victims? You mean the Gaillston boy?" Why else would he have told her about the family's tragedy?

Allard nodded, face grave. "The last place he was seen before the attack was a high-class gambling den. Half the victims have been rich young men who frequent such places."

He expected to go to those dens. He had publicly displayed enough wealth to be invited to games, and men often brought their mistresses to such places, another show of wealth. Allard could listen to the men's talk while Delphine gossiped with the women.

"Are you trying to get this magus, or the creature, to attack you?"

Was he bait? *Are we both?*

He looked down. "If need be. I owe a lot, nearly everything, to someone who wants this to stop. There aren't many magi who can. So I have to find the next victim or be the next victim. Almost."

Talon laid a heavy paw in her lap. She gave the drake a final scratch along his crest and rose. "Will my debts cause a problem?" *They're David's debts, not mine.*

Allard stood, stretching his arms over his head and yawning. "Don't worry about it."

Later, after Tanner had removed all the height and decoration from her hair and prepared her for sleep, Delphine lay and stared at the bed curtains.

Elemental beings. Magi. Allard had been hired to find them. *By whom?* What had she gotten herself into?

CHAPTER 15

The Ethics of Elementals

DELPHINE

In the morning, Bethie brought Delphine's breakfast to her rooms. After Tanner helped her dress, she wandered downstairs to the main floor. The manor felt too empty. Although it was always quiet, there was none of the usual background bustle. She could check the kitchens or look for Mrs. Halsey, but she had no reason to do either, except for the company. They had work to do, and she shouldn't interrupt it.

Allard was nowhere to be found. Where had he gone? Was he hunting the creature already? An old, familiar unease coiled around her stomach, and she took a long, deep breath to loosen it. Where Allard had gone was none of her business, and he wasn't David. He wasn't answerable to her, nor did he seem the type to waste time.

She retreated to the library, where the drakes lounged by the well-kept fire, tips of their tails swishing slowly. Both raised their heads to look at her. Talon heaved a contented sigh and went back to sleep.

Bored and restless, unable to keep her mind from Stokes and

Monteshreve, she poked around the library. She'd barely explored most of the shelves and titles nor the large, desk in the back, away from the fireplace and its sitting area. In a drawer, she found a deck of cards with the band on it. David had hosted informal card parties. The women would listen to music and enjoy the gardens while the men played the night away. She slid the band off the stiff cards, inhaling the familiar scent of the paper.

It was likely they would be visiting a gambling den; Allard had said that the Gaillston boy had been to one before his attack. The thought flustered her. At the opera, they'd been in a box for most of the night, separate from the crowd, protected. She imagined a gambling den as a wilder version of a card party, with drinks, cigars, and the ribald conversation that went with them. She would have to do more than stroke Allard's arm and smile at things he said. Moving freely at a gambling den would make her vulnerable to men like Lord Monteshreve and Mr. Stokes.

Nerves wound tightly, she sat at the desk and shuffled and reshuffled the deck, dealing out imaginary hands before sweeping them back into a pile to shuffle again. She knew the rules and tricks of David's favorite games. Poker hands and variations of bridge and euchre flew out from her fingers until they were sore.

But she wouldn't be dealing to a table. She'd only learned because it amused David. It had been a daring thing to know.

Still is.

She squared the deck and set it in the middle of the desk. She didn't even know enough about magi and their work to know what to listen for. The sense of inadequacy mounted but she refused to get caught in that. Sweet rivers, she was in a library. Surely, she could find something about magi and the arcane in here.

Delphine stood so quickly that she toppled the chair and startled the drakes, the spiny ridges on their necks standing up in alarm.

"Sorry."

They wrinkled their noses and thumped their ropey tails on the floor. Behind them, she caught the shimmer of the anima wards on the window again. She frowned. Wards ought to be invisible unless triggered, especially during the daytime. Torn between finding the butler, Morrow, and the fear that she was overreacting, she froze.

She had two large drakes with her. It was probably a bird or a small wild cat stalking the garden. She was jumpy.

Maybe.

She grabbed the poker by the fire and approached the window. Talon and Sable rose to follow, claws clicking on the wood floor.

Close up, she could feel the fizz of anima and glow woven into the window frame. The shimmer was gone, and she had a clear view of the garden beyond. It must be lovely during spring and summer. Even now it was tidy and well kept, inviting in a bleak way. Nothing moved except a few dried leaves stirring in the breeze.

Delphine lowered the poker. So much for not feeling ridiculous. "I'm not paranoid," she told the drakes.

Sable snuffled the frame before nosing her hand for attention. Absently, she scratched behind the curve of the drake's jaw. Surveying the garden again, she marked a few areas that would provide cover from prying eyes. Thicker scrubs and walls for climbing roses interrupted the line of sight, and a few areas were deep with shadows, even though the day was bright. Despite the room's warmth, a shiver scurried down her spine.

Unable to shake the sensation, she pulled the heavy drape across the window.

Books. She would find something on magi so she wouldn't feel so unprepared.

A large portion of the library was given over to history. Her brother Alastair would never have left until he'd read them all.

Delphine found a large volume of the peerage, although it wasn't up to date. Another section was on theology and philosophy, including several volumes containing essays by people she'd never heard of. If she ever wanted to know about the "Theory of Elven Descent" or the "Arguments for a Free Society", she knew where to look.

She found a book containing the founding and history of the University and another titled, "Ethical Considerations of Elemental Magic." That sounded beyond her. The others were more approachable: "Weaving Anima, An Introduction," "The Anima of Botanicals: A Course in Healing," and "Golden Pearls, an Exploration of the Power of the Great Elven Trees." The last one sounded the most interesting but was likely to be the least helpful.

Delphine laid them all on the desk. Together, they were an intimidating amount of information. Flipping through the introductory book on anima, she recognized some of the concepts. Anima could interact with the physical world. It could exude or absorb heat if the person had enough control. The section on the use of anima to wake glowlights and similar things was interesting enough, but not really new. She wasn't sure what she was looking for. The book on healing was far beyond her current knowledge.

She poked the book on elemental ethics with a finger before opening it. Ethics sounded boring, but if there were ethics, then there must be unethical things magi could do. It opened with an essay titled, "Elemental Creatures." A bit ominous, but it's what Allard had mentioned the night before.

The first subheading was "Earth," followed by an explanation that all the listed creatures were not made of their respective elements, but instead existed on—or *as*, a note said—the power or magic of that particular element. They were not corporeal, unless they wished to be.

So ... not physical? Touchable? Delphine was unsure what the author meant by the term, and reading on, she wasn't convinced the author knew what they meant either. It described creatures with less mind than the drakes at her feet, but capable of being as amorphous as glow or anima, or as solid as a rock. Or water, at least. She flipped to the next section, where someone had drawn a cunning picture of something a bit like a human with two fish tails instead of legs, webbed fingers, and disturbingly sharp teeth.

It was enough to put her off boating ever again, although another section, just below the illustration, assured her that these things could not "become material" without explicit rituals creating an entryway.

It was a relief that they wouldn't be lurking in the pond or river, but the idea that someone could intentionally bring them was disturbing. Why would anyone want to? She stared at the illustration, the claws at the end of the webbed fingers, the strange anatomy, and the needle-like teeth.

She flipped the page, happy to look away from it. The next illustration was of something more like a long, low drake with awkward stubby limbs and a thick tail. The face and forelimbs were vaguely human, and a corona of delicate flames in fading red and gold ink surrounded it. The caption said, "Useful for light and heat, but short-lived."

It looked mournful. Did magi bring such things here, only for them to expire in a world that must be too cold for them, like living—and dying—candle flames?

Earth, water, fire, and air she expected, but there were separate sections for metal and wood, followed by an essay questioning whether anima itself was a separate element with signature elementals like the others—even though this author disagreed with the previous section's claims that metal and wood were separate elements at all.

She rubbed her forehead. The intricacies of magery were not part of a genteel lady's education, beyond basic Skilling and adding the occasional Craft to appropriate things.

After the essay, it jumped to terms and concepts she knew nothing about: vertices, intersecting planes and points, angles of materialization, refracted elements versus reflected elements...

She was in over her head in more ways than one.

CHAPTER 16

A Thread to Pull

VARRICK

Varrick returned from his inquiries with Morrow in the late afternoon. They'd had no luck turning up connections between the Gaillston victim and any of the people he'd taken notice of at the opera. He'd hoped to find some connection to Lord Monteshreve; he wanted an excuse to pay the man back for distressing Delphine. Unfortunately, Monteshreve was the most banal of men: rich, greedy, and lecherous, but not playing with forbidden magic.

Varrick changed out of his muddy boots and left his coat and vest in his rooms. Going around in more than shirtsleeves all day felt confining. It was autumn and chilly, but the Torlish wore entirely too many layers.

Investigating Monteshreve had led to Mr. Stokes, and eventually, to discoveries concerning Mr. David Leighton. Dowries, inheritances, and debts were all a matter of record, if one knew where to look.

Morrow knew.

It had taken the whole, rainy ride back to Sayledon to cool

Varrick's temper. Stokes himself was just as tediously corrupt as Monteshreve. Varrick had wanted to track him down and confront him in his lair, but Morrow argued him out of it. Why waste time and effort; Stokes would find them soon enough and Varrick didn't need trouble with the Rockhaven constables.

But David Leighton.

Varrick paused as he descended from his room. Delphine was likely in the library. Talon's faint snores echoed from there, and the drakes adored her easy affection. He wasn't ready to speak with her. Instead, he turned the other way and went down to the kitchen for something warm. Their stash of Doonish coffee was small, but he preferred it to tea. It wasn't nostalgia, exactly—he was too young for that and hadn't visited his homeland as an adult. Tea just didn't feel like enough today.

Mrs. Edward bustled about preparing dinner, and he dodged around her to brew the ground beans before retreating to the dining room for a quiet cup.

No wonder Delphine was so closed off, so careful never to open her aura even a crack. Mr. Leighton had been a stupid man, to be so careless with what he had. Even in Elethen, where affairs were a matter of open discussion, a man who wasted his fortune was disdained. Be a fool for love but never be foolish with money. Leighton had been foolish with both.

Without Lady M's approval and funding, Varrick's life at the Scholarium would be finished. He didn't have anything of his own outside of that, except the drakes. He couldn't afford to be foolish with his heart. Someday, but not now.

It didn't keep him from taking his cup across the hall and quietly entering the library. Talon and Sable raised their heads, blinked at him, and returned to their napping. Delphine dozed at the desk, a book open before her and a few others in a stack to one side.

He peered at the book. "Ethical Considerations of Elemental Magic." No wonder she'd fallen asleep.

Her curls cascaded down one shoulder and obscured her face. He could see the curve of her ear to the tip of it, too pointed to be human. It had been clear that she didn't want to discuss her family history, which seemed odd to Varrick. It was generations ago; it harmed no one. Why should anyone care?

Except Rockhaven cared about everything, every glance, every move, every possible scandal. He was on display the minute he stepped out of the manor door until the moment he returned. He could challenge any magus in Torlund and hold his own. He could, from memory, trace sigils and recite incantations that would bring down even the best-warded walls. He could speak the secret names that would shape the waves.

He couldn't make Rockhaven see him as an equal.

Nor could Delphine, certainly not after their debut appearance the night before. He would feel guilty over it, except everything he'd discovered today painted the same picture: Delphine Leighton had been sliding away from respectability for years, dragged down by her husband's unraveling life. The debts to Mr. Stokes, and his vile solution to it, would have both ruined and imprisoned her. The requested boat to Elethen was her only escape.

The anger Varrick had worked so hard to contain bubbled up again. David Leighton had been born with rank and privilege, inherited money, had won a beautiful wife, and lost every bit of it. For what? The thrill of gambling? The novelty of another woman? One more bottle of wine? Even more frustrating, he'd actually been solvent on occasion, including the three or four months before his untimely demise. Then he'd sunk himself even deeper into debt. It was like he'd been trying to destroy his life at that point.

He'd succeeded, and torn apart Delphine's in the process.

Varrick and Morrow had nosed around the gambling den where Gaillston had been seen before his attack, but the proprietor had refused to speak with Morrow. Gossiping about clientele was bad for business. Gaillston hadn't even been much of a gambler,

Morrow had discovered from the family butler. He'd been invited that particular evening, but the butler didn't know by whom. One more dead end.

Varrick slipped into the chair on the other side of the desk and looked at the assorted titles Delphine had pulled. Nothing useful. He picked up the stack of cards and lifted a quizzical eyebrow. Not what he'd expected her to have, although he had mentioned gambling.

He liked the way the glowlights caught the purple undertones in her hair. He liked even more how she'd struck back at Lord Monteshreve the night before and kept her head while doing it.

He tapped her hand.

She jolted awake with a grunt and flinched, looking down as if he'd caught her doing something wrong. "Sorry. Last night was later than I'm used to."

Her reaction was one more part of Mr. Leighton's legacy, he was sure.

"You made good use of your time, I see." He picked up the book on the great trees by Lord Magus Professor Emil L'Mont. "This one is considered the definitive work on the subject. I wish I could have seen him lecture at the Scholarium. It was before my time."

"I didn't read it. It didn't seem as relevant." She made a face at the ethics book. "I didn't make it to any of the unethical possibilities in this one, though."

"There might be something in it, but it would be a slog. The easiest way to explain what's happening is to imagine someone capturing a wild beast and using it to maul people—but magically."

She picked up the book and flipped to a page with an old-style illustration of a minor aquari, with fish-tail legs and sharp teeth. "You mean someone out there has something like this and they're going around threatening people?"

"Not that particular creature, no, but that's otherwise an accurate summary."

She turned ashen under her freckles. "How can you be so calm? It's terrifying."

He took the book from her. "Because I know how to make them go away. It needs to be done, and quickly, before anyone else is attacked."

If Lady M hadn't noticed the pattern and signs, it might have gone on uncontested. The University of Magi wouldn't do anything about it. The victims' families were chasing ghosts, blaming accidents and too much alcohol. No one else had connected all the victims.

Yet.

He sighed and returned the book to her. "If I had one thread to pull, I could find the magus. He must be moving among the rich and powerful. Half our victims are from those families."

"And the other half?"

"The other half makes no sense. They seem random." He scratched his ear. "The lords had been robbed. These people had nothing. It's like he's doing it for sport."

Delphine traced the embossed pattern on the leather cover of the ethics book. "At the opera, you asked me to look for unusual auras. There was something, but I was so upset over Lord Monteshreve that I didn't think about it afterwards." She glanced at him, contrite. "It may be nothing, but I've never seen that in an aura."

"I'll decide if it's nothing." He'd been watching the crowd carefully during the performance, but he'd seen nothing out of place.

"There was a man afterwards. It looked like," —she motioned around her head— "little tears in his aura. Little black spots that weren't emotions."

Varrick looked aside, thinking.

Her words tumbled out. "It was late and I was upset, I might have mistaken some emotion for something strange. It was just a glimpse, I might have been imagining it."

"Like little pieces of..." He struggled for the right description. What she'd noticed was important. "Did it look like his aura was ill, as if pieces were going rotten, or more like bits of obsidian floating in it?"

"Obsidian." She grimaced. "Can an aura rot? That sounds horrible."

"Not exactly, it just looks like it. Like being infected with a parasite of sorts." But not really, since that type of elemental didn't do any damage to the aura. It drove the host to despair, sometimes fatally. But she'd said it looked more like obsidian chips. "Did you recognize the man?"

She shook her head. "I'm quite sure we've never been introduced. He was dressed like a dandy. Extremely wealthy, I'd guess from his clothes."

"Was his aura open at the time?" If she'd seen a completely ripped aura, the man wouldn't be walking around. If she'd seen a creature feeding on his aura, she wouldn't be so calm about this.

Delphine shook her head again. "Closed. I could barely see his corona. It really was just a glimpse."

"Describe him for me. Even if you don't know him, Morrow might." If he could find the man, or even name the man, they could start unraveling this.

He watched her animated hands as she described a man with brown hair, square face, and short sideburns. Every flick of her finger, or twist of her wrist was graceful. Elegant. She turned at a sound from Talon, the light gilding her profile, tracing the edge of her upper lip, the sweep of her lashes. He wanted her eyes to sparkle again, like they had before Lord Monteshreve and their discussion of Mr. Stokes had stolen their light.

"The Glass Gardens are opening a new section tonight," he said. Morrow had commented on it as they drove past the turn earlier. Even in Istalia, Varrick had heard stories of the complex magic used to create and maintain them. This might be his only chance to visit. "Whoever he was might be there. I'm, ah, told it's important for people to be seen at such things." He ducked his head, looking to the side.

"It is. They bring in extra performers for openings." She looked wistful. "I haven't seen them since my mother left. David thought they were boring." She broke off, pressing her lips together as if she wanted to take the words back.

"Would you like to go?" He would, less for the beauty and spectacle than the magic behind the displays, but more to see her delight in them. Her life must have held very little delight over the past few years.

She gazed up at him, twisting her hands in her skirts. "I would love to see them again."

CHAPTER 17

The Glass Gardens

DELPHINE

The Glass Gardens had started as a series of green houses and connected buildings for cold weather entertainment. No matter how miserable the weather outside, inside was warm and humid. Over the decades, the gardens had grown to showcase specimens of plants from all over the known world.

Delphine paused after she stepped out of the carriage. In the dreary night, the glass turrets and spires of the gardens shone. Multicolored glowlights twinkled, moving slowly like rainbow fireflies. As the greenhouses had expanded, so had the grounds around them. Evergreen trees and shrubs, resplendent in their glowlights, lined the walks. There were hedge mazes and a circular labyrinth, various stages for performers, and an area of booths selling roasted spiced nuts, hot sweetened tea, and fried sweet dough dipped in honey. The smell of them wafted enticingly through the entire area.

Oh, the walnuts toasted with honey and spices from Alladoon. She inhaled, regretting her full meal before they came. Beside her, Varrick sniffed the air appreciatively.

"Have you been here before?" She had come one last time with Alastair and Mama, a few nights before they sailed. They had bought rides on an exotic creature with a ridiculous, humped back, watched the jugglers, and laughed at a puppet show. It was one of her happiest memories.

Varrick shook his head. "I've been here barely a month." He scanned the towering glass building, mouth dropping open in awe. "Do you have any idea how much glow and anima they had to Craft into this? Not just strengthening the glass panes, but also weaving in this iridescence. I've never seen it done like that before. And the structural strength to have such height... the environmental control inside must be incredible."

Delphine laughed. He looked so different when he was enthusiastic. More approachable. Warmer. "Most people come for the performances and the flowers."

The entry fee to the grounds was only a few silver dahls. The greenhouses required a separate fee.

He sniffed again, ears relaxed. "And the treats, I assume."

"Always." She looped her arm through his.

It was easier tonight. Despite the numerous glowlights, the outside of the gardens was dim, granting an air of anonymity. Couples often took advantage of the mazes and labyrinths to steal kisses and more.

They strolled the main path as it curved between small stages and gardens cultivated around statues. The performers closest to the main entrance were the most sedate: jugglers and musicians who played in groups of two or three. Further on, the jugglers tossed flaming batons to one another. A solo performer used her anima to control water that coiled up from her feet, around her body and arms, and sprayed like a fountain as she sang.

Delphine tore her gaze from a sword-swallower to scan the crowd for the man she'd seen at the opera. He might not even be here at all. Would it be a wasted evening?

She glanced up at Varrick—it felt nice to look up at a man

instead of across or down. It only bothered her because so many of them took it personally, as if she'd grown tall just to spite them. He seemed to be trying to take in every performance while also analyzing the magic at play. He was especially impressed by the fountain lady; Delphine had to pull him away so he wouldn't quiz her on how she did it.

No, it will not be a wasted evening.

"It's probably a trade secret anyway," she said, laughing. "Like those illusionists who do such wonderful things with misdirection and sleight of hand."

"What do you know about those?"

"Enough to notice when people are trying to use it to cheat at cards." A stab of familiar sadness struck her, but it was only a needle tonight, not a knife. She could talk about it here. "David taught me to watch for it. It was fun, learning things like that." Unladylike things.

"So, I should be careful if I ever play cards with you?" Varrick twitched one ear, grinning.

"Only if you try to cheat."

A crowd of young men and women, merchant class from the look of them, blocked the way ahead. Delphine craned her neck to see something that resembled an enormous, ornate birdcage made of glow. Inside it, a pair of contortionists, one male, one female, in costumes that resembled exotic birds, flowed through a routine. Anywhere else, it would have been shocking.

Looking past it, she caught a glimpse of a familiar face. The man from the opera. She couldn't see his aura, it was too far and there were too many competing lights.

Varrick was murmuring to himself, something about intersecting weaves and self-sustaining structures. Delphine laid her hand on his chest. He broke off abruptly, eyes wide and ears perked, as if she were suddenly the only person in the world. He took in the whole spectacle of the Glass Gardens intensely, analyzing the magic at play. To have that focus turned on her should have been intimidating, but it felt more like the sun coming out on a cloudy day.

She pointed. "I think I saw our mystery man on the other side of the performance."

Blinking, Varrick surveyed the area. "The one with flowers embroidered on his jacket?"

"Yes, I think it's him." She'd only had a glimpse, but he was very similar.

Her hand rested on Varrick's chest, to one side of his cravat. His coat tonight was velvet, in the deep blue he favored, and the texture of it reminded her of how his hands felt. "You're quite adorable when you do that, you know."

"Do what?" He looked bemused.

"Bring your ears forward and make your eyes go all big." *Like a kitten.* She swallowed a giggle at the thought.

His ears flipped back, making him look grumpy, and she had to cover the next round of laughter with coughing.

"I think I see a way through," he said stiffly, and guided her through the crowd.

People moved aside and she floated along beside him. By the time they'd cleared the throng, the man in the embroidered coat was nowhere to be seen.

"He was moving toward those buildings." Delphine regained her composure. Had her observation embarrassed or offended him? *Adorable* might not have been the most diplomatic word, but it was accurate.

They passed a pair of performers playing a duet on violins.

"Over there?" Varrick nodded toward a side path leading to a newer building. It hadn't been there the last time she had visited.

Delphine caught a glimpse of the right coat. She hoped this was their man. He seemed to be with the same woman he'd been with at the opera; she had a similar build and hair color. "Yes, I think so."

"Do you know what that building is?"

Delphine shook her head. It was a grand feature, built from stone and wood, with curls at the eaves and symmetrical, stylized flowers painted around the door frames. There were no windows, though, which was strange. They passed another set of musicians and came around a looping curve in time to see their quarry disappear through the main doors. The sign above the doors proclaimed: "Maze of Mirrors."

"I've never heard of such a thing," Delphine said. Mirrors were every bit as costly as good glass, plus the price of silver. A whole maze of them would be prohibitively expensive.

"Do we follow? Or wait here for him?" Varrick glanced around. The new building was in a darker, less cultivated part of the grounds.

Had there been a band or group of performers nearby, Delphine might have voted to wait, but they were not far behind, and she was impatient. If they found him and discovered his name, they could spend the night enjoying the rest of the Gardens.

She wanted to explore them with Varrick. There was something catching about his enthusiasm for the structure, his desire to explain it to her as an equal. He assumed that she understood what he meant. She didn't, but she appreciated the assumption.

"Let's follow him." She tugged on Varrick's arm. "I want to see what this Maze of Mirrors is anyway."

CHAPTER 18

The Maze of Mirrors

DELPHINE

Varrick paid four silver dahls to the older woman working the door. She gave him a side-long look and a bit of a sniff but turned to the next couple without saying anything. Delphine stepped through the double doors and stopped short.

She'd expected a maze with mirrors, but the wall in front of her was one wide expanse of mirror, reflecting her rich blue gown and fur-trimmed capelet. She looked down the hall to meet reflections of her awestruck self looking back in infinite succession. Endless Varricks stepped up beside her, making her look small beside him.

He leaned close to the mirror, studying it. "I wish I could spend a week with the magi and Crafters who made this."

"It's on every wall." Delphine stepped slowly to the turn and blinked. Three separate paths branched from this point. She thought it was three, although the reflections blinked back at her, disorienting.

A group of four behind Varrick huffed, and he hurried to join her. "There's no way to tell which way he went."

And they couldn't go back. She gripped his hand. "Left, right, or forward?"

"Right every time until we can't, so we don't get lost." He pointed ahead.

They took it in measured steps. Delphine tried to read the other reflections for the man they sought, but it was too confusing, like trying to move through a living kaleidoscope. She reached out to check a side path, only to touch clear glass. People and reflections moved on the far side of it.

"Oh, that makes it more complicated."

Varrick poked the pane. It was extraordinarily transparent. "I think they wove some air glow in. It has the feel of it."

Delphine turned in a circle. They had two paths they could take. Glimpses of people moving, dark coats, bright skirts, pale hair and feathered hats, all passed the mirrors, innumerable people, but not the flowered-coat man or his companion.

Her excitement fizzled. She'd wasted his money and his time. Would he be upset? "I'm sorry. We should have waited outside."

"I wouldn't have missed this for anything." His eyes were bright.

"Truly? Even if we don't find any leads?"

"When am I going to get another chance to see this? Look, they've bound the silver with glow to make the mirrors unbreakable—or less breakable—and added something to make the reflections clearer, I think." He flushed, flattening his ears straight out to the sides.

It must mean he felt self-conscious. Delphine smiled, looking away so he wouldn't see her blush in return. It was endearing when he dropped the stiff facade.

"Well then," she said, "we must make a thorough exploration of the building. To be sure we don't miss anything."

He rumbled gently, eyes half-closed.

They followed the right-hand path again to a dead-end and traced their steps back. Another path turned out to be glass before they came to a six-way crossroad with a spiral staircase of tinted glass in the middle. The crowd milled about, waiting to go up, trying to move across. Women's wide skirts blocked movement. One lady's lace was caught on another one's brooch. A man bumped into Varrick hard enough to make Varrick step back. Delphine stumbled.

"Who let a swiving frog in here?" the man said. He wiped his mouth and sneered up at Varrick.

"The same person who let in a discourteous ignoramus." Varrick turned, shifting so he stood between Delphine and the man. "Must be equal opportunity slumming."

She regained her balance and touched his lower back. A room full of people and glass, no matter how enchanted and reinforced, was a terrible place for a fight.

If her aura had been healthy, she could have Skilled the man and soothed his temper. His cheeks were flushed, his nose red. Drunk. A few other men gathered, pushing the ladies back and egging on the confrontation. *Idiots*.

A lady next to Delphine sniffed as if something stank and pulled her skirts away, muttering, "Eletheni whore."

Delphine fluttered her eyelashes. "Jealous, darling?" She took a step closer, leaning over the woman. "I mean, you've no idea what he can offer over a mere human. So strong, so much endurance." Sweet rivers, she hoped Varrick was too distracted to hear what she'd said.

The woman flushed and gaped before grabbing the younger woman next to her and hurrying down the nearest corridor.

"Here now, none of that. You boys go your separate ways." The voice rang through the intersection, echoing off the mirrors.

Delphine turned, but a crowd of men blocked her way to Varrick, and a wave of women and young people pushed her away from him. She side-stepped into an offshoot to avoid being swept away and retreated again as a pair of disgruntled young fops dressed in pastels shoved past her.

In the mirrors further down the corridor, she caught a glimpse of the man in the flowered jacket. He must be only a few steps away. She followed the reflection, only to run up against a wall of glass. Turning, she glimpsed him again, that way, but that way led to a short flight of nearly invisible stairs. Three steps up and she found herself in a curving room full of mirrors that reflected distorted images of her back—narrow, wide, short, tall, wavy. But there was no sign of the man.

The distorted mirrors spiraled in like a snail's shell until she found a circular room just wider than the span of her arms with a glorious glowlight chandelier hanging from the two-story ceiling. A dead end, but a beautiful one.

She'd lost Varrick and was lost herself. Delphine spun to retrace her steps. Which way had she gone after the glass wall? She started out of the spiral and stopped.

Mr. Stokes.

"Well, well, Mrs. Leighton, I thought I saw you come in. I'll add my entry fee to your bill." He stalked toward her. "Lord Monteshreve was very upset. Yes, very. Me, now, I'll be happy to let your new patron pay me."

"I can give you a little. You can wait for the rest." Delphine stepped back, herded further into the spiral.

"I've given you time. I want my money." From his cuff, he drew a small knife that caught the lights, gleaming pink, then green, then gold. "You come with me, and we'll settle things up. I got someone will pay for the frog's leftovers."

Repugnant man.

She froze, transfixed by the light on the knife. "I'm not going anywhere with you."

She was in a public place. They could be interrupted at any moment. He couldn't force her away. With a twitch of her shoulders, she bloomed her two, weak anima arcs from between her shoulder blades, raising them over her head like twin snakes of pale light.

"Oh, sweetheart." Stokes chuckled. "That ain't going to do you a lick of good."

She knew it. Just maintaining her arcs was draining. There wasn't much more she could do with them, certainly not enough to physically harm him. If she were whole ... well, no use crying over what she couldn't regain.

"I am not going with you. You can't march me out of here at knife point. Even if Mr. Allard didn't see you, there are people everywhere."

How long could she delay him? Varrick had to be looking for her. Unless the confrontation earlier had gone badly. Her mind spiraled down a list of possibilities, sending her heart into a gallop.

Stokes took another step toward her, knife held low. She had no doubt he would use it. Blades did more direct, deep damage than anima. For most, they were a much more effective weapon.

He lunged. Delphine flinched to the side, away from the knife. His free hand clamped on her wrist, surprisingly strong for such a small man. He twisted it, the shooting pain sending her to her knees with a cry. Tears pricked in her eyes.

"Come along, my beauty. No need to be so stubborn about it." He applied a little pressure, making her cry out again. "I'll hand you over, and your frog can deal with Weber."

Brilliant gold light flooded the curving hall. The reflection blinded her. Stokes's grip eased enough for her to yank her hand away, bones aching.

"Mister Gary Stokes." Varrick's deep bellow reverberated. The mirrors shivered. The floor shook with heavy steps.

A wash of aura flowed over Delphine. It was Varrick, checking her for injuries.

The aura retracted, and the light eased enough that she could see Stokes, trapped in the deep brilliance of Varrick's anima like a cockroach in a spiderweb. Strands of it held his arms back and rooted his feet to the floor. Anima might not cut like a blade, but if someone was strong enough—Varrick obviously was—it made a wonderfully effective restraint.

Stokes started to babble about money and debts, that he was just a poor lender who needed his money.

"Shut up." Varrick's Istalian accent thickened. He wrapped a coil of anima over Stokes's mouth. "You will never touch her again. You will never speak to her. You will never set eyes upon her. You will forget she exists."

Stokes babbled muffled words.

Varrick emerged from the glare of his own anima, leaning close to Stokes's ear. "I can call the wind into your lungs until they burst. I know sigils that will turn your blood to steam in your veins. I can slide my anima under your skin and flay you alive. Do you understand me?"

Stokes's face turned gray. He gurgled an affirmative.

Varrick dropped the bookie, pulling four thick, powerful arcs back until they hovered above his head. Stokes fell to his hands and knees, coughing.

He grabbed for his fallen knife, but Varrick growled, a deep rumble that rivaled Talon's. Stokes stumbled away down the hall, leaning on the walls, leaving smears of sweaty fingerprints. Arcs out and ready, Varrick's glare followed him until there was not even an echo or reflection of him.

CHAPTER 19

Out of the Maze

VARRICK

Varrick listened to Stokes's retreating steps, erratic against the ornate floors, until they blended in with the general noise of the building. His aura locked, he took a deep breath to cool his crackling anger. When he'd agreed to come to Rockhaven, he'd known he would encounter ugliness and rejection like tonight.

He'd thought he could let it roll off, but it clung to him like bog mud. Someone had intervened and broken up the earlier confrontation before anything turned violent. He ought to be glad, but the fury simmered. He'd been so close to taking it all out on Stokes.

Stokes deserved it. Varrick had heard what the filth said to Delphine, echoing off the glass.

He offered Delphine his hand. "Are you alright? Did he hurt you?" He'd heard her scream.

"Not permanently, I think." She took his hand and rose, wincing. "And you? Are you all right?" Her eyes searched his face.

"I am—" *Angry. Hurt. Insulted. Enraged.* "Unharmed." It had been a sharp reminder that he did not belong here. The clothing, the affected manners, even his restraint, were fake.

She touched his cheek. "I'm sorry. I didn't mean to run off, I thought I saw the man from the opera, and I followed. I'm sorry."

"For what?"

"For leaving you alone. For causing all this trouble. For Stokes."

He'd been thrilled to get rid of Stokes. "I wasn't the one facing a thug with a knife."

She curled her palm against his face, as if her touch would somehow ease pain that wasn't physical. "Thank you."

"We should find the way out." His fascination with the structure was undimmed but no longer important.

They followed the spiral of the maze out and down the little staircase. Delphine stopped at the bottom, bracing herself against a column of iridescent glass. Another group was pushing down the hall toward them, five older ladies. They chattered non-stop about the sights, the contortionists, the violinists, the treats. Oh yes, they must try the treats as soon as they left the maze.

Varrick pressed himself against the wall. Delphine leaned into him until he wrapped his arm around her. The women barely glanced at him as they walked by, except the last one who gave him a brazen study from head to foot and back, then winked.

"Hah." Delphine sounded vindicated.

"What's that about?" He'd rushed through this part before and was unsure which way led back to the large, open hub in the center.

"Just a thought I had before the opera."

"Which was?" He was half-curious, half-worried about what the woman's wink made her think of.

"I might tell you later." She leaned more heavily against him. "Can I ask a favor?"

"You have someone else I need to threaten?" He was in the mood for it.

"I could make a list, if you wanted one."

He snorted.

"But truly, don't let go of me. Not until we're outside." She touched his chest again, as she had earlier, and the same thrill sparkled through him.

He caught his ears as they automatically came forward. What had Delphine said—*adorable?* With his temper still simmering, he felt anything but that. He was too big here. Every surface reflected back how poorly he fit in Rockhaven. He wanted to close his eyes and shut it all out or crawl out of his own skin and be something unremarkable for the night.

He met her eyes. He didn't look strange there, although he couldn't parse the mix of admiration and protectiveness in them.

They found the six-way hub and its spiral staircase after a few wrong turns. On a different night, Varrick would have wanted to continue exploring, but now he just wanted out, where he could put space between himself and humans. He touched the staircase and sent a blended pulse of anima and aura through the building. Everyone in it would feel a jolt, like the static off a wool rug. Delphine tensed.

He could feel the floorplan of the building. Normally, it would be impossible, but the Maze of Mirrors was so saturated with anima and glow, he could create a perfect image of it in his mind.

"We have to go upstairs to get out." He pointed up the glass staircase.

Delphine looked from the staircase to him. "You can tell?"

They started up the stairs, Delphine a little ahead of him to make room for her skirts. "The level of magic makes it easy to detect the paths and walls. Usually, I can only feel warded parts clearly." Explaining helped drain the anger. "Most places don't have enough Craft, especially on the interior, for me to feel."

"You can feel Craft?"

"If it's strong. And this is less than two years old, so it's fresh, so to speak."

"Fresh anima sounds like something I could buy at the fish-market. Cod, two cuers. Mackerel, four cuers. Anima, one dahl."

He chuckled, letting more of the fury dissipate. "Craft fades eventually, unless it's fed by something alive or refreshed."

They reached the top and stopped. Below was plain except for the columns, but up here, the edges of the mirrors were framed with glass birds and flowers, each gleaming with their own internal glowlights.

Delphine gasped and stepped ahead of him, still clutching his hand.

Someone started up the staircase from below, so Varrick didn't linger. He led Delphine through the maze more quickly than he'd like, but she didn't slow down or ask him to wait. They were between crowds. Sounds echoed up from the lower levels, but the people ahead had cleared out, except for a few stragglers who paid them no mind. He would love to come back when it was less crowded and explore it with Delphine, but there would never be a chance to see it again for the first time. Melancholy settled over him.

The exit led them to a large balcony overlooking the bay and another set of more private walkways. The widest one led back to the main greenhouses. Delphine heaved a sigh of relief as they took the wide, curving stairway back to the ground. Varrick echoed it silently.

She stopped halfway down, looking across the lawn to the illuminated walkway. "I think we've found our man."

The man in the flowered jacket stood with a woman who chatted with two others. The man rolled his eyes and swung his watch on its chain, bored and petulant about it. He noticed Delphine and gave her an appreciative nod.

"Can you see his corona?" Varrick asked. He couldn't, but she seemed to have a talent for it.

"Let me get a better angle." With an anxious glance up at him, she crossed to the far side of the stairs and descended two more.

She bent over, giving the man a flirtatious glance as she checked her ankle.

He stopped swinging his watch and straightened. The moment was cut short as his companion tapped his arm, apparently demanding they continue on their way.

With a glance back at Varrick, Delphine hurried down the stairs and strode toward the two women the companion had been speaking with.

Varrick hesitated. Should he follow her? They didn't quite look like ladies of rank. Their clothes were rich enough, but brighter and more ostentatious. In such a casual setting, he wasn't sure how to play his role. He descended a few steps and trained his ears on Delphine to catch the conversation.

"I beg your pardon," Delphine said, stopping them. She turned away from him, and her voice was lost in the background noise.

The shorter woman spoke, but the breeze blew her words away. Varrick heard, "Market," and "tonight."

Delphine tossed her head and gestured back at him.

The two women turned their scrutiny on him. Varrick lifted his chin, meeting their eyes and nodding slightly. It seemed to be the right response. Their study was far more than an evaluation of his looks, size, or race, and whatever they saw seemed to please them. Both smiled before hiding behind their fans.

He caught the murmur of conversation again, too low and competing with too many other sounds to hear. Delphine cast a fond gaze at Varrick; his pulse galloped.

The two women studied Varrick again, smiled at one another and turned to take the path back around to the front of the building. He did not want to know what those smiles had been about. Something embarrassing, no doubt.

Delphine returned to the bottom of the stairs as he finished descending. "It's definitely the same man. He had the same tears in his corona. They showed up against the light."

"Do we have a name?" He couldn't have easily asked the women for the information.

"Mr. Albert Bertram. He's the younger brother of the Duke of Fellinon, and he's quite the card shark." She looked pensive. "I met his mother briefly at one of my first balls." Melancholy tinged her voice.

He didn't like seeing her sad.

"Do you want to see the rest of the Gardens?" he asked. They'd achieved their official objective, but once again, her past had stolen her delight in the evening. "The new exhibit is said to be unprecedented."

"It will be a richer crowd." She ducked her head. "Do you think it will be safer?"

"No one will touch you." He thought he'd made that clear.

She adjusted the folds of his cravat. "Safer for you."

"Ah." She'd been the one at knife point, but she was worried about him? "I will be fine. Maybe I can strike up a conversation with this Mr. Bertram." And bring back her smile. "Morrow said the section of flowers from Alladoon has been expanded."

She traced his coat's buttons, obviously torn.

"I've heard the speckled orchids are quite spectacular."

There was her smile, a little watery, like the sun peeking through a rainstorm.

She smoothed her skirts and took a deep breath. "Then we should go."

He paid their entrance fee—a gold thalen each—and they wound through the warm greenhouses, which were no less incredible and beautiful than the outside grounds. The entertainment was more subdued; music played from an unseen ensemble. Performers were painted white and draped in matching clothes; they moved through slow, choreographed movements like living statues. Understated elegance and exclusivity permeated the air.

Delphine was attentive as they went through the section from Alladoon. The performers here had been painted and dressed to look like jade while the music was a ridiculous parody of what the Doonish actually played. Varrick gritted his teeth. He wanted to show Delphine a particular flower and hoped the display had one.

Finally, hidden away at the back of the section, he found it: a perfect bloom of the golden mountain orchid, the tawny yellow petals spattered with maroon spots.

"You must go very high into the mountains to find them, so they're quite rare and valuable. The stories say they grew from the blood of a goddess and mark the places where miracles happened or great deeds were done."

"Rare indeed, then." She leaned closer, careful not to touch the precious plant. "I've never quite smelled a flower like it."

"Prized by perfumers." He would have to find her a blend that included it.

The new section was crowded, the noise reverberating off the walls as people watched and cheered for a display of glass automatons powered by glow. They danced in a circle, bowed, changed places, and started again, new steps to new music.

It was intriguing, but he and Delphine exchanged glances and silently agreed that it wasn't worth plowing through the crowds.

CHAPTER 20

The Touch of Gold

VARRICK

They had left the Glass Gardens and Rockhaven behind before Delphine spoke. "Despite what happened with Stokes, I enjoyed tonight. Thank you." She stared out at the darkness. "I'm sorry for what people said."

"I should have expected it." He didn't want the anger to come back. He wanted to remember the fascinating way different types of power had been blended to create the wonders of the gardens.

He pictured Delphine's profile as she leaned over the orchid.

She rubbed her fingers over her nails, stopped, and made a fist. Taking a deep breath, she said, "My mother, brother, and I lived with my Grandpapa from the time I was five until just after I turned ten. Father was away almost the whole time, running between Elethen and Torlund on business. Mama would join him sometimes but I stayed on the frontier."

She broke off, and Varrick waited as she gathered her thoughts again.

"Grandpapa worked closely with the jaglin on the borderlands.

But Father came to visit. He was furious about it," she winced. "He called them ... that."

"Frogs." It wasn't as if he hadn't heard it. In Torlund, all the humans used it. In Istalia, it was only used for Doonish jaglin, like him.

She nodded. "Grandpapa threw Father out. Father sent us away and we never went back."

"Did you use it?"

She looked at him, horrified. "Of course not." Her voice dropped. "It was easy to think that Father didn't mean it or that things were different now, but he did, and they're not."

Varrick shrugged, unsure what to say. Tonight wasn't her fault. Her father wasn't her fault, nor was Torlund's history. Why had she made that confession? Did she think he'd regret driving Stokes off or want to part ways because some tipsy workman made a public fool of himself?

She looked how he often felt: caught between things, unable to be on one side or the other, always pulled apart or shoved away. He'd been born in Alladoon, raised among Doonish refugees in Istalia, then tried to fit in at the Scholarium, where the Istalian jaglin wanted nothing to do with him. He'd found support among the oldest, most cantankerous human scholars and magi, but he remained an outsider.

There was no safe ground for people who didn't fit neatly into the roles society insisted they play.

Moving across to sit next to her could tip the carriage. Instead, he bloomed a tendril of anima, thin as a blade of grass, and stretched it across the carriage to curl about her fingers. She clasped her hands around it.

This was supposed to be a business arrangement. All the cama-raderie and affection was for show. Nothing real, no hearts engaged. They weren't supposed to be vulnerable or open; he ought to pull back.

But he wound the anima vine around her wrists and up to her

elbows, patterning it to be warm. He slid hair-thin strands of aura with it, sending reassurance until she relaxed.

"Why tell me?" he asked.

"I needed you to know. My husband hid things and lied about things. Truth is important."

Her aura was closed and locked, as always, but with his against her skin, he could sense how unsettled she was.

DELPHINE

Delphine couldn't sleep. She ought to. It was late and the gardens had worn her out. She turned on her side and pulled the covers over her head. Why had she told Varrick about her father? Father was dead. Once they'd come back to Rockhaven, no one had mentioned why they'd left Elethen, or why they never went back. It was like it never happened. Five years of her young life had been wiped away.

As soon as she pushed that spinning memory out of her mind, Stokes pushed his way in. She rubbed her wrist. It was bruised, no worse. If Varrick hadn't come when he did, would she be in a very different bed tonight, unwilling, cries unheard?

Lord Monteshreve's face swam in her mind, the sound of him tapping his cane at the opera, how he'd looked at her. How often had she stood near him at a ball as a debutante? Had he looked at her that way even then, or only since she became—in his eyes— available?

The thought of that with Monteshreve made her skin crawl. He'd looked at her as if she were a meal to be devoured, any left-overs discarded. Mistresses could say yes or no to a particular patron. Stokes and Monteshreve had not even granted her that.

But Varrick had come. He'd stepped out of the blinding golden light like an emissary of the sun. He'd held onto her after-wards, through the mirrors. In the carriage, his anima had curled warm and prickly around her arms, like tiny sparks, gold as his eyes.

She'd come here thinking she'd be his mistress. Had that been true, what would it have been like to have his hands and anima on her body? He was so tall. Lying next to him would make her feel small. And safe. She would find how far down his stripes went, and if his whole body felt soft and flocked like the back of his hands.

Delphine flopped onto her back and pulled the covers off her suddenly hot face. A flush of the same heat washed across her breasts and between her legs.

For the love of ... no! They had explicitly agreed that it was all pretend. She ought to be relieved instead of whatever this was. They hadn't even kissed, not properly, and imagining more was ridiculous. He probably had a jaglin girl somewhere and was looking forward to going back to her.

The image of his fingers exploring her body, his lips on hers, refused to fade. They were very nice lips, especially when he smiled.

She wasn't going to get a wink of sleep, was she?

CHAPTER 21

The Shimmer of Wards

Delphine

For a week, Delphine tried to avoid spending too much time with Varrick, especially time alone. Dining was fine—the table provided enough of a barrier—but the library was too intimate. He seemed as reticent as she was. When they were alone, they fell into awkward silences. They had managed so well at the Gardens. Could they only connect when they were both pretending?

Over dinner one night, Varrick announced, "We have an invitation to a very exclusive card party hosted by Lord Everard."

"Everard? He's the richest man in Rockhaven." And had a dreadful reputation as a rake. He owned the land the skydock was built on, receiving payment from the elves who landed there to trade and from the local magi and tradesmen who wanted to buy elven artifacts.

"Yes. Mr. Bertram has also been invited."

"What do you want me to do?" She took a deep breath, hoping she didn't look nervous. "Other than be ornamental?"

"We need to be introduced." Varrick tapped the stem of his wine glass. "It will be easier for you than for me."

"And get him to talk to me." She could do that.

"Put him at ease. If he's comfortable and overconfident, he'll be easier to corner." Varrick nodded. "He's reputed to be a card shark. I'd like to play him."

"Do you play well?" she asked. He must, or this whole plan would fall apart.

He grinned, the first relaxed, real grin since the gardens. "I play well enough to lose when I want and win when I need to."

He looked wholly different when he did that; mischievous, a glow to his eyes. A fluttering heat spread from her belly to her thighs. She looked away. She knew almost nothing about his life or background. He'd been to Elethen and Istalia, had mentioned the Scholarium, but that didn't tell her anything about him.

He stood, spreading his hands on the table. "Shall we prepare to dazzle them once again?"

"Tanner has been setting out dresses and jewelry all day. She seems happiest when she can make me look like one of her baronesses." She rose with him. Arrayed in Tanner's selections, she could take this field like a general.

Varrick studied her. "Would you like to be a baroness?"

"I've no idea. I never actually met a baroness. My grandmother passed away when I was small, and my grandfather isn't the usual sort of baron." He planted trees, helped load lumber barges, and, according to Varrick, invented things.

And might live another century, because he was half-elven.

Varrick tipped his head. "I met a few. They're splendid. And terrifying."

"And I am not?" She certainly didn't feel terrifying.

A smile tugged one corner of his mouth. "You are splendid. You could be terrifying, if you let yourself." He looked away, ears flicking.

. . .

Later in the evening, Tanner worked her magic, dressing Delphine in a rich plum gown and piling her hair high. She pulled several curls out, letting them dangle down Delphine's neck and along her temples.

"Amethysts are too pale for this dress," she said, and draped a glittering collar of white, black, and brandy-gold diamonds around Delphine's neck, then started to add bangles.

"They aren't too much?" Delphine had worn one at most, but Tanner added three to each wrist.

"Not for this. You are bragging about Varrick's wealth tonight."

She suspected he wasn't wealthy. He played the elegant lord well enough, but he disdained coats in the house, and she'd even caught him barefoot once. Whoever had hired him was the wealthy one.

Who had enough money to casually buy her a wardrobe and enough power to have a magus at their beck and call? It shouldn't matter; she ought to be content with her stipend and passage to Elethen.

And when she was safely there? She would have to relearn everything she knew about society. The nostalgic memories from her childhood gave her no guidance.

Delphine looked away, staring out the dark window. "Tanner, when you lived in Elethen, did you know anything about the Bollenbaucher barony?"

"They're a long way from Elethen's capital, and I never left there." She began collecting her tools.

Delphine turned. "Did you hear the stories of Baroness Camillia Bollenbaucher?"

Tanner closed her kit. "Rockhaven would call it a scandal, no matter how long ago it happened, but in Elethen, they—"

"They don't care." *What would it be like not to care?*

"Oh, they care. It's a point of pride. Not many families can boast of elven blood."

"Boast?" Delphine stared at her. "Are you serious?"

"Elethen is not Torlund. They don't measure honor by your birth but by how you keep your word. They would challenge you to a duel for breaking a contract."

"How exciting." *How strange.*

The warding on the window flickered, shimmering to life before blinking back to invisibility.

"Did you see that?" Delphine stepped toward it, the room feeling suddenly cold. "The ward flickered. The one in the library has done that a few times since I've been here." She touched the window, squinting to see through it. The night revealed nothing.

"You're sure?" Tanner set her case on the dressing table, face grave.

"Quite sure." She hadn't imagined it.

"I will ask the staff. If you see it again, tell me or Mrs. Halsey straight away."

Her voice was calm, but there was severity to it that alarmed Delphine. "Is there something I should know?"

Tanner finished gathering her things without her usual precision. "Tell Mr. Allard. Tonight. Before you leave for the card party. He needs to know."

"What do *I* need to know?" How much hadn't they told her?

"He can explain it better." Tanner grabbed her hand. "But if you see anything else unusual, tell us."

"I will." She'd talked herself out of alarm before but wouldn't do so again.

Tanner squeezed her hand. "We will keep you safe, Mrs. Leighton. You're our responsibility."

"I believe you." Delphine squeezed back.

Varrick would keep her safe, as when he had confronted Stokes. But Stokes was a bookie, not a magus or a lord. A man with position, money, and power was far more dangerous than a knife.

After Tanner left, Delphine paced the room, casting nervous glances at the dark window. No shimmer, no sign of something trying to breach the wards, but fear seized her. She would wait for Varrick in the great hall, where servants would pass by and be within earshot.

As soon as she left her room, the tightness in her throat eased. She could breathe better. She hadn't noticed how oppressive her dressing room had been until now, but the whole house felt warmer and brighter.

Was it just her imagination? After Tanner's reaction, she didn't want to dismiss it. She didn't fully relax until she reached the bottom of the grand staircase, where she could hear footsteps and the occasional echo of voices. The image of her room, dark and isolated, with her bed an island in the sea of fears, made her shiver.

"This is silly," she chided herself in a whisper, but she didn't feel silly. She felt the same cold terror creeping around her as she had the last night in her lodgings off the alleyway. She could almost hear the echo of the poor man's screams, hear his hands scrabbling at her door in a desperate bid for safety.

"Delphine?" A heavy hand landed on her bare shoulder, and she shied away in alarm.

Varrick. Just Varrick.

"Are you quite alright?" He looked at his hand, then hid it behind his back, as if embarrassed that he'd startled her.

She wanted the floor to swallow her. "I am. I was occupied with my thoughts."

"Rather distressing ones, for you to jump so badly." He fussed with his cravat, tucking it slightly tighter before pulling it back and fluffing it.

"The window wards shimmered just now. In my dressing room. Tanner said I should tell you." She tried to keep her voice light, but even she could hear the shrill note under it.

Varrick narrowed his eyes. "On the second floor?"

Delphine nodded. The ground floor wards being triggered could be an animal, but what could have triggered them on the upper floors?

He paused, hands clasped behind his back, eyes on the floor, thinking, before he looked up. "We might be fashionably late tonight. Wait here while we check the house's perimeter."

She nodded. Perimeter was such an oddly formal word to use. It was the sort of language Alastair used when talking about military maneuvers and strategy.

The tall clock in the entryway tick-tick-ticked as the minutes passed. The footman strode through, giving her a polite but brusque nod. There were voices and clattering from the back of the house, where the stairs led down to the kitchens. Being stared at by strangers would be preferable to standing here alone, waiting to know what, if anything, was wrong.

After nearly half an hour, Varrick returned, looking windswept and rumpled. Morrow followed him to tidy his hair and retie his cravat, muttering to himself. Varrick looked blander than ever, like a statue of carved jade dressed in jet.

"Is everything secure?" Delphine wanted to grasp his hand or take his arm, any sort of touch to ground her in the moment and drive away the gnawing fear.

"We found nothing, but that doesn't mean it was nothing." He adjusted his cuff and wrinkled his broad nose.

"That's not very reassuring."

They held one another's gazes. Delphine broke first, looking away, but reached for his hand. She needed to feel safe before they plunged into the night. She couldn't do it if she thought she was coming home to some unknown threat.

It wasn't really home, but it was the closest thing she had.

Varrick tucked her arm inside his, enveloping her hand. Although his fingers were cold from being outside, it was comforting.

"The staff will make a more thorough search of the grounds. Everything will be in order by the time we return."

"I guess we'd better get out of their way, then." She mustered a smile, and some of the heaviness in his face lifted.

CHAPTER 22

Shuffling the Cards

DELPHINE

Outside, it was a rare, clear night. High above, the crossed ley lines hung in the sky, barely visible, shimmering curtains of silver. The manor sat on higher ground than Rockhaven, and outside the carriage window, Delphine could see the whole curve of the city around the bay, cut through by the river, to the far side where the university and airship dock loomed over lesser buildings. Only the towers of the House of Law rivaled them.

From a distance, Rockhaven was a place of dreams, full of adventure and potential. For a few bumps in the road, she felt like a debutante again, riding to town for her first season, eyes sparkling like the ley lines above. The road hugged the outer boundaries of the city, a quicker ride to the far side than dodging cabbies and other carriages through town.

Her debutante year felt centuries ago. Delphine expected the touch of melancholy that trickled into her heart, but not the accompanying relief. It had been an exciting, breathless time, but her whole future had turned upon one decision: whom she married. Now, she was on the far side of it all. The worst had happened, but she was still here, still alive.

Across the coach, the caps on Varrick's horns reflected the scant moonlight, and his eyes glowed briefly like a cat's. Delphine knew that jaglin saw better in the dark than humans. *How clearly can he see me?*

Three-quarters of the way around Rockhaven's outer limits, the carriage turned, catching a road that parallelled the river and brought them into an affluent part of town. The homes here had extensive gardens and grounds with high iron fences and thick hedges for privacy. Carriages waited outside several, but theirs didn't stop until it came to a darker street a little way from the busier estates. No carriages lingered here, and only a single glow-light hanging from a hook illuminated the drive.

"Do you know the house?" Varrick asked as they turned into the long, looping drive.

Delphine shook her head. "I've never been here. Private parties were usually too rich for my blood."

"For both of ours. Let's hope no one notices." He grinned, a flash of white in the darkness of the carriage.

Delphine shook the nostalgia and gloom away. She steeled herself to play her part, picturing a wholly different persona: effusive, bright, and flirtatious. Not Mrs. Leighton, but Baroness Bollenbaucher, there to outshine everyone else and not care a fish head for whomever she annoyed.

The carriage slowed to a stop. One of the horses snorted.

A footman opened the door and lowered the step for Varrick, who alighted first, before turning to offer her his hand. He wore no gloves and his hand was warm. She gripped it more tightly than necessary.

Unlike a ball, which would have had an extravagance of lights inside and out, the front entrance was lit only by two glowlights, just enough to indicate that the house was occupied. They mounted the short flight of steps and the door swung open before

Varrick could knock. Inside was barely better lit than outside, the halls suffused with dark golden glowlights.

A cacophony of voices echoed through the corridors as a thick-bodied butler stepped out to take their coats.

"Names?" he inquired, looking at Varrick with a lip curled in distaste.

"Mr. Varrick Allard and Mrs. Delphine Leighton." Varrick stared the man down. "We are expected."

"Yes," the butler said in a voice heavy with disapproval. "Follow me."

He led them through the vaulted main hall, past doors that must lead to a morning room, library, and others before showing them into a more private series of backrooms. Through perhaps four connected rooms, five or six circular tables were laid out, with groups of men intent over cards at each. Footmen walked through with carafes of wine or brandy, refilling glasses. Each room had its own sideboard of appetizers, but the men weren't frequenting them.

Dazzling women moved through the rooms, chatting, holding plates of food, or offering cigars to the playing men. Their dresses, like Delphine's, were cut low, and they dripped with expensive jewelry. Outshining proper ladies at the opera had been no challenge, but this was a different crowd altogether. Some of the women draped decoratively on men's shoulders. Others gathered in corners or on scattered sofas and divans, speaking without bothering to hide behind fans. The glowlights shone, clouded by the haze of cigar smoke.

"Varrick, would you like a cigar, a drink, something to eat, or all three?" She wasn't sure where else to begin. She would feel better if she had a small, specific purpose to start the evening.

"Brandy," he said, "once I'm seated."

A lull followed them through the room as they walked, but the conversations quickly resumed behind them. A pair of women standing near a curving staircase looked Varrick up and down before giving Delphine knowing smiles.

Sweet rivers, this wasn't the place to burn with maidenly blushes. She gave them a cool nod. Varrick paused, scanning the men.

"Ah, there's our host." He strode toward the table furthest from where they'd entered, aiming for a rather thin, sallow man with impeccably tailored clothes.

The thin man excused himself from a conversation and approached them. He shook Varrick's hand without any sign of disdain. "You made it. Here I was afraid my new showpiece wouldn't, well, show."

Varrick snorted. "I can't be that much of an anomaly."

"You'd be amazed at who wants the thrill of sitting at a table with such an exotic player as yourself." The host swept his hand at the back table. "They'll have a place for you in a few minutes. Meanwhile," he turned to Delphine, "introduce me to your lovely companion."

Varrick guided her forward. "Lord Everard, this is Delphine Leighton."

Delphine offered her free hand, keeping the other firmly on Varrick's arm. "So nice to meet you, Lord Everard."

He took her hand, kissing it with more ardor than she liked. "Whatever he's paying you, Mrs. Leighton, I'll double it."

There was no jest in his expression. "I've no doubt, but like your players here, I enjoy the novelty."

Varrick's arm shifted under her hand, but she didn't dare check his response.

Everard's grin took on a salacious air. "I cannot fault you for that."

"I hope not, as I'd hold it against you." She could do this, so long as she didn't have to look Varrick in the face. The ride home would be unbearably awkward.

Varrick laid a hand over hers. "I hope you didn't warn your players. Half the fun of a new player is testing their abilities."

"Wouldn't dream of it." Everard grinned, obviously looking forward to whatever the night held. "There now, the table is ready for you to join."

Varrick took the free chair and tossed a folded stack of notes into the pile in the middle. The four other men gave one another sidelong looks. The dealer at the table shuffled the cards, fingers moving too fast to follow. The men leaned into the game.

Everard stepped uncomfortably close to Delphine. "I cannot tell you how much I'm looking forward to the evening. If he wins, they'll have absolute fits. If he loses, they'll pat themselves on the back and let their guard down."

"I'll fetch Varrick his brandy." Was this a set-up or did Everard just enjoy defying convention by inviting a jaglin?

She dodged a few younger women arguing over a box of cigars and a portly man who was watching one of the other tables finish a game.

Everard was rich enough to slip out of social expectations, but he must be gaining something other than amusement from the evening. As the host, he'd keep part of the winnings, of course, but he would with or without Varrick. She watched him move through the crowd, chatting with ease. Every conversation was a chance to gather gossip and information. How many secrets did he pick up each night?

She hadn't asked Varrick how he liked his drinks, so she poured the brandy neat but with a stinting hand. She'd not seen him drink enough to gauge how well he held it.

"Why, Dellie! Never thought I'd see you here."

Delphine whirled around, more startled by the affectionate nickname than someone recognizing her. "Mr. Severson."

The gentleman tipped his head. He'd pulled his bright red hair forward so it hung in his eyes, a style often affected by the youngest fops. Too young for him, but he wore it with such aplomb, it wasn't off-putting.

He raked his hand through his hair, completely destroying the effect. "I thought I saw you at the opera, but by the time I was done with my, ah, business, you'd gone. I didn't have a chance to chat with you."

"I did see you, but we didn't linger afterwards."

"Damn it, Dellie, what are you doing here?"

The question was so unexpected that she answered without thought. "I am doing my best with what David left me."

He rubbed his jaw, at a loss.

"His debts, Mr. Severson. How am I to pay them otherwise?" By every god and star in the sky, David had lost to Severson often enough.

"If you needed help … didn't his family shoulder some of it? You could have come to me."

"No, they didn't." She couldn't respond yet to the second part. She hadn't seen Mr. Severson for nearly a year before David's death. He hadn't come to the funeral. How was she to know he would help? A lump lodged in her throat.

A group had started to gather behind him, probably for brandy, but possibly for gossip. Delphine stepped around him. "I should take Varrick his drink."

He followed her through the rooms to the back table. She glanced at Varrick's cards as she set the snifter down. A good hand, possibly an excellent one, depending on the game variation.

Varrick spared her a glance and a nod.

Mr. Severson dogged her steps, so she dropped a kiss on Varrick's smooth teal hair. "Let me know when you need anything else."

This time he looked into her face, as if remembering they were both playing roles. He laid a hand on her cheek. "Go enjoy yourself."

Delphine gave him an affectionate smile before strolling to one of the more out-of-the-way settees. Severson followed.

"Was it all that bad?" he asked as they sat.

"The debts? They were quite bad, yes. Took the house and everything in it." The pain of it seized her throat with long, icy fingers. "I am doing what women with no recourse have always done."

He frowned and crossed his arms only to uncross them immediately. "You should have come to me. Maybe I couldn't save everything but, damn it, Dellie—"

She hated that he called her that. It put her so neatly back into the box of who she had been.

"I could have saved you from selling yourself out to his sort. You can't be happy with it."

Delphine's laugh was bitter. "What does happiness have to do with any of it? Did you think I was happy when you brought David home, drunk, with a new pile of losses?"

He winced. "He loved you. The times he worried about being good enough for you—"

"Are gone. Were gone long ago." She refused to feel guilty over David and his professed love. He had broken her heart into too many pieces to count.

Severson leaned forward, elbows on his knees, head in his hands. "He never seemed to be able to stay away. Every night, he swore he'd stop, but he always came back."

"No mistress held his heart like cards. Nor did I. He chose what he loved."

"Let me help you now. If you're in a bad spot, tell me. Send a note to the club."

"I am in a better spot, as you put it, than I was a few weeks ago. Better than I have been for quite some time."

He looked woebegone, like a kicked puppy.

She relented. Like Edwina, his sympathy was mixed with

defense, but she couldn't afford another scene. "I thank you, Mr. Severson. Don't worry. Varrick is very generous and gentle."

He flushed. "That's good, I suppose."

"If you truly want to help, perhaps you could introduce me to a Mr. Bertram?" Their quarry wasn't playing with Varrick; she needed to find him.

"Bertie tends to be late, but he'll be here. Made a big fuss over Everard inviting a, ah, your Mr. Varrick. I doubt he'll miss it."

"Why aren't you playing tonight?" She'd never seen him hanging around the tables without dealing in.

"Got in a bit of a pickle. Have to get out again before I can bet anything. Doesn't do to run up the debts too high, y'see." He stared at the far wall. "Well, of course you see," he stammered. "You know."

"I'm glad you're being sensible about it."

"My dad cut me off. Makes it easier to be all sensible and boring."

"I approve of your father, then." She patted his hand. "You don't want to drown in your debts, I promise."

"Yeah." He flashed a bright smile. "Made for a dull evening until you walked in. You could have knocked me over with a feather. Well, not just me, practically everyone. Everard thought it was a hoot."

"I'm sure." She craned her neck to see the entrance to this back labyrinth. The disapproving butler stood there, looking as if he'd rather be drawn and quartered than watch such a filthy, decadent assembly of wastrels play poker.

He met her eyes, sniffed, and left his post, disappearing into the hall.

"I don't suppose you can introduce me around? I am new to these circles."

"I can. You'll want to meet the ladies." He rose and attempted to tidy his hair.

"And you know them all."

"You make me sound like a terrible cad."

"No. Just a man." She held her hand out to him.

CHAPTER 23

The Society of Mistresses

DELPHINE

Severson tucked Delphine's arm around his and steered her toward a pair of ladies who she'd seen on the way in. "They want to meet you. I'll bring Bertie over when he arrives."

Most men here would go home to wives. They might be joyful with winnings or furious over losses, and the women in their lives might be disappointed, or worried or indifferent. Maybe that was the best anyone could hope for in marriage.

The two women who'd given approving, knowing looks as she and Varrick entered were Octavia and Pearl. They could be sisters, for they had the same full figures, golden blonde hair, and wide mouths. There was an air of luxury to them that had nothing to do with their fine gowns or jewelry.

"Dearest," Octavia purred, opening her arms, "we always look out for new faces. We ladies must stand together."

Pearl, the taller of the two, stepped around Delphine before giving an approving nod. "You've a good lady's maid. So many are trained to only make their mistresses blend in."

"She was trained in Elethen." It shouldn't matter that they

approved, but it calmed her nerves. "She used to style baronesses," she said."

"I believe her." Octavia stood back, looking Delphine up and down one more time. "I might steal her from you, if we don't become friends first."

"We ought to be friends then." Delphine smiled, feeling at ease for the first time since they walked in. "I am very new to this."

Octavia nodded. "We heard the rumors. Your patron made quite a ripple, showing up at the opera with you. And you're a widow?"

"Yes." She glanced toward Varrick at his game. Every face at the table was intent on the cards. "I am looking forward to better times."

"We like to see a positive approach to our profession." Pearl opened her hand toward the nearest table of nibbles and drinks. "Most who come to it from higher society spend the whole first year in mourning."

Delphine followed them to the table, although she wasn't hungry. "I have done enough of that. Mr. Allard made an offer, and it appealed to me."

"We've heard rumors about him as well." Pearl plucked an oyster from a bed of ice. "You completely threw our betting pool off. We had odds on Juliette."

"*Juliette* had odds on Juliette. She was rather upset when he arrived with you." Octavia chuckled. She held her empty wine glass out to the footman attending the table.

"At the opera?" Delphine hadn't noticed any sour looks aimed at them.

Octavia took a sip. "Oh no, here. She took one look and whisked herself away to the back. She's probably sulking in the garden until Everard goes back to console her."

"Oh." Delphine chose a glass and nodded to the footman to fill it. She hadn't expected mistresses to have their own politics and rivalries. Foolishly, she'd assumed they would all make small talk but otherwise ignore one another.

"Was there some reason she was interested in Mr. Allard?"

Pearl tapped her nails on her necklace. "The novelty, I suppose. A foreigner? And not human? He garnered quite a lot of attention."

"She was asking a lot of questions, wanted recommendations and such." Octavia stared into her wine glass. "Vulgar, really."

"I rather stumbled into it." Delphine barely sipped her wine. She didn't want to be muddled. "How do men usually go about choosing a new mistress?"

"Much the same way a duchess hires a new lady's maid," Octavia said. "Maids keep their ear to the ground about a new, lucrative position, and we keep tabs on when a gentleman drops his mistress. Or a new gentleman comes to town."

Varrick had needed someone trustworthy, a woman who wouldn't complain about the ruse or gossip about his real aims.

He must have looked into her. Delphine considered that as Octavia and Pearl pointed out various ladies and which gentleman they'd come with. Not all were long-term mistresses, although her companions stressed that *they* were. Some women were escorts who sold each night separately. They charged different sums for what the gentleman wanted—one fee for the opera, more for a private party, and even more if he wanted her to join him in bed.

"Risky business, being just an escort," said Pearl, choosing her own glass of wine. "You never know if they'll turn from bargaining the price down to trying force. I knew someone, when I was younger, who was all but kidnapped by her admirer. Harrowing."

With the Maze of Mirrors fresh in her mind, Delphine shuddered.

"That happens with mistresses, too." Octavia frowned. "Just not as often."

"Men are more likely to shun a man who treats his mistress badly. They care less about escorts. It's safer if they work out of a house, instead of alone." Pearl shook her head. "Oh, there she is. I told you Everard would have her back in soon."

Delphine followed her gaze to Lord Everard and the woman on his arm. The woman's huge, hazel eyes were focused on Everard, beseeching, lashes wet as if she'd been weeping. Juliette was slim, short, and familiar. She'd been with the big blond man at the opera.

"Her hair?" Delphine whispered to Octavia. It was still blue.

"An affectation to look more elven."

Delphine raised an eyebrow. "Why?"

Octavia lowered her voice more. "Juliette rarely takes patrons. Mostly she runs a gambling den and escort house. The Indigo Elf. Very expensive, just to get through the door."

"Must be lucrative." The name wasn't familiar, but many gambling dens kept out unwanted players by running invitation-only games.

Delphine had spent her life denying the tipped ears and purple undertones in her hair that she'd inherited from the mysterious great-grandfather elf, and this woman was dyeing her hair to look like one. She was even wearing flashy silver ear ornaments shaped to look like elf ears.

Touching her own ear, Delphine rubbed the high tip of it. Irrationally, she felt awkward and huge compared to such a delicate swan of a woman, as if she herself were an imposter here.

Silly thought. Of course I'm an imposter. That's the point.

Everard escorted Juliette to the back table where Varrick played.

Pearl prodded Delphine in the shoulder. "You should take your gentleman a cigar now. Stand with him. Touch him. Make sure she knows he's taken."

Juliette sidled between Varrick and the player next to him; she traced the curve of Varrick's horn, stopping at the brass cap.

The blood rushed in Delphine's ears. How dare she fondle him! "Where are the cigars?"

Octavia handed one over. "Go on, go fawn over him. If it feels excessive, you're doing it right."

Pearl gave her an encouraging smile.

Delphine took a deep breath. She could do this. *Think like a baroness. Be a baroness.*

Passing between footmen and mistresses, she crossed the room to the table and slipped in beside Varrick. Juliette was currently cooing over the man on the far side of him, but her fingers still rested on Varrick's horn.

"Varrick." Delphine leaned on him, waggling the cigar next to his cards. "I finally found your favorite. Can I light it for you?"

The ride home would most certainly be awkward.

He looked up at her, the movement dislodging Juliette's hand. "I think you should."

There were cutters on the table. Finally, something life with David had prepared her for. She passed the cigar under her nose, inhaling the rich, dry scent, nodded, and cut the tip, making a show of it.

Varrick transferred his cards to his other hand and wrapped his free arm around her waist. He took the proffered cigar in his lips.

Everard handed Delphine a small box. "Match?"

"Thank you, Lord Everard. It's the only proper way to do it." She struck the match and lit the cigar. She didn't want to make enemies, but Juliette was pawing Varrick's horn.

"Stay with me." Varrick pulled Delphine into his lap, hand firm around her waist and stomach. Possessive.

Pleasure sparkled through her chest. Varrick was silently daring any man at the table to challenge them, and each one looked down or away. She relaxed, feeling safe even in such a precarious environment.

She lifted the cigar to his lips and leaned close to his ear. "Bertram isn't here yet, but he's expected."

His ear flickered, which she took for acknowledgement. "What do you think of my hand, Delphine? Should I play through or fold?"

She surveyed his cards. "Are you playing the serpents variation?"

"Reverse elven." He took a draw on the cigar.

"Play through." It was a good hand, but not a guaranteed win. She studied the men around the table, catching their eyes, looking for tells.

The man across kept darting his gaze to the left. The man on his left leaned back and puffed his own cigar. She couldn't see the man to Varrick's right; she sat with her back to him and Juliette.

The last man couldn't sit still. He drummed his fingers, shifted in his seat, and rolled his shoulders. He held a bad hand but had put too much into the pot to fold and walk away. He would stay in until he recouped his losses. If he ever did.

Delphine wrapped her arm around Varrick's neck and shoulders, steadying herself on the edge of the table.

"Oh, Mr. Allard, I didn't know you had a, *friend*, here." Juliette's voice was high, breathy, and grating.

Varrick ignored her.

Delphine enjoyed watching the game and keeping an eye on the men's tells. There was an excitement to guessing right. Maybe that was the thrill of gambling: making a guess and being right. Someone cleared their throat, and Delphine turned toward the sound.

Juliette had left Varrick's right side and come around to face Delphine. She fluttered her damp eyelashes. "I mean, I suppose some men like someone inexperienced because she's more malleable. I just didn't take him for the sort who would want to train his own."

Inexperienced. Malleable. Train. Juliette was working hard to dig a barb in. Delphine yawned. "I really don't know what you mean."

"He's training you, dear," Juliette said, steel finally showing in her voice.

Delphine considered pouring wine down Juliette's decolletage, but that would probably backfire. "Oh, my sweet, who's to say *I'm* not training *him*?"

Varrick chuckled. The small sound evaporated the last of Delphine's tension. She wasn't alone, and this was exactly the part she had been hired to play.

She turned away from Juliette. The way the small woman fluttered and swanned, she wanted everyone's attention. The best Delphine could do was remove it. She leaned close to Varrick's ear again, relaying her thoughts on his competitors. She didn't know if he wanted to win or lose, but the information would help either way.

The shifty man finally folded, looking morose. The one who kept glancing aside did as well, almost immediately after the first. The other man with the cigar planted his elbows on the table, grinning through the smoke. Juliette left to speak with Everard.

It was strange to have competition. Even when Delphine debuted, it had been the ingenues together against the glittering wall of society. This felt oddly personal.

CHAPTER 24

Dealing In

DELPHINE

"Excuse me," Severson's voice cut through the low chatter of the crowded rooms. "Hello, Miss Singleton, nice to see you this evening."

Delphine glanced over Varrick's shoulder as Severson bowed over Juliette's hand. She seemed unimpressed with him until she turned to his companion. Oh yes, that was Mr. Bertram. He was nearly as tall as Severson, but more solidly built, square-faced, and dark-haired. His tailor's work on the fit of his jacket and the embroidery on the lapels was exquisite, and designed to flaunt his wealth.

Juliette was back to fluttering as Mr. Bertram kissed her hand and murmured something. He had none of Everard's oiliness; he seemed bored, even with Juliette.

How was Delphine supposed to gain his attention and engage him in conversation when he seemed disinclined to speak with anyone?

Bertram and Severson stepped away from Juliette and Everard.

" ... lost a full five hundred in the first round," Severson said. "I thought he'd spend the night sulking over whiskey, but he won it back from—"

Delphine caught Severson's eye. He broke off and grinned. "I've got someone for you to meet, Bertie."

Taking her cue, Delphine slid off Varrick's lap and rose, waiting for the two gentlemen to approach.

Severson pulled at his collar. "Bertie, this is Delphine Leighton. You know, Davie's widow. Dellie, meet Albert Bertram."

"I wasn't aware you knew my husband, Mr. Bertram," Delphine said as he bowed over her hand.

"In passing," Bertie said. "I played with him at the club a few times when we were younger. Before he married."

He looked and sounded bored, eyes half-lidded, voice lazy. She had asked for an introduction. Severson had delivered. The rest was up to her.

"Are you married, Mr. Bertram?"

Bertram shook his head. "I've never been much inclined to it. To my mother's sorrow, I'm afraid."

"How is the dowager Duchess of Fellinon?" Delphine recalled her presence at a few of her early balls. "She complimented my gown at the first grand ball of my season."

He perked up at the mention. "That must have been one of the last years she was strong enough to go out. I'm afraid she's too delicate for much company or travel now."

"I'm sorry to hear it. She is a very elegant lady, and I appreciated her kind words." In those early days, Delphine had felt awkward and out of place, and the duchess's little favor, which likely meant nothing to her, had sent ripples through the room. Others had treated Delphine better because of the older woman's kindness.

"We bring musicians in as much as possible. She always loved music." He motioned to the nearest playing table, where the previous group had dispersed. Octavia and Pearl's patrons had found them, the gentlemen now fawning over their mistresses.

Bertram pulled a chair out for her, and she accepted the place. Varrick had said he wanted Bertram at ease and overconfident, but he already seemed confident, with that untouchable assurance of the rich and powerful that they were above consequences. Idly, Delphine picked up and shuffled the cards left after the game. The movement helped her think.

"I hope your older brother and his wife take good care of her." That oddness in his aura was a clue, and Varrick wanted him to be in an expansive mood.

He signaled someone for a drink. "Decently, I suppose."

Delphine arched the cards in a curve, the riffling of their edges making a satisfying rustle.

He accepted a snifter of brandy from a footman. "I would have sworn I'd met you before, Mrs. Leighton."

"I am quite sure I would remember meeting you. Perhaps you saw me at a ball or concert." Maybe because they'd followed him around the Glass Gardens a week ago. "I think your brother, the duke, visited my brother-in-law a few times, but never when I was there."

He swirled the golden liquid and sipped. "Michael Havemshire is far more my brother's sort, yes. I can't say I ever bothered with him."

She tapped the deck against the table. "It must have been elsewhere, then." She held up the shuffled cards. "A friendly game?"

Interest flared in his eyes. "Between the two of us?"

"Why not? I don't have the collateral to play the tables, and Mr. Allard is busy."

"You really are contracted to the jaglin, then?"

Nettled, she dealt a card too aggressively and it slid past onto the floor. "I fail to see how he differs from most gentlemen of my acquaintance. He gambles, drinks, likes pretty women and the things one does with pretty women. So what if he is green?"

He retrieved the card. "You have such a stellar opinion of our sex."

And he wasn't improving it. "Taught by experience, I'm afraid. A game of twenty-one, and see which of us can get closer without going over?"

He nodded. "What would the stakes be?"

"What would you accept, Mr. Bertram? A kiss? A promised dance? An honest answer to a question?"

"It's customary to ask for an entire night."

Delphine raised her eyebrows. "My time is contracted, so I cannot."

He grinned. He must have expected her refusal. "Honest answers then. I win, I get to ask you. You win, I answer."

"Very well." She dealt out the cards, two for herself, one face up, one face down, and two face up for him.

He stared down at his deuce of clubs and five of diamonds. "Hit."

She gave him another card, glancing at her lone eight of hearts and the downturned mystery card.

Jack of diamonds.

"Seventeen is quite close," he said. "Is it closer than yours?"

"Maybe. Do you want to risk another card?"

"No. Turn yours over."

If she had an ace or a face card, she would win. She had no idea what she would ask him. She turned her card over. "Five of spades."

"Do you draw, Mrs. Leighton?"

"I shall." Risk. Possibility. Was the thrill of it worth the trepidation? It must be for so many of the men here. Her anxiety boiled up but had nothing to do with the cards. She needed Bertram amiable, but she wanted to yell at him.

She took another card, holding it facedown to savor the tension of the moment and increase that burning light in Bertram's eyes. If she held something more than four and less than nine, she would win. The odds weren't good.

"Nervous?" he asked.

Yes. "Are you?"

"I am never nervous."

"I'm sure." What would it be like to live a life free of fear?

She turned the card over. Queen of Diamonds. She was at twenty-two.

Bertram grinned. "And now you owe me an answer to a question."

Delphine gathered up the cards, quick fingers covering her racing mind. There were things she couldn't answer honestly, and others she didn't want to. He might ask either.

"Do you have a question ready?" She tidied the deck with a satisfying thunk against the table.

"I shall have to think." He tipped his chair back. "The most natural question is why a lovely and well-bred woman as yourself has stooped to such circumstances, but I think I know that answer, in general if not the particulars." The angle of his gaze said her questionable circumstances had more to do with Varrick than being a mistress.

"Money solves many questions of taste and convention." Delphine tipped her head. "You must be curious about something?"

"Oh yes." He set the chair down and leaned toward her. "Why did you want to meet me, Mrs. Leighton? You didn't know I'd ever met Davie. We've never crossed paths, but you asked Severson for an introduction. Are you trolling for a new patron already?"

She'd twisted his tail somehow. "That's more than one question. Which would you like me to answer?"

"The first one, which might answer both." He narrowed his eyes, as if trying to study the edges of her aura. He'd have no luck.

"You are reputed to be one of the best players in Rockhaven. That's how I heard of you—David used to talk about your skill." A little flattery to help the mix of truth and lies go down easier. "Mr. Allard likes a challenge. He craves legitimacy." She leaned forward, lowering her voice until it was husky. "Why do you think he chose a human mistress?"

"He thinks playing me will give him that?"

"In certain circles, yes." She ducked her chin, looking up at him through her lashes, playing the coquette. "He doesn't just want to play. He intends to win. Build his reputation off yours."

"Like the depths he will!" Bertram's fingers tightened on the snifter.

Delphine froze, not even breathing. She'd meant to entice, not anger. Had she just ruined Varrick's chances of talking to him? No, she could salvage this. "So you refuse to play him?"

"I didn't say that."

His small lips pinched and his brows drew together. Did he think Varrick so much beneath him? A flash of defensive indignation rippled through her.

"Surely if you beat him, it will put him in his place." She fluttered her lashes, which she hated, but it seemed to work. "You can beat him, can't you?"

His mouth pinched more. He hesitated. "Of course."

"Shall I arrange it for you?"

"Just tell the frog I am ready when he is."

Varrick had wanted him to be overconfident. People said more in anger than they might otherwise, but his temper buffeted her, leaving her shaken. Delphine took a deep breath. He would do nothing to her here. She could work his anger against him, but only if she didn't let it rattle her.

"Vulgarity, Mr. Bertram? Are you feeling a bit intimidated, to throw around such language?" She arched an eyebrow at him. If she could Skill a person, she'd have prodded his temper higher. "I know human men feel *inadequate* compared to jaglin."

He finished his drink in a single, huge gulp and stomped away.

CHAPTER 25

High Stakes

Delphine

Heady from the confrontation, Delphine left the stack of cards at the table and collected a brandy for herself. The bubbly feeling in her chest sharpened her senses and threatened to twist into anxiety unless it burst. The brilliance of the lights, the thickness of cigar smoke, the background chatter, all surged around her like storm-driven waves.

She wasn't panicking. It was anger at Bertram's obvious disdain. It was tension over whether she was carrying her role well. A quieter, darker place would allow her to collect herself before explaining the wager and results to Varrick, but no such place was in sight. Varrick was still playing at the back table. Juliette's blue hair caught her eye. She was hanging on Bertram's arm, looking up at him with adoring, calculating eyes.

Maybe she would be happy with him and forget Varrick.

Delphine sipped the brandy, relishing the smokiness of it and the heat afterwards. It settled some of the bubbling. She would tell Varrick and let him take the lead. This was his hunt, after all. She'd beaten Bertram out of the bushes for him; it was up to him to give chase.

Forcing her shoulders to relax, she strolled over to Varrick. Bertram's animosity had unsettled her; it felt like a threat.

It felt like the window wards flickering when nothing was there.

Varrick was losing on purpose, folding despite better hands while his opponents chuckled at his apparent misfortune. Delphine leaned her crossed arms on his broad shoulders. It steadied her. He felt solid, immovable. He'd been sure he was Bertram's match. She ought to trust him.

Leaning her cheek against the smooth, cool curve of his horn, she sighed. He tipped his head, angling his ear up. An invitation to report.

"Mr. Bertram would like to play against you at your convenience," she murmured. "He is quite invested in winning the game."

Varrick nodded. The pot in the center of the table was enormous, full of bills and scripts for possessions. Whoever won that would have many people in his debt—if he didn't lose it all afterwards. Varrick asked for another card.

He already had two pair, and a ten or a six would give him a full house. Delphine ran her fingers along his other horn. The smoothness was as calming and satisfying as the brandy had been.

"He's offended by you," she added, whispering.

He placed the new card from the dealer in his hand. A six. Either he hadn't heard or he had a fantastic poker face, for he didn't even flick an ear.

The man across the table folded.

"Still in, Allard?" the man next to him asked, fanning his cards before pressing them back into a neat stack. "Call or fold."

"Call." Varrick looked to his right, at the man Juliette had fawned over earlier. "You?"

"I'm in." He leaned back.

The last remaining man shook his head. "Fold."

Did any of them have wives? Any of them might go home with devastating news, their household in grave danger from their debts. Sour guilt nagged at the back of her throat. If Varrick won, it might be more than a night's fun gone badly for some of them.

Delphine didn't care about the men, but their hypothetical wives, children, and servants had her sympathy.

They went around again, the bet raised, money added to that vast heap. She could have paid off David's debts and lived comfortably off that pile for years. She looked away, catching Octavia and her patron entering from the back. Octavia smiled and waved at Delphine, clearly content with her night. Delphine smiled back despite the chill creeping over her. Sharing Varrick's bed in truth might be easier than being part of this. These games destroyed lives.

Another man folded. Only Varrick and the man across from him remained. Delphine didn't want to be a distraction, but she leaned her whole weight on his shoulders, half sick should he lose, and just as ill should he win.

Varrick relaxed as each man folded. Whatever his plan, it was playing out as he wanted. She hoped the game with Bertram was also part of that plan.

The man across tapped his cards on the table. "Alright. Show down. We'll see if you're bluffing."

Varrick spread his cards, the full house making a tidy fan against the glossy wood. He clasped his hands, elbows on the table, and rested his chin on them. "Go ahead."

The other man hesitated, swallowed, and laid his cards down. He slid a finger across the pile so they spread into a line. Three deuces. Varrick's full house beat his three of a kind.

Varrick had won. That whole pot of notes and property belonged to him. The players around the table frowned, their dislike and anger simmering too close to the surface for Delphine's comfort, but Varrick didn't seem concerned.

"Are you ready for Mr. Bertram?" she asked into the uncomfortable silence.

A titter swept through the men who had just lost. They anticipated him losing in turn, and their debts would, very properly, be held by a Torlish gentleman instead of a jaglin outsider.

She suddenly hoped Varrick would take Bertram for every last cuer.

CHAPTER 26

Calling the Bluff

DELPHINE

The series of rooms was a chess board, the pieces suddenly rearranged for a fresh game. Women and their patrons swept in, exchanging empty glasses for full ones.

Everard, alone now, joined Delphine, offering a tall, slim glass of white wine full of bubbles. He sipped his own, satisfaction simmering rosy-orange at the visible edges of his aura.

She accepted the glass. "What do you get out of this?"

"Besides being thoroughly entertained by the drama?" he grinned. "I love rattling Bertie. He's practically boiling over, but he can't do a thing to me."

"That's a bit low-class, isn't it?"

"Please, Mrs. Leighton, allow me my innocent pleasures." He crossed his arms. "The moment I heard Allard wanted to speak with Bertie, I knew I had to set it up."

"He hates jaglin."

"No." Everard wagged a finger at her. "He hates that everyone here is treating a jaglin as his equal. That's a very specific type of animosity."

"And if that animosity goes beyond this game?" Bertram wouldn't be a gracious winner, and he was likely to be a vicious loser.

"It most certainly will, no matter who wins." He fairly oozed with pleasurable anticipation.

"What then?" Allard had magic and was physically powerful, but Bertram had money, connections, and strings that could be pulled.

Delphine sipped the wine to cover the chill creeping over her shoulders. Every time she convinced herself that this was a ruse she could relax and enjoy, something reminded her that it was indeed a dangerous game.

"Oh, I think Allard can handle whatever comes of it. Bertie tends to disappear to lick his wounds when he's humiliated."

"That only applies if Varrick wins." She took another sip of wine, then regretted it. Between the first glass, the brandy, and this, the room swam. She blinked, waiting for the dealer at the table to break in a new deck for the game.

Octavia had tiny flickers of gold excitement in her corona. Her patron's was more sedate, a soft, pink contentment, like someone who knows their evening will be satisfactory no matter what.

As people gathered, anticipation spread through the crowd, seasoned with the anger of those who'd lost to Varrick earlier. More people lost control of their auras; coronas became brighter and clearer, especially among people who had imbibed multiple drinks.

When Bertram stalked through the crowd to join the dealer at the table, the corona around his head appeared reversed. Instead of a slightly luminous color and a few tears, like at the opera, it pulled in the light and auras around it. Delphine blinked. This was much more noticeable than before. Was it because she'd riled him, or had the cause gotten worse?

He passed in front of a glowlight hanging from the ceiling and the black, negative aura was clearly visible for a moment.

Delphine glanced at Everard, who had finished his glass of bubbling wine and had a footman refilling it. If he'd noticed, he made no indication of it. No, he wouldn't have. He was too intent on the scene he'd set up.

Everyone else was talking, men were taking bets, some of the women too. The footmen topped off every glass, including hers. Varrick sat across from Bertram, inscrutable. This had to bother him. Everard was using him for entertainment and a stalking goat for Bertram. Betram obviously disdained Varrick and his kind, and it was all the center of a spectacle.

Delphine would hate it. Anger already licked at the edges of her mood.

How was he going to dig any information out of Bertram with everyone watching?

She moved away from Everard, strolling through the crowd until Bertram's head lined up with a glowlight on the far wall.

The black corona, a penumbra that apparently no one else saw, stood out in sharp relief.

Her father had trained her and Alastair to study auras and Skill them. They learned to analyze things others dismissed or didn't understand, but he'd never mentioned anything like this. If only she could catch Varrick before the game, but the dealer had already dealt the first cards. Bertram threw paper notes into the center of the table. Varrick followed.

Bertram glared at his cards, but that meant nothing. He was glaring at Varrick, the dealer, and Everard with equal hostility. His furious gaze met Delphine's and the wrath in it shifted. Not away from anger, but into a different sort, although she couldn't read the details. She tipped her head and raised her eyebrows, putting on an innocent, confused face. The confusion was real.

He dropped his gaze back to the game.

Pearl had stepped up on Delphine's right, cheeks flushed. Someone else joined them to Delphine's left. She assumed it was

Octavia until she turned to say something and found herself face to face with Juliette.

"You aren't going to go support your patron?" Juliette asked.

Delphine took too deep a gulp of her wine and ended up coughing. At least it gave her time to think.

"I wanted to give them room. Can't have Bertram accusing Varrick of anything underhanded because I'm hovering."

Juliette scoffed. "You look so lost, like a lamb wandering into a slaughterhouse." Her gaze traveled down Delphine's gown and back up. "Or maybe a calf."

Delphine's cheeks burned at the insult, although more from indignation than humiliation. What claim did the woman think she had on Varrick?

Delphine licked her lips. "I heard you wanted him as your patron. Lamb or calf, I'm obviously more to his taste."

Juliette pursed her lips, sipping her wine and scowling. If Delphine was veal, was Juliette fish? Duck or goose, maybe? Goose, Delphine decided. She'd been very hissy so far.

Heh. Instead of gryphons, Edwina could breed goose-phons. Delphine really had drunk too much, because the thought made her giggle.

"Oh, you find this amusing?" Juliette snapped.

"I certainly find you amusing." As a goose. The silly thought wouldn't leave and Delphine grinned, aware her own tension was part of it. "I'm over here because Varrick is quite capable of handling Bertie."

Juliette stepped in front of Delphine, blocking her view of the game. "You two have no idea what you're dabbling in," she hissed.

That was an interesting threat. What did Juliette mean? "I could say the same to you."

Black penumbras in auras. Summoned elemental creatures. Delphine's heart beat faster. Her aura had been torn to shreds, incapable of touching another person's emotions. Bertram's looked infected or corrupted but whole. If it wasn't connected with Varrick's investigation, it ought to be.

At the table, Varrick said something. Bertram bared his teeth. Delphine wished Varrick would bare his back, so Bertram could see how ridiculous he looked. Instead, Varrick raised, face blank but ears forward, intent. Bertram met the raise and both men took another card.

"This can't be new to you," Varrick said, rearranging his cards. "You must play for far higher stakes sometimes."

"My habits are none of your business." Bertram fished more notes from his wallet. "Raise."

"I heard you play for more than cash sometimes."

Bertram moved a card to the back of his hand, then returned it to its original spot. "What would you know about it?"

He was so obviously angry, Delphine ought to be able to catch bits of red-violet at the edges of his aura, but it stayed black, growing more intense with each outburst.

"Come now." Varrick motioned for two more cards, arranged his hand around them and discarded one. "The rich and the jaded, they like to play for experiences. The unusual or the despicable. Do you call or raise?"

"Raise." Bertram added the money to the pot and tapped for more cards. For a moment, as he stared at them, his aura flashed open. Black. Not like a shadow but like the absence of everything. Staring at it, the nothingness coalesced, thickening into something vaguely shaped like a long gryphon with tattered wings. It *blinked* at Delphine.

And it was gone, shielded again.

She glanced at Pearl. There was no alarm on Pearl's face or the fringes of her aura, nor in anyone else's. They'd seen nothing.

It had seen Delphine, whatever it was. Nothing in the books back at the manor had shown anything like that. She swallowed rising panic.

Varrick made a long show of considering his cards before discarding one and tapping for a replacement from the dealer.

"Some rather odd incidences in certain card houses lately," Varrick drawled as Bertram scowled.

Bertram didn't respond, but on Delphine's left, Juliette flinched and finished her wine as if it was a shot of whiskey.

"Are you familiar with the local card houses, Miss Singleton?" Delphine asked. Unlike Bertram, Juliette could flounce away from the conversation at any time, but she seemed like the sort who enjoyed the last word.

Juliette shrugged. "If you have to ask..."

Delphine swirled her wine. "Quite a lot of money trickles through them."

"Far more than a trickle. And far more than money." Juliette curled her lip in disdain.

"Really?" Juliette seemed in a forthcoming, if sour, mood, so Delphine took advantage of it. "What sort of other things?"

"Anything that can be bought and sold is bet at gambling establishments. From any sort of market. Black. White. Mundane. Magical." She brushed a stray blue hair behind her ear, highlighting the luminous golden pearl of her earring.

Golden Pearls. That had been in the title of the book on the great elven trees. Anything grown on or near the trees, including pearls, was nearly priceless. They weren't just beautiful, they contained raw, usable anima. Juliette was showcasing her power and wealth, but why?

Or was it a patron's power or wealth? "What lovely jewelry."

Juliette preened, rolling one pearl between her fingers. "No one can find new ones anymore. The elves stopped trading them."

Keeping them rare would keep the price high. "You must have gotten them some time ago then."

Juliette narrowed her eyes, and Delphine realized she'd implied the other woman was old.

"Almost no one." Juliette touched the pearl again. "A few have connections."

"Through a particular club or card house?" Delphine pretended ignorance of Juliette's ties. "You must be familiar with many of the most exclusive ones."

Juliette studied her again, considering. "I don't gossip about my patrons or clients."

"I suppose Mr. Bertram frequents many of them."

She side-eyed Delphine, smiling slightly. "Not anymore."

For the first time, real emotion showed in her aura. A spark of rose-gold satisfaction blazed near her pulse and faded. Delphine focused on that spot, just below the golden pearl of her earring, but it didn't appear again.

Varrick won the first hand. A footman set a generous glass of brandy beside each man. Bertram gulped at first, then mastered himself, taking a smaller sip and setting the rest of the glass aside. The decorative cuts in the side of the glass spread the light across the table in an array of tiny dots, bright yellow and deep gold against the glossy wood. Bertram wiped his mouth with the back of his hand, staining the lace at his cuff.

The dealer shuffled and dealt them two cards each. Varrick retrieved his from the table but didn't look at them. "Ever played at the Iron Dragon Club over by the university?"

"What of it?" Bertram licked his lips but kept the scowl off his face. Whatever had rattled him, he'd shaken it off. He was serious now.

Varrick turned one ear back and finally checked his cards. "There's been strange goings-on down there. Nasty stuff."

"Magi piss and elf shit, you mean," Bertram said. Several men guffawed, especially those who had lost to Varrick. "Put your money in the pot. Swiving gods, put *everyone's* money back in the pot."

Varrick smiled and added his bet. "Two more cards."

There was a pause in conversation as the two men received their cards. Varrick discarded one and asked for two. Bertram held his.

"And down there among the piss and shit, as you say," Varrick said, "maybe you saw something that has nothing to do with cards." He dipped his finger in his untouched brandy and drew a circle on the table around his discarded card, then a larger circle around that.

Bertram's hand shook.

"Can't walk away now," Varrick said in a low voice. His eyes glinted, yellow and gold like the scattered light from Bertram's glass. Varrick dipped his finger in his brandy again and added a dot between the two circles, right at the top.

"Waste of good brandy," Pearl murmured.

Delphine squinted, trying to make out the design.

Varrick added another dot on the opposite side of the circle, at the bottom. Bertram stared, transfixed by whatever it was. One to the right, one to the left, one for each cardinal direction.

Bertram swallowed. "I think—I think I am not well. I need some air." But he didn't rise, didn't even push himself away from the table.

"Were you bored and looking for amusement? Until you heard the incantation?" Tap tap. Tap tap. Four points of brandy outside the bigger circle at each point of the compass.

The room stirred. Out of the corner of Delphine's eye, a few men walked away, shaking their heads. Everard crossed his arms, intent on the scene. He was getting his fill of drama. Pearl quietly excused herself, but Juliette looked as pale and transfixed as Bertram.

"Answer my questions, and I'll give you my winnings for the night, to distribute as you see fit. Or not." Varrick caught Bertram's eye and held it. "Answer, and I won't finish the pattern."

"Not here," Bertram croaked. He tugged at his collar. "Some-where private."

"Everard? Can you arrange it?"

"Of course," Everard grinned, "But what happens if you finish your little doodle there?"

Varrick rose, pinning Bertram with his stare. "I'll have to replace your table."

Those at the front of the crowd stepped back.

CHAPTER 27

Check in the Dark

DELPHINE

Bertram lumbered to his feet with Varrick looming over him.

"Well, can't have you damaging the furniture." Everard tsked. "You can continue the discussion in the library." He nodded at the butler, who looked even more disapproving than before.

Delphine hesitated. Should she join Varrick or stay? He caught her eye and shook his head.

Stay. She could keep an eye on Juliette. Disappointed, she turned to catch Juliette's reaction, but the blue-haired woman was gone. Not even a glimpse of her in the crowd.

Damn, and Varrick and Bertram were disappearing through a door, escorted by the butler. Delphine could mingle, but that felt useless. She needed to know more about the strange aura.

Several gentlemen had cornered Everard, probably concerned about how the debts would fall out if Varrick transferred them to Bertram. Well, they'd have to wait. Delphine required Everard's attention now. She approached the pack, tapping the first gentleman on the shoulder and favoring him with a brilliant smile.

"I need to speak with Lord Everard." She slipped past him, doing the same to the next man until she could grasp Everard's hand. "Sorry, gentlemen, Lady's prerogative."

"That's right." Everard made a shooing motion with his free hand. "We can settle debts and payments after Mr. Allard and Mr. Bertram have made their peace."

Once they'd dispersed to drink and grumble, Everard guided her to a different exit than Varrick had taken. "There's a second floor to the library with a gallery and balcony. The acoustics channel sound to it amazingly well."

"Thank you, Lord Everard." Delphine offered him a genuine smile, grateful for the quick solution.

"I'll put it on Allard's tab." He whisked her to a smaller staircase, the sort children and servants might use if they didn't want to disturb anyone in the front of the house. "Turn right at the top. It's the first door on your left."

She started to thank him again, but he cut her off. "I want to hear all about it, but I can't leave my guests." He pointed up the stairs. "Off you go, and do remember everything for me."

Delphine started up the steps before looking back. Everard was gone. Was this merely something to break the ennui of the rich for him? There must be more to it.

She found the door to the upper floor of the library and turned the knob slowly to avoid alerting the men below. Bertram might not hear the snick of a bolt opening or the soft click of the door behind her, but Varrick would.

As soon as she opened it, Bertram's voice drifted up from below. She couldn't see the men from here, but Everard's promised acoustics came through. Once inside, she pulled the door not quite shut and curled into the darkest corner near it.

"—was too damn drunk to remember anything," Bertram said. The thump of someone slamming a fist down sifted dust from the stacks. "Can't even make sense of what I do recall."

"Try," Varrick said, voice deep and commanding.

Delphine couldn't have disobeyed that voice even if she'd wanted to.

Slowly, she eased forward on her hands and knees to the railing. Although she had a good view of the first floor stacks and the single glowlight, she could only see the back of Varrick's head and the occasional gesture from Bertram.

In the shadows between two freestanding bookshelves, someone moved. She held her breath.

"It was months ago, but yeah, the Iron Dragon." Bertram plopped into a chair facing Varrick. "The game was over and a magus came in. He started drawing on the table, double circle, like what you were doing."

"In what?"

"Huh?" Bertram looked up.

Delphine squeezed her eyes shut, as if he couldn't see her if they were closed. *Silly.* She opened them again.

The figure between the stacks moved closer to the edge and seemed to be crouching down.

Varrick snorted. "Water, spirits, wine, blood? What substance?"

Bertram shrugged. "Something dark. Thick. Maybe blood, I don't know. It was late. It's hard ... hard to remember."

"Did you see his face?"

Bertram shook his head. "No, I can't. Can't remember. I can't remember how I got home, or what I was doing earlier that night. I lost money I can't remember." He covered his face. "I can see his hand, tracing the symbol."

The person below shifted slightly into the light. A round, golden earring gleamed in the dark. Juliette. She touched the earring and a shimmer of rich gold anima slithered around her hand, briefly illuminating it.

Varrick's back was to her. Bertram wouldn't be able to see from where he sat.

Varrick waited. Bertram wrung his hands.

"I could use another drink," Bertram said, looking to the side.

Varrick shook his head. "When we're done. What did you see?"

"He finished that symbol. It was all glowing, but black. Glowing black. Something came out of it, I don't know, a sluggy fish cat thing, all oozy and dark and bits of nothing drifting off it." Bertram rubbed his face in his hands. "Like how oil floats around in water, but it was just floating through the air."

Varrick leaned forward, hands on the table. Delphine pushed herself up a few inches, squinting into the gloom for a better view of Juliette. The shimmer of anima was gone now, and she was just a hunched shadow.

"Did any of it touch you?" Varrick demanded, voice rising.

Juliette crept closer.

"I don't remember. Maybe? What if it did?"

"Try to remember." Varrick leaned closer, letting his aura blaze. The bright pulse of it hit Bertram and washed over him like liquid fire.

Bertram flinched and cowered, his own aura responding in instinctive defense. Black. And the long nothing-creature with tattered wings reared up from his chest with an audible hiss. Delphine shivered. What was the horrid thing?

"Oh, you touched one," Varrick muttered. His anima bloomed between his shoulder blades, a shimmering golden tendril of power that wrapped around his arm and finger as he started to trace a glowing circle in space.

Delphine watched with parted lips as he etched a symbol into thin air, crisply enunciating words she'd never heard before, and dearly hoped never to hear again. Every syllable spun through the air like a burning spark. Her skin shivered as if under a caress, under the beating heat of the sun, cold and hot, desire and fear sliding through her.

Juliette lunged to her feet, arm outstretched, double strands of anima blooming. She took a deep breath, loud enough to hear over Varrick's chant.

"Watch out!" Delphine cried as Juliette's anima flew like spears at Varrick's back.

He spun. Juliette's strike missed, passing over Bertram's head and crashing into the fireplace mantle behind him. Bertram scrambled to the side, chair toppling.

Juliette twisted to gaze up at Delphine, eyes dark with fury. It was a mistake.

Varrick didn't pause; his anima sliced smoothly from the ruined symbol he'd drawn to strike Juliette in the chest. She stumbled back and fell.

Bertram crawled away, white as milk.

Delphine scrambled to her feet, scanning the room for a way down. There it was, at the back, far from Varrick and Bertram. She twisted her skirts up in one hand and ran as Varrick called Bertram back.

"It will only keep eating at you," he said, voice calm, as if the terrible thing hadn't hissed at them all.

Bertram's ragged gasps and Delphine's footsteps echoed in the thick silence. Where was Juliette? Delphine leaned on the railing and scanned the room. She'd attacked Varrick—to protect Bertram, or cover up what he knew?

Delphine swung around the corner of the railing and took the stairs in a clattering rush. Varrick's chant started again. Bertram was crying and gasping. Golden anima light filled the room, making the shadows darker.

Delphine reached the bottom and stumbled over her own feet and gown. Juliette had been right there, fallen between two bookshelves, but now there was nothing between the stairs and Varrick but worn carpet.

The anima symbol hanging in the air grew brighter, sending sharp shadows about the room as it spit sparks of power into the air. Varrick twined bits of his aura into it, like a farmwife adding wefts of wool to her spinning.

Delphine stopped at the shelves where Juliette had hidden. The dark space between them was empty, but an open door at the far end let in a slice of light. She'd fled. Delphine pressed her hand to her chest and caught her breath.

Bertram made a choking noise, like someone swallowing against vomiting. Delphine felt little sympathy for him. His opinions of Varrick had been vile. If he knew the whole of her family history, he'd think the same of her. But it wouldn't change the lust in his eyes. *Odious man.*

Sick, green-gray light pulsed through the room. Delphine's stomach churned, sour and queasy. A wave of gold and clean blue swept past, easing the sensation.

Bertram retched. The sour reek of bile followed the light.

The room returned to its calm, dim state, the glowlight giving off a steady gold-pink light. Bertram's quiet gulps broke the silence, but the table hid him from view.

Delphine stole up the main walkway toward Varrick. "Is that dark thing still here?"

He blew his breath out in a long sigh. "No. I bound and dematerialized it."

Closing her eyes in relief, she clutched the bookcase for support. "What was it?"

"I can explain when we have more time." He rubbed his horn. "I will settle up with Everard and we should go."

Cautiously, Delphine stood on her toes to peer over the table at Bertram. "Will he be alright?"

"Eventually." Varrick leaned over the table. "I recommend several weeks of rest. Go to the southern seaside or to your hunting lodge. Choose good company."

Bertram laughed softly and bitterly, ending in a sob.

"That doesn't sound like something the seaside could cure,"

she said. If he opened his aura, would it look like hers, gray, torn to shreds?

The thought that something like that shadow-creature might have touched her aura, coiling itself around her heart, sent a wave of icy horror over Delphine. Could it be there, without her knowledge? Bertram didn't seem to have known. *How would I know?*

CHAPTER 28

Dead Man's Hand

DELPHINE

Despite the smell, Delphine stayed in the library, leaning against the bookcase near the main entrance into the hall as Varrick spoke with Everard.

Everard couldn't be a random man who happened to host card parties. He must be an ally of sorts. Varrick could have told her. Then she would have known she had someone she could trust in the crowd.

Varrick's power ...

She'd known he was a magus. His knowledge and his confrontation with Stokes demonstrated that, but this was beyond anything she'd imagined.

Delphine pressed the back of her hand to her mouth. This had been no small hex or conjure, nor Skilling or Crafting. She'd felt the power radiating from the symbols, thick and strong, as overwhelming as a rip current.

Sweet rivers, Varrick's spell ... there was a sparkling, honey-rich pleasure to the power that had strummed every string in her. It woke a bone-deep craving for life in her, as if she could drink vitality from the world. It was eternity crying sweet, empty promises in her ears.

She closed her eyes. Aura use didn't do that to people. Aura interactions were like conversation, persuasion, a give and take. Basic Crafting, like Tanner warming her blankets, didn't create the agonizing high and subsequent emptiness. Did magi feel that every time they did whatever they did? No wonder they guarded their work so zealously.

"Ready, Delphine?"

Varrick's voice at her shoulder jarred her out of her thoughts. She opened her eyes. "Yes. I've had enough."

He held up her coat and helped her into it, as if he were the sour butler, who was nowhere to be seen. He was probably arranging for maids to clean up Mr. Bertram's mess.

No one was there to see them off, not even Everard. Delphine would have liked to say her goodbyes to Octavia and Pearl, but the carriage was ready. Everard's staff had provided hot bricks for their feet and blankets woven with warming Craft. She couldn't fault his hospitality.

"Are you comfortable?" Varrick asked before they rolled away. "Warm enough?"

Delphine wriggled further into the coat and rugs, enjoying the heat and quiet. "Yes."

He thumped the roof and the carriage lurched forward. They followed the long curve of the drive out to the street and through the elegant neighborhood. Some of the balls and parties carried on, glowlights adorning the drives and yards, strains of music drifting to them as they clattered past.

She waited for Varrick to say something but he seemed morose, staring out at the night and rubbing the velvet of his cuff between his fingers.

They rumbled away from the houses and grounds and onto

the main road looping around the outskirts of Rockhaven. She'd resigned herself to his silence when he spoke.

"Thank you for the warning. Casting sigils like that takes a great deal of concentration. I can't keep track of everything around me." He glanced at her. "I'd rather you hadn't seen it, but it would have been messier if you hadn't come."

Messier? Hadn't it been messy enough? "What was it? That black creature?"

"A residue, like the stickiness on your fingers after touching pitch, and just as hard to be rid of."

Delphine rubbed her fingertips together. "Residue of what?"

"Something I would much rather discuss behind wards I trust." He ran his finger along the edge of the carriage window. "I suspected he had one, from your description of his aura, but I didn't think it would be so large or well-entrenched."

"It had grown since the opera and gardens. Before, it was just a few spots, but today his corona was completely black." The blackness had looked at her. The term *residue* felt inadequate.

"You shouldn't be able to see it in the corona at all." Varrick sat back with a thud, making the carriage rock. He grimaced.

"Why not?" Was something else wrong with her? Reading auras was one of the few talents she had left.

"They should only be visible if an aura is completely open. Most people never reveal that much of themselves. That's why I had to force him to open it before I could purge him."

"It was easy to see when he passed in front of the glowlights." She leaned forward. "I saw it. When you upset him during the game, I saw that thing, its wings, its eyes. It looked back at me. It blinked."

Varrick tipped his head, doubt shifting through his corona.

She was too tired to face his skepticism, not when she had enough of her own. "I can't draw hexes in the air like you—"

"It wasn't a hex."

"—but I can read auras. I know what I saw." Fatigue rolled

over her. She didn't want to fight. "I don't care that it wasn't a hex. I know it wasn't, but I don't know what it was. I didn't know you could do that." He was capable of everything he'd threatened Stokes with. His raw power had frightened her, but she was more disconcerted that she'd liked the overwhelming feel of it. Varrick fully displaying his power was captivating.

"I'd hoped it wouldn't be necessary. It's a messy business, dealing with summonings."

"So I noticed." *Summoning.* One summoned servants and messengers, not inky horrors from some other world.

He scowled. It should have been intimidating, but it was nothing compared to his intensity while that chant had rolled from his tongue.

"The residue, how dangerous is it?" *Do I have one?*

The wheels of the carriage clattered on the bridge. Halfway home, where whatever had triggered the wards lurked.

"Not—"

The carriage lurched. The driver cried out.

A horse screamed.

They hit a bump.

Everything tipped.

Delphine glimpsed the bridge railing and the river far below as they toppled. She grabbed for the ceiling handle and missed. The tumbling of the carriage tossed her away from the handgrip. Her anima bloomed instinctively, thrusting out to steady her.

Falling.

Weightless.

Brilliant gold exploded as they hit. The carriage cracked.

Icy water rushed in.

The shock of cold drove the air from Delphine's lungs. Her heavy skirts tangled around her thrashing legs, dragging her down. Black water closed over her head, cutting off light and sound.

Gold wrapped her. Anima held her, pushing her up with the bubbles until she broke the surface. Caught in the current, she swirled away from the bridge. A moment later, her foot hit solid ground. Delphine dragged herself onto the muddy bank and huddled among the coarse grasses. The anima vanished, not even sparks of it left hanging in the air.

"Varrick?" Her teeth chattered. The night wind bit bone-deep through her wet clothes and skin. She gulped for air and tried again, louder. "Varrick!"

The river was black, only the silver edges reflecting the moonlight showing where the current rippled and tugged.

No carriage, driver, or horses.

No Varrick.

The bridge loomed above her, far away, disorienting until she realized they'd fallen off the upstream side and she stood downstream by a good bit. Figures gathered on the arch, leaning over the railings; faint shouts reached her.

Ice seeped into her bones, setting her teeth on edge. Turning, she crawled on stiff hands and knees through the dry grass until she found the edge of an old walkway and pulled herself up onto it. She'd lost a shoe and the uneven stones hurt as she limped back toward the bridge. There would be steps up to the road.

"Varrick?"

She tripped, stubbing frigid toes, yelping at the pain. Varrick must be here somewhere. His anima had caught and guarded her as they hit. Hers had been useless.

But the gold was gone now.

Black water rushed by, muttering like an old drunk. Was he under there somewhere, drowned? Or washed further down, perhaps to the opposite side? She stumbled again, hitting both knees hard. Her scraped fingers felt distant, even as she curled them to grip the stone wall on the bank-side of the walk.

How she hated the cold.

Over the murmuring of the river, the grass rustled. Delphine froze.

"Varrick?" Her voice was going. She coughed, unable to project more.

A deeper cough answered.

"It's me." He rose out of the mud and pale grass, a looming shadow in the night.

"I thought you'd drowned." She lurched toward him.

"Near thing." He coughed again.

She reached for him. He had to be as cold as she was. How could they make it up to the bridge shivering like this? Even if they made it and hailed a cabbie, it wouldn't be full of heated stones and rugs. The ride back to Sayledon Manor stretched endlessly long in her mind.

He staggered onto the path, shaking water off his ears. It dripped from the tips of his horns. His long coat and vest clung to him, the heavy velvet slapping at his thighs.

"I'm spent," he said. "Signal for help. Use your anima before you're exhausted."

She couldn't focus enough. Anima took energy, and she was freezing.

He reached the wall and sagged against it. A dark trail followed him from the bank and across the stones. *Blood.* "Send up a flare. So they see where we are."

He was cold and bleeding. No matter how strong his anima, both would sap whatever was left. Delphine gripped his hand and focused on the bloom between her shoulder blades. If she had one of Juliette's pearls, she wouldn't lack for power.

Her weak anima stretched above them. She focused all her energy into a round light. Someone on the bridge shouted.

"There you go," Varrick whispered and squeezed her hand. "I knew you could."

"You don't get to scare me like that, doubt my word, dump us into a river, and then get away with it. You'd better hold on. Or else!"

Her mind reeled with possible injuries: impaled by a broken

piece of carriage, detritus in the water, or his own broken bone. She had to stay angry, or she might cry.

Shouts came closer and boots thundered on the pathway. A boat scraped against the shore.

"Make sure they take us back to Sayledon." Varrick squeezed her hand again.

"You'll need a physician."

"To the manor..." he trailed off.

They were suddenly surrounded by shouting men. Bargemen who'd seen the carriage go over scrambled out of the boat. The thundering feet were constables.

"He's injured. We're both freezing." Her limbs dragged like bags of sand. Her anima fizzled, its light fading out. "There was a driver. Did anyone see our driver?" She didn't even know the man's name.

"We'll look," one of the bargemen said.

"Did you see what happened, ma'am?"

"Can we fetch someone for you or deliver a message?"

"He's a big one, ain't he? How're we gonna move him?"

The conflicting voices spilled over her. Someone wrapped a warm, smelly jacket over her shoulders. Delphine blinked up at the constable. "We need taken back to Sayledon Manor, then a message to Lord Michael Havemshire. From ... from his sister-in-law, Delphine Leighton."

"You're with this ... man?" another constable asked.

Two or three men gathered around Varrick, whose hand had gone lax in hers.

"Yes! Stop the bleeding, get us back to our manor and send for Lord Havemshire." If she said Michael's title often enough, they might overlook that Varrick was a jaglin. "Failing Lord Havemshire," *Who?* She didn't know any of Varrick's contacts or allies. "Contact Lord Everard at his home on the northern side of town. We just left there."

She squeezed Varrick's hand and was relieved when he

squeezed it back. The water may have made the trail of blood look worse than it was. He'd been coughing more than she had; he must have swallowed too much of the filthy river water.

"—cut on his leg." someone was saying, "Get it wrapped up, and get him to his feet—"

On his leg, not his guts or chest. To his feet. That was good. She pulled the coat closer and clung to Varrick's hand.

CHAPTER 29

The Magus Folds

Varrick

The constables wrapped Varrick's leg half-heartedly in a dirty kerchief. He waved off their offers of help and supported himself on the wall. Looking too vulnerable would invite as much harassment as looking too dangerous. The oldest constable let Delphine lean on his arm. Varrick felt them watching him, halos of anxious fear around their heads. He clenched his teeth and risked putting weight on the injured leg to keep up.

They couldn't seem to decide if he was a threat or not. Two hovered close but never touched him. The others kept their distance, looking back at him every few steps, tensed for any sudden move. It would have been amusing in different circumstances.

It could have been deadly in different circumstances. If he hadn't been dressed like a gentleman and in the company of a lady, he would have been left for dead or locked up. Delphine had been smart enough to drop both her brother-in-law's name and Everard's. That should give them enough credit to get back on their way. The last thing he wanted was to be stuck in the constables' custody, at the mercy of their prejudices.

The wreck was too coincidental to be an accident. An attack? But by whom? Or what?

Delphine and her escort reached the top of the stairs before he did. Normally, he'd be able to support himself with anima, but he was drained. He'd caught Delphine and the hired driver, kept himself afloat, and pushed the frantic horses to shore further down. He'd barely had enough left to get himself to shore. A deep chill that said he'd gone too far crept through him. The dull, pulsing ache spread across his shoulders and down his spine to his legs.

Delphine stood shivering in the breeze as the constables and random men who'd been out late gathered around the stone half-wall. They had found the driver miserable and shivering on the far side. He held his arm oddly. *Probably broken.* Varrick limped to stand next to Delphine, shielding her from the biting wind.

She hunched further into the thick wool coat the constable had lent her. "Can't they send us back to the manor?"

He wrapped his arm around her shoulders, pulling her closer. Although they were both drenched, the combined body heat eased some of the cold. She fit comfortably under his arm; he didn't want to let her go. "Are you alright? Other than the cold?"

She nodded.

He ducked his chin. "They have to satisfy themselves that it was an accident." It couldn't have been. The bridge was clear, but they'd certainly hit something.

"Was it?" She looked up at him, her eyes black in the night.

He could lie, reassure her that the driver must have been drinking or a horse threw a shoe, but that was unfair. She deserved to know that the stakes had been raised.

Varrick made a rumbling sigh deep in his chest, not quite a growl. "No."

A cab with twin glowlights hanging off its front corners rolled up the road. The cabbie tipped his hat to the nearest constable. Good. The sooner they were off, the better. Too long in the cold and he wouldn't be any good to anyone.

"Can we go now?" Varrick called. "I'd like to get Mrs. Leighton out of the cold."

"Bet you would," one of the younger men quipped. A few of the constables laughed, but the older one in charge didn't. The laughter died down.

Varrick laid his ears back. He and Delphine were playing such parts, but it sounded dirty in the men's mouths.

"You can go soon, Mr. Allard." The oldest constable jerked his head to send the others away. "I just have a few more questions. Mrs. Leighton can wait in the cab."

Once Delphine was safely in the cab, Varrick turned to the constable. "Ask away." Damn, he was tired. The wind seemed to be pulling the very life out of him.

"That was a neat trick, making sure no one died in the fall," the constable said.

Varrick looked down, unsure how to take the praise. "Did the cab hit something?" There had been a bump, but it hadn't felt like they'd gone over an obstacle.

"The driver says something spooked the horses. A fox or a cat, maybe." He scratched his head. "Now, what's the likes of you doing with the likes of her?" He nodded at the cab.

Varrick didn't have time for this. Collapsing would make the night worse, and his legs were shaking. "Mrs. Leighton is my employer."

"And what sort of employment would that be?" His eyes slid to his colleagues further down the bridge. "Nothing inappropriate for a nice lady, I hope."

"Protection. She is a widow and that draws scavengers and predators. I had to deal with one recently at the Glass Gardens. In the Maze of Mirrors." Varrick imitated the man's folded arms and stance. "I hope you are not implying anything untoward about

Lord Havemshire's sister-in-law." He could use their ridiculous notions of propriety against them.

The constable shifted from foot to foot. "No. Nothing like that. A bit unusual, is all."

"You can't claim I didn't do my utmost to protect her."

"No, of course not."

"Do you wish to ask Mrs. Leighton if she is satisfied with my work?" Delphine was smart enough to play along, even without warning. "It will keep her out in this chill. Might I have your name, in case Lord Havemshire inquires?"

"No, not necessary." The constable rolled his shoulders. "The driver's story makes sense. If anything suspicious surfaces, I will find you at Sayledon Manor, yes?"

"Yes, that's where she's currently staying." Goddess, he hoped the man didn't look into it too closely. Lady M would be displeased, and Lord Havemshire had made his disgust with Varrick quite clear. "If I may go now?"

The constable waved him away. No one wanted to be out in the wind.

Varrick joined Delphine in the cab. "If anyone asks, you hired me as your bodyguard."

She sat hunched over, arms wrapped around herself. "I did?"

"Yes." His ears were back again. He was too tired to control them.

As he raised his hand to signal the cabbie to go, a movement near the edge of the bridge caught his eye. The shape slipped along strangely, not scuttling or stalking like a rat or stray dog. If a slug moved like a snake, it might look like that. The light hit it and sank in instead of reflecting.

A residue. Now he knew what had spooked the horses, but where had it come from? He knocked the ceiling.

The cab began to move before he spoke. "Something startled the horses. Combined with the uneven surface, it threw us over."

His voice was dull and soft. He didn't have much more in him for the night.

"Do you believe that?" She didn't look like she did.

He shook his head. He didn't want to lie, but he didn't want to frighten her. Not until he had answers. "I don't think they were startled by accident."

Delphine leaned back, pressing her arm against his. She wasn't shivering anymore, but her eyes were wide and round. Confused. Scared. She'd probably never seen an active sigil, nor experienced the backwash of power it produced, and he didn't have the energy to explain it. It could be overwhelming. Intoxicating. Painfully sweet.

Her arm was warm against his. Her leg pressed against his, body heat radiating through the layers of sodden skirts and undergarments. It eased some of his frustration at the constable, his fury at whoever had tried to kill them.

She laid her hand on his thigh, sending a thrill through him. "Thank you for catching me."

He cleared his throat, unsure how to respond. She saw him as the hero. It was a little balm to his wounded pride, having to play himself off as a hired man when a human magus would have gotten bows and respect. Either way, the attention of the night felt odd, like dangerous exposure more than accolades.

She looked up. "I mean it. I could barely brace myself, and I couldn't have gotten to the shore alone."

"I brought you into this." He shifted his gaze to look straight forward, heat rising in his cheeks. "Keeping you safe is my responsibility." He could accept that accolade.

If he'd lost her in the water … a hollow carved itself in his chest, as if his heart had been drained out like his anima. He wrapped his arm around her, and the way she leaned into him without hesitation helped fill the hollow.

They finally rolled up to Sayledon. Varrick paid the cabbie in soggy notes and let Delphine help him limp up the steps to the door. He expected Morrow or Henry to be up, but Bethie, the maid, was the only one about.

She stared at them, eyes round in alarm, as they limped into the main hall together.

"There was another alarm on the wards, about twenty minutes ago, down by the kitchen doors. Talon set up a terrible ruckus." She bobbed her head. "Everyone went out to check."

"And left you here alone?" Delphine asked.

Bethie pursed her lips. "I'm not helpless, ma'am. I can help you into your nightdress since Tanner's not here." She looked back at Varrick. "You need something for that leg, though, and I can't stand blood."

"I can take care of him." Delphine looked up at Varrick. "Just make sure the fires in our rooms are built up."

Varrick shook his head. "The library is fine."

Bethie tsked. "The bedroom fires are going, since we expected you'd be out late. It will take forever for the library to warm up." She blinked and looked away from him and his bleeding leg. "Go on, I'll bring up what you need to clean it." She strode off toward the kitchens.

"Just help me up the stairs. I can tend it myself," Varrick said. Delphine shouldn't have to deal with blood and muck on top of everything else. "You should change and warm up."

Delphine shook her head. "You're just as wet and cold as I am. I'll see to your leg and get that wet coat off you, at least."

"It's not—" he fumbled, his cheeks and ears growing hot, "it isn't the proper thing for a lady to do, is it?"

Her face flushed. "It's not like I can get any more ruined than I am. In the eyes of society, I mean."

That hadn't been his worry, despite the snickers of the younger constables. If they threw their contract to the wind, just for one night, what would happen? It was tempting. "You can run for help if I tumble."

"We've tumbled enough for the night."

He huffed a short laugh and leveraged himself up a few steps, rested, and repeated the effort. Delphine did little more than hover nearby, but if she hadn't been there, he would have just sat down and slept on the stairs.

"What you did in Everard's library, drawing the symbol with your anima ... it's draining?" Delphine stumbled over the words. "When you drove the thing out of Bertram?"

He paused to rest. How to explain a complex process that involved pulling two types of existence together? "Torlish doesn't have a good word for it. It's sort of cleansing the aura, in the sense of squeezing the pus out of an infected wound so it can be treated. Purging is the closest term. Yes, it takes a lot out of me." He frowned at the rest of the stairs above them. So many stairs. "Keeping everyone alive in the accident, that took more."

She stood on the stair just above him, hands out, unable to help. If he fell on her, he'd squash her, even if she was tall.

"The accident that wasn't an accident," she said.

"There was another residue on the bridge. I'm not sure how it got there." It had to have been with the carriage. There was no other way for it to know their route and when they would leave. Residues weren't very intelligent, not until they'd fed on someone for months. If it was sent with a purpose, it had to be under a magus's control. That was no small feat.

Delphine supported his elbow. "Mr. Bertram striking back? Or Miss Singleton?"

"Bertram won't be in much shape for anything for a while. He'll heal. Eventually." Varrick took one of her hands, although he leaned on the banister for support. "I don't mind leaving him to sweat over it a bit." There had been no magi at Everard's.

They navigated the last few steps that way, fingers starting to warm, the ache from the cold fading from his joints. His shoulders and legs felt as stiff and heavy as river clay, dogged by bone-deep fatigue.

At the top, Varrick checked his injured leg. The slash traveled up one calf to a gash just above the outside of the knee. It didn't look deep, but it hurt like fire. He must have been bleeding the whole ride home. Blood saturated his stocking, and he'd left a trail across the floor of the entry hall to the stairs.

Delphine bent for a closer look at the injury. "It's messy, but not as deep as I thought it might be."

"I can clean it up and wrap it once Bethie brings the supplies. You can change."

Her hair had fallen out of its high coif, wet locks spilling down her shoulders, the tiny hairs along her forehead starting to curl as they dried. He wanted to see it completely loose, flowing down her back, and run his fingers through it. *Which is why she ought to go to her room and I should go to mine.*

"I've tended cuts and scrapes." She followed him as he limped to his door. The oozing under the kerchief was becoming a trickle. "Once she brings the supplies, I'll do what I can."

"You don't need to." He didn't want to embarrass himself by passing out from exhaustion. Or saying—or doing—something he'd regret. And she looked so *undone* already.

She put her hands on her hips. "But I'm going to. Let's get you to a chair."

He grimaced down at the injury. She wasn't going to relent. "Just until it's wrapped properly, then."

CHAPTER 30

Tending Wounds

DELPHINE

Delphine opened the door for Varrick and helped him to one of the chairs in front of the fireplace. He sat, looking grumpy, ears flat out, and let out a long breath.

Bethie followed with a basket containing a bottle of cheap whiskey, a jar of some ointment, and several bandages. She carried a steaming kettle of water with a strand of anima.

"There's a basin by the bed," she said, eyes half-closed so she wouldn't see the blood. She handed the basket to Delphine, set the kettle by the fireplace, and fled.

Varrick stretched his injured leg out in front of him. "I am never going to hear the end of it from Mrs. Halsey," he muttered.

"I'm sure the blood will come off." She set the room's basin on the floor beside him and poured steaming water into it. Kneeling between him and the fire, she pulled the remains of his stocking and trousers away from the gash and cut.

David's nights had often ended in brawls. Once, he'd come home with a rapier stick through the shoulder. He'd accused a lord of cheating and the man had insisted on a duel. The way that had bled! Delphine had sent for a physician, but until he could come, she'd cleaned David up and kept pressure on the wound to try and staunch the bleeding. Varrick's wasn't nearly so serious.

The heat from the fire beat against her back, easing the chill from the river. She didn't trust her stiff fingers to sew the wound up, but she could clean and wrap it well. Varrick hissed through his teeth as she wiped the blood away with hot water and rumbled in his chest when she followed it with the sharp, raw whiskey.

"Sorry," he said as she finished.

Delphine glanced at him. "You didn't kick, hit, or curse me, so not bad."

He frowned and shifted uncomfortably in his chair. "I wouldn't. Ever."

"I didn't think you would." She didn't want to explain to him that David had never taken nursing calmly. Even in early years he would have shouted to the rafters. The last time, he'd come close to striking her. "Some men aren't as stoic about it."

He rumbled again, a different tenor. "It stings. Nothing more."

She ducked her head. Something he hadn't said hung between them, keeping company with what she hadn't said either. "I should have read the book on healing. Maybe I would have found something useful in it."

"It wouldn't have helped much. That's very specific training." He inhaled and held his breath as she finished cleaning the wound. "Mrs. Halsey can, when she gets back."

Delphine opened the ointment, recognizing a tingle of anima in it. "You studied at the Scholarium D'Arcanis in Istalia, right? Did Mrs. Halsey as well?" Nowhere in Torlund would teach arcana to a woman, much less a jaglin.

She unrolled a generous amount of gauze and wrapped the knee and calf well. Once finished, she sat back, exhausted and reluctant to move from the fire's warmth.

Varrick fussed at his remaining boot, trying to remove it

without bumping his injured leg. "I did. I don't know about Mrs. Halsey."

"How did you end up in Istalia?" She gripped the heel of the boot and pulled it off. It sloshed. "Your toes must be freezing."

"They've gone numb." He bent to remove his stocking. "I was born in the mountains of Alladoon. A mudslide wiped out my village."

That wasn't the start she'd expected.

"How old were you?" He didn't have a Doonish accent. She waved his hands away from his stocking. "I'm already down here. Let me help."

She'd wondered how far down his stripes went. All the way to the tops of his feet, where the darker banding was more distinctive than it was on his hands. The skin of his legs and feet had that same pleasant, flocked texture. It was cool but not clammy under her fingers.

His sudden intake of breath made her look up, thinking she'd found another injury. His ears were full forward, his normally slitted pupils round and wide. The firelight reflected off him like the anima light had earlier, casting him in sharp relief. Gold, green, and black. She recalled the deep rolling chant he'd used earlier, and he was suddenly some forest guardian from her mother's old stories, mysterious and powerful.

Delphine swallowed, mouth dry. The light on his horns gleamed like liquid gold. "Would ... would you like help with your jacket?"

"I do, but I'm not sure if you should." He stroked her cheek, fingers warmer than her face.

A flood of doubts and misgivings filled her mind. They had an agreement, signed and legal, but it was just his fingers on her face. Nothing untoward.

She tipped her face into his warm palm. "Help me up."

His hands were surprisingly steady as she used them to rise. Her soaked dress weighed her down. The dress was her whole life, years wrapped in sodden brocade, dragging her further and further down with no way to shed the burden. She froze, hands in his, the fire at her back and him before her, caught in the detritus of the night and swirling waters of her life.

"Firelight becomes you," he said.

"I—" She bobbed her head, unable to receive or return the compliment. The firelight gilding his face was doing uncomfortable things to her. Heat that wasn't from the fire washed over her. "You'll warm up faster once you're out of the wet clothes."

"So will you." Tugging at the wet cloth, he untied his cravat and pulled it off, sighing at the stained silk. He tried to peel off the heavy coat.

Delphine took his generous velvet cuff and held it so he could pull his arm out, then passed behind him to do the same with the other. He swiveled his ears to follow her movements, even as she laid the ruined jacket and cravat over the other chair. They would always carry the water stains. His chair creaked behind her. She whirled.

"Don't you dare try to stand on that leg." She stopped short. He was still seated, but he'd leaned closer to the fire.

"Wouldn't dream of it." Their eyes met. He broke the connection first, looking down so the firelight caught his forest-dark lashes.

She swallowed again, watching the divot at the base of his throat flash as he breathed. She ought to stop looking. This was fatigue, the wind-down from the excitement and danger of the evening. Enjoying the feel of his fingers on her face, the feel of his skin under hers, was merely seeking comfort.

She shouldn't look anymore.

"I should go." If she started thinking about the commanding timbre of his voice, the rolling power of his spells, while he sat there, wet shirt clinging to his broad chest, ears focused on her every move ... hadn't they agreed the relationship was for public show only?

"Three," he said. "Or four."

"What?" Three or four what?

"That's how old I was when the mudslide came." He looked away. "There weren't any other survivors."

It was an offering. He'd chosen to give her a little piece of his past, that he'd been alone before he'd even begun to understand what that meant.

"I—" What did one say to that? Was he still alone?

He pulled the tie out of his hair and held out the dripping length. "I don't really remember anything except the refugee ship."

"To Istalia?" How did a refugee end up studying at the Scholarium?

"Eventually." His gaze swept over her again. "Do you need help with your dress and hair?"

She could do it herself, but she was reluctant to return to her room. Even if it was bright and warm, she would be alone. Isolated. After the shadow-creatures, the accident, Varrick's spells glowing in mid-air, and the mystery of the window wards, she couldn't be on her own.

She smoothed the cravat over the jacket and turned back to him. It was her turn.

"I don't want to be alone." Her tongue tripped over the rest. Just admitting she wanted company was enough. She wanted to know what she'd seen. She wanted to know how much danger she was in. She wanted to know how to protect herself against shadows and people who could trace symbols and summonings of power in the air.

He held his hand out to her. "Then don't go. Stay here with me."

She reached for him, but hesitated before taking his hand. How often had she done that tonight? Her earlier sallies and bold-ness came back. She'd sat in his lap. Said she liked the novelty of him. Her cheeks burned at her brazen flippancy.

Yet ...

He could have told her to go. He had not. Biting her lower lip, she made a decision. The brass buttons on his long vest had taken on some of the heat of the fire, a sharp contrast to the clammy chill of the fabric. Pushing them through the buttonholes took more effort than she'd expected.

"Lean forward for me to take the vest off." With the weight of his clothing, it was a wonder he'd made it to shore.

"Help me stand." He steadied himself on her shoulder and used the arm of the chair to push himself up.

"Don't fall on me." She'd catch him. Then she'd be squashed by him. But what would it be like to be held by him, someone taller than she was, who made her feel safe?

Once up, he shucked the sodden vest, tossing it carelessly on the same chair as his coat and cravat. She made an aborted movement to retrieve the discarded clothing.

"In a minute." He fumbled with the buttons on his shirt, fingers clumsy.

She brushed his hands away, working the tiny buttons through their loops, revealing him inch by inch. She stole glances at the stripe of green skin and velvety hair down the midline of his chest. It grew paler in the center, and the hair denser and longer as she moved down past the firm muscles of his stomach. He tensed when she brushed his skin.

She paused as he exhaled.

They were both exhausted, worn down from the night and the accident. Emotions already ran high without tempting fate.

He peeled off the shirt and held it out like a bedraggled creature, looking sheepish. "I don't think the lace will ever be the same."

"If you'd kept your winnings tonight, it wouldn't have mattered." It didn't matter either way.

He looked down at her, huge pupils reflecting all the light in the room, but she held his gaze, too shy in the moment to look at the broad expanse of his green chest. They stood frozen as she fumbled for words. She was too close to him and silence rang all her alarm bells. Silence was dangerous. She rushed to fill it.

"The lace, I mean..." He wasn't David. He wasn't drunk. She'd had more to drink than he had. But she didn't know how he would react to the night going so well, then so badly, and she'd just criticized him. A shiver seized her, hands and shoulders shaking from remembered fear more than cold.

"We should have warmed you up first." He touched her shoulders again, tentatively. "I could have waited once we stopped the bleeding."

It wasn't the cold, but she let him think so. His hands were warm, and the pressure kept her mind from tumbling down old paths.

"Do you mind my help, or should I ring for Bethie?" he asked.

"Help me." She could hardly breathe. *Why let him? Why not Bethie?* She looked up at him, his bulk and height at odds with how careful and gentle he'd been. "Start with the pins."

She guided his hand to them so he could deftly remove the pins holding the gown to the stomacher, placing each one in the padded arm of the chair, and let the heavy gown drop in a heap. The room felt colder for a few moments until the heat from the fireplace warmed her damp stays, skirt, underskirt, and petticoats. She tugged at the ties for the skirt; the water and movement had pulled them into a hard knot. Her fingers ached and the angle was awkward.

He laid his hands over hers. "Let me."

She barely breathed as he loosened the knot, plucking and pulling until it gave way and her skirt joined the gown on the floor.

We agreed to keep our clothes on.

She turned so he could work on the underskirt knots at her side. So much weight shed with each piece. If only she could shed her past as easily and forget old reactions and fears.

Underskirt off, petticoats followed.

She stepped out of the pile of gown, skirt, and petticoats and scooped them into her arms to lay aside with his wet things. Heaped like this, it all felt unbearably heavy and unruly, sliding out of her arms in sloppy swags. She stumbled and dropped everything in the pile with his discarded shirt and vest.

He limped up behind her, untying the tight cording on her stays and helping loosen them. Delphine shivered from the cold, each layer of body-warmed, wet clothing exposing more of her damp skin. The final wash of warm air as she wriggled out of the stays made her sigh with relief. She rubbed her bare upper arms.

Varrick's fingers brushed against her back, just her chemise between them. No, she did not want to be alone. She wanted to be touched and held, like his arm around her after the accident. His breath drifted across her neck and shoulder, followed by a warm kiss.

All her questions fled. They'd agreed not to do this, they'd signed a contract, just business. *We are playacting.*

She couldn't have rejected his affection if her life depended on it.

She turned to look up at him, trying to read his expression and aura, and his eyes searched her face the same way.

Delphine laid her hand flat against his chest, the texture of his hair thicker and softer than on his hands or legs, the damp nearly gone. His body heat radiated over her. "Don't stop."

He bent his head. The warm rush of his breath flowed over her collarbone and between her breasts.

He kissed her neck, then her mouth, hot and hesitant.

A kiss was easy to accept, easy to relax into and return, although it was strange to kiss someone after so long. Strange to open her lips and let his tongue inside, let his teeth nip her lower lip. She leaned into him, enjoying how solid and warm he felt. The smooth, soft texture of his skin caressed hers, luxurious, enticing. He smelled faintly of cigars, and there was a smoky touch of brandy on his breath.

Uncertain at first, he pulled her in more firmly, one hand pressing at her waist, the other tangling in the mess of her hair.

His aura pressed against her shields, more keen and intimate than his hands. Vibrant, questing tendrils curled deep magenta passion around her neck, twined around her arms, and slithered over her breasts like warm, trickling water. Had her aura been open, she would have melted like spring snow.

She pressed her breasts against him and slid her fingers into the thick silk of his hair. She wanted her own hair loose to tumble down her back.

"Open up to me, Delphine," he whispered. His aura engulfed her, seeking chinks in her shield, pressing against her weak points, seeking reciprocating emotion. "Let me see a little of your heart."

Panic roared in her ears.

"No." Delphine pushed away from him. "That's too far."

He let go and withdrew his aura, face confused and hurt.

With her aura so damaged, staying shielded was her only defense against being Skilled. She'd be so engulfed in his emotions, her own would drown. She wouldn't know where her desire ended and his started, or if it was hers at all. He could overwhelm her without intending to, without even realizing it.

"My apologies," he said stiffly, bewilderment and hurt clear in his aura, peppered with guilt.

"No, you didn't do anything wrong." She clutched herself, hunching forward. "It's just too much."

It would always be too much. Anyone could get in, take over her heart, make her feel what they did, what they wished. She could never let her guard down.

"We don't have to touch, but you never let me see even the faintest glimmer of you, not even a corona. Can't I even catch a glimpse?" His aura shimmered around him, deep pink desire close to his heart but darker swirls of confusion further out. "I've never seen anyone lock themselves up so tightly."

"I can't." She couldn't expose herself. "I'm sorry."

CHAPTER 31
Lessons in Trust

VARRICK

Limping, Varrick retreated behind his dressing screen. He'd frightened her. Or pressured her. He'd never had lessons on how to woo or flirt, and Rockhaven had different rules than Istalia. He'd done something wrong. He flung on a heavy dressing gown. He needed food and rest to replenish his anima, and Delphine obviously needed space. She would be better off away from him.

He returned to her, carrying a second thick dressing gown. She knelt before the fire, hands out to warm them. She was shaking, but not from the cold, he suspected. He draped the dressing gown over her shoulders. She slid it on without looking up. It engulfed her, sleeves going to her fingertips.

She looked as small and vulnerable as a newly hatched chick in the voluminous swath of fabric. He wanted to gather her up and protect her. Rescue her.

Damn it, Tanner was right.

"Thank you." She clutched it around her shoulders but kept her eyes on the fire.

"My chairs are both wet," he sighed. "We could sit on the floor in front of the fireplace, if you want company. Or, your room wouldn't have all this mess." *Please stay.* But he wouldn't make her if she didn't want to.

She gazed up at him. "How is your leg? Will sitting on the floor be comfortable?"

Getting down might not be a problem, but standing up would. "I would prefer the settee in your room. If you want my company." She hadn't wanted to be alone, but she might have changed her mind.

"Yes, I want company." She glanced at the window. "The settee is a better idea than the floor."

She wrapped the generous dressing gown around herself and plodded toward the door.

"There's a shorter way." Varrick pointed to the panel on the wall that hid a private passage. "These are the lord's and lady's rooms. They're connected."

She blinked at him. "I think I should have been apprised of a secret passage between our rooms."

Yes, she should have. He'd never used it. Never even considered using it until tonight. "I never would have taken advantage."

Delphine shook her head, sighing so heavily he thought she might crumple right there. He wasn't the only one who was exhausted.

He worked the mechanism hidden in the panel border and stepped into the warm, stuffy passage. Delphine followed, feet silent on the thick rug.

He found the latch on the inside of the door to her room. It clicked and warm firelight flooded the passage. Varrick stepped through and aside, sweeping his hand out to let her lead the way to the settee. Her rooms were smaller than his and the lively fire had warmed them more thoroughly. She pressed herself into one corner of the settee, pulling her legs up under the dressing gown. Varrick lowered himself slowly, wincing as he stretched his injured leg out in front of him.

She watched him trying to get comfortable. "If you'd rather rest in your own room—"

"You want company, and I can explain things." He rubbed one horn with his thumb. They'd gotten off-track, forgotten the contract. "You wanted to know about the creature afflicting Bertram."

"Among other things." She half-hid her face in her oversized sleeves.

"What Bertram witnessed was a summoning. That's not quite an accurate word for it, but it's the one we use. Um—" He flicked his ears forward, then back. *Simplify it.* "Summoning suggests calling something from somewhere else, but it's more giving substance to something that didn't have it. Manifesting it or materializing it."

She pulled the folds of the dressing gown more securely around herself. "What is it?"

"A shadow elemental. Which is also an inaccurate term, it's really more." He stopped and looked down, grimacing. *Simplify it.* "You don't want all those details right now."

"Not really. Someday, you can tell me about all the inaccurate labels you want."

She could jest with him, so he hadn't irrevocably offended her. He half-closed his eyes, rumbling in his throat. "They're dangerous and hard to control. Summoning one is strictly forbidden."

She shuddered. "You said the thing in Bertram is a residue. Was it a part of that elemental? Or an offspring?"

Close enough. "Remember he described black blots of nothing floating off of it?"

"Rather vividly, yes." She pulled her knees up to her chest and wrapped her hands around her toes. "Your spell was a bit..." she paused, "terrifying."

What had been in that pause? He stared at the fire and rubbed his chin. He didn't like being terrifying, not to her. He pushed aside the desire to ask her about it. "Offspring is a good term. They aren't independent the way we are, more like gryphons or foxes. All instinct. Bertram touched one, or it touched him, and it followed that instinct."

"Which is?"

"We say shadow, but these ones are more a manifestation of emptiness. It looks dark to us because it's empty of light as well as everything else." He was over-explaining. *Simplify.* "Emptiness craves to be filled. They are hungry." True while also inaccurate.

Her whole body had gone tense. She took a long, deep breath and lowered her hunched shoulders. "I don't like the sound of that."

"The residues aren't deadly, but the original, the one that mage summoned, can be." He pressed his lips together into a hard line. What fool would risk it? They were notorious for escaping. "I suspected a shadow, but not one big enough to produce residues."

"What do the bigger ones do?" Delphine had gone pale under her freckles.

"The same. Try to fill the emptiness. They feed on auras." He fell silent. It was an ugly business, and they already had a long list of victims. The university had moved to protect their reputation rather than admit the attacks were magical.

"Auras?" Delphine clutched her chest, gasping as if the room had no air. "The victims would remember, wouldn't they?"

It was too much for her. He should have waited until morning. They were both exhausted. "If they survived, no. Even Bertram had memory gaps, and he just witnessed it."

Her breathing grew ragged.

"Delphine?" He reached for her. Her face crumpled, but she squeezed her eyes shut and mastered her breathing with visible effort.

Varrick leaned forward abruptly. "You said you could see the darkness in his aura even when it was closed."

She flinched. "In his corona."

He shifted his jaw, eyeing her. He was better than most at

reading auras, but he hadn't seen anything odd in Bertram's corona, not at the opera, not at the Gardens. But Delphine had, even with her own locked down. How?

"Juliette's defense of Bertram means she's probably connected with the summoner as well."

"She runs a place called the Indigo Elf." Delphine rubbed her face. "Octavia said that Juliette wanted to be your mistress."

"Excuse me?" The pushy woman that had her hands all over his horns? He'd been annoyed at the time—thank Ashanti for Delphine's timing—but if she was part of the summoner's work, that put her attention in a whole new light.

"You'd put word about for a mistress. There were bets being placed on who you'd choose. Juliette was sure it would be her, according to the other women." She rocked, holding her toes again.

He sat back, arms crossed, ears back. That was embarrassing.

"That bad, is it?" Delphine looked sympathetic, although amusement tinged her voice. "Honestly, if she hadn't attacked you in the library, would you have considered her?"

"Not after I'd met you." He met her eyes and looked away. After he'd met Delphine, he couldn't have accepted anyone else, but he shouldn't feel that way. He must remember that the relationship was fake. Pretend.

He wanted it to be real.

The realization washed over him like the river water earlier, an irresistible current, sweeping him toward her. He'd been angry about leaving his research. He'd fought so hard for the respect of his peers, to be regarded as an equal at the Scholarium, and his absence would damage that. But tonight, for the first time in his life, she'd looked at him and he'd felt seen. Recognized. *Known*. For the first time in his life, there was something, *someone*, more important than his research.

The thirst to know and analyze everything around him had always been a search for someone willing to understand him.

When Delphine looked at him, she appreciated what it meant to always stand between two worlds, to always be pulled this way and that, never content, never accepted.

Delphine rubbed her face, serious again. "Can the residues give off distress signals?"

"I don't know. Studying them is difficult and risky." They'd only learned theory, never actual application.

"But you can contain them, right?" She leaned forward. "Purge them?"

"The residues, yes. The original won't be hiding in someone's aura. The magus will have it contained in something and, hopefully, under their control." He rubbed his thighs. It was easier to talk about this than try to sort out what had almost happened in his room. This was a safe topic. He knew this. His desire for her was uncharted territory. "We dematerialize them. They can't harm anyone if they're not physical. Half the attacks we know about can be traced to gambling dens or gentlemen's clubs."

He spoke more to himself than to her now, verbally sorting through information. If he threw himself into the puzzle, he wouldn't have to analyze his feelings.

Juliette Singleton had tried to stop him from interrogating Bertram, which meant she had something to hide. The name Indigo Elf hadn't come up before, but it couldn't be a coincidence that she ran a gambling den.

Varrick moved his hands as if manipulating a physical puzzle while he wrestled with the mystery. "I wish I understood why the magus is doing this."

"What would anyone use one for?" Delphine asked. "Can they control people?"

"The elementals? No, I don't think they can directly control anyone. Push them to despair, maybe." He shook his head. "For the person tasked with finding this thing, I don't know enough."

She wriggled her toes. "Juliette's attack and the carriage not-an-accident sound like the magus knows we're looking for him."

"I considered that." He didn't like the implications of it. "I don't see any gain in allowing an elemental to feed on people."

"Could the thing he summoned kill him?" Her eyes went wide and dark again. "Would it turn on him if it wasn't fed regularly?"

He frowned. "Existing here is painful for them. It's attracted to strong emotions. Passion. Anger. Excitement. Fear. It will feed where it finds them, but it will want him eventually." The victims must have been terrified, and their horror would have driven the creature's hunger.

Delphine started to ask something but closed her mouth on the words.

He tried to explain. "They drain auras. The residues do it slowly, so the aura never really dies, but the larger ones will tear it out. The person is left staring blankly at the world. No emotions. No memories. They can't even speak or feed themselves."

Delphine was rocking again, losing control of her breathing, panicking. She closed her eyes, face twisted into a grimace.

He was scaring her. He never wanted to scare her.

"There was a man," she whispered. "In the alleyway outside my door. He screamed and begged for help..." She covered her mouth, muffling a sob.

Varrick touched her knee. "I'm sorry, I didn't mean to tell you so much, not so soon after everything tonight. You look like you might faint. Please don't faint. Please don't cry."

She pressed her face into her knees, pulling herself into as tight a ball as she could. Varrick winced at her first muffled, choking sob.

He sent a tendril of his aura to her. *Concern. Worry.* He couldn't hide the wisp of guilt. *Comfort.* Most of all, comfort.

"I need to show you something," she whispered, muffled by her knees. "But you have to lock your aura up tight first."

He drew his aura in, locking it as securely as hers. "Alright."

She peered at him with one eye, searching for a corona or any cracks in his shield. "You must promise to keep it that way."

"I will." He reached to hold her hand.

She shook her head, shrinking back. "No, no touching either. When you see, you'll understand."

Leaning back, he crossed his arms. "I won't touch you, then." He wanted to touch her, hold her, and make everything right and safe

He laid his ears half back in frustration but stayed still as a rock.

She opened her aura.

Varrick's shoulders went taut. He sucked in his breath, and his lips twitched. She'd been aura torn. Not completely, or she wouldn't be able to move or speak or be herself, but the remnants of it drifted in ragged gray wisps about her, like smoke. Of course she'd stopped him earlier. She wouldn't dare let herself be swept up in his emotions.

"How long?" he said softly.

She swallowed a sob. "Nearly nine months ago."

CHAPTER 32

The Forgotten Night

Delphine

Nine months ago, there was a gap, a night Delphine had gone to bed furious with David for being out so late, again. Hurt because she knew he was losing money or spending the night with an opera dancer. She'd woken up two days later with a shredded aura, and David trying to coddle and comfort her. Acting guilty.

They'd never spoken about it. He'd said he came home and found her ill and feverish. She had no memories to naysay him, although she'd had nightmares for months afterwards. Black things with empty eyes had stalked her through mazes of streets, dead hedges, and empty rooms. A world of voids.

Varrick lurched to his feet, cursed, and sat back down, wincing and holding his injured knee.

Opening her aura was like peeling off a bandage and letting cold wind sear a wound. Delphine felt the ragged edges of herself drifting around her, the pent-up, unexpressed emotions bubbling against her ribcage. They were pale things, like sightless frogs who lived in caves, bereft of light or comfort.

She pulled the wisps of it back in and focused on her shield. It was too raw and painful to leave it open any longer. Now he knew how helpless she was, how constantly vigilant she had to be. He would know that he could compel her into any emotion he wished.

He grimaced. "I ought to get you something."

"Tea won't fix it. Brandy won't numb it. Heat, comfort, and sympathy won't change anything." She had an answer of sorts, finally, but even that offered no solace. All she had were more questions and the sure knowledge that the creature that ravaged her was out there. She wanted to dissolve, to not exist until she could control herself inside.

"Can you talk about it?"

"No!" She pushed herself up and wavered there, unsure what to do next. "I would never have shown you except—" Delphine waved her hand to indicate everything they'd spoken about. "I don't remember anything." The last part came out in a wail.

"We hadn't traced any victims before six months ago," Varrick said. "Please ..."

"That man. Right outside my door. It happened to him. I heard him clawing at the wood." She flung her arms out. "It was right outside my door."

Varrick rose more carefully this time, putting weight on his good leg. He caught both her hands. "I will find the magus behind this. I will banish the creature that did this."

"Varrick, you don't understand. It doesn't matter. The damage is done." She forced control into her voice. "I can't be fixed."

She couldn't touch someone with her love or calm a frightened child or reassure the suspicious. She could feel but never share it.

"You are afraid, so of course it matters." He leaned toward her. "You matter. And you can help me catch him. Will you?"

Blinking back tears, she nodded.

"Please. Sit. For the sake of my leg, which you did yell at me about standing on."

"I didn't yell." She lost the fight with her tears. One coursed down her cheek. She wiped it away, only for another to follow.

"You did, but I will overlook it if you sit with me." He tugged her closer to the settee.

She wiped her cheek. "Fine."

He returned to his seat and focused on her in that ears-forward, expectant way, hands out to support her or catch her. Delphine perched in the middle of the settee, not touching him but close enough that she could. The push and pull of it rocked her. She wanted to be held, wrapped up in someone else's strength for a change, but she didn't dare. What if she chose wrong? If she let herself be weak for a moment, would she be able to be strong again?

She stared at Varrick's expectant face. "What do you need?" she asked him.

"If you remember anything from before it happened, it might help."

She slumped back on the settee. The wooden edge along the top dug into her shoulders. "David went out. He hadn't for a while, but then he'd fallen back into old habits. He said he'd found a new group to play with, and he thought his luck was up." She glared at the fire and wiped away another tear. "He always thought his luck was up."

"Do you know who he was with?" Varrick flexed his hands.

She shook her head. "Mr. Severson might."

"Mr. Leighton came home?" Varrick prompted.

"Obviously, but I wasn't awake for it." *Damn tears.* Recounting her scant memories was hard enough. "I gave up waiting for him long before he died. I went to bed. I think I woke up when he came in. He was talking, you know, how drunks talk when they're trying to be quiet and utterly failing. I must have gone back to sleep."

With a deep breath, Varrick reached out and brushed another tear from her face. "How do you remember feeling?"

"I—" she touched where he'd touched. "What does that have to do with anything?"

"It might help."

"Mmm. Lethargic. I'm sure I heard him come home, and usually I would get up, but I couldn't, like..." Like being in the river earlier, dragged down by her dress. "Like having a pillow suffocating me all over."

She had tried to explain it to David when she woke up, but he'd shushed her, hiding his reluctance to hear it under the excuse that she should rest. She waited for Varrick to dismiss it or tell her it didn't mean anything, but he watched her with that intent yellow gaze.

"Anything else?" he asked.

"Not that night. When I woke up, everything was dull. Washed out." She waved her hands, trying to explain something she couldn't quite describe. There had been a veil over the world. "All the color came back eventually, but not my aura." She'd been dead inside, alone, unable to reach out for help or comfort. "I didn't know how to keep it well shielded at first."

Before she'd perfected her control, David had tired of his broken, bewildered wife. He'd forced her into cheerfulness. No mistress he'd taken, no lie he'd ever told, had been such a deep, unforgivable betrayal.

"Mr. Leighton never said anything about the night?"

"Nothing useful. Excuses and apologies. He'd lost a lot." She stared down at her hands. "I'm sorry. You wanted a mistress and a spy, and all you got was a woman with a sob story and no other options."

"Who followed me even though I told her not to, warned me about an enemy at my back, noticed things I couldn't, and just revised my entire timeline." He trailed his fingers down her jawline and lifted her chin until their eyes met. "You're not broken, you need extra care and protection."

She inhaled and held her breath to keep the tears from flowing again.

"You deserve that care and protection." He shook his head. "I can't believe your husband didn't try to find answers. I'd have torn the city apart."

"I was supposed to be the object of envy that he could parade around, the wife with connections that would benefit him, someone who would raise his status." Although it hadn't worked out that way, as Torlund's alliance with Elethen soured. "What he got, eventually, was the daughter of a dead ambassador to a country we are at war with, who was unwelcome in most venues and, eventually, wouldn't leave their home." She hadn't dared. Anyone could have Skilled her. She couldn't block out the deluge of emotions present in the world until she perfected her shield.

Varrick rested his hands on his knees. "Do you want me to leave? I can make sure the room is secure, and Sable and Talon can sleep in here if you'd like." His corona flickered dark bloody red before he slammed it shut. *Rage.*

"No." She deflated. "I can't, I need ... I don't want to be alone."

"If you'd rather Bethie, she could sleep in here."

But could Bethie expel those creatures? "I would like you to stay." She placed her hand on his. "Although I'd like the drakes in here, too." There was something very comforting about knowing their teeth and claws would be on her side.

He nodded. "I warn you, Talon snores."

She laughed a little. "I think I can survive it."

Varrick rose and limped to the door, opened it, and whistled a low sequence. The thump and scrabble of clawed feet echoed through the halls, and a moment later, both drakes slipped into the room. They snuffled at Varrick, paying special attention to his injured knee, receiving his gentle pats and praises, before coming to investigate Delphine. Sable rubbed her face against Delphine's legs while Talon assumed his usual position, flopped on his side in front of the fire.

Varrick closed and locked the door before returning to the settee.

Delphine scratched Sable between her nostrils. "I ought to have gotten up for you."

"They wouldn't come to you." He leaned back into the corner of the settee, sighing deeply, and closed his eyes.

Delphine leaned on him, gratified when he laid his arm across her shoulders. This was comfortable. She relaxed into the warmth of the fire and his body, only slightly disturbed when Sable clambered onto the settee as well, draping her head over Delphine's hip and a forepaw over her legs.

She might not be able to move, but she was well guarded.

CHAPTER 33

Morning

DELPHINE

Pale gray light filtered under the drapes before Delphine felt Varrick stir. She finally felt thoroughly warm and, despite Sable's heavy head on her hip, had no inclination to move. The night before drifted in her mind like a bad dream, and she wanted it to stay that way.

"Mrs. Halsey is here to check my leg," Varrick murmured, shifting out from under her. "Sleep some more. It's early."

"Mmm, alright. I'll allow it." She scooted into his place, claiming the warmed spot on the settee; the fire had burned low during the night.

Varrick's limping step moved around the room, and a moment later, a thick bedspread draped over her.

"That's a poor substitute," she said, and pulled it over her shoulder. She drifted back to sleep to Talon's monotonous snores.

It was much later when Delphine woke again. The door clicked shut behind Tanner and Bethie, who set a tray on the bed.

"We knew neither of you would be down for a proper breakfast after such an *eventful* night." Tanner's voice was more brusque than usual.

Delphine sat up, wincing. She felt every bump and bruise from the fall and all her sore muscles from crawling out of the water and back to the bridge. The night's conversation rolled back, leaving her emotions raw.

Bethie slipped out. In the silence after the click of the door, a chill settled on the room.

Scooting out from under Sable's head, Delphine stood and held the blanket around her shoulders. "Tanner, is something wrong?" Varrick's leg had bled profusely, but she'd cleaned and bound it well.

Tanner crossed her arms. "Mrs. Leighton, I like you, and so far you've done a fine job playing your part, but you signed a contract specifying the limits of your affections toward Mr. Allard. There was to be no after-hours frolicking."

Delphine blinked at her, considering the ridiculousness of Tanner using a word like *frolicking*.

"Everyone but Bethie was away. I cleaned up his wound and we got out of our wet things. That's all." Embarrassment prickled along her cheeks. Nothing had happened, but not for lack of opportunity or desire. "Did he tell you the carriage fell into the river?"

Tanner's arms stayed crossed. "Bethie told us. Mrs. Halsey has seen to the injury. Coming home to a trail of blood was alarming, but you two don't seem too worried."

Delphine felt like a little girl being chastised by her nanny. Childish petulance warred with her better sense. Sense won, barely. "I am sorry, Tanner. The night didn't go as planned and we were both rattled."

Tanner motioned to the tray. Delphine skirted the settee and sat next to where it lay on the bed, sipping the tea while it was hot.

Tanner must have more to say, since she didn't usually linger like this.

"We can't do this without Varrick," Tanner finally said. "No one else on this continent has his command of anima and knows the elemental spells well enough. We need him focused."

We? "And I have become a distraction." Irritation prickled along her neck. She hadn't started the *frolicking* last night. She'd stopped it.

"He's young, and you are beautiful. It's like sparks and tinder." Tanner sighed. "I will let you eat, then come do something about your hair."

"How young?" Delphine asked. He must be her age, more or less. He didn't act like any of the young men who frequented balls and gambling halls—never serious, never looking ahead.

Tanner paused at the door. "Varrick is twenty-six. A bit of a prodigy."

Four years her junior. "Oh." She hadn't expected that. "I'd guessed him to be older."

"I thought so." Tanner left.

Delphine picked at the food, chewing her toast slowly and poking at the porridge without much appetite. She couldn't push away the resentment that the responsibility for last night's kisses was being placed on her head. She was older, but she hadn't known she was older.

If she closed her eyes, she could still feel his breath on her skin. Young men were impulsive, and the night had been a mess, but if she was honest with herself, she had fanned those flames.

She didn't regret it.

She knew so little of him. A prodigy, Tanner had said. A Doonish refugee child, an orphan, raised in Istalia. How had he entered the Scholarium? She knew little of Istalia except that they produced exceptional wine, and the Scholarium rivaled the university.

She hadn't known David any better before she said her vows.

Name, birth, family connections, as those were public, but nothing about his hobbies and proclivities. Knowing someone was a charming dancer meant little.

Bethie returned for the tray, and Tanner entered as she left. Delphine felt a bit more contrite than she had earlier, but not enough to apologize. She would make peace with Varrick but not be scolded for responding to his overtures.

"Let me see your hair." Tanner sounded weary instead of cross.

Between the number of pins and stitches, the rats for padding, and the soaking in the river, Delphine's hair looked like something a crow had built to nest in.

She grimaced at it in the mirror. "The river did it no favors."

"Neither did sleeping on it." Tanner began removing the few surviving hair pins.

Hint taken. "Tanner, who brought Varrick here to hunt the summoner?"

Tanner made a noncommittal sound.

"Was it the university?" Delphine could not demand to know their secrets, but the more she tried to fit pieces together the less she knew.

Tanner removed the thread that had stitched a rat into place. "As I said, no one here could do it. After last night, I'd think you'd be grateful he was."

No one else on the continent had the power and knowledge to do this, according to Tanner. Delphine shuddered. "Yes."

Pins and rats removed, Tanner took the wide-toothed comb to the snarls and knots in Delphine's hair. "Your connections and knowledge have proved helpful, Mrs. Leighton."

"We have a few leads to follow." *Juliette and Severson.*

Tanner nodded but didn't reply.

At least she was useful. "How did Varrick get into the Scholarium?" She met Tanner's eyes in the mirror. "I know he was born in Alladoon, grew up in Istalia, and visited Elethen, but nothing else."

Tanner raised her eyebrows. "Ask Mr. Allard."

"Which is another question. *Allard* is definitely an Eletheni name." So was *Varrick*, but first names drifted over borders more quickly than surnames.

Varrick's hunt for the summoner and shadow would not last forever. When it ended, she would sail to Elethen. She would restart her life in a world vastly different from this one. She ought to look forward to it, but the thought lay heavy on her heart. Where would Varrick be going?

Tanner laid her hands on Delphine's shoulders. She'd brushed Delphine's hair until it flowed loose and smooth down her back, although it was already trying to frizz.

"You may ask him whatever you wish, but please, keep yourself cool to him in private," she paused, "as you agreed."

"As agreed, yes."

She hated to say it.

Tender Sensibilities

DELPHINE

Once Delphine was properly dressed with her hair braided and pinned up, the previous night felt even more surreal. Sayledon Manor lay peaceful around her. Rare autumn sun streamed through the windows of the sitting room, making the thought of shadow creatures and the magi who summoned them feel distant. If the black things she'd seen were creatures of emptiness, were there opposite creatures of light or fullness?

She checked the windows. It was too bright to see the wards, but she could feel them buzzing slightly when she ran her fingers along the sill. Outside, the sharp shadows had the expected shapes and depth.

She had one answer at least. She knew what had happened to her, although she didn't know why. Was it too much to hope that Severson could tell her anything more?

Talon clicked into the sitting room, circled the perimeter, then clicked out after casting her a reproachful glance. Apparently, she was in the wrong room. She followed him to the library but paused at the door. Muffled voices echoed from further down the hall, in the direction of Varrick's study.

"Just a moment," she murmured to the drake.

She crept down the hall, heart thundering in her ears. She shouldn't pry, but the more she knew, the more she could guard against future threats. Guard herself and Varrick.

The door to the study was closed but raised voices reverberated well. She held her breath, listening.

"—do not need to remind you what is at stake." That sounded like Mrs. Halsey.

"Not likely I'll forget, since they tried to drown us both," Varrick rumbled.

"Can Mrs. Leighton continue to be part of our plan when she's also the first victim?" Tanner said.

So he had told them.

Victim. A mix of sadness and relief washed over her to hear it acknowledged that way.

A chair creaked. "First that we know of. But it changes how we look at this. If the first attack was nine months ago, we've been looking at the wrong events."

"Nine months ago—" Tanner started.

"Peace treaty talks started." That was Morrow's voice.

An irregular thumping passed the door. Delphine tensed, ready to rush back to the library.

"Stop pacing and sit down," Mrs. Halsey said. "That makes it a bigger tangle."

"It's not her fault," Varrick said.

Delphine took a slow, silent breath.

"It can't be a coincidence that the creature fed on her, and then she came to us." Mrs. Halsey's voice rose. "I don't believe in chance."

"Quiet," Tanner said. "We'll put together the pieces we know and decide where to go next."

"We don't know that it has anything to do with the treaty," Morrow said. "The timing could be completely unconnected."

"Your only job here is to track down the magus and his creature and deal with them," Mrs. Halsey said. It sounded like she was pacing now.

"I know," Varrick said softly. "Do any of you have any substantial complaints about my work here? Does Lady M?"

"I'd rather not find you half-naked on Mrs. Leighton's settee again," Tanner said dryly. "Don't lay your ears back at me, young man."

Delphine choked back a nervous giggle.

"She's far too vulnerable," Tanner continued. "You cannot take advantage of that."

"If that hadn't happened—and nothing that you think happened, happened—we wouldn't know about her aura." Varrick rumbled in his throat. "And I would never, will never, take advantage of her."

Quiet fell, with both women murmuring reluctant agreement. Delphine shifted, intending to return to the library and give in to Talon's demands, but the doorknob to the study jiggled. She wouldn't have time. She slipped into the next room, which was dark, chilly, and unused, pulling the door nearly shut as Mrs. Halsey and Tanner strode out of Varrick's office.

Morrow's voice echoed from the study. "It could be pure chance that she heard about the position."

"To be a governess," Varrick said.

"But maybe it wasn't."

A chair scraped the floor; Varrick standing? "She can see signs of the creatures in coronas, even when they're shielded, maybe because of what happened to her. It makes her more qualified to watch my back than anyone else."

"I am less strict than Tanner is regarding your affections," Morrow said. "I think Lady M would be too, so long as the job gets done."

Varrick grunted. "Do you actually think someone stalking gambling dens and attacking young, rich men is trying to influence the peace talks?"

"No. I think we've missed something important." Morrow sighed. "It's hard to know what we don't know until we know it."

"Clear as mud. Thank you, Morrow."

Morrow laughed. "When we find the right piece, it will fall into place. In the meantime, we have some leads, and you have a lady of tender sensibilities to comfort."

Tender sensibilities? Delphine would apply the term to Edwina, not herself. She hadn't been allowed to be tender since ... she couldn't remember when. What would it be like?

Now that she knew what had happened to her, she had every reason to want the summoner and his creature dealt with. If they found them, she might finally find out why. Why had they come into her house, into her room, and ravaged her aura? Why had David allowed it? She couldn't rage at him anymore or hold him accountable, but she wanted answers.

"What is our next move?" Varrick asked.

"I want to pin down the woman. Juliette Singleton," Morrow said.

There was another pause, then the door opened and closed, and footsteps retreated down the hall. Delphine waited, fingers growing chilly, to see if Varrick would follow, but his chair scraped again, followed by the sound of papers being shuffled.

She crept out of the empty room and walked as quietly and calmly as her heart would allow. Mrs. Halsey's suspicions annoyed her. She had come here by chance, simply an overheard and misconstrued conversation in a haberdashery.

Morrow might want to find Juliette, but Delphine wanted to speak with Severson. He'd hung on the longest as one of David's friends, and perhaps he remembered that night.

She idled the afternoon away in the library again, mostly

because Talon and Sable whined and looked pathetic every time she rose to leave. She wasn't sure Varrick would want to see her; it couldn't be anything but awkward after the night before. As the light outside faded, Tanner fetched her to dress for dinner.

"I don't know why we do this when it is just pretend," Delphine grumbled as Tanner twisted her hair into a more elegant style.

Tanner stepped back, studying Delphine's hair, then added a silver comb to the back. "Company might arrive. If so, we want to all look the part."

She turned from the mirror to look at Tanner. "Is everyone still cross at me over last night?"

"We are not cross," Tanner said, although her tone was strict enough. "We are cautious."

"Understandable."

"This is not without risks—to all of us. And we don't want unnecessary entanglements." She replaced the brushes and combs.

"I will be sailing for Elethen when this is done." *I should be looking forward to that.* "As per the contract. I am not entangling anyone."

Tanner lifted her chin. "Dinner will be served directly. Mr. Allard has some plans for the next few days."

"I look forward to hearing them." Delphine rose, stealing a glance in the mirror. Irritated or not, Tanner had done a splendid job.

Most likely there would be company for dinner.

When she descended the stairs that evening, Mr. Severson and Lord Everard waited in the entry hall, chatting with Varrick about horses. Delphine raised one eyebrow. She'd suspected that Everard was some sort of ally, but Varrick hadn't known Severson before last night. How had he managed to invite them so quickly? At least

things were moving along. She would not spend day after day waiting, feeling useless.

"Ah, there she is!" Severson grinned up at her. "You look amaz-
ing, Dellie." He'd styled his red hair over his eyes again and worn
exactly the wrong shade of pink coat, every inch the dandy.

"A treat for the eyes," Everard agreed. He wore black, although
he couldn't make it look as sinister as Varrick did.

Varrick clasped his hands behind his back, but when his eyes
met hers, his ears perked forward. After last night, she knew it was
no act, and pleasure at his admiration made her smile.

She paused on the staircase, gathering herself before playing
the proper hostess. "What a pleasant surprise to see you both." She
favored them with smiles. "I did not realize we had company, or I
would have come down sooner."

"I'm afraid that's my fault, Mrs. Leighton," Everard said.
"Your message from last night reached me, and I thought we ought
to check on you." He stepped forward to take her hand.

"Goodness, I'd forgotten it in the aftermath." She had for a
time, then she'd been a little embarrassed about it; they'd made it
back to the manor without aid.

"I am pierced to the heart." Everard kissed her hand, but the
effect was ruined by Severson rolling his eyes in the background.

"I am glad you're here," Varrick said. "I have to ask for favors
from both of you gentlemen."

"Had to check on Dellie, y'know?" Severson held his hands
out to her.

Delphine extracted her hand from Everard and clasped both of
Severson's, swallowing a sudden lump in her throat. His profession
of loyalty the night before had hit her harder than she'd expected.
"I have some important questions for you. I hope you can help me
with them."

He glanced at Varrick. "Anything."

Varrick cleared his throat. "Shall we go in to dinner, Delphine?
Everything is ready."

He kept his hands behind his back until she moved up next to him, as if unsure that he would escort her in. Tanner's scolding seemed to have chastened him more than she expected.

CHAPTER 35

Fishing at Dinner

DELPHINE

The staff had adjusted to the gentlemen's arrival with aplomb. Usually, Delphine and Varrick's meals were casual, with no ornamentation on the table, and smaller placemats instead of a full tablecloth. Today, a white damask cloth covered the table, and elaborate sculptures of glass and silver flowers in vases lined the center of the table, catching the light from the glow power in the chandelier, which shone brighter than usual. The table was set for four, wine glasses filled for the first course, and as soon as they sat, the footman brought the soup.

A brief silence fell as they ate and tasted the wine. Everard glanced from Varrick to Delphine, then to Severson, and back to Varrick, as if he expected tension but found none. Severson watched Delphine, although he tried to be covert about it. Varrick had returned to his bland poker-face, even his ears relaxed.

Everard finished his wine and gave the empty glass an approving study. "What sort of questions, Allard?"

Varrick tapped the table. "Tell me about Juliette Singleton and whose company she keeps."

"Whoever pays her the best for her company is who she spends time with." Everard raised his glass for a refill.

"Hardly helpful," Delphine said, meeting his eyes. "After all, so do I, but you know who my patron is." It was becoming easier to slip into that role.

Severson opened his mouth to say something but stopped himself.

"I don't have much to do with the woman," Everard said. "Frankly, I don't care to get in too deep with her."

"You keep track of people who enter your parties, though." Varrick stirred his soup. He'd barely eaten. "And if you're smart enough not to deal too much with her, you know something about her."

Everard half-smiled. "Flattery will soften my heart, but get you nowhere."

"Then tell us about the Indigo Elf," Delphine said.

Severson dropped his spoon.

Everard shrugged. "I don't need to go out for a good game. And I don't think she'll soon forgive me for showing Mrs. Leighton to the library."

"But you've no idea who she's been around these past, say, six months?" Delphine tried to sound casual, but she needed a name, just one name. "Her regulars?"

"Indigo Elf is by invitation only. I've never been on the list." Severson spread his hands. He met Delphine's eyes by chance and looked away too quickly.

Varrick sighed. "I would appreciate it if you'd help Morrow and I narrow down some names, Everard."

There was a pause in conversation as the soup was removed, and fish served.

Everard took a drink of wine, swirling it around his mouth to savor it. "I'm sure we can negotiate a fair price. I'll add it to my bill for the visit."

Delphine pushed the flaky fish around the plate with her fork.

Severson was getting twitchy. He was drinking more than eating and avoided her eyes. Everard shrugged again, but Severson sucked on his lower lip and looked off to the side. *What does he know, and why won't he say it?*

"Are you well, Mr. Severson?" Delphine tried to catch his eye again. "You seem unsettled."

"I came to check on you, Dellie. And my offer from the other night hasn't changed." He tapped the table with his fingers. "I was worried, and you need a friend."

She'd needed a friend nine months ago. Five months ago. Four weeks ago. Where had he been?

"That's very kind of you." Varrick trained his ears toward Severson, making the redhead shift his chair back. "I think Delphine hoped to reminisce about old times with you."

Delphine lifted her wine glass. "Yes. Most of my acquaintances have distanced themselves. It has been lonely."

Severson stared at the tablecloth as if the weave were suddenly the most interesting thing in the world. "Well, you know, no one cares much what I get up to, so long as I keep my nose clean."

"You could enlighten us on what you're doing here, Magus." Everard lifted his glass to Varrick. "It might be worth more of my time and thoughts than another stack of thalens."

"No," Varrick said.

Everard gave Delphine a beseeching look. "Come now, Mrs. Leighton, surely you can convince him to drop me a tiny secret or two."

"No, I will not, Lord Everard," she said. "I am afraid you must remain in the dark."

Severson squirmed in his chair. He knew something, but Varrick was pinning him with that intense, yellow stare, and Severson was losing his nerve.

"We can catch up privately, Severson, just the two of us." Delphine crossed her fork and knife to indicate she was finished, although she'd barely tasted the fish. "Remember that one night last spring? David was excited about an important game."

Severson's shoulders tightened up to his ears.

"I'm sure Mr. Allard and I can find something to chat about," Everard said. "He might know something interesting about Istalia, for example."

The footman removed the fish. Varrick was the only one who had finished it. No one spoke as squab and roasted turnips were served, nor as they ate. Everard seemed amused by something, although she'd no idea what. Severson looked like he might fall over in his chair if someone walked too close.

Delphine's mind whirled, always coming back to why. Why hurt people this way? Why attack her? Father used to soothe tempers or aim people toward the solution he wanted. What had he said? People fell in line for money, power, or love—or the trappings of love. Whatever this summoner wanted, it was simpler than continuing a war. He wanted money or power. The people who would gain either from war didn't need to skulk around in the shadows. They would use other levers to steer Torlund: bribes, blackmail, and backroom agreements.

The only thing that granted more power than money was magic, like Juliette's golden pearl earrings.

Rare, elven pearls full of anima, their value driven higher because the elves refused to sell any more. They were magic and money all in one tiny gem.

"Pearls," she mused.

Three men looked at her with complete confusion.

"Juliette's earrings." Had all three missed them? They'd been in plain sight. "They were golden pearls—elven tree artifacts. She drew anima from one when she attacked Varrick."

Varrick's pupils widened, then snapped to a narrow line. Everard leaned back and whistled, while Severson rubbed at his jaw, distressed.

"Those are nearly impossible to find," Everard said.

There was something important about the pearls and Juliette, but Delphine couldn't make the connection.

"Do you know something about them, Severson?" she asked. He'd been fidgety all evening. If Varrick and Everard would leave, she could quiz him.

"No. Nope. Not particularly. You don't usually see them used for jewelry." He emptied his wine glass.

"She was certainly using them for more than decoration." Delphine had thought they were just Juliette showing off, until she used one. Had Juliette come to Everard's party prepared for trouble? Had she expected Varrick to be there? He'd been more than she could handle, but now she knew what he could do.

Everard looked like a gryphon with a fish, pleased with this bit of information. Varrick frowned. The footman took the plates away. He inquired about bringing up the cheese platter, but Varrick shook his head. Conversation was the order of the night.

Delphine rose without waiting for a gentleman to move her chair. "Varrick, Mr. Severson and I will catch up on old times in the library, if you don't mind."

Varrick cocked his head, raising his eyebrows. "I don't mind at all. Would you like the kitchen to send coffee or brandy?"

"Tea in a bit." She turned a brilliant smile on Severson. "Come along. It's been ages."

Severson swallowed but stood and joined her.

Everard took out a slim, metal case and offered Varrick a cigarillo. "Best tobacco Alladoon can grow."

Varrick's ears flattened. "No, thank you."

Severson took Delphine's arm and guided her out of the dining room and back to the entry hall. Sable and Talon rose from their places at the bottom of the staircase and circled around them.

CHAPTER 36

What Severson Said

DELPHINE

"They're quite tame," Delphine told Severson. Judging by his grip on her arm, the two large drakes made him as nervous as Varrick did.

"I'd like them better if they had fur or feathers. They look too much like the illustrations of dragons in my childhood books." He held out a tentative hand for Talon to sniff.

"They don't shed, and they're not nearly as destructive as gryphons. Edwina has several, and her poor couch was taking the brunt of them last time I visited." A twinge of guilt struck her, remembering what she'd said to Edwina last time they met.

He rubbed Talon's nose. "When was that?"

"Before I accepted Mr. Allard's offer." She stepped away from him, noting the alarm in his eyes as both drakes converged on him. It was just Sable wanting her fair share of scratches, but he didn't know that.

"You should get out of all this, Dellie. Although I don't think Allard is a bad sort, for a frog—" He stopped with another nervous swallow. "You don't want anything more to do with what he's into."

"What do you mean by *more*?"

He caught her arm, then dropped it when Talon growled. "You don't remember? When you mentioned that night in spring—"

"Tell me." She crossed her arms. Her whole reason for wanting to speak with him was about that gap in her memory, those missing days that coincided with her torn aura. "If you know something about it, tell me."

"You've got to get out of this. Go to the country. Take a ship to Alladoon. Go somewhere else." He raked a hand through his hair. The sudden move made Talon growl again.

Delphine balled her fists. "Not unless you tell me what you know."

"Maybe not in the middle of the entry hall?" He tried to step around the drakes. "You don't want both those gents overhearing."

"I suspect you don't." Let Varrick overhear, but Everard had no right to her past.

Severson followed her to the library. He tried to slip in without the drakes, but she shook her head. "They come with us. It's their favorite room."

"You guarantee they won't take my hand off?"

"Probably better to keep your hands off me if you want to keep them." She'd no idea what either drake might do if they thought she was threatened, but Talon had already growled twice.

They settled in the chairs before the fire. The drakes sat at her feet, heads in her lap, giving Severson gloating side-eyes.

"Now, tell me about that night." He was acting too guilty to not know something.

Severson laid his hands on his knees. "David had been away from the tables for a while. Months. It was the best he'd ever done at walking away."

Delphine nodded. He'd gone out most nights but only came home drunk, not with a pile of new debts.

"Then he got his invitation. A special game. High stakes, big rollers. I had no idea why they'd want him. He didn't have the money." He leaned forward, forlorn. "Swiving gods, I couldn't even corner an invitation. Davie took me along, but I wasn't welcome to play."

"At Everard's." If the sardonic little man was involved, Varrick ought to know.

"No! No. Everard runs a clean card party. It was at the Indigo Elf."

"Juliette."

He nodded. "There were a few others there. Bertie and another fellow. Bartholomew Weber. Big as Allard, blond. I'd never seen him before."

"I don't know him." But ... big, blond. It had to be the man she'd seen so often, the one who seemed so familiar for no reason. He'd been at the opera with Juliette. *Weber.* Stokes had said the name in the Maze of Mirrors.

He shrugged. "They got David hooked, let him win and kept him drinking until he was in deep. Then he started to lose and lose more."

"But there was always the promise that he might start winning again." She knew the cycle. It took a shipload of bad luck to convince David he couldn't win it all back.

"Of course." Severson sighed. "Cleaned him out, then refused to take his signature on a promissory note."

"So he took out loans?" That would explain why he owed so much to Mr. Stokes.

"I wish." He buried his head in his hands and said something she didn't catch.

Delphine touched his shoulder. "Say that again."

"Weber wanted you." He gave her an anguished stare. "I swear on my mother's blood, I didn't think David would go for it. I thought he'd walk away."

The little she'd eaten churned in her stomach like cold surf. David hadn't walked away. "He lost."

"I fought with him over it, offered to cover his debts, but he wouldn't hear of it. It was like he couldn't say no."

"He was Skilled." It must have been subtly done and might not have been Weber. It could have been any player at the table, or the dealer, anyone in the room. "Didn't anyone else find it strange, or reprehensible?"

"From that crowd?" He spread his hands, helpless. "Men gamble with their mistresses' favors all the time. No one thought much of it."

All the time. Sick fury roared through her. "I wasn't his mistress. I was his *wife*."

"Yeah." He had that same look Varrick had sometimes, staring through the wall and into somewhere else.

"That's all you can say about it?" She rose, upsetting the two drakes. "You stood there while my husband gambled me away like a horse!"

Startled, Talon and Sable growled, raising the sharp hackles on their necks and shoulders.

Severson pressed further back into his chair. "Swiving gods, Dellie, call them off!"

"I didn't call them up." She loomed over him. "You'd better tell me about the rest of that night, or I'll walk out that door and leave you alone with them."

Severson clutched his hands over his chest. "Weber won, and he wouldn't take money in lieu of what David had bet—"

"What specifically?" She had a sinking feeling she knew.

"A night with you. Payable immediately."

All the old ashes of her anger and frustration at David blazed to life. The neglect. The secrets. The debts. The lies. The insults.

She'd endured, covered for him, smiled for his family and pretended everything was well.

And he'd bargained away her virtue in a single night. Her hands shook. Her knees trembled. She wanted to scream and throw things, to hurt something the way she hurt now, but it would just bring Varrick and Everard crashing down on them, and she'd have to explain everything. It didn't matter that he'd been Skilled. The betrayal was too deep for forgiveness or mercy.

"Dellie. Dellie, listen, it wasn't what you think. He didn't touch you, I promise. I went along to … I don't know, to do something." He looked down, right into Talon's face and flinched. "You should have had this pair that night."

"Sounds like they would have been more helpful than you or David." She clenched her hands until her nails bit into her palms.

"Weber's a magus. A powerful one. He had a creature with him. You were asleep." He stopped, refusing to look at her.

"Keep going, damn you." She couldn't look at him. She knew how horrifying the small creatures had been. A large one like Bertram described would have been terrifying, but she still blamed him. David was dead and she needed someone living to vent her rage on.

"It was hungry. I heard it, like nails on iron, screeching in my head. He let it out of its metal ball, and your aura was so bright." He slumped back, miserable and pathetic. "It was always so bright, so strong, even when you had it shielded, your corona shone."

No longer. "Severson."

"David was too damn drunk to do anything, and I tried to grab Weber. He knocked me into the wall so hard, damn near broke my head."

"Forgive my lack of sympathy."

He winced. "This shadow-beast-thing sucked every bit of color out of your aura. It was all coiled around you like a great snake."

She couldn't remember, but something in her, her bones or

her lungs or her muscles, did, because she felt it squeezing, felt the cold horror sinking into her heart, stealing all her feelings but fear.

He rubbed his face. "I told Davie to fess up, but he wouldn't. He didn't want anything to do with me after. I knew too much, and he was afraid I'd tell."

"You should have told me. I woke up and had no idea what had happened to me. I had to lose my husband, my home, and my respectability before I found out anything." She paced to the door of the library and back to him, trying to gain control of her voice. "And no, I will not be stepping back or stopping. I'm going to help Varrick find him and take him down."

"Did you hear what I said? He's a magus. He'll kill you or worse. Just get out of Rockhaven and away from all this."

Delphine shook her head, dismissing his worries. Weber was a magus? So was Varrick. "Juliette too. You can't convince me she wasn't part of this."

"It's just her place. She probably didn't know anything about what Weber was up to. I don't know why you think she does."

She glared at him until he dropped his gaze. He hadn't seen Juliette spinning anima out of her earring to attack Varrick. She might have been loyal to Bertram, but that made little sense.

She'd dismissed Juliette's animosity as jealousy. Severson's story rearranged the pieces into a more coherent order. Juliette was working with Weber. Weber was following Delphine. He'd been at her rooms the day she and Tanner retrieved her things. He'd been at the opera and used Stokes to corner her at the Glass Gardens. Where else had he tracked her? And why?

"I need a moment," she said. "Please go find Varrick."

He rose and stood there, deflated. "I'm so sorry, Dellie."

"Go." She pointed to the door and didn't look until it closed behind him.

CHAPTER 37

The Making of a Magus

DELPHINE

Delphine ought to have returned to the drawing room, where the men would be gathering with cigars and drinks, but she slumped back into the chair in front of the library fireplace. Sable wrapped herself around Delphine's feet, so covered in skirts that only the drake's tail peeked out. Talon laid his head in her lap with a contented sigh.

"I wish I'd had you two there." She leaned forward, pressing her forehead to his.

He licked her chin and purred deep in his throat. The low vibration shook loose everything she'd been holding inside. Hot tears coursed down her cheeks.

She'd wanted to know. Now she did. Was she any happier, knowing the depths of David's betrayal?

No.

Everything was painful. Her old hurts rose from the graves she'd buried them in. All her emotional ghosts keened for peace. Her breath came in short gasps. David's criticisms and excuses echoed in her memory.

Some things could never be made right. Some wounds could never be healed. They weren't scar tissue, but raw, bleeding gashes, incapable of closing. She gulped for breath, clutching at Talon's sinewy neck. There was comfort in the simple, animal strength, the silent, undemanding support. She would never need to explain anything to him. He would never reject her because her aura was gone or her reputation ruined.

The house grew quiet, the silence of night seeping in with the chill. Footsteps in the hall jolted her out of her grief. She wiped the tears off her cheeks, sniffing. The gentlemen *would* show up when she was scattered and out of sorts.

The knob jiggled but didn't turn. She wrapped her arms around Talon.

"Severson said she was angry and upset but wouldn't explain why." Varrick's voice drifted under the door. "I want to check on her."

Delphine hiccupped, trying to compose herself. At least Severson hadn't told the whole story to Varrick and Everard, but if it was Everard outside the door, she couldn't face him.

"I can see her to bed." *Not Everard. Tanner. Thank goodness.*

"When I'm done," Varrick said, steel in his voice.

"If she's upset, it may be better to let her rest before making her talk about it." Tanner sighed. "If you want to protect her, protect her from what's out there, not the people in here who want to help."

"I think a cup of tea would be in order," Varrick said.

"With milk and sugar. I mean it. Don't push." Tanner's staccato footsteps retreated.

Delphine stared at the doorknob until it turned, and Varrick slipped in, silent as shadows. He closed it behind him but stayed there as if unsure what to do.

"I know his name." She held tighter to Talon. "Bartholomew Weber did this to me. He's your summoner."

Varrick closed his eyes and nodded. "Severson just said you'd talked about your husband, and you were upset."

"He's a master of understatement." She saw the appeal of gryphons; warm fur would be comforting.

Varrick was warm and had fur, sort of.

"Do you want to talk about it?" He took a hesitant step forward.

"You're trying very hard to follow Tanner's advice," she smiled sadly, "but I'll tell you after the tea comes."

He nodded and approached her as if she was a wild drake. "I could hear you."

She exhaled heavily. Of course he had. "I was not trying to be quiet."

He sank into the chair, leaning forward with his elbows on his knees. Sable's tail thumped, but she made no move to leave Delphine's skirts.

"Traitors." He rubbed Talon's neck. "Give you a pretty face and you abandon me."

"I think I'll have to keep them." She would miss both drakes.

"They know when you need them." He wriggled his fingers and was rewarded with a nudge from Talon.

"Weber sought me out. He trapped David into a bet for me. Why?" Maybe it had nothing to do with her, just that David was foolish and easy to catch, but that felt off.

"Tell me from the beginning, then maybe I can shed light on it." He thought for a moment. "After the tea. Tanner's orders."

"Wouldn't dare disobey."

"Certainly not."

"You know all about me. Tell me about you while we wait for the tea." She'd had enough mysteries to fill a lifetime.

"I only know your history. Not the important things. I don't know your favorite flower, or what you like to do on rainy afternoons, or read about, or how to ease your sorrow." He clasped his hands and stared at them.

"That's a nice list of important things." She relaxed a little, still clutching Talon. "I know where you were born and where you were raised, but not what you like to read." She thought for a moment. "You probably like to read books about magical theory and philosophy."

He flicked his ears and his eyes narrowed, looking as pleased as Talon. "I told you about the mudslide. There were ships helping the Doonish jaglin escape a push northward by the Torlish. The Sisters of Our Lady of the Jungle put as many orphans on board as they could."

"They took you to Istalia?"

"Not at first. We stayed on Maythem Island for, oh, two years? There was food and shelter, and the refugees all took care of each other." He half-smiled at her. "But the island hadn't been prepared for us. When the offer came to relocate to Istalia, most took it."

"Maythem Island explains why you have an Eletheni name."

"I was too young to tell anyone my name, so I was given one by the human family who cared for me. Their name was Allard." He looked bleak. "I worry about them, with the war there. Their children were grown, and they would have kept me."

"When I get to Elethen, I'll have connections and resources. I can find them for you." It was so easy to promise, but how hard would it be to find one family?

"I envy you, having a family to go home to."

He looked so wistful, her heart ached for the child he'd been. "You must have people waiting for you in Istalia. How did you ever go to the Scholarium?" There was a vast distance between a displaced child and a powerful magus.

"I was clever. I had powerful anima. And I was trouble." He laughed. "I wanted to learn so much, but school was expensive. Books were expensive. And among the Doonish, men don't become magi. Crafters, yes, but not magi. My community thought I was foolish."

"That doesn't sound like trouble." She pictured Varrick as a child with small horns and ears too big for himself.

"I figured out how to undo wards and locks." He scratched his head, flushing with embarrassment. "I stole a lot of books, but I always put them back after reading them."

"You broke back into places a second time to return the books?"

"It was the knowledge I wanted, not the books themselves."

"When did you get caught?" He must have been caught eventually.

"Not until I was fifteen. I tried sneaking into the Scholarium's library. If I got in just before they closed, then I could hide and spend all night reading." He stretched, favoring the injured leg. "I thought it was a perfect plan."

"But it was not." Oh, fifteen sounded so long ago. She'd been awkward, embarrassed about her height, and convinced she'd never marry because of it, at that age.

"The night librarian caught me. Quizzed me. And instead of turning me in, arranged for me to have a benefactor to pay for me to stay and study." He stared out the window. "The other refugees cut me off. I could go to the Scholarium or stay Doonish, but not both."

That was too close to the arguments among Mama, Father, and Grandpapa, just before her family returned to Rockhaven for good. *Choose one. You cannot be both*, Father had said to Alastair.

"I'm so sorry," Delphine whispered. He'd lost everyone. Twice.

"I'd never really been a part of the community. I didn't have a family or village connection to any of them, and I was strange. I fit better at the Scholarium." He lifted a flap of his coat. "Although I wasn't well-tailored for that, either. Too Istalian for the Doonish, too Doonish for the Istalians."

"And nowhere to just be yourself." That, too, felt familiar.

"Once, I spent a year at sea with the elven privateers." He smiled at the memory. "I didn't feel out of place there."

"You were a pirate?" She meant it as a joke, but he twitched his thick eyebrows and nodded.

He cocked an ear at the door. "I am a passable sailor."

"But you weren't there to learn sailing. Or pirating, I hope." She wiped a stray tear off her cheek.

"I was working with elemental summoning, specifically air and water. Hands-on experience."

He spoke so casually of power that, if misused, destroyed lives. The image of snake-like darkness constricting her, devouring her dreams and desires, flashed in her head. She couldn't pursue it. "Tanner thinks I'll distract you."

"Um," he squeezed her hand. "It isn't a wholly unfounded fear."

Delphine was saved from responding by Tanner bringing in a tray of tea. She must be worried, to bring it herself. *Distraction*.

Tanner eyed Delphine with equal parts concern and suspicion.

"Do you want me to stay to pour?" Tanner gave Varrick a sharp glance.

"I can pour." Delphine lifted the teapot. "It's been a draining few evenings, but I am not that fragile."

Tanner smiled a little. "Very good. Ring when you are finished."

The door clicked closed.

"How likely is it that she's listening at the keyhole?" Delphine poured herself a cup. She wasn't sure how to read Tanner. She understood jealous wives and protective mamas, but Tanner was neither. Her protectiveness extended to Delphine.

He aimed an ear in that direction. "She's not."

Delphine poured him a cup, set down the pot, and added milk to her tea. After tea, they'd said, and now the tea was here. She blew on her cup as he added sugar to his.

"You can wait until morning if you don't want to talk about it now." He took a sip, then added another spoon of sugar.

"Maybe if I talk about it, it won't run around my head all

night." She couldn't forget Severson's words, but she was grateful she could not remember the attack. "There doesn't seem to be much to tell."

"You have a name. What else do we know?" He took another sip.

"David was invited to a game at the gambling den run by Juliette Singleton. I think he was Skilled." She hoped he had been Skilled. "It was a set-up so he would lose, so Weber could bring that creature in and let it feed—on me."

She'd thought she had a grip on her emotions, but her hands shook. She set her cup down before it slopped on her skirts. Why had he targeted her? What did she possess that made such a scheme worth it? Or rather, what *had* she possessed? Whatever it was, she no longer had it.

She turned her eyes up to Varrick. "Why did they want me?"

"Maybe convenience. Maybe to blackmail Mr. Leighton." He trailed off, rubbing his chin and frowning at the fire. "I suspect it has more to do with your heritage."

Delphine took a sip of tea, still hot despite the milk. Heritage. *Being an ambassador's daughter? Half-Eletheni? No.* With a start, she knew. "My great-grandfather."

"Elves have incredibly strong auras. I'm sure it considered you a feast." He watched her. "Weber may have known your family history."

History they thought hidden from Rockhaven. "My great-grandmother took a sea captain for a lover, bore a child out of wedlock—"

"Perfectly acceptable for a baroness of Elethen."

But not here. "We buried it. We had to bury it." She covered her ears that hinted but didn't quite confess. "Not even David knew."

"That doesn't change that you were a banquet, where the average human is a few bites of cake, at best."

"I like any other theory better." She rubbed her forehead,

knowing she was wrong. Weber had seen something in her he could use.

"The gambling den was the Indigo Elf." She couldn't escape her heritage, but she had no reason to hide it anymore. "Juliette is in league with Weber."

"We suspected it." He set his cup down. "You may have been a convenient meal for his creature, and someone whose damage wouldn't make ripples, because your husband would hide it."

"He's following me." She had too many emotions tonight. She wanted to go back to talking about his childhood. "Why?"

"I don't know." Varrick looked grave. "Maybe he thinks you can identify him. But we know him now. We know where we'll find him. We can put an end to this."

End Weber, end the hunt.

Would it end this little spark between them?

CHAPTER 38

Lessons in Desire

DELPHINE

Delphine poured herself another cup of tea. Varrick had people on his side. He had Morrow, Tanner and Mrs. Halsey, who had gone out hunting for whatever triggered the wards. He had the person who hired him.

Weber had Juliette.

Varrick was powerful and educated. What had Tanner said? He was the only magus on the continent strong enough to do this job. Weber couldn't be his match.

Varrick scratched behind one ear. "Something doesn't make sense. If it fed on you nine months ago, your aura should have started recovering."

Delphine almost dropped her cup. "What?"

He removed her cup and steadied her hands. "It didn't consume your whole aura, or you'd be comatose."

Like the man in the alley. Delphine clutched his hands, horrified at what might have happened. "I don't understand."

"Think of it as a tree. If you cut down a tree, it can grow back from the root, but if you tear out the root, it's truly dead." His ears swiveled forward. "Your roots are there. They just need a chance to regrow."

"But they haven't." She would have been ecstatic at even the thinnest wisp of healthy aura.

"Grief can stunt it. I didn't want to give you false hope, so I checked before saying anything." He released her hand to touch her cheek, fingers trailing down to her lips. "I have a suspicion, but I don't want to scare you."

"Can it be worse than what has already happened?" She shouldn't have asked; his expression grew grim.

"Yes, because that is all in the past, and this is—might be—ongoing."

Cold, seeping terror slipped up her legs, coiled about her trunk and squeezed the breath from her lungs. Delphine inhaled, but her chest refused to take it. It felt like even her heart had frozen in fear.

"Might be, Delphine. Might. Please." He lunged awkwardly to support her as she floundered. "Breathe."

"Tell me." She tumbled into his grasp, heedless of Talon and Sable scrabbling out of the way. *Ongoing. Sweet rivers.*

He lifted her into his lap as if she was made of air.

She flung her arms around him. "Your leg?"

"Will survive. Mrs. Halsey did wonders." He pulled her against his chest, so the thunder of his heart beat in one ear. "Can I explain now?"

His voice reverberated through her. She closed her eyes and nodded. If she was not safe here, in his arms, with the drakes at their feet, where would she ever be safe?

"Do you have any other blank spots in your memory?" he asked.

She wanted to hold onto the baritone comfort of his voice, not search her memories. There had been nights when she didn't recall going from her evening sitting room to bed. Days she'd woken up late, not understanding why. Even brief moments during walks where pieces of the day were missing. She'd dismissed them as grief.

"Yes." Delphine wanted her earlier anger back. Anger felt hot and powerful, so much better than sick, icy fear.

"I think Weber's creature has fed on you during these other times. As soon as your aura starts to regrow, it finds you and—"

She turned her face into his chest, heedless of the brass buttons and fine embroidery on his coat. She didn't want to hear the end of the sentence. It was stalking her, biding its time before pouncing on her.

"I suspect it's been testing our wards. That's why you've noticed them tripping, but we can't find anything. It's like trying to find a shadow in a forest at night." He tucked his face into her neck.

Delphine curled more tightly into him. She didn't want it to be true. How many times had it come? How many times had she been vulnerable and not known it? "How do I stop it?"

"I have to dematerialize it." He leaned his cheek into her jawline, careful to keep his horn away from her face. "I have to do my job, and do it perfectly, and soon."

"Why soon?" She did not like the sound of that.

He sat back and met her gaze. "If you want out of this altogether, we can arrange for you to leave for Elethen early. It would be a longer route, but you'd be safe."

She could leave everything behind and follow Mama and Alastair. The instinct to flee fought with how much she wanted to stay here in Varrick's arms. How could she leave him to face it?

She searched his face, looking for anything that would urge her to go or ask her to stay. Reaching up to follow the curve of his horn around, Delphine knew she wouldn't leave until it was done. She couldn't. She would spend forever looking over her shoulder, forever wishing she'd stayed.

"Use me as bait," she said.

He shook his head. "No."

"Draw in the creature and do whatever you do with them. Find Weber after."

"It's dangerous."

"It won't do anything more to me than it already has. If it wanted to glut itself and leave me blank, it could have several times already." For some reason, Weber didn't want her finished.

He rumbled in his throat. "I don't like it."

"I won't leave." She gripped his horn. "I have broken our contract. My heart is involved."

He caught her hand, turning it wrist up and brushing his lips where her veins showed. Her pulse beat a wild rhythm. He moved up her inner arm and kissed it again, running the tip of his tongue along the place so the kiss tingled hot and cold. Delphine held her breath, afraid to break the moment.

"Mine too," he whispered. "So I refuse to risk you."

The flush of his body heat washed over her. Teeth brushed against the tender skin of her inner arm. Fear evaporated. Thoughts evaporated. She caressed the thick silk of his hair, then the velvet softness of his ear, all the way to the tip, where the fine hair grew longer. His breath shuddered and his hands tightened.

She wasn't supposed to do that. "Sorry."

"You are allowed."

Her fingers traced down the lower side to the back of his jaw. His pulse drummed under her fingers, fast and strong.

His tongue traced a path to her inner elbow, where he brushed another kiss. Heat flushed down Delphine's chest to a warm coil in her stomach and below. Grasping both horns, she turned his face to hers and kissed him.

They needed to stop. They had Weber to find, and his creature to catch, his connection to Juliette to unravel, but Delphine pulled Varrick closer. She was tired of needs. She was ready for wants, and she wanted Varrick's mouth on hers, their bodies skin to skin with nothing between them.

The golden radiance of his anima flooded around them. The lock on the door clicked.

"No interruptions," he murmured.

He'd locked the world out. His anima wrapped around Delphine, warm, fizzing like strands of bubbles in sparkling wine. Tendrils of power slipped under the edges of her neckline and down her back to touch her own anima bloom between her shoulder blades. A ripple of sparks ran down her spine.

He pulled back, both of them breathing heavily. "I don't want to risk you, but I don't want to send you away."

"I'm not going away." She wouldn't think about what they'd do after. He'd promised her passage. She would sail over the horizon without him. *No. Together. There must be a way.*

Anima coiled around her neck, tipping her head back so he could kiss her throat. Delphine leaned back into the strength of his hands, the lines of his anima cradling her. He found the divot at the base of her throat and licked it, a low purr vibrating through them both.

Delphine bloomed her anima, twining the personal energy around his shoulders. She used it to pull the ribbon out of his hair so it tumbled across his shoulders. It smelled faintly of his cologne, spice and fresh oak blending with the scents of books, leather, and fire that permeated the library. She breathed it in, trying to memorize it.

They could continue what they'd started the night before, shedding the last of their clothes, sharing their bodies, all of their bright energy curling around one another. His mouth moved back to hers, the touch of his anima washing down her neck and over her body. She closed her eyes. If only they could push away the world and its demands long enough to explore one another, to know how it felt to lay her bare skin against the incredible texture of his body, all the way to her toes.

He nipped her lower lip. Her eyes flew open, the simmering desire threatening to come to a boil.

"Be careful," she murmured. "I know what I'm doing."

His chest heaved under her. "Good," he breathed. "I don't."

Delphine released his horns to run her hands through his hair.

How was she going to resist doing that every chance she could? It flowed thick and sleek over her fingers, the color of a green sea on a stormy day.

Regretfully, she slid her hands to his broad shoulders. "You mean we should stop?"

His hands tightened on her waist. "I mean I don't want to stop, but this is—" he searched for words, "—it wasn't included in my lessons."

Oh. *Ohhh*. She curled her fingers around his lapels. More things she didn't know about him. She'd assumed every young man had learned about bedplay. His golden eyes were serious, pupils wide and intent. When she'd been in such a position, what had she wanted from David?

She didn't want to think about David, not now, not ever again.

"What do you want to do?" she asked. "There's no rush."

A dark flush crossed his cheeks, rising to the tips of his ears, which he rotated back, then forward. "Touch me again, like you did last night."

"Under your shirt?"

He blinked and nodded. "Use your anima."

She pulled it from where it wrapped his arms, pale threads slipping under his coat, under the vest, between the gaps left by buttons to touch the center of his chest where his aura grew. Rooted, he'd said, like a tree.

"You can open it if you want." She spread her anima across his chest, savoring the distant sense of it touching solid muscle, smooth skin, and that fine, flocked hair. "It won't break my shield."

"You're sure?" He brushed her temple, fingers lingering on her cheek.

"Let me see you." She slid her anima slowly down the center of his chest, to the tip of his breastbone, over his tense stomach to his navel.

Deep magenta desire swirled all around them, turning the

library into a pink haze. Streaks of rich purple arousal drifted by in softer pools of pale pink. *Affection. Even love.*

Delphine ached to offer it back in the same way. The aura's center at her heart pulsed painfully. Her eyes burned, threatening tears.

"Tell me," she gulped, "if you want to stop. Or slow down."

"Please don't stop." Another wave of purple flowed out of him.

Talon pressed against her leg. A good reason to use a bedroom instead. She could slide her anima lower, below his navel, following the trail of hair down, but she wanted to savor this moment first.

Talon loosed a full-throated, ear-shattering bay. Sable followed. They lunged at the window, where the ward flashed.

Varrick pressed his forehead against Delphine's shoulder and growled a curse. His aura snapped closed as his anima blazed between them and the window.

Someone was pounding at the door.

Sweet rivers, damn it!

The drakes bayed full volume, hackles up. Still holding Delphine, Varrick rose and set her on her feet. His breathing was uneven, and he stumbled over the first incantation he tried, stopping to repeat it. His anima pulled away from her, racing down his arms as he traced a blazing circle in the air, flung it wide and traced a second inside it.

CHAPTER 39

The Hungry Void

DELPHINE

Sable and Talon backed against Delphine's skirts, howling and baying. The pounding on the door grew louder and more insistent.

Delphine rushed for the door and turned the lock.

Tanner, Mrs. Halsey, and Morrow burst through, brushing past her to flank Varrick. They wrapped anima around their arms, thick, brilliant lines of power.

As they poured their anima into Varrick's, he began etching symbols in the space between the first and second circle. Along the windowsill, the ward shifted from pale gold to dark red to black, darkness pulling at the frame.

Delphine pushed her back against the doorframe, not willing to flee, even though everything in her said she should. Hackles up, Talon retreated on stiff legs to press against her legs. His deep growl shook her. Sable stood in front of them, a last line of defense.

The darkness seeping through the window frame dribbled to the floor, coalescing into five or six slug-like creatures with tattered wings and empty slits for eyes. They kept melding into one another and reseparating as they oozed and bubbled across the floor, high pitched hisses screeching across Delphine's mind. Behind them, the entire window—-panes, frame, spacers, and sill —were consumed by a larger darkness. Wood popped and splintered. Glass shattered unseen as the shadow broke through.

Its attention riveted on Delphine. A wave of pure hunger swept over her. Her stomach felt hollow; her limbs trembled, weak, as if she hadn't eaten for days. The gnawing, starving, ravenous demand to be filled, to grasp and take what it could not create for itself, overwhelmed her. Her strength drained away, and she feared her flesh would follow until she was nothing but bones.

The large one was held at bay by the gleaming circles and Varrick's chant, but the smaller ones slithered past his feet, creeping toward her. Their hisses turned plaintive, like the screeching cries of hungry gryphon kits.

Sable backed away from them. Delphine cast about the room for something, anything that could help. Could she catch them? Contain them in something? If she ran, they would follow, and she couldn't create anything like Varrick's glowing sigil and runes.

But the teapot wasn't so far out of reach. She inched to the side, eyes on the slug-creatures. Talon and Sable shifted with her, holding a defensive line. If she went around the back of the chairs, she could snatch the teapot and do something with it.

The slugs didn't correct their course toward her. She took a breath, gauged the distance to the teapot, and darted behind the chairs. She lunged forward to catch the delicate porcelain handle before turning to face the hissing, mewling things.

One was pawing at Sable, who danced about to keep her feet from it. Another half-rose like a snake preparing to strike, twisting this way and that. Searching. For her. Its empty, see-through eyes landed on her and it shot forward with a cry. She tore the lid off the teapot. Heedless of the spilling tea, she held it between herself and the creature, tipped forward so the opening would scoop it up. *I hope.*

It twisted, tried to dodge. Delphine batted at it with the lid to herd it inside. It was determined to take the most direct path to her and plunged straight into the pot. She crammed the lid on afterward, catching both wings and part of the body. The parts left outside dissipated like morning mist.

Talon and Sable had two of the slugs occupied, but two more lumped and slithered to her feet. *Hungry. Hungry. Hungry.* Their cries thudded with her heartbeat, chanted with her pulse. Tiny claws tore at her skirts. The creature in the teapot pushed and snarled at the lid, crying now, hissing again, pleading and demanding in turn, no words, only feelings.

How did one fill such bottomless emptiness? It was nothing but a void. What was that quip Alastair used to infuriate her with? *You're not cold, little sister, you just lack heat. It's not dark, we just lack light.*

Lack. Light. Heat.

She flung the teapot into the fire.

It shattered in the flames. The creature twisted and writhed. Delphine pressed her hand to her mouth, equal parts horrified and guilty, as if she'd thrown a kit onto a bonfire.

It didn't burn, crackle, or curl away. It devoured, sucking in the flames until the darkness of its body was flickering red and yellow. Full of fire. For how long?

Varrick's chant rolled through the room like summer thunder.

The creature in the fire rolled, ecstatic, making squeaks of pleasure. The two harassing the drakes perked up. Far quicker than they'd attacked, they scurried toward their fellow in the fire. The two clawing at her feet paused, then did the same, until all five leapt on the rapidly dying flames, fighting and hissing at one another. The room already felt cooler.

If they destroyed—devoured?—the fire, what then? It wasn't harming them, just satisfying their hunger for a time.

Varrick's circle had lines crisscrossing it like a spider web. It pushed back at the nothingness that threatened to consume every bit of light, magic, life. The large creature's cries scraped across her mind, claws on metal, that same blend of pleading and threatening, infinite hunger.

Want. Need. Desire. Desire. You. Bright. Tassssty.

If she fed ...

Devour.

If she fed the fire, it might keep the smaller ones satisfied.

Never. Satisfied.

Delphine steadied herself on the chair. Hunger sucked at her movement, pulled at her, drew her, a maelstrom trying to suck her to its bottom. One step, then two, three, four, to the fireplace and the stack of split wood beside it. The coals were fading as she curled her fingers around a piece and shoved it into the deepest, hottest part of the dying fire.

Nothing. She shook as the voice beat on her. Tiny flames licked at the wood and the piece caught. She fed another to the coals, and the little nothinglings scurried around the inside of the fireplace like shadow squirrels.

The larger darkness twisted and churned, formless and seething, held at bay. Varrick advanced step by step, pushing it back. It snarled but couldn't escape the sparking power of the circles and runes. Delphine fed stick after stick to the little fire as the keening, boiling darkness fled out the window. Varrick pressed his circle into the wall, tracing connections between the empty sill and the intricate web of power pulsing across the circles.

The room fell silent except for the contented hisses of the residues in the fire.

The golden light of the anima circle faded to a soft glow. Tanner, Mrs. Halsey, and Morrow drew their anima in, the threads barely a shimmer in the air.

Varrick withdrew his still-bright anima from the circle. The circle etched in the wall and the web in the middle persisted, flickering like a candle but holding.

All four turned to look at her. She was a mess, huddled by the fire, tea spilled down the front of her gown, shattered pieces of the teapot on the hearthstones, and five horrid creatures in the fireplace, lapping up the flames as quickly as she fed them.

Tanner tsked. Morrow's eyebrow rose to his hairline, and Mrs. Halsey's mouth twisted into what might have been a smile before she smoothed it away.

"We're trying to be rid of them, not feed them." A tinge of amusement colored Tanner's words.

Delphine added another piece of wood. "I wanted them to stop trying to feed on me."

Varrick came to hunker beside her, careful of the broken porcelain. "They're more intelligent than I thought. They know to wait for the wood to catch well."

"We are not studying them," Mrs. Halsey said.

Varrick spun a sphere of anima, hollowing it out into something like a birdcage. "But think what we could learn. They're little. Controllable. Maybe trainable."

Tanner shook her head. "And when they grow?"

Varrick sighed, then nodded. "I'll dematerialize them." He spread his hands, the cage expanding with them, and opened his aura. He pushed it into the cage, making it pulse bright blue with curiosity. Bait.

"Let the fire go out," he whispered.

Delphine nodded. They were quickly devouring the remaining flames, the fire dying back to coals and the pieces of partially-burnt wood. The room cooled again. They sucked the heat from the stone of the fireplace as they fought over the last of the flames.

"Look over here," Varrick murmured, widening the opening of the cage. Runes began to glow in the spaces between the anima bars.

The fire gone, even the coals going black and cold, the residues whimpered in scratchy little voices and hissed at Varrick. He grew his swirling bit of aura so it filled the cage. Like before, it took them a moment to understand, then they converged on his aura in a wave, right into the cage.

Delphine startled as he snapped the anima shut around them and withdrew his aura. They screeched, but the cage shrunk, tighter and tighter, until all five collapsed into a single creature, a ball of oblivion, a pinpoint of darkness, then they were gone.

Varrick pulled his anima in and blew out a long breath.

"Mrs. Halsey," Tanner said. "Get Bethie to help clean this up. Morrow and one of the stable hands will board up the window until it can be replaced." They both nodded and left. "Mrs. Leighton—"

Delphine rose, refusing to wince or shudder. "Tanner."

"I will see you to your bed." She put slight emphasis on *you* and *your*. The word *alone* didn't need to be said.

Delphine disliked being made to feel like a debutante who'd wandered too far into the gardens with a gentleman. "May I take Talon and Sable?"

Tanner's stiff shoulders relaxed. "Yes. We will reinforce the wards on your windows as well, but I suggest you avoid—" she glanced at Varrick, "—strong emotion."

Varrick flicked his ears back, face bland.

Strong emotion was certainly one way to describe what had been happening. "Did that draw it here?"

"It had to have been close," Varrick said. "I have a suspicion. Not an encouraging one."

Delphine swallowed. Even Tanner looked worried.

"I don't think Weber has control of his creature. Not this one, anyway."

"There might be more than one?" What an appalling thought. The small ones had lost some of their impact, but the one that forced its way through the window, crying hunger into her mind …

She felt like she'd plunged into the river again, darkness and cold closing around her.

Varrick laid his ears back. "If he lost control of the first one, he might have summoned a second one to use, yes."

Delphine steadied herself against the mantelpiece over the fireplace.

Tanner looked at her hands. "Do we need to find more help?"

Delphine turned to Varrick. Tanner was asking if he was strong enough to dismiss two of the creatures and deal with Weber.

"We don't have time. If Weber can summon one or two, he can summon more. We find him, then we deal with the shadows." He stepped toward Delphine but stopped when Tanner caught his arm.

"You are sure?" she asked.

"I am. If we wait, more people will be attacked and hurt. We'll start with Weber and the Indigo Elf."

CHAPTER 40

In the Dark

DELPHINE

Talon and Sable happily draped themselves across Delphine's bed, grunting when she pushed them this way and that to make room under the covers. Although scaly, drakes produced plenty of body heat when they chose. She wouldn't even notice if the fire went out.

She turned, elbowing Talon between the shoulder blades so he'd move over and stared at the canopy of the bed several feet above. The drakes made her feel safe, but they didn't alleviate loneliness, nor did they satisfy everything else that had been stirred up earlier.

The passage between the rooms loomed large in her mind. She could creep through there with no one the wiser. She could just stretch out next to Varrick and enjoy his warmth and company.

Talon snored. Sable's tail thumped her ankles.

She was fooling herself. If she curled up under the covers with him, they wouldn't be circumspect. They wouldn't want to be. *He* wouldn't want to be. He'd made that clear. A girlish pleasure flushed through her. It was strange and wonderful to feel desired again. She'd been an object to men like Lord Monteshreve, but Varrick saw her as precious and important. It had been too long since she'd felt that.

She pulled the covers up to her chin. *I know what I'm doing.*

'Good. I don't,' he'd said.

He'd never had a lover. She covered her face.

Well, he was young, four years her junior. But men started experimenting early, didn't they? David and his friends had laughed over their youthful conquests when she was supposed to be out of earshot. She had assumed that Varrick would have had a lover, or at least a night of passion. What was she supposed to do with a man who didn't know what he was supposed to do?

And she'd quipped to Juliette about training him ... If only the bed would swallow her.

Although he'd been doing just fine. He certainly knew how to kiss. He had a deft touch—with both hands and anima. His aura ...

She rolled to the other side, making Talon snort. Her aura could come back. It wasn't completely gone. If they finally destroyed the creature, she could share her aura with him without fear of being overwhelmed. They could fully taste each other's passion and desire. But only if they caught Weber and the thing that had come for her tonight.

Varrick was confident he was strong enough, but Weber was dangerous. Juliette could be as well. Men dismissed pretty women, especially if they looked small and delicate. But a woman who ran a gambling den like the one Severson had described wouldn't be weak. She would be smart and cutthroat. She would have to be.

Juliette knew Bertram. Severson said Bertram was there the night David lost so badly. The night he'd described to Varrick might not have been his first time witnessing Weber's work.

Delphine sat up, disturbing both drakes, who looked at her with despairing eyes. "Bertram said he didn't remember who the magus was," she said to them. "But he was at the Indigo Elf when David lost to Weber."

She doubted he was holding back, not after Varrick started lighting up the room with anima and runes. So, Bertram hadn't remembered or hadn't been certain. He might have said more if Juliette hadn't interrupted. That might be why she interrupted.

They should go after Juliette first. Delphine slid out from under the covers and set her feet on the chilly wooden floor. Just going to the Indigo Elf wasn't enough; they had to corner her and find out what she knew before they confronted Weber. She padded across the floor to the passage door and stopped.

Varrick would be asleep. He had used a lot of anima tonight, even if he'd had support. Her convictions could wait until morning. She stood there, toes growing cold, wrestling with sense. Nothing good would come of waking him, and Tanner had warned against strong emotions.

Rubbing her face, she turned back to the bed. The creature had been driven back, but it was out there, possibly prowling the grounds, looking for her. The thought was better than a bucket of cold water for controlling her less ladylike desires. It didn't ease her inclination to go crawl into bed with Varrick. She'd feel safer with him. Drakes could warn but not defend against the creature.

She touched the cunningly hidden knob, nearly flush with the wall and matching the intricate border of the paneling. She had plenty of practice reining herself in. She'd bitten back her words and hidden her thoughts often enough. She could make herself go back to bed.

She could.

She would.

She should make sure Varrick was well, first. Just make sure he was sleeping peacefully. She wouldn't wake him. She would come right back.

The knob turned with barely a click. Delphine left the door open and trailed her fingers on the wall through the stuffy passage. In the pitch dark, she fumbled until she found the knob to let her into Varrick's room.

It rattled but didn't turn. Locked.

He'd locked her out.

The warmth in her chest drained away. It had been a silly ruse to pull on herself anyway. They both needed rest, and they'd signed the contract. The attack tonight must have convinced him it ought to be followed to the letter.

Delphine trudged back to bed. She shouldn't have tried to visit him. Then she wouldn't be fighting the tight misery in her throat.

Talon rearranged himself with several grunts when she crawled back into bed and curled up against him. Her toes and shoulders were chilled again. Why was sadness so much harder to push away than fear?

She slept eventually but only knew it because she woke up when early light sneaked under the bed curtains.

Tanner came in early, briskly laying out a day dress for Delphine and selecting combs for her hair. Delphine pulled the bed curtain back and frowned at her. It was tempting to behave like a petulant lady, except Tanner wasn't really her lady's maid.

"No hurry," Tanner said. "I need to be ready for the day, but you might be out late, so a little more sleep would be in order."

"I won't complain." Delphine pulled the blanket away from Sable who made a grumpy noise and plopped to the floor.

Sable nuzzled at Tanner until Tanner opened the door for her, prompting Talon to thump down and follow.

"Trust me," Tanner said, "you want them to take their morning constitutional earlier rather than later."

"Is Varrick up?" Delphine's stomach rumbled. She'd barely picked at dinner last night.

Tanner looked back from the door. "I'm sure he'll be up soon. The kitchen can prepare breakfast if you're ready."

Delphine's stomach gurgled. "Yes, please."

"I'll be back." Tanner stepped out and shut the door behind her.

The pitcher and basin by the vanity had been filled, and Delphine splashed water on her face. In the daylight, the events of the night before felt distant and surreal, like an opera she'd watched while drunk. There'd been a beautiful heroine, a strong hero, an assortment of villains—if she wanted to cast Severson and Everard as henchmen—and a legendary creature come to devour the maiden. Although she was hardly a maiden and had come close to making herself less of one.

Maybe Varrick was the maiden.

She missed her splash of water and sent it straight up her nose, which left her snorting and trying not to laugh. She could picture herself in the gentleman's role, out to save his lady-love, who was big, green, and hid his innocence better than one would expect.

Delphine dried her face. She struggled to regain her composure before Tanner returned but didn't think she could watch another opera with a straight face. In any case, she couldn't rescue Varrick. What did he need to be rescued from? He had a place at the Scholarium, an education most people couldn't dream of, and a clear purpose in his life.

Beyond this hunt, he needed nothing from her.

The accomplishments of a Rockhaven lady had never felt so empty; she would have been better off learning how to handle a crossbow or musket than languages and deportment.

"I envy you." He had a place, but not people. Not truly. Could she give him that?

Tanner returned to help her dress.

"When you said a late night," Delphine asked as Tanner worked, "did you mean we'll be going to the Indigo Elf tonight? Or somewhere else?"

"I hardly think Varrick is going to receive a gilded invitation, so you may be crashing their party," she grinned, a sharp edge of glee in her voice.

CHAPTER 41

An Uninvited Guest

DELPHINE

After yesterday's events, the household had dropped all pretenses. Mrs. Edward herself brought a tray of crumpets to the table and Tanner and Mrs. Halsey joined Delphine. Bethie scurried through a moment later with a covered tray for Varrick.

Delphine took her seat. "Is this where you all put your cards on the table?" Sitting with the two other women at the dining table, while they both wore their uniforms, felt stranger than walking on water.

"The creature is stalking you." Mrs. Halsey took a crumpet and buttered it. "That increases your risk considerably."

"How comforting. Before, I was just at risk of being dumped in the river." Her risk hadn't changed. It had been stalking her before she ever met Varrick. Only her knowledge of the risk had changed.

Mrs. Halsey exchanged a glance with Tanner. "We decided it was better to explain what we know."

Delphine took her own crumpet and spread butter and jam into the nooks and crannies. "The wretch summoned a monster, attacked me with it, may have lost control of it, summoned another one, and is attacking other people and destroying their auras. Varrick was brought here to stop him." She took a bite. "You're here to help him and make sure he doesn't run off with some tart."

Tanner's lips pinched, but Mrs. Halsey snorted so hard she nearly dropped her crumpet.

"She's not wrong, Gertrude." Mrs. Halsey poured herself a cup of tea. "And Varrick's virtue isn't our responsibility. Or business."

"It is while we are hunting down a dangerous magus and who-knows-how-many elementals." Tanner glared at the crumpets. "He needs to stay sharp."

Mrs. Halsey handed a cup to Delphine and pushed another to Tanner.

"Thank you." Delphine sipped. "So, what should I know that I don't already?"

"Just a moment." Tanner rose and left the room, returning with a large roll of paper, which she spread out on the table. It was a map of Rockhaven, with several places marked, each labeled with a date. "Your story explains why the pattern didn't make sense. Where were you living when you were attacked?"

"Our home was here." It sat among the smaller townhouses of the city. The Leighton family had lost its country estate long before.

There were three marks within blocks of where she'd lived with David, and not one but two in the streets near her squalid room. She shuddered.

Tanner took a tiny ball of fabric from her pocket, spun a trace of anima into it, and stuck it where Delphine had indicated on the map. The three marks around it were all from after her initial attack, the earliest from when David was alive. She pressed her fingers to the base of her throat to stop the sick fluttering. The creature had been there all along.

The other marks were all past Everard's and the other sprawling city estates, where the high-class billiard rooms, gentlemen's clubs and gambling dens stood on a road that bordered the university grounds. Magi liked to gamble, too. Seven marks dotted that neighborhood, with two more in the residential area bordering it.

Only five had happened close to where Delphine lived. Even after she'd moved, they followed her. Five—six, if she included herself—over nine months. And she'd had odd turns and blanks in her memory at least twice a month.

"All those marks, were they people who'd been fully, ah, devoured?" she braced for the worst answer.

Tanner nodded. "None of them will wake again. One was dead, although he died of exposure, not the attack."

Delphine pressed harder against the fluttering. "Which one?"

It was the last man, the one that had clawed at her doorknob, desperate for an escape. It had to be.

"The black one." Tanner pointed.

Yes. Just outside of her lodgings. If she had opened the door for him, would his life have been saved? But if the other victims never woke, death wasn't much worse. Like trees ripped out by the roots, Varrick had said. They wouldn't grow back.

"Why didn't it do that to me? Was I just lucky, or did Weber rein it in?" Its voice echoed in her memory, the screeching sound of iron nails on stone. Its hunger lingered on her tongue, raw and salty, like blood.

"Only Weber can answer that." Mrs. Halsey came around the table to stand beside Tanner. "We were puzzled over how the attacks were clustered, but it makes sense now. The escaped creature is following you, while Weber has the other on a leash."

"Where's the Indigo Elf on here?"

Tanner tapped a spot further up the border street between Rockhaven and the university grounds. It was far enough inland to be in the better part of the city, but not on the hills where the richest citizens lived. All the club attacks were within a few blocks of it.

"Regarded as a respectable club." Tanner snorted. "That's all Rockhaven cares about. Presentation and appearances."

Delphine sighed. "Respectability." The little markings on the map mocked her. "I hope this hunt of ours was worth giving up all of mine." She shouldn't care, but she couldn't shake the conditioning of two decades off her shoulders.

"Respectability is a poor substitute for what truly matters," Mrs. Halsey patted Delphine's hand. "It is a capricious currency at best."

"Most capricious. It can evaporate at one wrong word."

So why was she trying to hold onto it?

"And self-pity is a poor ornament for either lady or mistress." Tanner rerolled the map. "You needed money, and now you have it. We agreed to find you passage to Elethen, and we will."

Delphine would have a chance to rebuild her life as the granddaughter of Baron Bollenbaucher. She would be introduced to a society full of new rules and faces. Mama and Alastair would be there. She would have a place in the world again.

Without Varrick. "What will Varrick do when this is done?"

"He will return to his studies in Istalia. He was quite upset that they were interrupted." Tanner nodded curtly and took the map away.

Mrs. Halsey finished her crumpet and chose another.

The heavy echo of the front door knocker startled her. The sound of the door opening and Morrow's grave tones followed, then a familiar voice.

Delphine stared at Mrs. Halsey. "What is Edwina doing here?"

Mrs. Halsey set her crumpet back on the platter and gathered up the extra plates. "I don't know, but I imagine she'd be shocked to find you breakfasting with your housekeeper." She marched out as Morrow entered.

"Lady Havemshire is here, Mrs. Leighton. Will you receive her in the sitting room?" A lift of his brows and a glance to one side told her she ought to.

"Yes, please." She wasn't properly dressed for company, but Edwina was family, and hadn't she just been considering the advantage of being outside of proper society?

Why does it still bind me?

CHAPTER 42

Snowdrop

DELPHINE

Edwina stood in the middle of the sitting room, clutching a covered basket and looking like she expected beasts to lunge at her any moment.

"Edwina?" The guilt that Delphine had been ignoring since the opera poured over her.

Edwina placed the basket on the settee and flung her arms around Delphine. "Oh Dellie! I've felt just awful since we saw you last. I begged and begged Michael to do something." She broke off, too distraught to go on.

Delphine closed her eyes, struggling to keep her aura's shields tight against the swirling tide of Edwina's emotions. Guilt. Grief. Fear. Anticipation? Delphine patted Edwina's shoulder awkwardly.

"It's—I'll be alright." Life had been easier when she could have wordlessly Skilled Edwina calm, assuring her, heart to heart, that she didn't blame her. "I was unforgivably nasty to you at the opera. I am so sorry."

Edwina sniffled, pulling a hanky that was mostly lace from one sleeve and uselessly dabbing her eyes. "Already forgotten."

"What are you doing here?" Delphine asked. Seeing Severson the night before had been shocking enough; she'd never thought she'd see Edwina again.

"I got your message the other night. The constable came and said you'd been in an accident." She daintily blew her nose. "You might have been killed! I felt so guilty after you left the house that day. I asked Michael for help. I wrote you—"

"I have your letter." Delphine guided her to sit on the settee next to her basket.

Edwina dabbed her eyes again. "I begged him to see you, but he wouldn't. I even asked him to give you my next allowance, and he said no. That he'd take it away from me."

Just for that second, it was good that Delphine's aura was shredded smoke. The bleak, black hatred that roiled up for her brother-in-law could not have been hidden. She sat in the chair opposite Edwina and took a long slow breath.

"You did what you could." How dare Michael threaten Edwina for asking him to be generous! Delphine clasped her hands together to keep them from shaking.

"I didn't then, but now I have." With a final dab and sniff, Edwina tucked the hanky back up her sleeve and set the basket on her lap. "Michael will notice if I sell jewelry, but he doesn't care about my gryphons."

The basket chirped.

Anticipation. What had Edwina been planning?

"I am touched." Delphine couldn't take her eyes off the basket. "That you're here, that you're trying to help, but Mr. Allard is helping me sort things out."

"But you have to—" Edwina looked away, blushing bright red. Her voice dropped to a whisper, "—have to do *things* with him. I had to help."

"So you're saving me from the horrors of bedding him?"

Ironic, that Edwina wanted to rescue her from something that hadn't yet happened. *Not for lack of temptation.*

"Must you say it that way?" Edwina looked reproachful. "The kits are big enough to leave their momma and Chrysanthemum is ready for them to be gone, believe me."

She opened the hinged lid on the basket and lifted out a tiny gryphon kit, pure white feathers unmarked by banding, fuzzy coat showing only the palest gray striping on the tail and toes. It yawned, laying back black-tipped ears.

"She's the most perfect of the litter. As a breedable female with impeccable lineage, she's easily worth five thousand thalens to the right buyer. Possibly more." She offered the kit to Delphine with both hands.

Instinctively, Delphine held her hands out to take it.

The door swung open with a crash as Talon and Sable bounded in, making a beeline for Delphine. Edwina screamed. The gryphon screeched. Delphine held it above her head, unsure what the drakes would do.

The gryphon, unable to climb higher, took flight, wobbling on its wings to the nearest perch on top of the tall grandfather clock in the corner. From there, it took another leaping glide to the top drapery rod, out of Delphine's reach, and hunched down to growl and glower at the drakes.

Too well-mannered to jump, Talon pranced and bounced, rump wriggling, tail thrashing. Edwina wailed and hid behind Delphine.

The door flung open a second time, a wave of golden anima bursting through a heartbeat before Varrick barreled in. He held one hand in front of him, wrapped in his anima, ready for battle, no vest or coat, cravat sliding off to the floor.

Edwina screamed again, her wide-open aura, pure and bright with fear, crashed over Delphine. Talon and Sable bounded to Varrick, then back to Delphine, quite proud of the chaos they'd wrought.

Varrick stared at his anima-wrapped hand, then at Edwina. He retracted the anima and tucked his hand behind his back, as if that would undo his threatening entrance.

"Dellie," Edwina whispered. She pressed into Delphine's back, trying to hide.

Delphine reached back, caught Edwina's hand, and squeezed it. "Edwina, I'd like to introduce you to my—my patron, Magus Varrick Allard. And his drakes."

"Pleased to meet you, Lady Havemshire." Varrick bowed his head, flushing, embarrassment shining in his corona. "I apologize for my alarming entrance, I heard screams and assumed there was a threat."

Edwina whimpered. "Threat?"

Trying to explain the elementals and attacks to Edwina wouldn't be easy. She didn't want to alarm the sensitive woman more. Best to gloss over it.

"The drakes surprised us, and she's not used to such large creatures inside." Delphine inched to the side, pulling Edwina up beside her.

Talon tried to snuffle her, making Edwina squeak.

"Scratch his crest and he'll be your friend forever," Delphine said. "They're gentle giants."

"Is he?" Her hand stretched toward Talon, but her glance darted to Varrick. She could have been asking about either.

Talon slurped her hand, and she yelped.

Varrick cleared his throat. "Talon. Sable. Place."

They trotted to the room's fireplace and sat.

Edwina fanned her face, still clutching Delphine's arm. "I thought they were going to eat poor Snowdrop."

"Snowdrop?" Varrick's ears swiveled and he cocked his head.

Delphine was just as confused until it dawned on her. "The kit." She pointed to the top of the largest window. "The drakes scared her."

"She's just a baby," Edwina whispered.

Varrick rubbed his chin, ears going forward and pupils growing wide. Snowdrop huddled at the top of the drapes, peeping in distress. "Ah."

Edwina was too distraught to help, and Delphine would need her aura to coax the tiny kit down. "Can you get her?"

She guided Edwina to the nearest chair. It was the least she could do. Edwina adored her gryphons. There was no greater gesture of care and concern her sister-in-law could have made. It made Delphine more ashamed than ever of losing her temper at the opera.

Approaching the curtains slowly, Varrick made cooing noises until the gryphon peered over the edge of the drapes. It cheeped at him and cocked its head for a closer look.

"Come on now, sweet little girl." Varrick opened his aura to let a strand of reassurance brush the creature. "Come down and I'll take you to your lady."

He reached up, Skilling it with his aura, sending gentle waves of calm and security so it trusted him. It kept its eyes on him until his aura coaxed it down the drapes to his hand. Nudging his fingers and rubbing its head against his palm, it relaxed.

"There now, sweetheart." Varrick scooped it up with one hand and cradled it close to his body.

Delphine felt, rather than saw, the ripple of surprise followed by relief and admiration that flowed from Edwina's aura. Her own heart melted watching him fuss over the kit. He cooed and clicked at her, moving slowly and gently so she wouldn't take fright again.

Snowdrop sunk her claws into his forearm before relaxing into his chest.

"Pretty girl." He stroked it between its eyes until he was rewarded with the curious high-pitched purr of a gryphon. "Let's take you back to your lady."

Edwina reached for the gryphon, her aura swirling with gratitude. "You saved her!"

"She's beautiful." Varrick stroked the gryphon between her wings. She trilled in contentment.

Delphine dropped into the other chair, watching the emotions crossing Edwina's aura. There was a sort of wonder there, as if the moment had opened a whole world of thought in her sister-in-law. Was it simply surprise that a man might care about her pets?

Edwina took Snowdrop from him. "She's the best of my litter out of Chrysanthemum and Snowpeak. She's Delphine's."

Varrick turned a brilliant, hopeful look on her. "She's a gorgeous little thing."

"Snowdrop is just eight weeks old. She'll impress on you in no time, Dellie." Edwina handed the kit over. "Her pedigree papers are in the basket."

Snowdrop chirped at Delphine and glided to Varrick's shoulder.

Delphine met his eyes. No matter what Edwina said, the kit has decided to be Varrick's. "Thank you, Edwina. We will make sure she's well taken care of."

Edwina smiled, looking down at her lap. A wisp of sadness swirled through her aura, but she pulled it back. "I must go. It has been an interesting visit, but I should be home before Lord Havemshire returns."

Delphine rose. "I'll walk you out. Snowdrop is happy right where she is."

In the foyer, Edwina pulled on her gloves and adjusted her hat. The sadness swirled through her aura again. "I do hope things go well for you, Dellie. I will miss you."

CHAPTER 43

Planning the Hunt

DELPHINE

Delphine returned to the sitting room, where Varrick had coaxed Snowdrop from his shoulder to the crook of his arm.

"You've fallen in love, I see," she smiled, as much at him as at Edwina's well wishes.

He blushed, ears out. "Is that so obvious?"

"You know, Edwina gave her to me so I could sell her and pay my way out of a fate worse than death."

"She knew about Stokes?"

In Varrick's arms, Snowdrop lay calm and purring. If gryphons acted like this more often, she wouldn't mind owning one.

Delphine would be purring if he held her like that. "No. She meant you, although you did the one thing that would change her opinion." *I'm jealous of a gryphon.*

"Nothing else important from Lady Havemshire?" He cooed at Snowdrop.

Smitten. No doubt, Snowdrop would be as well-behaved for him as Sable, who lay by the fireplace with Talon.

"Just Snowdrop." She reached out and stroked the kit. Snowdrop rewarded her by purring more loudly and kneading Varrick's arm.

Michael wouldn't notice that one of the kits was gone, but the situation left her uneasy. She couldn't repay Edwina, and the glimpse into her marriage with Michael was uncomfortable. Had Delphine been so wrapped up in her misery these past few years that she never noticed Edwina's?

"You look sad," Varrick said.

"When things were bad with David, I used to wish I'd married someone like Michael. Dependable. Responsible. I was jealous of Edwina."

"But not anymore?"

Maybe there is no happily ever after. "No. Not anymore."

She ought to ask him where he would go when this was done, but she'd rather pretend they had a chance of happiness. If she didn't hear his plans, she could imagine him joining her in Elethen.

Mrs. Halsey entered and raised her eyebrows at the sight of Varrick and Snowdrop. "If Lady Havemshire is gone, perhaps you two would join us in plotting how to approach Weber and Singleton."

Varrick lifted Snowdrop to his shoulder.

Delphine joined Mrs. Halsey near the door. "Plotting makes it sound so nefarious."

"Well," she said with a smile, "one must be a bit wicked when dealing with the unscrupulous."

"I should like to be downright malevolent." Let the creature devour Weber before Varrick pressed it into a point of night and dispatched it. Let him feel her fear, beat for beat, until his heart stopped.

"That's the spirit." Mrs. Halsey walked beside Delphine as they crossed the entry hall, Varrick trailing behind them.

Delphine glanced at Varrick, but his face had gone closed and blank, the only part of his aura visible was a strand keeping Snowdrop calm.

Tanner and Morrow stood at the desk, looking down at the same map Tanner had brought out that morning. They'd marked the Indigo Elf with a little blue circle. When they spotted Snowdrop, Tanner shook her head while Morrow grinned.

"Weber is probably working out of the Indigo Elf." Morrow tapped the map. "Getting in is the quickest way to find him."

"We can't just show up," Delphine said. "Clubs like that are members or invitation only. After what happened at Everard's, we'll never get Varrick through the front door."

Morrow drummed his fingers on the table. "Perhaps we can convince Miss Singleton to speak with you."

Delphine shook her head. "Women don't go to those places alone. Not even mistresses or widows."

"They'll let you in." Varrick said. "Weber wants you."

Gooseflesh crept up Delphine's arms. "Will he, now that he knows you're hunting him?"

"He needs to regain control of his first creature." Varrick leaned over the map. "So long as it follows you, so will he."

Delphine shivered.

"How can you be so sure?" Tanner asked. "I doubt he cares who it hurts."

"They aren't meant to be physical. It's starving and in pain, and he's the reason." Varrick clasped Delphine's hand. "Eventually, it will attack him. It's inevitable as sunset."

"I wish I knew what he's actually gaining from this," Mrs. Halsey said.

"Some people just like to hurt others." Tanner walked around the table, as if studying the map from a different angle would help. "Cruelty might be the point."

"Why doesn't matter," Varrick said. "Only stopping him does."

"We could trick her into helping us." *What would entice Juliette to allow me inside?* "Morrow, do you know anything about her? The other mistresses at Everard's said she manages escorts, not just gambling."

Morrow cleared his throat. "Most such places have ladies, and sometimes young gentlemen, for the entertainment of players."

"Oh." Delphine looked at her fingers.

"Winners celebrate. Losers get consoled," Morrow continued.

"Don't elaborate," Mrs. Halsey said.

Morrow looked bland but not contrite. "If Miss Singleton thought you'd parted ways with Mr. Allard and needed money—"

"No." Delphine shook her head. "She won't take pity on anyone, and certainly not me." At least she hadn't called the woman a goose to her face.

"Not pity," Morrow said. "But gloating? You interfered with her at Everard's. I think she'd love the chance to humiliate you."

"You want to send Delphine in alone?" Varrick flattened his ears. "How does that get me in?"

Tanner folded her arms and exchanged an unhappy glance with Mrs. Halsey. "You think Singleton will serve her straight up to Weber?"

"That's what I'm afraid of," Varrick said. "You can't send her there alone. She doesn't have enough anima to defend herself."

Delphine winced. It was true. "I go in, I talk with Juliette, plead for ... what? To be one of her escorts? And she sends me to Weber? Do you have a plan beyond that, Morrow?" She'd told Varrick to use her as bait, but she'd pictured him ten feet away in the shadows, not outside while she was trapped in the bowels of a brothel.

"I mean, if you don't have your own anima, Mrs. Leighton, black market is fine." Morrow raised his eyebrows at Tanner, who sighed and nodded.

"I don't understand." Delphine said, bewildered.

"Artifacts of stored anima," Varrick said. "Like the pearls Juliette wore. I wasn't aware you had any, Morrow."

"We have a small selection." Tanner spoke over Delphine's

head to Varrick. "Your patron was unsure of Weber's strength and wanted to be certain both the creature and the summoner were dealt with."

Varrick's patron. The mysterious person of rank.

"I'm going to assume that you're using the term patron in a different sense than Varrick and I have been using it." Delphine was so tired of guessing at things.

Varrick's ears went even flatter, a dark flush rising across his cheeks. "Benefactor. Not Patron. So, if we send Delphine in with an artifact, what is she supposed to do once she's trapped with Weber?"

"I vote for blowing out a window—a signal and an entrance." Morrow grinned.

"I've no idea how to use an artifact." Delphine wasn't sure Morrow's plan would go so smoothly, either. "What if there isn't a window? Or I can't signal Varrick in time?"

"Varrick can teach you, and Morrow can scout the building so we know as much about it as possible," Tanner said. "If—and only if—we can send Mrs. Leighton in safely, we will proceed. Otherwise, we will find another way. Agreed?"

Delphine agreed, but Tanner was speaking to Morrow and the others, who, after a pause, also assented.

CHAPTER 44
Lessons in Magery

DELPHINE

"You know," Delphine said the next morning, "when I took this position, I was promised pretty dresses and glamorous events, not breakfast before dawn and emergency training in the arcane."

"I recommend coffee." Varrick set a steaming cup in front of her and took a seat at the dining room table. "It's not actually arcane training. It's merely powerful Crafting."

Snowdrop stalked along the top of the drapes, chirping to herself. She'd followed Varrick down from his room.

"I'll take your word for it." It was less intimidating to think of it as Crafting. She'd woven heat into blankets and prolonged the life of cut flowers. Bashing a window out sounded easier than either.

She sipped the coffee, aware that Varrick was watching her. She had gotten better at reading his facial expressions even when his aura was locked. Ears forward, pupils half-dilated, brows scrunched together. He was worried about her. Sweet rivers, who else had been truly concerned about her lately? Apart from Edwina.

"Are you sure you want to follow through with this part?" He held his cup but didn't drink. "Juliette may be as dangerous as Weber."

"Except I could beat her in a wrestling match." Weber looked like he could throw Delphine across the room; she'd rather deal with Juliette.

Varrick's eyes grew distant.

"If you're picturing such a match, I'm going to kick you," Delphine said. Distraction indeed.

"I was not." His ears laid back. "Not with Juliette. Not Juliette with you. You, um."

"Mmm-hmmm." She took another sip of the coffee. It was an acquired taste, but she could picture having it every morning, perhaps with milk. With Varrick.

Where? Did she expect him to come to Elethen with her and live at Grandpapa's? He had a life, a place, at the Scholarium. He wouldn't want to give that up. And what about his mysterious benefactor?

His kisses were more than kindness, and the passion and desire in his aura could not be faked. Was there anything to stop him from joining her if he wished?

Did he wish? The question stuck in her throat.

Varrick drank his coffee. "Tanner has prepared some things for you in the library."

Artifacts. They would not leave her vulnerable, exposed like a fawn in a field while hunters waited for the lion to pounce. "We'd better go see them."

In the library, an ornate wooden box sat on the large desk, radiating a faint golden light.

Tanner nodded at Delphine. "Juliette's access to elven artifacts concerns me. It makes her far more dangerous. But she has shown her hand, so we can prepare for her."

"She isn't the only person with access to artifacts." Varrick tapped the box. "I'll teach you to use the ones we have."

"I only know basic Crafting. I can weave warming into a cup of tea or freshness on a plate of cake, but not much else." Depleted anima was a different loss than her aura, but she'd locked it up and stopped using it just the same.

"The artifacts carry their own anima, and it's easily accessible," Tanner said. "So long as you can bloom the weakest strand, you can use them."

"That's why they're so valuable," Varrick commented. "They can be used without draining yourself. I'll be carrying one."

He expected to need that reserve. The thought set Delphine's heart thumping. Finally, they would corner Weber. Unless he knew they were coming. Unless it was a trap.

She didn't want to be the center of all this, but she felt like the bullseye, and Weber was taking aim. Would Varrick snatch her from the arrow at the last moment? Would he be quick enough?

"Are you sure you want to go through with this?" Tanner asked. "We know our quarry. We could put you on a ship and finish this without you."

They could send her off across the sea.

"Could we ensure the loose creature wouldn't follow me onto the ship?" The desperation to be free of Rockhaven and its memories had faded, even though the risk had grown. Her gaze slid to Varrick, his eyes reflecting the gold shimmer of the box. No, she did not want to leave yet.

Tanner's mouth made a grim line. "No."

"Then I'm sure. We have to finish it here."

How big was the bullseye? How deadly the archer? She must place all her trust in Varrick and believe he would ensure she came to no harm.

Varrick met her eyes. "Put me in a room with Weber, and I'll finish it."

Delphine gulped her worries back down. Varrick had protected her when the carriage went into the river. He'd defended her from Stokes. He'd stood between her and the attacking shadow. He wouldn't let Weber hurt her.

She took a deep breath. "Teach me how to use the artifacts."

Varrick

Varrick opened the wooden box to display an ornamental hair comb. The goldenwood formed delicate petals and vines of a rose-like flower, each tine of the comb thin and perfectly curved. Live anima pulsed in the grain of it. Elf-work: far more than just wood, the artistry exceeded human or jaglin ability. Where had Lady M found it?

Delphine came up beside him, a wisp of rose perfume lingering in her hair. She held her hands above the table as if afraid of damaging the artifact.

"It's beautiful," she said. "Where did it come from?"

"You'd have to ask Tanner. The elves limit how much of their goldenwood they trade, to keep it scarce." He ran a finger over the ornament, gauging the strength of it by the prickle of power. "There are professors in Istalia who would kill over something like this."

"Not truly." She gave him a rueful glance. "Right?"

"Oh, truly. For this or Juliette's earrings." He picked it up. "It might be best not to know its provenance."

Delphine traced the edge of the comb, then withdrew her hand and looked at her fingertips. "You don't know, or you don't want to tell me? Or aren't allowed?"

"I don't know." Varrick looked to Tanner, but the older woman crossed her arms and shook her head. "And wouldn't be allowed to tell if I did."

"By your benefactor?" Delphine's voice was soft, eyes on the comb, as if the question wasn't important.

Aware of Tanner's scrutiny, he shook his head. "I don't know."

He'd hardly had time to puzzle over the mysterious Lady M. Rich? Definitely. Influential? She must be, to arrange this. Why she'd paid for his education was just one more question he couldn't answer.

"Feel free to chime in any time, Tanner," he said.

Tanner tsked. "I'm just a servant. I can't speak out of turn, Mr. Allard."

"If I succeed, I'm going to demand some answers," he said.

Tanner pointed to the comb. "You have more important things to do right now."

Delphine sighed. "How do I use it?"

Varrick shook himself. He could demand answers from Tanner and the others later. Delphine needed to know this now. "Bloom your anima."

She did, her two arcs pale and thin. They'd been weak after the carriage accident, but he'd assumed she expended herself during the fall. "Have your arcs always been like this?"

She looked away, lacing her fingers together. "No. They used to be stronger, but after the attack on my aura, I can only do this much."

She was one-eighth elven. She ought to have brilliant, powerful anima, even after three generations of dilution. Certain elementals fed on anima, but not the shadows. He'd have to think about that.

He offered the comb to her. "Hold it and channel your anima through it. Lightly."

One pale arc touched the deep golden surface of the comb. Her eyes grew wide and round. "It's so much."

"Touch the far wall with the anima channeled through the comb." He bloomed and stretched his own out.

She followed him, a much thicker, deeper gold arc drifting away from the comb. Furrowing her brow in concentration, she brought it to touch the same spot on the wall.

"Hold it there." He pulled his anima back to his wrist.

This part was tricky, but it was also the easiest way to show someone how to manipulate the stored anima of the artifacts. Most people were used to slogging through mud; the artifacts changed it to sprinting on a smooth road. It was easy to overdo it.

He wrapped an arm around her and clasped her wrist where her anima swirled around it. Under his fingers, her pulse raced. "Close your eyes and feel how I'm manipulating the energy."

"Am I supposed to do something with it?" Her voice rose in pitch.

"No, just hold it, right there, as steadily as you can." The perfume on her hair surrounded him as he channeled his own anima into hers, blending the two. She gasped, blinked, then squeezed her eyes closed again.

It was not the awareness of shared auras. He could only guess at her emotions, but there was a fizzing connection when their anima joined, a sense of her shape and body that fired his nerves and imagination.

Not the best situation for concentration. She would be aware of him in the same way.

"Um, Varrick?" She took several short, deep breaths. "What am I supposed to do?"

Turn around and kiss me. No, this lesson might save her life.

"I'm going to form a shield with my aura, channeled through the comb to boost it. You should be able to feel how I do it, then you can try on your own." Shields were simple material projections. Once mastered, the same technique could be used to attack.

The bare curve of her neck was tantalizingly close, warm golden skin an inch away.

She nodded and gulped.

He formed it slowly, conforming their combined anima to the image in his mind. Flatten it. Spread it. Temper it hard so it would hold up to both the summoned creatures and anima attacks from others. Her body relaxed against him, helping her anima flow more freely.

"Now I'm going to pull it back. Bring your anima back to your hand." He pulled his own in slowly, shrinking the shield and sliding his anima away from the thread of hers.

The bubbly heat of their connection faded, but he was aware of her breathing, her racing pulse, the languid way she leaned against him.

Delphine swallowed. "I experienced what you did but describe how you concentrate on it. Explain what your mind was doing."

"When you Craft something so it's warmer, you picture heat. You have a pattern for heat in your mind. It doesn't matter what the pattern is, just that, in your mind, it means *heat*."

"Right." She'd gone breathless.

"So, the picture of a shield is simple: broad, flat, whatever shape and size you want, but you have to create a pattern for strength and solidity." His hand hovered under her wrist, even though he'd pulled his anima further back.

Her anima grew brighter with her focus and confidence. It was still thin and pale, but not so hesitant. Had she locked it away along with her aura, afraid to use it or show her weakness?

"Try it," he said. "I'll move in and support you if you need it. Channel it through the comb."

Her anima stretched toward the opposite wall again, bolstered with the deep gold of the comb's reserved power. It pulsed into a blob, retracted, and Delphine took another deep breath.

"Picture what you want," Varrick murmured.

Her anima stretched into a tall rectangle as big as a door.

"Thicken it."

Concentration sent tension through her shoulders. The shield grew from paper thin to as thick as his hand was wide. Varrick felt the shift in the anima as she imposed the idea of solid strength on it. The projected image took on a metallic cast.

Varrick released her and stepped away. "Now hold it. I want to test how solid it is."

Her gaze flashed to him and back to the shield she'd created. "Test?"

Varrick stretched his anima out and around the front of the shield. "I'm going to hit it."

"Um." Her shield trembled and lost its metallic sheen.

"Relax into it. Tension restricts your control." His arc paused a foot in front of the shield.

She kept her eyes on the shield, steadying the anima and returning the strength to it.

"Focus on holding position and staying whole." When she nodded, he struck the shield with his arc, just a tap to start with.

The anima sparked as it clashed, but her shield held.

"I could feel that," Delphine said.

"I'm going to strike it again, harder. With the comb's stored anima, I am not strong enough to break it unless your pattern fails." That might boost her confidence, which would be key if she needed to manifest a shield quickly. "Ready?"

"Yes." Her voice sounded stronger, less shaky.

Varrick put more power into the strike this time. Not his full strength, but enough that it could shatter her concentration if it caught her off guard.

Delphine flinched, but the shield held. For a moment, she stared at the intact form of it before breaking into a grin.

"Again?" Varrick asked.

"Full strength?" She raised an eyebrow. "I assume you can pull the punch if I don't hold it?"

"Of course." He'd trained back and forth like this often enough, and control was the first lesson. She trusted his control, and the realization sent a flush of delight through his chest.

The strike splashed against the shield, spilling sparks of anima on the floor. Delphine retreated a step, but the shield didn't waver. He hit again, a quick succession of attacks like a flurry of punches. Delphine squeaked but didn't flinch this time. *Good.* She needed to see that she could do it.

He drew his anima back. "How do you feel?"

"Better than expected. I thought I'd be exhausted." She studied the comb. "How much power is in it?"

"Quite a lot. More than you'll need." He hoped. "Better to be over-armed than under."

She explored the comb with her anima, probing the nooks and crannies of the design. "It's bound in there strangely. I've never seen anything like it."

"Most items that are reservoirs for anima have taken it from somewhere else and just stored it in an object," he said. "Artifacts from the elven trees are holding their own anima in. It's a more natural process, but it can only be done with their trees."

Delphine ran her fingers over the carved surface. "I didn't know anima could be stored at all."

Unsurprising, since the process was difficult, required a prepared object for storage, and, unless someone was preserving their own anima for later, potentially fatal for the donor. In Istalia, ripping anima from the body was a punishment for some crimes.

He'd seen it done. He even knew the incantation and sigils for tearing it from the victim. He couldn't imagine using them. The person could live, forever cut off from that power. Few had the fortitude to remake a life after it.

Like Delphine had after losing her aura. "You said your arcs were stronger before the attack?"

The shadow that always accompanied that memory crossed her face. "By a great deal. I assumed losing my aura affected it. Or the grief."

Logical. Grief and depression sapped anima, preventing it from reconstituting as quickly and making its use more exhausting. Without a healthy aura, it would have been doubly so, but ... a suspicion tugged at the corner of his mind. "How strong were you at your peak? How many arcs could you bloom?"

"Four, usually. Six, if I concentrated." She tipped her head. "Why?"

Pieces fell into place. "I know what he's doing. I know what he wants."

"Weber?"

"Yes. It makes sense with the reported injuries, who was targeted—you especially." He'd thought the attraction was her aura, but it had been her anima. It was diabolical. He turned to Tanner. "He's making his own. He's stealing anima to store it. The creature is just to keep the person helpless and wipe away any struggle or memory. Once the person is comatose, there's no way to know if they have their anima."

Delphine blinked. "I need to sit down."

He caught her elbow and guided her to the nearest chair, where she leaned back, slightly crumpled. "Why would he?"

"He'll sell them on the black market." Varrick paced in front of the fireplace. "They'd be cheaper than authentic artifacts."

She followed his pacing with her eyes, face growing more and more grave.

"What are you thinking?" Varrick asked.

"If he took my anima, then how much of me is being traded around the city?" She stared at her hands, as if imagining her fingers being taken and passed around. "Would it all be in one object? Or scattered, all mixed up with someone else's anima?"

Horror crept slowly over her face, and he had no comfort for it. A part of herself had been stolen. It lay in someone else's hands. Auras could heal; anima could not regrow any more than a lost limb. Weber might as well have cut off her hands.

He knelt on the floor and clasped her hands. They were small in his, and cold despite the anima work they'd just done. He wrapped his fingers around them to warm them.

"Delphine." He wouldn't tell her it was fine, or that it would be fine.

Her hands curled into fists. "We'd better finish the lesson, because I intend to destroy him."

The Blood of Elves

DELPHINE

Delphine had never thought of herself as vengeful, but she wanted to hurt Weber. A deep well of aching rage boiled inside her, so fierce and wild it didn't even feel like hers. Some other, older blood thundered in her heart, calling her to revenge.

She lay on her bed after the exertion of the lessons, memories from her years in Elethen with Grandpapa bubbling to the surface. Stories of Grandpapa's father, the elf. The sea captain. *The scandal.*

Grandpapa had collected the faded flowers from his mother's grave and let her hold them as he told her about the elf, a pirate captain. On the high seas of the world, pirates fought each other as they assailed merchant vessels for treasure and goods. Once, Great-Grandfather Pirate Captain had been captured, his ship sunk, his crew dead.

Lying safe in bed in Sayledon Manor, Delphine could remember the breathless fear and excitement she'd felt as Grand-papa told her the story.

"What did he do?" she'd asked then, and she asked now, aloud, to the empty room. What had her ancestor done when someone had taken everything from him?

"He blew up their ship. Sank them. Then—" Grandpapa had grinned. "He snuck onto another ship in the archipelago, seduced their lady captain, and got clean away."

He'd kissed the top of her head. "Never let them get away with it, darling."

Never let them get away with it.

They'd left Elethen soon after, but the words stayed with her. It had been a strange story to tell her. Grandpapa must have been trying to give her some sense of her Eletheni family history to balance out the strictures and social rules of Rockhaven.

Never let them get away with it.

She'd been lied to. Robbed. Violated. With Varrick's help, she'd sink Weber.

And sail away. Off to Elethen, to see Grandpapa again.

Without Varrick. It always came back to a life without Varrick. They both avoided facing the looming end, ignoring it when their desire flared. There was no harm in enjoying one another until they parted, was there? Varrick wasn't resisting the temptation any more than she was.

They'd just begun that tentative lovers' dance, and it was nearly over. If things went well, it might be finished in a few days. Weber would be in custody or dead.

A chill crawled over her. She'd never truly wished someone dead, but now …

Someone with his power couldn't be contained or held. He would escape and hurt more people or come for revenge. The desire for his death sat uncomfortably in her mind.

No doubt Great-Grandfather would have no such scruples. Would Varrick? When face to face with Weber, would she? She wouldn't know until it happened.

Delphine rolled onto her side, weary, but too restless to sleep. Her mind played out endless loops of possible scenarios, imagined confrontations with Weber or Juliette, and she could not make them stop. She wanted to rage against someone, wanted them to repent, but even in her imagination, Weber laughed. How could she win anything if she couldn't even imagine victory?

Finally, as the day faded, a knock at the door broke the stillness and Tanner entered.

"Morrow is back from scouting." she said. "You should join us."

Morrow wore workman's clothes, his face smudged with coal and dirt, looking rough and dangerous. He and Varrick studied a hand-drawn map of the Indigo Elf and surrounding buildings.

The Indigo Elf was a U-shaped building, wider at the bottom of the U, which faced the street, than it was on the two longer sides, which flanked an interior courtyard with a wall at the open end.

Morrow indicated the wide bottom part. "This is the main area for gambling. There are tables in the second floor gallery for games too. Private games are held on the ground floor rooms along each leg of the building."

"How many floors?" Varrick asked.

"Two for the main section, three for the other parts. The third floor is all servants' quarters. The second-floor rooms are for ... different types of private games." He cleared his throat, not elaborating on that.

Delphine studied the sketch. "There has to be an office and a safe box for money and ledgers."

"In the side of the main section that butts up against the courtyard." Morrow pointed. "You can't get to the third floor from the front. You have to go upstairs from the end of the hallways, away from the streetside."

"Dare I ask how you discovered all this?" Tanner said.

"Well, everywhere has maids to clean up and bundle things out to the rubbish bin." Morrow looked pleased with himself. "A little silver incentive and sweet talk, and one was happy to answer all my questions."

"Where are the doors?" Varrick asked.

"The main entrance is here." Morrow thumped the center of the bottom of the U. "Each wing has a hall with rooms on both sides and a door at the end. There are doors at the back of the kitchens that open into the courtyard. Four exits in all."

"What about windows?" Delphine was supposed to blow one out.

Morrow met her eyes. "Every room has one, except the main room."

Silence fell, the four of them staring at the map. Delphine felt detached, as if someone else would be knocking on that door and walking into danger.

"We don't even know if Juliette will speak to me." Delphine gave it even odds.

"If she doesn't, we try something else." Tanner drummed her fingers on the table. "Shall we get you dressed for it?"

"We're going tonight?" She'd expected to have another day at least.

Varrick reached for her. "Every night that passes increases the chance of another victim, and another attack on you by the loose shadow."

She stared at him, the sense of detachment growing. A different woman, standing on the shore as the storm surge swept in, not her.

"If I have to take the building apart brick by brick to get to you, I will." Varrick opened his aura so she could see how earnest and confident he was.

"Morrow will accompany you inside, if possible," Tanner added.

"And I will be right outside." Varrick swiveled his ears back and forward.

He could hear better than humans. "Can you hear through brick walls and a crowd?" she asked.

He hesitated, uncertainty staining his aura before confidence bloomed in it. "Yes."

"I guess I'm ready then." *As ready as I ever will be.*

Tanner dressed Delphine in a plain blue skirt and overdress of fine quality. "If you look too fancy, she won't believe your story. Have you thought about what you will say?"

"She'll know about the carriage accident. I'll say that risking my life wasn't part of my contract, and Mr. Allard and I have parted ways." Delphine stood, checking her silhouette in the mirror. "I'll butter her up, say she's so well-connected and intelligent."

"The more desperate she thinks you are, the quicker she'll pounce," Tanner pinned the stomacher to the gown and arranged the ruffles just so, "and the sooner Weber can be dealt with."

"Varrick's benefactor must want this done quickly." If the end was coming soon, she wanted to know who was pulling all the strings. "What will happen to him afterwards?"

"It's not my place to say." Tanner looked grave.

"What hold do they have over him? Why did they involve themselves in all this anyway?" She wasn't ungrateful that someone was taking on Weber and his shadows, but she wanted to know who had such authority over Varrick.

"Someone has to keep an eye on misused magic," Tanner said. "The university won't. Those artifacts Weber is making are probably being sold to students and professors there."

For money and power, the university turned a blind eye. For money, Delphine's world had been razed.

"We don't know how many artifacts he might have with him." Tanner wound Delphine's hair around a hair rat and pinned it all into place. "Don't take any chances you don't need to. Weber must be powerful himself, even without the use of artifacts."

"And has no scruples." He'd targeted multiple people of high rank. He wouldn't hesitate to kill her or Varrick.

"None," Tanner agreed. "If you are present when Mr. Allard confronts him, escape. It will turn violent, and he can't do his job if he's trying to protect you."

And he would try to protect her. And she would want to stay and help protect him. She pushed it out of her mind. She didn't want to face the decision until it happened.

"Morrow will be there for you and for Mr. Allard."

There would be back up. Varrick would be just outside.

Tanner placed the wooden comb in Delphine's hair. "You can use it without touching it. Just channel your anima through it. And don't give it away too soon. Let her underestimate you."

"She'll notice the comb. It's shimmering." It shone like a beacon in her dark hair.

"Hats are quite fashionable." Tanner produced an ornate tricorn hat with plumes, silver stitching, and a draping net veil to cover her face and sweep back over her shoulder. Tanner settled it on her head, secured it with hat pins, and stepped back with an air of satisfaction.

Delphine admired herself. The veil was the same dark blue as her skirts, partially obscuring her face without interfering with her vision. The air of mystery it produced ought to catch Juliette's attention.

Delphine tucked a curl behind her ear. Juliette was very invested in the idea of elves. The colored hair, the ear ornaments ... Time to show her the real thing.

Never let them get away with it, darling.

Morrow joined her in a rented coach. He looked sinister, despite the footman's uniform.

He nodded at her. "I'm here to watch your back, Mrs. Leighton."

"Thank you, Morrow." Of course, she knew he wasn't an actual butler, but she had no idea how much protection he would be.

Varrick climbed in after him. He was dressed as a sailor, in ankle-length slops, sturdy shoes, and a rough woolen vest and coat over a loose shirt. He looked younger, more relaxed, and somehow larger, as if he was letting himself expand beyond his original role.

"It's easier to move quickly in these," Varrick explained.

Morrow tapped the roof to signal the driver to go.

They rumbled down the road in silence. Varrick watched the dark countryside go by, but Morrow watched her, as if sizing her up.

"Have you spent much time in Rockhaven, Mr. Morrow?" Delphine asked to break the tension.

"I grew up here." He laid his hands on his knees. "Our employer hired me about fifteen years ago for my varied and useful array of skills."

Delphine glanced at Varrick, but he hadn't moved. Hadn't appeared to notice Morrow mentioning their benefactor.

"Who are they? And what do they have to do with Varrick?"

Owed them nearly everything, Varrick had said.

Varrick's ears trained on her.

"She pays for his place at the Scholarium D'Arcanis. Has for a decade, I believe."

Varrick's ears rotated toward Morrow. "Yes."

Morrow followed her gaze. "Do you have anything to add, Mr. Allard?"

"Am I allowed to?" He shifted uncomfortably. "I can't go back to my studies if she stops paying."

"Lady M is private but not vindictive," Morrow said. "She is extremely proud of you, in a distant way."

Varrick's chin sunk to his chest and he frowned. "I am fully aware of what I owe her. I am here, at her beck and call, because I owe her." He met Delphine's eyes. "I'm not free to walk away."

Morrow flexed his fingers. "You should speak with her."

"I want to," Delphine said. "Tell her that." She glanced at Varrick, but he stared at his hands. "Before I sail."

"I'll pass the message along." Morrow inclined his head to her. "Tomorrow."

CHAPTER 46

The Indigo Elf

DELPHINE

"Are you ready for this?" Varrick asked as the coach rolled to a halt.

Delphine's heart galloped and her throat constricted. It had sounded simple when they'd discussed it, but looking out at the dark street and alleyway, lit by a single glowlight, a dozen doubts assailed her. The enchanted blue lantern left the area feeling ominous.

"As ready as I'll ever be." Other things piled up in her throat, words she wanted to say but could not. *I don't want this to be over. I don't want to die. I want time, a chance. I am afraid of losing you.*

She swallowed them back down. Afterwards, she could say those things. And if it went terribly wrong, they wouldn't matter.

Morrow stepped out of the coach first and held up a hand, stopping Delphine. He washed the area with a pulse of aura, nodded, and held out his hand to help her down.

He held both her shoulders, staring intently at her face. "Do not back down. Go in there and act like you have every right to be there. Do not let her rattle you."

Delphine nodded. "I can do it."

She had allies. She wasn't just a destitute widow: she was the granddaughter of a baron. Her ancestors had fought duels and taken lovers, carved a life out of the frontier and made allies where others saw none. The blood of elven pirates beat in her veins. She could handle one woman.

But could she handle Weber?

She gathered her skirts in one hand and followed Morrow to the door under the blue light.

"Be mysterious and nonchalant," Morrow whispered. "It's more intimidating."

She took a deep breath as he knocked on the door.

An eye-level slot in the door opened, revealing the upper half of a man's face. "Password?"

Morrow was the picture of calm. "We are not here to play. My mistress is here to discuss business with Miss Singleton."

"What sort of business?" The man inside sounded big, his voice heavy and his accent thick with the docks.

"The sort discussed between ladies, not with doormen and bouncers," Morrow said.

"Then it's the sort that stays on the doorstep." The man started to slide the slot shut.

"You may tell him." Delphine kept her voice calm, even though her heart pounded in her ears and sweat dampened her palms. "Just not the particulars."

"As you wish, Ma'am." Morrow gave her a nod and turned back to the half-open slot. "My mistress has a business opportunity Miss Singleton might find interesting. She will not discuss more with anyone except Miss Singleton."

The man behind the slot looked to the side, eyes shifting as he thought. "Does your mistress have a name?"

Delphine froze. She didn't know if she should give her actual name or something false. Morrow must have anticipated this.

"Tell her it is the lady whose acquaintance she made at Lord Everard's salon so recently," he said. "She will know."

The man behind the slot snorted and slid it shut.

"That will add veracity," Morrow said, clasping his hands behind his back.

"I hope so." She couldn't calm her heartbeat. Even breathing slowly wasn't helping.

Time crawled by as the alley grew colder. Apprehension gathered in her shoulders, tying knots along her spine. Delphine looked back at the coach, barely visible around the corner. Varrick would hear every word clearly.

Finally, the door opened. The bouncer stood beside it, but a handsome young man—barely more than a boy to Delphine's eye—bowed to them. "Follow me."

The boy wore tight breeches and his billowy shirt was open nearly to his waistband. His long, fair hair flowed down his back, and he wore a metal cuff on each ear, pointed to look like elf ears.

They entered an open room with a sunken floor. Several tables dotted the room, but only a few had card games. Most customers seemed to be merely drinking and enjoying the company of the young men and women who moved about, bringing drinks, cigars, and food to the tables. The women wore sheer chemises with short stays over them and skirts tied up to show their stockings and knees underneath. Like the boy escorting them, every server wore long hair and elf-ear jewelry.

Delphine curled one hand into a loose fist to keep from touching her own ears and their tell-tale tips. No one here would recognize her. She scanned the crowd for anyone she knew or the unmistakable bulk and blond hair of Weber. *No.* If he was here, he wasn't in the front room.

There were other rooms for private games like the one David had attended, rooms where the beautiful young men and women offered services that had nothing to do with card games and drinks. She watched a man slide his hand up a girl's thigh, under her chemise, and a prickle of revulsion stuck in her throat. The girl didn't look old enough for a debutante ball.

Her step slowed, but Morrow touched her elbow, a reminder of their purpose tonight. She focused her eyes on the guide's long fall of pale hair, ignoring the room.

Their guide led them up a curving staircase to the second-floor gallery and around to the back directly above the bar below. The clink of glasses broke through the chatter.

The guide tapped on a pair of ornately carved, thick doors with panes of colored glass too textured to see through. The door swung inward without a sound.

Thick carpet muffled their footsteps as they approached the heavy desk of dark wood. Shelves of books lined the back wall, and a high-backed chair, turned away from them, sat between the desk and shelves.

The books all looked new, unworn and uncracked. A show, if they were real books at all, and not hiding places.

"Your man can wait in the gallery." The chair turned slightly, enough to show Juliette's dismissive wave.

VARRICK

The door to the gambling den closed with a solid thunk. A rush of panic washed over Varrick. Weber might be in there. Juliette would certainly have guards. Delphine was walking into a trap. A single day's training wasn't enough, even with the power of the artifact. Would Morrow be able to protect her?

He leaned out of the coach window enough to see a slice of the alleyway and drummed his fingers on the sill. How long should he wait before worrying?

He was already worried.

Beyond the blue glowlight, shadows swathed the far end of the alley. Rats scuffled for food, their squeaks and screeches echoing off the bricks.

Then they didn't.

Varrick trained both ears toward the end of the alley.

The darkness thickened. It moved. It blinked at him.

The loose elemental had found Delphine.

He opened the coach door. The glowlight dimmed. The creature would be attracted to the light but couldn't feed on it. It had been summoned nine months ago and had fed seven times. It would be powerful and intelligent enough to recognize him.

Smart enough to hold a grudge.

He slipped to the ground and bloomed his anima under his clothes. He couldn't afford to put it on guard. It had taken four people to repel it last time. Dipping his hand into his pocket, he gripped the short, thick wand of goldenwood, full of stored tree anima, and waited for it to attack.

Like a sinuous mass of shadow-snakes, the darkness swooped down on the glowlight, snuffing out the blue light. The creature sped toward Varrick and reared above him, twisting into something like a winged serpent. Varrick began murmuring the binding and dematerializing incantation, pulling on the anima stored in the wand. If the shadow struck, he would have only seconds to fling up a shield.

It held there, ten feet above him, wings billowing like torn sails in a gale, empty eyes focused on him. Varrick began the first binding circle.

The creature screeched in his head, steel on cold iron, and twisted away over the building.

He dismissed the circle and incantation. "Damn." Varrick paced along the street side of the building, searching the dark skies for blocked stars. "Damn, damn, damn."

He'd lost it, and it knew Delphine was close.

Resolute, he scanned the side of the building and the skies above it and pulled himself up on the first window ledge. The creature would be testing the windows and doors for wards, slithering around for weak points. Roofs were rarely well-secured.

DELPHINE

Delphine paused long enough for Juliette to snap her fingers in irritation. She nodded to Morrow, and he stepped out of the room, followed by the guide, who shut the doors behind them.

"He's not a very pretty one. Where's your big green fellow, Mrs. Leighton?" Juliette turned her chair, a tumbler of golden liquid in one hand, lips twitching with annoyance.

Delphine pulled the veil back over her hat. "May I sit?"

"I shall not stop you." Juliette gestured to the chairs on Delphine's side of the desk. "I am surprised to see you at my door."

"A woman has to survive, and you're obviously good at it."

A spark of interest lit Juliette's eyes. *Good.*

"So, you show up with, what? A hired man? To make me an offer?" Juliette sneered. "What could you possibly offer me?"

Her question echoed Delphine's thoughts, not just toward Juliette, but toward Varrick. What could she offer a man who loved learning?

She half-closed her eyes and traced the curve and point of her ear while she collected herself. Like her workers, Juliette wore jewelry to imitate pointed elven ears. Delphine wanted to be sure Juliette noticed hers.

"Mr. Allard and I have parted ways," Delphine said.

Juliette smirked. "You found him untrainable? Or did he find you lacking?"

"Magi battles and falling in rivers put a pall on the arrangement." With her hand near her ear, she could feel the tingle of anima from the comb hidden under her hat. It bolstered her confidence. "I've no desire to die for his secrets."

Juliette leaned forward, setting down her drink and focusing on Delphine. Her sharp face, gaunt around the eyes, took on a ghoulish cast for a moment, her corona flashing dark green greed around her head.

"I heard something about an accident," Juliette said. "Quite a fall. I was surprised you survived."

"As was I." Delphine relaxed in the chair, leaning back. "Since I am looking for new employment, I thought your little elf-themed endeavor here might need some authenticity."

Juliette's sneer congealed. "My little endeavor?"

Delphine tapped the point of her ear. How strange, to have what she'd hidden her whole life become an asset. The scandal was all moot. Her family was gone and she would be leaving. Elethen would not bat an eye. But Juliette didn't know that.

"The dyed hair and ornaments are rather cheap imitations. Surely the genuine article would be a bigger draw." She pulled a curl out in front of her face, letting the light catch the undertones.

"I've spent years building this place, and you think you can walk in here and ask for a favor because you've got fancy ears?" Indignation flared around Juliette's head.

"I don't need any of your favors." Delphine let the curl fall. "But you might want a valuable asset."

The smaller woman took a sip of her drink and set the tumbler directly between them. "You're a bit old for my clientele."

It was meant to sting, but if Delphine let it, she'd lost. "Well, most of them are a bit old for me. Let the girls handle the bedrooms and give me a table and cards."

Juliette leaned forward, narrowing her eyes. "A dealer?"

Hooked.

Delphine smiled. "Set me up as something special, only for the most private, exclusive games."

"It's not just handing out cards. Dealers have to know the games, their variations, how to catch cheating—"

"I've dealt for parties." Ha, who'd have thought those lessons would actually be useful. "Try me out. Give me a table."

Juliette tapped her nails against the desk, considering. "There's a private game starting soon." She pulled a deck from a drawer and tossed it to Delphine, cards scattering across the desk. "Show me what you can do."

Delphine swept the cards into a stack, riffling them together. "Pirate Hold 'em? Serpents variation? Reverse elven with aces high?"

"Basic seven-card stud," Juliette said. "Beat me, and you can deal a real game."

Delphine flicked the cards to Juliette, set the deck aside, and arranged her hand. The stakes had never been so high.

CHAPTER 47

Hunting the Shadow

VARRICK

Varrick pulled himself over the edge of the roof, the goldenwood wand gripped in his teeth, and balanced on the steep slope. The night's damp left the wooden shingles slippery. The three-story building sprawled in a landscape of peaks and dormers, creating too many hiding places for the creature. He froze, listening for its mind-scraping voice, watching for shadows that moved or were too thick.

Carriages rumbled by. A thread of music drifted past, fading as an argument on a distant street grew in volume. Voices in the building beneath blended together. Varrick picked his way to the nearest dormer, testing the wards with his anima. Old, but solid. The creature would find the weakest one and break through like it did at Sayledon.

Then it would find Delphine.

Were the elementals capable of obsession? The literature was spotty, the best sources ancient, fragmented, and suffering in translation.

He crept to the next dormer and froze as a cold breeze whispered across his skin, despite the night being still and heavy. Wrapping a hand around the edge of the dormer for stability, he pulsed his aura across the roof. Empty—unusually so. No pigeons. No rats or cats.

It was here, but he couldn't find it. It might bypass wards altogether if it found enough cracks in the structure or a victim to use as a host. If he guessed wrong...

Another puff of cold breath washed over him. A snarl like winter wind hissed in his head—no words, but it wanted him to go away.

"I can't do that." Varrick pulsed his aura again, feeling for hunger. Fury and fear tickled at the far corner of the roof.

There.

Varrick pinpointed it and navigated the dormer, pulled himself over the nearest peak and oriented himself toward the sensation. It hung there, waiting for him, either in ambush or anticipation. The peak led down to a narrow interior courtyard. Beyond that far peak, a seething piece of night prowled the rooftop. It paused on top of a chimney, a swirl of sentient smoke and night grinning at him. Was the chimney warded?

No shimmer lit the night.

Damn it.

It poured down the unwarded chimney until nothing was left but smoke from the fire below and Varrick's heartbeat rushing in his ears.

DELPHINE

Juliette swigged the last of her drink as Delphine dealt the last card to each of them. Neither's up-cards were very impressive on their own, but the three down-cards could make or break a hand.

Delphine set the deck down and picked up her cards, heart in her throat. She collected her four up-cards, two sevens, a five, and a jack. Juliette had a nine, two sixes, and a four, all different suits.

"Nervous?" Juliette had locked her aura down, but her sneer was easy to read.

Delphine picked up her first down-card. A jack. That gave her two pair. "Not particularly." She discarded the five.

Juliette plucked up two cards at a time, smirking as she arranged them into her hand and discarded one of her originals.

Delphine's next card was a deuce. No use. She discarded it. Juliette seemed pleased with her last down-card, smirking at her hand. Delphine hovered her hand over her final card, face-down on the table. If she lost, could she demand to see Weber? Pretend to sell a secret? If that card was a jack or a seven, she had a good chance. Depending on what Juliette had.

She lifted it.

A jack. Delphine grinned.

She arranged her cards and fanned them face-up on the table. "Full house."

Juliette's smirk congealed. She laid out a straight, ten-nine-eight-seven-six. Close, but not quite beating Delphine.

"Well, I suppose you can try a real game." Juliette made a show of gathering up the cards, her movements short and sharp. A halo of anger glittered around her head before she locked it down again. She slammed the drawer with the cards and stalked to the doors.

"Do you really have elven blood?"

Delphine rose to follow her. "My great-grandmother was adventurous."

Juliette pulled the doors open. As Delphine passed through to the gallery, she felt the woman's scrutiny and skepticism.

Morrow was not there. The mask of confidence Delphine had built threatened to crumble. "Where's my man?"

"I'm sure he's at the bar. I'll have one of the boys tell him where you are." Juliette strode past her, aiming for the stairs. "Come along."

If she quibbled or stalled now, Juliette might get suspicious, and she hadn't seen Weber yet. She followed.

The room was even busier than it had been. Most tables were between games. A group of women danced on a stage in one corner as two musicians played. Ankles flashed. Skirts were hiked for glimpses of knees and hips. She scanned the crowd for Morrow, to no avail.

Juliette led her under the gallery to the hall of one long leg of the building. The thick runner rug muffled their steps. Glowlights shed a soft purple radiance, lending an air of luxury to the space.

The noise from the main room faded and Juliette slowed her pace. "So this adventurous great-grandmother ... how'd she catch an elf?"

Alastair had told her that part of the story. "He danced with her at a ball, then seduced her in the library." When Delphine had been younger, she'd found that part hard to believe. People didn't just do that, did they? She saw the same skepticism in Juliette's corona. "He visits her grave and leaves flowers on it."

Juliette turned to look at her, skepticism shading into anger and envy. "No need to embellish it too much."

Delphine shrugged. She'd seen the grave and flowers. Arguing would be counterproductive.

They came to the end of the hall, where a heavy door led outside and stairs went both up and down. Morrow hadn't mentioned a basement or cellar. Most of Rockhaven was too close to the water to safely have them.

"This way." Juliette started downstairs. "Some games are more private than others."

Delphine took a few steps down. There was no light at the bottom and the air smelled chilly and damp. The utter darkness reminded her of the river closing over her head, of the shadow bursting through the window.

Juliette reached the bottom and kindled a glowlight with her anima, purple like the ones in the hallway. Delphine shook off the impressions and continued until she came to a shorter basement hall with a low ceiling. A runner graced the floor, and the five doors were identical to the ones above, brass knobs gleaming dully in the light.

What was she supposed to do if there was no window?

Juliette opened the fifth door at the end of the hall and stepped in, blocking Delphine's view. She caught a glimpse of a table and the small chandelier of glowlights above it. She touched the comb under the edge of her hat, reassured by the well of power in it. Morrow was here somewhere. Varrick was right outside.

She followed Juliette.

The door slammed behind her, blocked by a bright shield of anima. Weber sat in a chair to one side of it, hidden until she'd entered. His anima held the door fast.

Breathless, she scanned the room. No windows.

He stood, looming over her. "Hello, Mrs. Leighton. So nice to see you again."

CHAPTER 48

Shadowfall

VARRICK

Varrick ran for the courtyard side of the roof and skittered to a stop by a dormer. The window was boarded up and warded, but he pushed his anima against it, finding the way the ward had been woven and undoing it, like untangling a knotted skein of yarn. The ward unraveled into dissipating wisps of gold.

He slid his anima under the nailed edges of the boards, forming the pattern for a wedge, expanding, pushing.

The boards fell in a clatter, sliding down the roof to fall into the courtyard. By the time anyone investigated, he'd be inside.

Varrick pushed the entire window frame into the dark room beyond. It was a servant's room, unoccupied but not unused, with several narrow beds along the walls. The door opened easily into a hallway that echoed with distant voices and music. The smell of stale cigars and food clung to the threadbare carpet and wood.

Where was Delphine? The creature could be anywhere from the next floor down to the kitchens. Rushing down the hall and the narrow flight of stairs took him to a better kept hall with polished floors, a colorful runner rug down the center, and blush-inducing murals on the walls. Moans, giggles, and the squeaking of beds leaked under the doors.

An older man in fine clothing came around the corner at the far end, accompanied by two scantily clad women. The shorter of the two women saw Varrick first. She stumbled, her mouth forming a circle. Varrick straightened his shoulders, unsure he could pull this off, especially dressed as a sailor.

He strode toward the trio as the other two also saw him and stopped. "Miss," Varrick boomed, "I am extremely displeased with the service in my room. It's an absolute mess."

The first woman opened and closed her mouth a few times, but the second set her jaw. "Well, what did you pay for?"

"The same as this fellow." He waved a dismissive hand at the man, who looked irritated by the interruption. "I won't delay his pleasure for my displeasure. Direct me to Miss Singleton."

The creature wouldn't be with Juliette, but Delphine would be.

The woman rolled her eyes. "You've got to go to the main floor and ask."

Varrick snorted and strode past them. A nearby staircase curved down to the main floor. He stepped to the railing of the gallery instead, scanning the tables of men playing and drinking. Music drowned out any distinct voices.

A shriek, followed by several others, sliced through the noise. Two boys and a woman fled the area behind the bar. Several apron-clad cooks followed, yelling for people to run.

He'd found the shadow.

Varrick slung himself down the curving staircase and fought against the tide of people rushing for the exit. Darkness filled the doorway to the kitchen, billowing like a sail in the wind, bloated.

He couldn't contain it while the crowd stampeded around him. A serving girl tripped over his foot and sprawled, crying out when someone else stepped on her in the crush. He threw his anima in a shield over her as the crowd bunched at the main door.

Shaking, she stumbled to her feet and darted away toward a side hall.

The shadow pulled free of the door, forming a dragonish shape, wings unfurling, fading and reforming. How many people hadn't survived the kitchen? He fought free of the last of the fleeing crowd and drew his circle. It would escape again if he didn't work fast.

Second circle. Runes between the two. Start the chant.

The shadow hissed and pounced on the bar, scattering bottles and glasses to shatter on the floor.

Varrick flung the binding circle wider, hurrying through the chant. Almost ready—

It whipped across from where he stood and paused at a hallway entrance. With a screech, it plunged down the corridor.

Varrick broke off his chant and rushed for the doorway, boots crunching in the shattered glass. He reached the hall, but the shadow was gone.

Delphine

"Juliette, be a dear and hold the door." Weber advanced, forcing Delphine back step by step until she fell back into a chair along the side of the room. "That's better. I want you to be comfortable while we wait, Delphine. Can I call you Delphine?"

Behind him, Juliette used her anima to block the door while Weber pulled his in.

Delphine swallowed. Wait for what? But waiting gave her time to think. "If we're going to be friendly, *Bartholemew*, why don't we talk about you?"

Juliette leaned against the door, anima fizzing under her. "Just let the thing finish her. I don't see why she's so important."

Weber cast her a glare.

"Actually, I'd like an answer to that question," Delphine said. Could she blow down the door with Juliette's anima blocking it?

If she screamed loud enough, would Varrick hear? She must put Weber off-guard first.

Weber sat down again. He took a metal sphere from a satchel beside the chair and held it in one hand like a trophy.

Varrick said the summoner would have the second creature under his control; Severson had spoken of a metal ball. It was in there. Weber spun the sphere in one large hand.

"You were a mistake," he said. "Such a brilliant aura. So much anima to take. And that pathetic husband of yours let me do whatever I wanted."

"You Skilled him," she hoped.

Juliette laughed. "Didn't need to."

Weber glared at her again. "My pet was hungry."

"So why was I a mistake?" Delphine watched Juliette's corona, resentment simmering fire-orange. Weber's glittered with irritation. If they were focused on one another, they wouldn't watch her as closely.

"Oh, that damn redheaded dandy got in the way. Your husband lost his nerve, and a well-fed shadow gains power fast." He spun the sphere again. The symbols etched in the metal caught the light. "I allowed myself to be distracted."

"And lost control of it." It had only grown since then. *How powerful can it become?*

"Do you think your frog can control it before it finds you? Where is he?" Spin, spin, spin.

Delphine caught herself before she reacted. "We've parted ways. Whatever he's doing, it's too dangerous."

Juliette laughed again.

Weber grew more annoyed.

"Although, if I'd known that I was walking further into the fire, I wouldn't have come here."

Weber kept spinning the sphere. It made her stomach hurt.

Juliette smirked. "He said you'd find him, I just didn't think you'd be this stupid."

Weber leaned forward, elbows on his knees. "Shut up."

Juliette stepped away from the door. "Do you hear screaming?"

Weber stood again and rolled his shoulders. "Maybe you should go check it out, Jul."

Screams and the thunder of running feet filled the air. Delphine gripped the arms of her chair; she bloomed her anima, sliding it up her back and into her hair, where it wrapped around the comb under her hat.

"Swiving gods, this had better not be someone busting up my place." Juliette yanked the door open.

Roiling night enveloped her.

Delphine shrieked. Would Varrick hear?

Cursing, Weber struck Delphine across the face. The force of it toppled her to the floor and knocked the wind out of her.

The shadow pushed into the room.

Miiiiiine.

Shield. She needed to form the shield, but her head was ringing from the blow. One of Weber's anima arcs pinned her in place as he drew a sigil with another.

"Come on, finish your meal," he hissed.

Shield.

Delphine caught her breath. She poured her anima through the comb and flung her arm out. Strength. Width, Protection. Anima spread in an irregular blob, gleaming like polished bronze, but the shadow ignored her.

It swirled in front of Weber, darting first to one side then to the other as he chanted desperately. Rearing to the ceiling it formed a face, long, with jagged teeth, snapping at him. Blobs of residues slipped off its tattered edges only to be pulled back.

"You want her," Weber shouted between chanted lines. "Take her!"

It turned empty eyes on her and blinked.

"I didn't bring you here," Delphine whispered. Existing here hurt it, Varrick had said.

In a single, majestic swoop, it spread across the ceiling and dropped on Weber.

His chant rose to a scream, loops and sigils of anima gleaming gold in the folds of darkness.

CHAPTER 49
Call the Wind

VARRICK

Varrick was two flights up when he heard Delphine's shriek.

Below?

Delphine was below him. He spun and plunged back down the stairs. On the ground floor, he could hear chanting. Weber, starting the binding sigil.

One more flight down and the chant was clear. A seething shadow obscured the end of the hall, only sound leaking through.

It had nowhere else to go. Varrick braced his feet and traced his circles and sigils for the second time that night, speaking the words that would pull the creature in. He spread it across the breadth of the hall, blocking any escape.

Make the trap.

Bind it in.

Weber was shouting, but he faltered, faded, and restarted.

Where was Delphine? That cry had been hers. If she was in the room, it would feed on her.

Gripping the goldenwood wand, he poured its power into his spell. The golden circles deepened, sizzling with power. They drew the darkness in, wisps and threads of shadow unspooling from the creature. It writhed, screeching as the edges of the circle bowed around it, the pattern inside dividing, forming bars, compelling it into the growing sphere of anima.

Varrick stepped back, pulling it with him. As the sphere closed to contain it, he glimpsed Weber through the doorway. Juliette huddled on one side of the hall, shivering.

Where was Delphine? He had to finish the dematerialization.

The power flowing through him set his hair on end, fizzed across his skin like bubbles. His teeth ached. Sweet as sunshine, burning like brandy. The very edge of life, fully aware of every sense, nerves alive with it, one heartbeat from going too far.

He pressed the sphere smaller, sparks spitting as spaces closed. The shadow inside twisted to stare at him with one baneful eye as he compressed it to the size of a melon, a turnip, a radish.

It sighed in relief and release and dissolved into nothing.

Juliette pushed herself up on unsteady feet, dyed hair in disarray. She touched a small gleam of gold by her ear. *Pearl earrings.*

Lashing his anima like a whip, Varrick slapped her hand. The earring tore from her ear and skittered across the floor; Juliette darted past him and fled.

DELPHINE

The shadow twisted and screeched in Delphine's mind as it was dragged out of the room. Varrick's chanting and the wash of his power hit her like a pounding surf. With the shadow retreating, Weber stood and shook himself. His anima glowed around one fist. He held it out, forming a heavy hammer.

"Jul was right," he rasped. "I should have killed you." The anima hammer fell on her shield, jarring her bones.

Delphine clenched her jaw, pouring her anima through the comb as the hammer fell again.

MISTRESS AND MAGE

Weber grimaced. "When they find your body, who do you think they'll be looking for?"

"Shut up." She barely had the breath to speak.

The hammer fell.

"Do you think they'll just hang the frog, or will they strip him of his anima and send him to Alladoon? Put him in the glow mines?"

Her teeth clattered as the next blow fell.

Varrick stripped of his golden life and power. Her shield wavered. Varrick chanted, the light of his anima brighter and deeper. He was just outside the door.

"He's going to exhaust himself." Weber struck again. "Then I'll gut him like I did Stokes."

He killed Stokes?

The hammer cracked against her shield, sending a hissing spray of anima across the floor.

Varrick in the mines. Varrick gutted.

Stokes gutted.

The images swirled in her mind.

Weber's bulk loomed over her. "Then I'll finish what I started with you."

Finish ... being engulfed and devoured by the shadow while he stole her anima. Old panic and anger rose in her heart.

Delphine's concentration shattered. She lost her connection with the comb.

Her shield evaporated as the hammer fell again, a jarring blow to her arm that sent pain shooting through her shoulder.

The whipping coil of Weber's anima wound around her, wrenching her throbbing shoulder back. It snaked hot up her neck and face, burrowed into her hair, and found the comb.

Weber chuckled as his anima pulled it out and delivered it to his hand. "That's the real thing, that is."

The darkness outside the room winked out. Delphine glimpsed Juliette scrambling away.

"Varrick!"

VARRICK

Varrick scooped up Juliette's earring with his anima. The moment it touched his palm, he felt the wrongness. The power in it wasn't from the trees; there was none of the distinctive feel of flora and sea that goldenwood always radiated. This was human anima. *Stolen. Hoarded.* He snarled in visceral disgust, but he might need the power.

Weber held Delphine fast in his anima, the comb in one hand, an iron sphere for containing elementals in the other.

Varrick caught his breath, his fear for Delphine crackling into fury at Weber. "Let her go."

Weber pulled Delphine between them, holding her bound, her toes brushing the floor. "You'll have to go through her to get to me."

With the goldenwood comb, Weber had enough power to counter a direct attack, and enough skill to hurt Delphine while doing it.

"The first shadow is gone." Varrick studied the small room. How to disarm him? "You don't need her anymore."

Varrick had worked with air and water more than any other elements. There was no water here. Using air would catch Delphine in the backlash or suffocate her.

"I'm not daft, you swiving frog. The minute she's safe, you'll hit me." Weber tightened his anima on Delphine's neck. "Walk away."

Weber had enough power to burn her throat away or strangle her. The fury clenched in Varrick's chest turned to cold, hard rage. Even walking away wouldn't guarantee she'd live.

He'd found someone for himself, someone who made him feel at home. He'd promised to protect her.

The pearl earring clenched in his fist hummed. Delphine's

desperate gasps scraped the silence. Anima, air, and a prepared receptacle. Stolen anima. He'd seen it done, he knew how, but he needed to play for time.

"Say I walk away," Varrick slithered his anima to the floor, one hand holding the earring, the other at his side, tracing a subtle pattern. "Then you'll release her?" He turned slightly to the side to hide the sigil.

Weber sneered. "You can retrieve her tomorrow."

Delphine's eyes grew round. Her weak anima pulled futilely at Weber's, her fingers clawing at the golden light around her throat. Weber trapped her wrists with his anima, pulling her hands away.

My lily, my orchid, my trout. Trust me. If he kept Weber distracted just a little longer, he'd be ready.

"Unharmed?" Under Varrick's fingers, the elemental air tingled, cold and ready. He twisted it around his anima, murmuring words for being as unseen as the wind. He covered it with a growl.

"I'll let her live." Weber loosened the coil around Delphine's throat long enough for her to cry out and gasp. "You can have what's left, if you still want it."

Aura gone, anima gone. She'd have no memories, no awareness. She'd fade like the flowers she was named after.

"Not good enough. I walk away. I end this hunt, and you give her back to me unharmed." Wrapped in air, invisible, his anima snaked along the floor, curved around behind Weber, and reared high, level with Weber's bloom.

Weber laughed and hefted the iron sphere. "You have nothing to offer me. You can leave, or you can feed my pet."

Varrick struck. His anima sank deep into Weber's bloom, into the center of his life's energy.

Weber dropped Delphine as his anima splayed wide. Varrick chanted the reversal and pulled, draining Weber's power, drawing it to himself and coiling it tightly into the earring. Without the prepared jewelry, the battle would have been a tug-of-war, but

Weber couldn't regain what Varrick trapped inside the earring any more than he could put blood back in a body.

Delphine crawled to the doorway, stumbled to her feet, and flung herself behind Varrick. Weber's scream drowned out her sobs.

Varrick kept pulling. Every strand, every thread, every last wisp of Weber's power came to him, like twine off a spool. Weber gripped the comb he'd stolen from Delphine, making an aborted attempt to draw on its power.

"Not without your own," Varrick growled. The anger wouldn't abate. He dragged at every last thread, so Weber could never threaten Delphine again.

Weber fell to his knees, cursing. The delicate comb splintered as he pounded it against the floor, precious anima dissipating in the air as the binding spells lost power. The last whisper of his anima drifted away from his back, curling through the air to be sucked into the earring. The iron sphere rolled to Varrick's feet.

"I should thank Miss Singleton." Varrick closed his hand over the pearl. "Without the prepared earring, I couldn't have done that."

Weber gasped for breath, chest heaving. Varrick turned to Delphine. She staggered, shaking, into his arms and buried her face in his shoulder.

"I've got you. I've got you," he murmured.

Hunched on the ground, Weber trembled, holding himself. "You bastard. You swiving frog bastard."

He lunged, a blade gleaming in one hand.

Without thought, the words for air and flame spilled from Varrick's lips, driving a storm into Weber's face, the spoken name for hurricane made the wind rage, the sigils for desert heat scribed in the air turned the gale to a furnace blast.

Weber's skin blistered. His hair shriveled, stinking and crisp. The table behind him blackened.

"It's enough, Varrick." Delphine gripped his wrist. "He can't hurt anyone anymore."

The blast roared.

Her grip tightened. "It's enough."

Shaking as the last of his fury was spent, Varrick let the words and wind die.

He retrieved the sphere where it lay at his feet. The shadow in it was contained. It could be dematerialized after he'd rested. "We need to go."

She nodded.

Weber's groans and mumbled curses followed them out.

They found Morrow halfway up the stairs. His coat was ripped, one eye blackened, and his lip split, but he was standing guard over a resentful Juliette. She held one bloodied ear. The other lobe was empty.

"I didn't want her catching you from behind," Morrow explained, offering Varrick the other earring.

Delphine gulped. "What happened, Morrow?"

"Her bouncers tried to remove me." He rubbed his bruised cheek and winced. "I recommend we exit out the back door."

"What about her?" Delphine tipped her head at Juliette.

Varrick looked back at Weber. There was no telling how deeply Juliette was entangled with the man, but Varrick's part was done. "If you follow us, bother us, raise the alarm, or call for the constables, I'll burn the place down."

Juliette glared at him. "Get out."

With Morrow guarding their backs, they mounted the stairs and stole outside.

CHAPTER 50

Lessons in Love

DELPHINE

Delphine expected to feel relieved or giddy, but as the coach rolled up to Sayledon a wave of sorrow and fatigue washed over her. It was over; the danger was gone. It was over; she would sail to Elethen.

It was over; she might never see Varrick again.

She had their memories. The opera. The head turning and gossiping amused her now. They had the Glass Gardens. He'd been so enthusiastic about the magic that created it. She'd enjoyed his excitement.

Tanner and Mrs. Halsey met them in the entryway. They congratulated Varrick, asked if Delphine was injured, and hurried Morrow off to be tended. There was no lingering or discussion about the future, not even when Tanner prepared Delphine for bed.

"You can rest easy tonight, Mrs. Leighton. The shadow is gone. We'll be hearing about your passage to Elethen any day now."

Any day now. "Thank you, Tanner."

After Tanner left, she stared into the fire. How many nights did they have left? There was no blockade against Istalia. Varrick wouldn't even sail on the same ship.

Was he thinking the same thing? Did he dread their separation like she did?

The hidden passageway to Varrick's room was right there. If it was locked, she would have an answer, wouldn't she? There was no reason not to go to him.

Decision made, she wasted no time finding the catch. She stepped in, hand on the wall for steadiness.

Something ahead clicked. A vertical line of light widened to a rectangle, suddenly blocked by a familiar, tall figure.

"Varrick?" She could barely hear her own dry whisper.

"Delphine." A blushing, curling frond of his aura caressed her, his intent and desire, clear.

She leaned into it, understanding the question behind the emotion. "Yes."

When he hesitated, she took his hand and led him back down the passage to her room. They stopped between the passageway and bed, as if unsure where to go.

He wore his dressing gown, but it was open to the waist, and he wore no nightshirt under it. The firelight caught the fine, velvet hair on his skin, the thicker, pale green plush of it in the center of his chest. She buried her fingers in it, luxuriating in its softness, admiring the strength of his body beneath it.

He pulled her closer, kissing her cheek, catching her mouth with his, as if trying to convey every feeling in one moment. He brushed her again with his aura, the soft pink of it deepening to magenta and rich purple, the yearning becoming a physical ache.

He withdrew it and broke off the kiss, forehead pressed to hers, brass tips of his horns cold on her cheeks. "I don't want ... I won't flood you with me."

"I feel it too. I wish I could share it with you." By the time her aura had fully healed as he said it would, they would be worlds away from one another. "Flood me. Overwhelm me. Wrap your passion around me so it's mine too."

He trailed his fingers down her jaw and released his aura, letting it crash over her, coil around her, saturate her in his longing. Instinctively, her shields resisted until she dropped them, riding the waves of his desire like a ship in a storm, surrendering to it. She floated within it.

She spread her palms across his chest and slipped her arms around him, pressing into his strength. Desire, lust, and yearning were simple things, but the complex swirl of interest, affection, and devotion that rested against her skin was something she hadn't hoped to find.

He pulled the ribbon from the tail of her braid, undoing the thick locks until they cascaded in waves and curls down to the small of her back.

"I've wanted to do that for so long," he whispered, voice rough with need. He ran his fingers through the dark mass of her hair, buried his face in it, and inhaled.

"We both have." She couldn't reach around him to undo his braid as easily. "Turn around."

It was like unbraiding the finest silk threads. The strands slipped over her fingers, smooth as water, the color of peacock feathers. She ran her hands up his back, feeling his shoulders shift under his dressing gown, letting the flow of his hair cover her arms. He tipped his head back into her touch, purring.

She bloomed her anima, sending the gold tendrils over his shoulders, sparkling down the chest, gratified at his sharp inhalation and the deepening intensity of his desire, until her arcs found the tie to his robe.

She paused. "May I?"

"Please." His whole body trembled in anticipation as her magic pulled the tie loose.

The dressing gown fell open. He shrugged so it uncovered one shoulder, then the other, slipping to lay rumpled on the carpet by the dressing screen. Delphine traced the dark line down his spine and explored the breadth of the stripes that branched off it. The pattern was fascinating and beautiful, and the longer she touched them, the tighter his muscles bunched and the faster his breath came.

"As I recall," she said, "Tanner didn't want to find you half-naked on my settee again, so that's sorted."

He gulped and snorted, the tension easing.

"Now that you're fully naked." She parted his hair and kissed the place between his shoulder blades where the darkest hair whorled over his anima bloom. The skin tingled against her lips. She kissed it again, savoring the sensation and how it sparked warm pleasure down her chest and between her legs.

Laying her cheek against his back, she caressed the spot. It did fascinating things to his breathing and heartbeat. "She was obviously right about the settee. It will be far too narrow. We'd better go to the bed."

He turned, stepping back so she could appreciate the full display of his body, taut and ready. He ducked his head, flushing. "Seems unfair, Trout."

She raised her eyebrows. "What does?"

"That you've still got your nightgown on."

"Then come take it off."

He stretched one deep golden anima thread between them, trickling it down her neck to the buttons holding the gown shut and undoing them one by one. It fell in a soft sigh of linen.

Delphine backed to the bed, beckoning him with one finger. The tingling arc of anima stayed with her, coiling around her arm, encircling her waist as she stretched out, letting him see every full, soft inch and curve of her body.

He was more himself out of his formal clothes, more at home with his height, comfortable with the span of his shoulders. He stretched out on the bed, facing her, and kissed her again, but there was a question in it.

"I believe you said you'd train me." He wound a tendril of her hair around his finger. "Show me what to do."

Oh, he remembers that, does he? She'd best keep her word on it.

"Like this." She guided his hand to her breast, showed him how to tease her nipples. A quick study, he followed his hands with his anima, letting the warm fizz of it explore her body as she drew his hands lower, to the curls between her legs, to the soft skin between those lips, how to stroke her so all the aroused tension of his body was mirrored in hers.

While her hands directed his, her anima explored his body, and she basked in the rolling waves of his aura. She traced the angles of his ears, the cords of his neck, and made him shiver and gasp as her arcs ghosted down his chest.

"Not too much too fast," she whispered. He was young and eager, and she didn't want it over too soon.

"I need you. I can't wait." Varrick pulled her against him, the lengths of their bodies pressed close, his erection hard between them.

She eased him onto his back so she could stretch a leg across him and lower herself, fitting them comfortably together. With his hands and anima holding the full curves of her thighs, she moved with him until the final pleasure rippled, a brilliant storm of colors cascading through his aura, through his body, across her.

They lay side by side, bathed in the muzzy glow of Varrick's aura, thoroughly pink and satisfied.

"This will make it harder," Delphine said, watching the ceiling instead of him.

He rolled up onto his side. "Will it?"

"I was braced to go, but now all the walls I built up are gone and it will hurt." She ran her fingers down his chest. "I wouldn't choose not to, but it will make boarding that ship harder."

"What if I'm with you?"

It wouldn't be hard at all. "You can't walk away from the Scholarium." She would never ask him to.

"I'll think of something." He lifted her chin and kissed her. "I was coming to tell you that I wanted to go with you."

"And got more than you bargained for." She kissed him back, tempted to fall back into sensuous affection instead of talking.

"I got exactly what I bargained for." He caressed the curve of her bare shoulder. "I've done good work for my benefactor. That should count for something."

"We'll speak to Lady M. There must be a way. Morrow said that she was proud of you." Everyone wanted something. His benefactor would have a price.

"I'm not her slave. She can't hold me." His anima embraced her and pulled her closer to him.

Delphine blinked to keep the pricking tears away. "Don't throw away what you have for me. If you have to go back to the Scholarium, I will find a way to you."

"It's home, but it's lonely." He pressed his forehead against hers. "Until I met you, I was content to live my life under someone else's direction. I was doing what I wanted to be doing."

"What you still want to be doing." She kissed him. "What I think you ought to be doing." She'd seen his face at the Glass Gardens. He wouldn't be happy if he wasn't learning. "Let's just enjoy what we have."

She didn't intend to let him go without a fight.

Delphine woke to the door opening. She squashed the immediate urge to be embarrassed or defend herself.

Tanner stopped and stepped back.

"He's not *half*-naked, and he's not on the settee," Delphine pointed out.

"So I see." Tanner flushed. "I shall come back later, shall I?"

"I think so."

CHAPTER 51

A Baroness and a Lady

DELPHINE

Once Varrick had retreated to his own rooms to dress, Delphine rang for Tanner. A wisp of an idea had formed in her mind. It might work.

As Tanner laced her stays, Delphine started her campaign. "Tell me about Lady M and Varrick."

"I'm her servant, which means I won't be speaking out of turn." Tanner tightened and tied the stays.

Delphine turned and held her gaze. "Then tell her I want to speak with her. Before I sail. Today, preferably."

"You can't just order my lady around."

The idea caught fire. "You will tell her that Gentlelady Delphine Bollenbaucher of Elethen wishes to speak with her." The title for the granddaughter of a baron should catch Lady M's attention.

Tanner's lips thinned. "Very well."

Once she left, Delphine leaned on her dressing table and took a deep breath to steady herself. Lady M could be any powerful woman in Rockhaven society. If she was a reasonable sort of person, she would listen to what Delphine had to say. If she was unyielding, then Varrick was better off cutting ties.

When she descended the stairs, there was no sign of Varrick, but Morrow was bustling about, dusting the main hall even though there wasn't a speck of dust to be seen.

She paused on the last step. "Morrow?"

"Mrs. Leighton. Or would you prefer Gentlelady Bollenbaucher?" He twitched his eyebrows.

"I'm a gentlelady today. Will Lady M be coming to speak with me?"

"I think there is a very good chance," he smiled. "I hope she will."

"If she doesn't, I shall have you deliver me to her door." After facing Weber and his shadows, she could challenge one lady.

The front door banged. Morrow whirled. Delphine rushed forward a few steps as Tanner marched into the hall, brows down, aura exuding irritation. A thin old woman in an elegant coat and hat followed. She stopped in the middle of the hall and surveyed Delphine from head to toe.

She raised an eyebrow. "Gentlelady."

"Lady M," Delphine inclined her head.

Lady M swept her coat off and handed it to Morrow, then removed her hat pins and gave the hat to Tanner. "You are very demanding for someone who was hired for a bit part."

"This isn't about me. I want to talk about Varrick." There was something familiar about the old lady. They'd attended a ball together somewhere or run into one another at the opera or a private soiree.

"Then where is he?" Lady M demanded.

"He is out with his drakes." Morrow indicated the sitting room. "I'll have Mrs. Edward prepare some tea while you wait for him."

Lady M narrowed her eyes. "Very well." She stalked through the sitting room door.

Tanner caught Delphine's arm as she made to follow. "What do you think you're doing?"

"I'm following your advice. You told me to act like a baroness." She intended to discuss Varrick's future.

Their future.

Lady M sat in one of the chairs, so Delphine settled on the settee. Snowdrop crept over her skirts to curl in her lap.

Lady M sniffed. "Are you dissatisfied with your payment, Mrs. Leighton? I was generous, and your passage has been arranged. No small feat, I assure you."

"I have no complaints." She was curious how such a stiff, prim woman had been able to pull strings for that. "You've paid for Varrick's education at the Scholarium."

Lady M nodded. "The university here has no place for men like him, nor women like me. The Scholarium gives anyone with the talent and desire a chance to learn, if someone pays for it." She drummed her fingers on the arm of the chair. "And the university loses the money and connections I could have given them."

"Connections that allow you to privately eliminate threats and hire ships to Elethen." What sort of connections would those be?

"Exactly." Lady M lifted her chin. "I am quite proud of Varrick. He has exceeded all expectations."

Delphine mirrored the woman's posture. "I hope you've told him so."

"We did not meet until recently. We would not have, if this didn't require his skills."

Delphine stroked Snowdrop. "You should have told him. Often."

Lady M shrugged. "We traced Weber's history." Her face softened as Snowdrop peeped. "He was expelled from the university for dangerous practices that cost another student's life. But Rockhaven dislikes cleaning up its own messes."

"They just let him out into the world to wreak havoc on others?" How dare they? Instead of containing or stopping him, they'd let him prey on the people of Rockhaven like a tiger on sheep.

Lady M nodded. "They couldn't take responsibility for him. Not without losing face."

Morrow brought in the tea and cakes. "Mr. Allard has returned, Ma'am. He'll be in directly."

Lady M ignored the tea tray. "Tanner told me you and Varrick have formed an attachment of sorts."

The clatter of drake claws on marble echoed from the main hall, followed by Varrick's footsteps.

"He can tell you himself," Delphine said.

He entered a moment later and sat beside Delphine. Snowdrop abandoned her for his lap. "If I'd known you were coming, I wouldn't have been out so long."

"I hadn't intended to." Lady M glanced at Delphine. "I received an abrupt invitation."

"She's concerned about our attachment," Delphine said.

Varrick clasped her hand. "If I choose not to return to the Scholarium, that's it, isn't it? I can't go back."

"You were the one who complained about leaving very important studies." Lady M snapped her fingers. "No, you do not get to walk away after ten years. To do what? Waste your brilliance?"

Varrick put his ears back. "How much of my life will be lived at your beck and call? Last night I nearly killed a man for you."

"From what I heard," Lady M said, "it was as much for the gentlelady as for me."

"Varrick." Delphine laid her hand on his arm and turned back to Lady M. "What if he wasn't leaving, just taking a sabbatical?"

"You don't take such things on a whim," Lady M said. "Nor for leisure and tomfoolery."

"The Scholarium won't agree unless it brings in knowledge or money," Varrick murmured.

Delphine rose. What she had planned was better done standing. "The Bollenbaucher Barony of Elethen formally invites Magus

Varrick Allard of the Scholarium D'Arcanis to visit. They should like him to study—" What had Varrick described that first night? "New applications of glow in reference to water travel."

"Such an invitation ought to go through the Scholarium," Lady M said.

"But you could pull him from his current project?" A sabbatical was only temporary. He would be returning. Why couldn't the woman give an inch?

"You know." Varrick spoke slowly. "No one has gotten permission to study Baron Bollenbaucher's designs. As the magus who saved his granddaughter, I think I might be the only one allowed."

"Are you actually a descendant of the baron, girl?" Lady M gave her another study, more keenly this time.

"Delphine, daughter of Lady Florentina Bollenbaucher, daughter of Baron Florian Bollenbaucher, son of Baroness Camillia Bollenbaucher, daughter of—"

"Enough. I thought the invitation was a ruse." Lady M shook her head. "Varrick, do you want to go to Elethen? And do you want to return to the Scholarium afterwards?"

"Yes and yes." He looked up at Delphine. "I might need bigger quarters when I get back, though."

Delphine beamed, flushing.

"If you were anyone other than Florian's granddaughter, this would not be happening." Lady M stood. "A one-year sabbatical, and you bring back something incredibly clever."

"One year from our arrival in the barony," Delphine insisted. "Do you know my grandfather?"

"One year from arrival, fine." Lady M sighed. "I know his father. It's complicated."

"How—?" Delphine started

Lady M rose. "Passage for you two, two drakes, and the gryphon?"

"Yes." Varrick confirmed before Delphine could say anything.

"Then we are finished." Lady M swept past them to the door.

Delphine followed. "How do you know my great-grandfather?"

"Young lady, take care of my magus," Lady M said. "He's valuable."

"I will, but—"

"You have him. You don't get other answers." She walked out, taking her coat from Morrow and hat from Tanner.

Varrick came up behind Delphine and wrapped his arms around her. "We won, Trout. Leave it for now."

"Only for now," she tipped her head back to look at him, "Kitten."

He leaned on her. "I beg your pardon?"

"If you want to call me Trout, that's what you get."

Epilogue

BOLLENBAUCHERS

DELPHINE

The barge navigated the last bend, the tall trees on either side of the river giving way to a wide swath of farmlands, roads, and the familiar manor house at the top of the slope above them all. Humans and jaglins called from the docks. A man directed the barge to its place with flags.

"Word was sent ahead, right?" Varrick asked.

Delphine squeezed his hand and nodded. She'd sent a letter from the capital.

The bargemen threw ropes to the dockhands, who pulled in and secured the barge. Delphine squeezed Varrick's hand again. It was ridiculous to be nervous.

"Dolphin!" A dark-haired young man pushed his way through the workers, arms spread wide, grin equally wide.

Delphine laughed, nerves evaporating. "Staircase," she shouted to her brother.

The dockworkers gave the signal that all was secure, and Alastair offered his hand so she could step across the gap. He swung her into a hug, lifting her off her feet.

Talon and Sable leapt onto the dock, prancing and wriggling. Varrick followed, Snowdrop securely perched on one shoulder.

Delphine squeezed her brother. "Where's Mama? Did you get my letter?"

"She should be on her way down from the house, and Grandpapa is here somewhere." He set her down and turned to Varrick. "Magus Allard?"

Varrick ducked his head. "Yes, sir."

"None of that." He held out his hand to shake. "Alastair. And there's Grandpapa, who will be delighted to explain everything to you. Sweet rivers, it'll stop him from turning the rest of us cross-eyed."

Delphine caught Varrick's arm and peered through the chaos of the dock. Alastair was dressed like the workmen, and when she spotted Grandpapa, so was he. He grinned and waved. Mama came up just behind him and stopped, blinking back tears.

Alastair did the rounds of introductions as Grandpapa ushered the group to solid ground, well away from the bustle. The drakes took off in a sprint, the workers cheering on their favorite to win the impromptu race. Delphine's head spun; she'd forgotten how boisterous everything was here.

Mama drew her aside as Varrick began fielding questions from Grandpapa. "What happened to David?"

"Oh Mama, I have such a story, but it needs several bottles of wine to be told." She wasn't even sure where to start.

Mama embraced her again. "Later. You are here and you are happy, yes?"

Delphine looked back at Varrick, who was deep in conversation with Alastair and Grandpapa. "Yes, completely happy."

Meet The Author

Among other things, Blythe has been a theater kid, English teacher, and homeschool mom. She is a self-taught artist who draws her own character art and mini comics. Her first literary loves were *The Lord of the Rings*, *Les Misérables*, and *The Three Musketeers*, with a heavy dose of *Pride and Prejudice*, *Rebecca*, and *The Scarlet Pimpernel*. Her stories reflect her love for other worlds, swashbuckling adventure, magic, and romance. She'd take the mountains over the beach, unless the beach is rocky, foggy, and overshadowed by a mysterious forest. She lives in rural Wyoming with her husband, six children, three cats, and one very tolerant dog.

Other Titles from
5 PRINCE PUBLISHING